THE DEVIL'S
EVIDENCE

Also by Simon Kurt Unsworth

The Devil's Detective

Collections
Strange Gateways
Quiet Houses
Lost Places

THE DEVIL'S
EVIDENCE

❧ A NOVEL ❧

SIMON KURT UNSWORTH

DOUBLEDAY
NEW YORK • LONDON • TORONTO
SYDNEY • AUCKLAND

Book design by Michael Collica
Jacket design by Michael J. Windsor
Front jacket images: (flames) plyapongrot / Shutterstock;
(gun) Sami Sarkis / Getty Images
Back jacket image: (vine) bellenixe / Shutterstock

Library of Congress Cataloging-in-Publication Data
Unsworth, Simon Kurt.
The Devil's evidence : a novel / Simon Kurt Unsworth. — First edition.
pages ; cm
Sequel to: The Devil's detective.
ISBN 978-0-385-53936-4 (hardcover) — ISBN 978-0-385-53937-1 (ebook)
1. Private investigators—Fiction. I. Title.
PR6121.N795D48 2016
823'.92—dc23
2015031479

MANUFACTURED IN THE UNITED STATES OF AMERICA

1   3   5   7   9   10   8   6   4   2

First Edition

For Rosie, who makes me whole and who owns my heart now and forever.

For Ben, my dude serious, my son, fellow watcher of *Doctor Who* and by far and away the best thing I will ever have a hand in creating.

For Mily, stepdaughter the elder and all-around cool girl.

For Lottie, stepdaughter the younger, who's still happily living in the la-la land that only she understands.

The four of you are my life, and wherever you are is home and is where the world feels safest and best. Without you, there would be no stories worth telling, and this book is for you with all the love I have.

THE DEVIL'S
EVIDENCE

PROLOGUE

It was a building, and it had burned.

"How many does this make it?"

Fool ignored the question, lifting his hands to his face and rubbing, and the skin of his palms smelled of soot and scorched flesh.

"I don't know," he said eventually, dropping his hands from the exhaustion that his head had become. *How many fires* have *there been in the previous days and weeks?* he wondered, and then stopped wondering and tried to remember. *I should know,* he thought, *I'm an Information Man. I should act like one and not like the Fool I was.* So, how many? Certainly five, when he sifted through his mind he found that many, but possibly more. Almost certainly more. He was tired, the images in his head jumbling, blurring together, at least five but more, definitely more. Six, maybe seven, or even eight. Buildings, burned and damaged.

"It's eight," said Marianne at his side, and Fool turned to her, focusing, pulling himself back to now, looking at her with his officer's eyes. She was young, only several months old despite her adulthood, freshly harvested from Limbo and made into one of the new Information Men, and she was already beginning to understand her role. She was already good.

"Eight, yes," he said, "this is the eighth. And the links between them?"

"Fire," Marianne replied immediately, "obviously. Fires that have been set, that haven't happened accidentally."

"And?" It was unfair, really. Fool didn't have any great insight; even after the previous seven investigations, he was simply hoping that her eyes might have seen the ground differently than his own. She was smart and sharp, and only rarely did she act around him as the other human

Information Men did, with that irritating deference. Now, however, she looked at him without speaking, unable to answer, shoulders hunching slightly into a shrug. Sighing, he turned away from her and looked at the burned thing at his front and thought back, over the whole fucking smoking mess of the investigation. Eight fires, eight things burned to soot and spindle and ragged chaos, and what did he know?

Mr. Tap crouched in the corner and watched, impassive.

Fool's officers, his *troops* as the Bureaucracy now insisted on calling them, were distracting him, pushing and poking and talking. Each time he tried to focus on the details the sound of them shifted his attention, or one of them would amble into his eye line and he would lose the threads that were starting to form behind his eyes. They weren't helping, weren't finding clues, assuming there were any to find; they were simply creating more chaos, more disorder, blurring the narrative the building was trying to tell him. "Out," he said finally, waving his hand at the door.

"Sir?" asked one of the demons, its black uniform hanging awkwardly over a body that appeared to be formed solely of twists and kinks. Fool could hear the disgust in its voice. This little demon, part of a lineage of the infliction of pain and suffering, was taking orders from a human, and it hated it; *hated* it. Never mind, it would learn, or it would be taken away. That was how things were now.

"Out," said Fool again, this time more loudly, jabbing his finger at the doorway. "All of you. Wait outside."

Fool watched as his Men left, their feet and claws leaving puffs of ash behind them, weapons and bags clanking, until they were finally gone and an almost-silence seeped back in around him. Only Mr. Tap remained, still in the corner, still crouched and watching. Its skin seemed slick in the hazy light, its mouth open and tasting the air. Fool, as instructed, tried to ignore it and turned back into the dead structure and tried to read its corpse.

The problem now was the same as that first time, when he had been sent to an outbuilding burned away to shadow and grime. He saw it, it was there around him and in front of him, but the fires made things jumbled and he didn't know how to investigate them; he'd never had to before. There was little or no *information* here, nothing to link the burned places besides the fires themselves. Fool understood, to some degree anyway, how to investigate the deaths of humans and even the deaths of demonkind, but the burning of buildings? He didn't know where to start.

Maybe that's the trick, little Fool, he thought. *Treat this not as something new, something separate, but as a variation of what you know, what you learned investigating the Fallen. Treat it not as a burning building but as simply another death, the death of a building where the weapon was not claw or rock or tooth, but fire.* The death of a building, its murder. He could investigate murder, had learned that trick over the last months, his understanding of the *how* and the *why* growing as he became more skilled. *This is murder,* he thought. *Look at it that way, little Fool, and see it with an investigator's eyes.* So, what could this new Fool, born over the previous months out of death and pain and loss, see?

The fire had been set by humans. Fool had seen enough flame from demon and angel to know that those fires were different, they were either directed and specific or all-encompassing, and this was not. It had spread evenly, he thought, starting in the far corner where the damage was most severe and reaching around almost to here, by the door, before petering out. It had moved constantly, burning hard but slow, sinking its teeth through to the center of the wooden walls and posts carefully and patiently and worrying at the building until it came apart.

Fool walked to the corner where the fire had started. Pieces of the roof lay scattered on the floor, all but consumed. He kicked them aside, revealing a pile of greasy ash in the corner. Kneeling down, he sifted through it with a sliver of wood, working his way slowly into its still-warm heart. What few fragments he could identify were the remains of twigs and branches, piled together to create a womb for the fire's first stuttering breaths. This was a fire created and tended by a man or woman, fed fuel and brought to life with patience and care.

Clever Fool, he thought, *working out where it started. What use is that?* And the answer was, as ever, *No use at all.*

He went through to the rear room, to the bodies.

There were four of them, lying under the room's only window. All four were long dead, their bodies charred into brittle, black memories by the heat. The flames had pulled them into fetal curls, clenching their arms in front of them and drawing their legs up into tight-kneed angles, their skin split and re-split. Fool crouched over the first corpse, feeling the sick warmth still radiating from it, and as he watched some internal flame still cooking through the dead body's flesh escaped, splitting away a flap of skin across one of its shoulder blades and flickering briefly before dying. The flap was curved like a smile, its edges crusting away, and it breathed out a tiny puff of air that smelled of the roasting meat they were sometimes served for their meals as it yawned to reveal muscles and fat that had been dried out to the consistency and color of old leather.

"They couldn't escape," said Marianne from behind him, her voice toneless. She had returned, unable to keep away, the officer in her overcoming the orders he had given.

"No. The fire was set at the front of the house; it must have been burning fiercely by the time these poor bastards realized what was happening." It was impossible at first to tell if the bodies were of men or women, so badly damaged were they. It was only when he rolled one over that he saw the victim was male, which meant they were all male; men and women didn't live in the same houses in Hell.

"It must be an awful way to die," said Marianne. Fool, who had seen enough terrible death in Hell to understand that there was little to decide between various types of awfulness, said nothing.

"Why didn't they run?" asked Marianne, her voice still toneless but now brittle and hopeless and starting to crack. He looked at her, slim in her black uniform, hair shaved close to her head so that the shape of her skull shone through her stubble like a secret inner reality. He reached out, intending to put a hand on her shoulder, to try to reassure, but dropped it. What could he say that would make this better? Nothing. Better to take refuge in facts, and the trail that facts opened out before them.

"By the time they realized things were burning, I'd imagine it would have been too late, that the flames already had the house in their grip." He thought of thick, clinging smoke filling the rooms, and his lungs clenched in a little itch of sympathy. The fire had eaten the workers as surely as any demon might, leaving nothing Fool could use.

"They came here but it was too late, the glass was too thick to break or they were too weak to break it. They died together."

"What should we do?"

"Do? We look around. We see what's here and what's not, we see if it points anywhere. We investigate." *But not using the bodies,* he thought, *not this time.* There was no point in sending these corpses for questioning, there simply wasn't enough left for Hand or Tidyman to talk to.

By the end of the day he had to accept that there was nothing new, no trails or clues, there was simply Fool and Marianne and the other Information Men moving around a murdered building holding in its heart murdered men, and Fool was again their witness and the recorder of their fate even though he still had no idea why he had been sent to investigate this particular crime. It was how Hell worked, even now, layer upon layer and each reshaping what was above and below; the Bureaucracy gave instruction, not explanation, and expected him to fill the gaps in a structure whose outlines he could rarely see. All he could do was look and guess and report, and hope that the patterns of Hell, the language he was supposed to understand, might become clear to him at some point.

The murder of four humans, and the murder of another building, and still he understood so little.

He knew one thing, though, from the earlier fires, the ones they had arrived at while they were still burning: fire had a *voice,* it talked in a constant bitter mutter, the sound of something chewing its own teeth, a one-sided conversation that babbled as the flames burrowed deep into wooden frames around now-glassless windows and ate warping doors buckling in their mounts. And as the fire talked and drew itself on, it *cleaned,* leaving no spore or trail that Fool could track or read, and in doing so it became for him a thing of frustration and anger. Its glowing red heart beat in a rhythm Fool could see but had no way to understand, and as he stood in this latest burned place he thought, *I will make sense of you soon,* and hoped he wasn't lying to himself.

"Is this how it always is?" asked Mr. Tap, finally straightening up, standing. It was tall, its head scraping against the low beams of the ragged building, its skin a mess of ridges and furrows in which the drifting ash had caught. Tiny worms wriggled along the furrows and gnawed on the ash.

"Sometimes," replied Fool.

"I came to observe the great Fool," said Mr. Tap, "so I might learn how to be an investigator, but now I wonder if you have anything to actually teach me?"

"Note it all," Fool said to Marianne, ignoring the jibe, and started out of the building. Mr. Tap followed, kicking thick clouds of ash up as it walked.

"Perhaps, Fool, you aren't as good as I've been led to believe."

"Perhaps," agreed Fool. *Don't respond except with deference, don't rise, don't argue.* Fool had no idea why he had been told to take Mr. Tap with him; the instruction had been in the canister that morning along with the details of the fire and deaths. It was another of Hell's jobs, another task, to take this tall, skinny demon with its warped and melted face and uneven eyes with him and to answer any questions it might have.

"And will you make any arrests today? Or possibly shoot any of my brethren?"

"No."

"You're sure, Fool? You have a reputation for that, after all. Fool the demon killer, I've heard you called, Fool the slaughterer."

"I'm sure." Voice still flat and uninflected.

"And you know nothing?"

"Nothing useful, not at this point."

"Then perhaps I can help, yes?" Mr. Tap stopped and bent, scooped up a clawful of burned material, and placed it in its mouth. Chewing, it spoke through the black mess that dripped around its teeth.

"It doesn't taste like demon, Fool," the demon said and then stopped. When it resumed chewing, it did so more slowly, and when it spoke again its voice was also slower, more thoughtful. Fool had the sudden idea that it had originally intended to condescend to him, to prove its superiority, but had then found something unexpected.

"It's human but it tastes strange, Fool. Sharper, bitterer. Why is that?"

"I don't know, I don't eat the crime scenes, I'm not sure how they should taste," said Fool and immediately regretted the flippancy.

"Perhaps you should," said Mr. Tap and grinned, revealing row after row of crooked teeth like warped nails. Wet ash like black mud spilled from its mouth and fell to the ground, smearing its chest as it fell. More of those tiny bugs burrowed into the mess, so that the demon's chest rippled slightly as they ate. It leaned in close to Fool and whispered, breath burned and sour, "All these fires, Fool, and you haven't got a thing to tell us. You aren't anything, Fool, are you? You have this position bought by the slaughter of demons, you think you are important, but you are not, Fool, and you should watch. Watch carefully, Fool, because I am coming."

With that the demon strode past Fool and left the remains of the building. Fool followed after a moment, trying to ignore the looks on the faces of the Information Men outside as he emerged. They had all heard Mr. Tap, of course; the demon's whisper had been a staged one, loud enough to cut the air on blades of sibilance and threat. Fool was now the Commander of the Information Office of Hell, in charge of all the new Information Men, but the demon Information Men still looked at him like he was shit to be eaten or scraped off their feet, and most of the human Men still looked at him as though he was something unclear, to be deferred to or stared at in equal measure.

Nothing changes, he thought as he walked away, Marianne following. Above them the spires of Heaven gleamed in Hell's sky, clouds swirling around the white towers, their light falling to the earth in glimmering waves like delicate rain. Fool looked up at the city, thinking of angels that fell and demons that walked in his shadow and crouched in the corners, and felt small and alone and weighed down.

Somewhere in the distance there was a terrible low ripping sound and a leap of orange as something else caught aflame. As Fool and the others turned to watch, tongues of fire reached into the sky as though to scorch Heaven's feet before falling back, muttering angrily.

Starting toward where the new fire was birthing, Thomas Fool, Commander of the Information Office of Hell, thought, *It's an irony, of course. Hell, the place is flames, is burning and I don't know why.*

PART ONE
REMAINS

1

The transport pulled to a halt before the building, and for a moment, Fool simply sat and looked at it. It was small, old, its paint peeling, nestling back against a series of smaller hills covered in a thick mess of scrub and trees, and its front door was open and its windows were broken. The glass was still lying along the sides of the building, he saw, its broken faces clean, catching the morning light and spitting it back toward him. Newly broken windows, he thought as he exited the transport, waving a hand backward to halt the emergence of the other Information Men he had brought with him.

The canister had arrived that morning wrapped with tangled red and two yellow threads, one bright and the other paler. As near as he could make out from the guide to thread colors in the *New Information Man's Guide to the Rules and Offices of Hell,* ten fat leather-bound volumes filled with dense, tightly packed script setting out the rules in a layering of clause and sub-clause and counter-clause that had been issued to him to replace his old *Guide* as part of the growing of the Information Office, it meant that several murders had taken place and that the deaths were quick rather than prolonged—no torture or eating of the corpses, at least. He had nodded to himself then, almost relieved to be back investigating murder rather than one of the increasing number of fires that had been burning recently and slightly disgusted at himself for the relief, and put on his uniform jacket and buckled the holster and the gun it contained to his leg. This was murder, and murder he understood.

Out of the vehicle, he could smell the blood. The scent of it was baking in the day's growing heat, thickening into veins drifting through the air that Fool felt like he could touch if only he reached out and pressed his fingers together. He moved through it, going first to the corner of the building. There were fresh scratches on the wall, scrabbles under the window that meant . . . what? Something had clambered up the side of the building to the window, broken the glass, and entered that way. Several somethings, he thought; there were similar marks below each of the three windows on this side. When he crossed the front of the building and looked at the three windows on the other side, he found the same things there. At least six, then, he thought, and finally waved his troops from the transport.

"You," he said, pointing to a demon whose name he couldn't remember but who he knew could sketch, "go and draw the marks under the windows." He could look at them later, set them side by side to look for hints about what might have made them.

"You and you," to two other demons, "go and see if there's anyone about, anyone who saw anything. Marianne and the rest of you, with me." Then, taking a deep breath, he led the woman and the remainder of his troops inside, to where the dead were waiting for him.

Inside, the stink of blood was far stronger, curdled like overboiled soup. It was dark despite the six windows and the gas lamps strung along the wall in fixed brackets. The flames, sputtering, added the scents of burning tallow and wick to the miasma. The glow the lanterns gave out was sallow and weak, even with the flow of gas set at its highest, giving shape to the shadows filling the room rather than banishing them.

The space that lay before Fool was long, stretching back from the entrance, and he realized that the building was cut back into one of the hills, its rear end burrowing into the earth like a grub. Down the center of its length were two long rows of trestle tables, surfaces scarred and pitted. Wooden racks lined the walls, simple frames filled with folded clothes and piled bolts of rough linen. Needles and threads and large bobbins of twine on stands were spaced regularly down the center of the trestles, knots of frayed twine like old snakeskins gathering dust on the floor under them. Chairs were pushed up under the tables, the spaces in front of them neat. Fool saw that the needles were connected to the table with thin chains, delicate locks threaded through the needles' eyes and the chains' links.

It was a Seamstress House. His uniform came from a factory like this one, all the uniforms did, all Hell's inhabitants' smocks and trousers and thin underwear did. Working in a Seamstress House was considered to be a good job because it was generally warm and safe. He wondered if the dead had had a chance to appreciate the irony of that, and doubted it.

The first body was seated halfway down the table; it was a man and he had been decapitated. His head had been placed on the table, turned so that it was looking back at the body it had come from, and the floor and chair and table were thick with drying blood. The body was rigid, the left hand still clamped around a needle and the right around a piece of cloth now soaked red. The man was naked. Beyond him, a second figure was sprawled on the floor, another man, judging by the hairiness of the part of the back and single arm that were visible. Whatever he had been stitching together had fallen on him and covered him like a shroud, reminding Fool of the gray tarpaulins the porters used to take bodies to the Questioning House or the Flame Garden. Patches of blood showed through the material, odd blooms like the petals of a flower he hadn't seen before. He didn't bother to peel the cloth back; there were other bodies to investigate, two or three of them on either side of the tables and more beyond them.

The worst were gathered in a pile at the far end of the table: a tangled mess of naked limbs and blood and pieces of material. The attack had happened toward the end of the night shift, had caught only the straggler workers, those who hadn't finished their jobs for that shift and hadn't yet been allowed to leave. There was space at the tables for at least fifty workers, but Fool could see only nine or ten distinct bodies in total, counting torsos to find the tally. All of them were naked, and his first thought was that they had been stripped after death until he remembered that nudity was a condition of working for the seamstresses to prevent the theft of material. He had been to a Seamstress House once before, somewhere on the other side of the industrial area. He had visited during the day and had found it unbearably hot, the air dry and hard to inhale because of the dust of tiny fibers hanging in the atmosphere, but still a better place than most of Hell. *At least it's covered*, he had thought, *at least they're not wet and cold*. Most of the workers' hands had been bleeding, he remembered, covered in cuts and peeling dry skin and punctures that left spots across the clothes they were stitching. The supervisor, a painfully thin woman, had told him that was normal even as she beat the workers' shoulders with a flat stick for getting blood on the garments they sewed. *Everything we wear is bound in blood,* he remembered thinking, *little bloody Fool.* Despite their bleeding hands and the beatings, most of the workers had looked, if not happy, then at least less miserable than the heavy-industry workers or farmhands.

Calling Marianne to his side, pulling her away from her study of the table and what lay under it, but noting her interest and hoping he'd remember to ask her about it later, Fool said, "So. Tell me."

Marianne looked around, visibly gathered herself, and said, "Whatever happened here happened quickly. There's no blood near the door, meaning that the dead hadn't had time to run. Something came in through the windows fast and savaged the workers, tore them apart."

She paused, waiting. He nodded at her, encouraging her to go on, thinking, *She saw the windows. Good. She's getting sharp, seeing it clearly, learning to understand the story.*

"It was fast and brutal but not about torture. The dead have been killed but not too badly mistreated."

"Apart from being murdered?"

"Apart from being murdered," she replied, ignoring his sarcasm, the ghost of a smile twitching across her face and then vanishing. "There are bodies at the back of the room, piled, but there's still no sign of mutilation or torture, they were simply killed."

"Were they driven to the back of the room and slaughtered like cattle, or did they simply run that way because the other direction was toward their attackers?"

"Neither. They were killed close to where they were sitting or standing, then piled at the back. There's blood beneath the table where there are no bodies, and bloody footprints on the floor."

"Human?"

"No. Maybe. No, I don't think so, they're distorted, smeared, but I still think demon, although what sort I can't tell."

"Good, you've done well," he said, then turned to the rest of the troops and called out.

"This is a Seamstress House, a place of sewing and repairs. Look around, see what's here, decide whether it should be, and if it shouldn't, or it looks wrong in any way, tell me. Do you understand?"

There were muttered responses and the Information Men began to spread out, scattering through the space and peering about themselves in exaggerated shows of looking around. So far, apart from Marianne, who was now back to looking beneath the table, few of the demons or humans that had been given a role as Information Men showed any aptitude for the tasks it entailed, simply carrying out Fool's orders in stolid silence. They could sketch, some of them; others took accurate notes, could encourage people to talk, or even managed to drag information from the demons that walked Hell's streets, but it was still Fool who collated everything, tried to discern the patterns that lay below the surface.

Fool went to the pile of bodies at the end of the room, trying to take in the whole scene as he did so, trying to let it talk to him. As Marianne had said, the bodies were, by Hell's standards, not badly abused. Most seemed to have been beheaded or torn apart, but there was something almost surgical about the injuries; there were no defensive wounds and little sign that the bodies had been interfered with following their deaths. They had simply fallen where they stood or sat, set upon by assailants who murdered them and moved on. Even the pile of dead flesh seemed to have been created more as a convenience than anything, the shoving together of the dead so that a walkway around the end of the table was still passable. A small horde of flies droned about the splashes of part-coagulated blood in noisy hunger, landing and alighting in delicate waves. Streaks and gashes through the liquid might have been made by the feet of the attackers, but if so, it would be impossible to gain any knowledge about them as the blood had seeped back in before drying, the edges of the marks furred and unreadable.

What else? There had to be more, more openings leading away from this initial scene, paths that he could follow.

The dead were all naked and few, so he knew it had occurred at the end of the shift. He could find the time the shift usually finished and pinpoint the violence to sometime around then. What else? There was more, there was always more, it was what he had learned these last months, more trails unfurling from every point that he could try to track his way along. There were blood streaks under the windows and on the frames, so the assailants had left the building the same way they had come in. Why? What would be the purpose in that? Coming in that way Fool could almost understand, it would be shocking, fear carried on the sound of breaking glass, but leaving that way? It made little sense. "Think, little Fool," he said aloud, ignoring the look the nearest Information Man gave him, "think."

These were workers, sewing the clothes that they all wore, naked so that no thefts could occur and, he suspected, to rob these workers of what little dignity and safety their job might offer them. What had the supervisor in the last place like this he had been told him? About clothes?

No, not told him, shown him, her seniority marked out by the fact that she had been clothed, that she was not a worker and therefore not naked. He looked again at the corpses and saw that all were bare, clothed only in blood and flies. Workers, but no supervisor. Had the supervisor fled? How could he? The swiftness of the attack, the carnage around him, seemed to show that no one had escaped. Fool tilted one of the gas lanterns, casting its light about him as widely as he could. How long had the dead been dead? An hour? At least that. The blood was crusty and dry at the edge of the pools, but in the center of the mass it was still thickly sticky where the flies landed and lifted off, so no longer than three or four hours. The tube had arrived at the office around two hours ago, so between two and four hours, he thought.

There was no more blood in the room, nothing near the door, just these overlapping pools that formed a single irregular mess across the factory floor. What else was there? Racks of finished clothing along either side, their contents folded neatly, next to fresh cloth rolled around huge poles and piles of cut fabric awaiting stitching. An open tub containing new bobbins of thread, another next to it containing the empty bobbin centers. If he couldn't see, could he listen?

No. It was pointless, the distant thrum of heavy machinery and the sound of his Information Men, demon and human both, cluttered the room. He had to keep looking.

There was nothing, just the racks, each four shelves high containing pile after identical pile of folded articles of clothing with separate sections for the bolts of cloth.

Identical? No, the rack closest to him was different, wasn't completely neat. The clothes on the lowest shelf were ruffled up, bunched into a lump toward the wall at its rear. Nearby, a chair lay on its side and a whistle was on the floor by the chair, its bell cracked. The chair was bigger than those by the long table, had a padded seat and arms. Not a worker's chair, but a supervisor's one. So where was the supervisor?

Fool approached the rack and crouched by it, staring at the bulge of messy clothes. From out of a shadowy gap, a pale eye stared at him, and then the mound took a hoarse breath.

Fool started and fell back off his haunches and onto his ass, hand jerking automatically toward his gun. The mound took another breath, the clothes shifting slightly. The inhalation sounded as though it was coming from a long way underwater, was thick and phlegmy.

"Who's that?" said Fool, finally wresting his gun loose from its holster. His hand was shaking, the barrel of the gun jerking back and forth as though unable to decide where to focus its attention. The mound shifted again, the top piece of clothing slipping, gliding sideways. It slithered off the shelf and to the floor, revealing the top of a head, hair thin and tangled and dark. Fool scrambled around, flapping back his Men, wanting them to stay away. "On with your work," he said loudly, but most ignored him, standing and watching him with thick, uninterested eyes.

Fool turned back to the mound, crouching again. "It's okay," he said, knowing it wasn't okay, this was Hell and things were never okay. He put his gun away, holding both hands out in front of him in a gesture that he hoped was unthreatening, safe and secure.

There was another soggy inhalation. The eye blinked and something at the base of the mound began to move, pushing out from the inside, knocking the clothes aside. A hand emerged, pale and old, the skin dry and cracking. Fool took it and the hand clenched tight; carefully, he began to knock the remaining clothing aside.

It was an old man. He had crawled onto the shelf and wedged himself against the wall at its rear, pulling the thin jackets and trousers up over himself. Fool brought the man into the room's dirty light, seeing as he did so that his face was pale and greasy with sweat, froth bubbling at his lips with each shallow, moist breath. He tried to speak but what emerged was a long, low groan. His eyes stuttered, leaping from Fool to a place over Fool's shoulder and then back again, and the fear in them was clear.

"It's okay," Fool repeated, "they're gone." He looked over his shoulder, the fear in the old man's eyes contagious, suddenly convinced that he'd see some demon swooping down toward him, but the room was empty. He leaned in, wrapping his free arm around the man and taking as gentle a hold as he could. The man groaned again as Fool began to pull him out, and the man began to tremble.

It wasn't a uniform tremble; it was as though each part of the man was reacting to a different pressure, shivering at a different rate. Fool felt the man's heartbeat under thin ribs, its rhythm ragged and loping. The man's eyes rolled again and, close to, Fool smelled breath that was sour and harsh. More spittle bubbled over his lips as he tried to breathe and he tightened his grip on Fool's hand. His skin was rough and hard, calluses grating against Fool's palm, nails tearing into the skin on the back of his hand, more injuries, the tales of Hell written in crescents of his blood. Fool tugged again, wincing as the man groaned a second time and clenched his fingers tighter, and then managed to drag him free from the shelf.

He was tiny, a bone and skin person, and he was dying. His breath was coming in shorter and shorter bursts, his skin yellowing almost as Fool watched. His other hand came up and pulled at Fool's jacket, fingers dragging at the material and then falling away. His knuckles struck the floor with a dull, grisly crunch. People in Hell didn't die like this in front of Fool, and he had no idea how to react or whether there was anything he could do. He dealt with the dead, not the living, not the almost-dead.

The man's face was coloring further, becoming a darker red, veins bulging in his neck and visible across his scalp through his thin hair. He opened his mouth, breath rattling, liquid slathering his lips, eyes terrified and pained. Fool wished he could do something, that he had some skills or knowledge that would be useful. The man's eyes jumped from Fool's face and looked along the room, then came back.

"What did you see?" asked Fool, the Information Man in him taking over. "What was it?"

The man exhaled, his lips working, chewing at the words but failing to form them. He was trying, though, his tongue licking out and trying to remove the spittle from around his mouth, his throat clenching and unclenching. It was painful to watch. He tried again, gulping at the air and then exhaling, tongue and lips writhing around words that the air from his lungs was too weak to create.

Do something, stupid Fool, do something now or he'll be gone, thought Fool, brushing the man's hair back from a brow that seemed both feverish and clammy at the same time. The man's eyes rolled again, carried on rolling, the pupils contracting and expanding as though he was trying to focus on Fool but failing, his vision slipping to some other depth, some other place.

The trembles were spreading more widely across the man's body, becoming shudders, rippling out from some place inside him and shaking him apart. It was coming quicker and quicker now, this thing. *Was this what death was like when it was allowed to occur naturally,* Fool wondered. *Was this what it was like shriven of the terrors of Hell and the freedom of Heaven and its host of angels? Was this freedom, to be able to die like this?*

And ultimately, did it matter? That wasn't the job, the *deaths* were the job, the deaths and the reasons for them. Fool needed answers.

"Hold on," said Fool, brushing back the man's hair again, trying to soothe him. "Please, try to hold on."

Behind him, one of the Information Men said something and there was laughter. Fool looked back over his shoulder, saw the speaker was a demon whose name he did not know, and decided that, when they were finished here, the demon was finished as an Information Man. He pointed at one of his other troops and said, "Bring water. Now."

A moment later, the man brought Fool a glass of cloudy, warm water, which he held to the supervisor's lips, gently tipping it into his mouth and letting the liquid roll down his throat around the struggling exhalations.

"What did you see?" asked Fool. The man grimaced, tongue darting out wetly and lips pulling back from teeth that were little more than brown stubs.

"Please," said Fool, trickling a little more water into the man's mouth. The man was calmer but his breathing was still shallow and uneven, choppy, its smell wretched; he was still dying. The man blinked and tears rolled from the corners of his eyes. He nodded at Fool gently.

"Thank you," the old man said, the words stretched and half formed, almost unrecognizable. He lifted a hand and stroked Fool's face, his touch like being caressed by twigs wrapped in parchment.

"What did you see? Can you describe them to me? Please?"

The old man nodded again, took a deep breath, and then let it out. A terrible shudder racked him as he exhaled, almost shaking him loose from Fool's hold, the words "They danced" slipping past Fool on a tide of torn and stinking air.

"What did?" asked Fool. "What danced? What?" The old man did not reply, his body shivering violently until it became stilled and limp. Cradled in Fool's arms, he died and was gone, more anonymous flesh, more death.

"Fuck," said Fool. "Fuck and shit." He let the man's corpse down to the floor slowly, freeing his arms from the man's tight grip, and then sat back on his haunches.

Fool looked at the piled dead around him, and then back at the man's corpse. He'd need more men with tarpaulins and stretchers. The corpse might talk; Tidyman or Hand might get something from it yet. From *him*, Fool amended.

It was as he was walking to the pneumatic tube in the corner of the room to send a message to the porters that Fool heard the noise. A scream from outside, a crash, and then the babble of voices that Fool had come to know only too well these last weeks.

The Evidence was coming.

2

If the door to the Seamstress House had not been open, they'd have kicked it in and entered in a rush of sound and splinters, Fool was sure of that. It was, he had come to realize over these last weeks, how the Evidence operated—grand gestures, visible, thrusting themselves in front of everything so that they became the foreground of Hell in those moments, everything else falling to scenery. The Evidence was the expression on the face of the new Hell, one of scrutiny without pity and judgment without thought. And now, they were at Fool's crime scene.

Even without a door to crash through they contrived to make an entrance. First their shadows appeared in the doorway, three of them, stretching across the factory floor and creeping up the edge of long tables, as the sound of their gibbering swelled. Behind the shadows and noise shapes formed against Hell's glaring light, furred at the edges at first and then sharpening into solidity. They were small, bristling, and hopping, two shapes dragging a third between them. The other Information Men stepped back from them, Fool saw, pressing themselves into the racks so that there was no way they could be accused of getting in the Evidence's way. Although the Evidence held equivalent rank to the Information Men, there was no doubt who had the power, who had Hell's favor. There was no doubt who would be *noticed* if a conflict occurred, and what that notice might mean.

The Evidence was the latest development in the ranks of Hell, one that had emerged from the Bureaucracy almost fully formed with little fanfare, as though they had been standing on some sideline merely waiting for their call. A message had arrived one day several weeks previously in a tube without a ribbon, dropping into Fool's office with a sound like teeth clicking together on air, a missed bite. The message inside the canister read simply, *There is a new department. They are the Evidence. They will investigate.* Fool wasn't sure whether the Information Office was equal to the Evidence, whether as Commander of the Information Office he should have some authority over them, but he knew that in reality he had no control over them at all.

Worse, he was as frightened of them as the rest of his troops were.

The first time Fool had seen the Evidence was several days after the arrival of the canister that heralded their formation. They had come to the crime scene he was investigating. He had been trying to determine where the murderer of a Genevieve had entered and left the room the body had been found in, when the door had crashed open and two demons entered.

They strode through the crime scene as though it wasn't there, driving a wedge through the room until they came to a halt in front of Fool. The first was smaller, coming up to just above Fool's waist, and was nearly naked except for a cloth hanging around its waist that covered its groin. After peering at him for a moment, it grunted and turned away, muttering as it went around the room, pulling furniture away from the walls and tearing up the grimy floor covering, throwing pieces of it over its shoulders. When one of the Information Men got in its way, he was pushed aside and then snarled at when he protested. The little demon had huge tusks that pushed their way out from behind lips that were torn and scratched by the teeth, and strings of bloody saliva ran down its chin and dripped to the floor.

The second Evidence Man was Mr. Tap.

The demon seemed even taller, as though its new role had increased it, its head bowing to prevent it from banging against the ceiling. It was thin, terribly thin, like corpse branches and decayed bones wrapped in leathery skin, and its face was warped as though it had existed in some vast heat, melting and then resetting as the flesh dripped down so that its three eyes were unevenly spaced and its mouth was a thin slit in which Fool could just make out the hundreds of needle teeth ridged in uneven rows that descended back down its throat and that moved in waves as it spoke.

"Hello, Fool," it said, coming over, its voice like dusty ratchets grinding. "I told you I'd come back."

"Yes."

"Good, Fool, good. It's important you know me. It's important that you understand that my word, Fool, my word is absolute and you can trust me. It's important that you understand that I am everything and that you are nothing. I am Mr. Tap, Fool, and I am head of the Evidence."

"'The head'?" repeated Fool, watching as behind Mr. Tap the other demon crashed away from them and carried on destroying the crime scene. "And that's the body?"

"One of them, one of many, Fool, with me as brain and guide. The head of the Evidence," said Mr. Tap.

"Good for you," said Fool, "and I'm Commander of the Information Office of Hell."

"You are," said Mr. Tap, leaning in very close to Fool's face so that his watery, sour eyes filled Fool's vision. "You're Commander of the Information Office, commander of facts and details, but I am the head of the things that are coming, Fool, the head of what is already here. The Evidence is mine, Fool, all of the Evidence is mine. I intend to put those valuable things, those facts and details I learned watching you, to good use in running it. After all, I had lessons from a master, didn't I?" And then it turned, ignoring Fool and watching the thing it had brought with it.

The littler demon went to the body and yanked it up, wrenching it so hard that the dead boy's head crunched dully against the wall. The demon licked the dead flesh, sucking at the blood that was coagulating on the boy's skin.

"What—" Fool said, but Mr. Tap interrupted him, reaching out a long arm and wrapping a thin, rough hand around Fool's neck without looking at him. Fool's hand, dropping without thought to his gun, was immediately gripped in the demon's other claw, tight enough to leave marks that lasted into the next day. Mr. Tap finally turned back to Fool and pushed its face close to his, close enough that Fool could smell its breath, smell the rank odor of excrement and blood wafting from its mouth, see the striations across its skin and the tiny worms wriggling within them, tearing into each other. At the lowest edge of his vision he could see the teeth in Mr. Tap's mouth undulating back and forth, more worms writhing in the narrow gaps between them.

Mr. Tap peered at him for a moment as though he was a piece of half-chewed food that he had discovered on his fingers, and then it spoke. "We are the Evidence," it said, "and we will find the things that need to be found, and you will not ever stand in our way unless you want us to find you. Unless you want *me* to find you."

Its voice rasped, as though the hundreds of teeth lining its throat and mouth were tearing the words before they emerged from it, and it was *hot*, a heat that came off its flesh in waves like dry sweat. Mr. Tap squeezed Fool's throat just a little tighter so that he felt the pressure against his breathing and then the demon let go, turning back to its little companion and watching it with a smile on its face that seemed oddly delicate and soft, Fool and the others now dismissed. Burning with embarrassment and anger but knowing he could do nothing, Fool had left Mr. Tap's little demon to its search and returned to the Information House.

And now they were in the Seamstress House.

Mr. Tap wasn't with them, which was how things generally were; it was as though, that first time, it had attended so that it could impose itself on Fool and the others, but since then it had been seen only on rare occasions and had mostly left its Evidence Men, as Fool supposed they must be called, to investigate for themselves. Only, they didn't investigate, they simply tore things apart and reached conclusions that made little or no sense, and then executed justice on the spot.

Fool had seen them take people from the street for infractions of minor rules, things buried in the pages of the new *Guide* that Fool managed to find reference to only after searching carefully. People had been vanished for things like walking in front of a demon without acknowledging it or wearing the wrong type of clothing for that day or showing disrespect by having a dirty face or hands, for the infringement of rules that they didn't even know existed. Where before the people of Hell had feared its lack of justice, the violence that came and went without check, now they feared the laws themselves.

Fool wasn't even sure what the Evidence Men were, demons or something else. Certainly, they were solid when they needed to be, but he had heard stories of them leaning out of the shadows, emerging from thick walls or closed doorways, and grasping people, leaning back and vanishing and taking the person with them. Were they ghosts, or something between ghost and demon? He supposed it didn't matter, not really; they were real, actual, whether or not they were solid all the time.

There were two of them today, dragging a semiconscious human between them. It was a man, his hair hanging down in front of his face and blood seeping from an ugly gash that ran across his scalp. A flap of skin hung down, revealing the white and pink fleck of bloodied bone. They dragged the man before Fool and looked at him, expectantly.

"What?" asked Fool.

"Did it," one said, its voice liquid through blood and spittle and tusk.

"Did what?"

"This," said the thing, jerking its head in a tight circle to indicate the dead flesh scattered around them.

"No, this was done by something that wasn't human. Besides, there were lots of attackers, not one man," said Fool and pointed at the piled dead at the rear of the room. "And a man couldn't do this."

"Not alone?" said the Evidence Man, and turned back to the drooping human still held tight in its grasp. It leaned in so that its face was close to the man's head and said, "Who?"

The man mumbled, tried to raise his head, lifting a face that was battered and swollen to his questioner. One of his eyes was a protruding, angry swollen bulge that wept blood.

"Who?" asked the Evidence Man again and the man shook his head.

The little demon leaned in closer still, its mouth opening wide. A tongue the color of old turds slipped out and licked the blood from the man's scalp, lapping wetly at the liquid as it oozed from the torn skin. The man groaned and tried to twist away, but the other demon holding him pushed him forward and the first kept lapping, digging its tongue under the flap of skin, burrowing into the man's head. Fool stepped toward them, hand going for his gun, but before he could do anything else the little demon's jaws opened wider, cracking audibly and stretching obscenely apart, and then it clamped its tusks into either side of the man's head, biting. Something ground for a second and then there was a crunch like the splintering of old wood.

The man screamed.

There was another crack, blood squirting out from the side of the demon's mouth, and Fool could still see the tongue working its way through the blood, ragging at the skin. The man's head was changing shape, squeezed thin, forehead and rear bulging as the pressure increased. Fool drew his gun, feeling the demons among his troops tense, sensing their hunger, their envy, their anger, their *desire*.

"Let him go," said Fool, pressing the barrel of the gun against the Evidence Man's neck. The demon ignored him, kept sucking and licking, its jaws grinding, those tusks splintering their way through the man's skull. *Can he even be alive now?* Fool thought, and as if in answer, the man made a noise that might have been a weak, torn shriek.

It was the shriek that decided it, really. It was hopeless, less a cry for help than an acknowledgment that this was it, the end that everyone in Hell faced sooner or later, that they all knew was coming to them. Fool angled the gun up, faced it away from the man, and pulled the trigger.

The demon's head exploded.

The other Evidence Man let go of the man and leaped back, the man collapsing to the floor, and Fool knew that somewhere between the intention and the shot he had died, knew it from the loose way he fell and from the gray and red morsels that spilled in torn chunks from the wounds in his head. The dead demon, head now simply two flapping wings of flesh covered with coarse hair, spun away and crashed into the edge of the trestle, banging back from it and ending up collapsed in the blood pool, another body decorating the factory floor.

For a brief, tense moment no one in the room moved, and then the remaining Evidence Man sprang. It was nimble and agile, seeming to rise straight into the air, hair standing out from its head in a shock wave of bristle, its claws extended and its mouth wide open. Fool, expecting the attack, had already stepped back, arm swinging around, gun extended and new bullet formed. The Evidence Man landed in front of him and Fool fired again, not at the demon itself but at the floor at its feet, the shot driving it back as the wood splintered and the sound wave exploded around them.

"Stop!" Fool shouted. "Stop, in the name of the Information Office of Hell!"

The Evidence Man kept coming, scuttling on. Marianne stepped forward but, hemmed in by the other Information Men, couldn't get her gun out and instead yanked a bag off the arm of the demon next to her and swung it in a wide, fast arc that caught the demon in the face. Whatever was in the bag broke with a crash as the demon was shunted back, tumbling in an ungainly sprawl to the floor. Fool stepped between it and Marianne, pushing her behind him as she drew her gun, and then the other Information Men, the humans at least, were moving, surrounding the demon, pinning it and holding it.

None of the demon Information Men joined in the melee.

Fool shouted again, wordless, and pushed his way into the mess of struggling bodies. He managed to force his gun against the demon's forehead and then, twisting the barrel so that it drew its flesh into a tight circle around the muzzle, said, "Everyone be quiet."

The silence that fell was brittle, fragile, and Fool thought that the demon might not have much life. Speaking quickly, he said, "You're not stupid, you know I'll fire if you keep attacking me, don't you?"

The demon nodded, the gesture cut short by the force with which Fool was pushing the gun against its head.

"When my men let you go, stay calm or I'll kill you. Do you understand?" Another nod.

"Then we're doing well," said Fool. He stepped back, still keeping the gun trained on the Evidence Man, feeling rather than seeing Marianne step to his side, gun also outstretched, and then motioned his Men away. They let go of their captive carefully, each of them moving out of the thing's reach as soon as they had let go of it. It clambered to its feet, eyes never leaving Fool, its chest rising and falling in ragged anger, breechclout swaying. It raised a hand to its nose, ruined and pouring blood from the impact of the bag Marianne had swung, and then bared its huge teeth at him, bloodied spittle dribbling down the ivory curves and spattering to the floor. Fool kept the gun pointing at it and, over his shoulder, said, "Marianne, put your gun away."

"Okay," said Marianne, and Fool risked a brief glance over, seeing her holster her weapon. Marianne's voice was shaky, and at the sound of it the Evidence Man tensed further, one long-nailed hand rising to its twisted nose.

"No," said Fool, voice low and careful. "She is an Information Man, one of mine, and if you move against her I shall see it as a move against me, and I will kill you for it. Do you understand?"

The Evidence Man glared at Marianne a few moments longer, as though memorizing her for future consumption, and then finally nodded and deliberately turned its back on Fool and his troops, going to its fallen companion and gathering the body in its short arms, snarling as it did so. It snapped its teeth together, growling, and tugged its dead companion into a clumsy lift and then, half carrying, half dragging it, backed out of the factory. No one got in its way and no one spoke as it went. The last Fool saw of it was its shadow, stretching down the table toward him, and its silhouette in the factory's doorway and then it was gone.

The tension didn't lessen with its leaving. Instead, the Information Men began to tighten into two ranks, human on one side and demon on the other. Fool watched as claws unsheathed, mouths opened, hands dropped to weapons, and then he stepped between the gathering lines.

"Does anyone think what I did was wrong?" he asked. No one replied, but he could feel the hate coming at him from the demons, another mark against him, a human who commanded demons, who killed their kind. *What have I done?* he thought, and hoped the fear he felt didn't show in his voice.

"It killed this man without provocation," he continued, pointing at the mangled corpse, still bleeding on the floor in front of them.

"It said he was guilty," said one of the demons, sullen. It was long-faced, its mouth a curve that took up the lower part of its head filled with a mass of square, gray teeth below a snout that flattened back to huge black eyes that had neither iris nor cornea. *Orobas*, thought Fool, mind flickering over names, lineages, wishing again that Gordie was alive, Gordie with his memory and his understanding and his knowledge. *I'm sure it's called Orobas.*

"He's not," replied Fool. Even a few months ago, he could have said, *Humans don't kill humans*, and it would have been true, but now? Everyone killed everyone, it seemed, in the new Hell.

"How do you know?" When Orobas spoke, its teeth clacked together with a sound like dropping plates, punctuating each word, breaking it into pieces. Its ears were curling points reaching up from its flat head, turned as though to catch the sound from everywhere. It should have been comical, something to make it seem preposterous and weak. It didn't.

"Because no human could inflict this kind of damage," said Fool, "not even in a group. This was fast, organized violence. This man isn't even armed, the footprints don't look human. You're Information Men, you have to learn to *see* this; you have to learn to read the places we visit, to see the truth of them, not the lie of what you want them to be. You are the line that divides truth from lies, and even in Hell the line has to exist. You have to *see*."

"Could have dropped his weapon," said another voice, this one high and breathy.

"It could have hidden the weapon, or hired someone," said Orobas, and now as it clacked and spoke it drooled, strings of thick saliva spilling over the teeth, making them glimmer in the torchlight. It was only short but the body in the ill-fitting uniform was solid, the arms extending from the sleeves capped not with hands but with clumsy, uneven hooves. It flexed them now, the dark curves of solidity that it had instead of fingers splitting, twists of hair tangled between each segment, and then the demons were drawing together, taut and rigid. Orobas took a step forward, lifting its hooves, and the ends of the bony arcs were filthy, looked solid and sharp. It smiled, black lips pulling back without humor.

Whatever authority Fool had previously had, it was ebbing from the room moment by moment. He had killed not just a demon but a fellow officer of sorts, a mere upstart human thinking he had the authority to challenge the demonkind. How high would this feeling go? he wondered suddenly. All the way to the top? To Elderflower, assuming Elderflower *was* the top? His usefulness would not, he thought, protect him if Hell thought he had stepped too far. And then there was Mr. Tap to think about, and Fool pondered, not for the first time, whether the most dangerous thing in Hell for Fool was Fool himself.

"Fine," he said, thinking fast. "We'll send him to the Questioning House along with the others and tomorrow morning they'll ask the flesh what they need to ask, and if this man killed the people here and the Evidence Man was right and I'm wrong, I'll take whatever punishment is required of me. Agreed?"

A pause and then nods, an affirmative noise under them, sullen and mistrustful, and Fool saw Orobas hesitate, try to gauge the mood and then decide that now was not the time for open rebellion and it, too, nodded and lowered its arms, and Fool thought, *I hope you're right, little Fool. I hope you're fucking right.*

Fool returned to his room in the Information House and stripped, trying to shed the stress and fear of the morning but they clung to him, wrapped around his skin like old cobwebs. Dropping his dirty clothes in the hall, where one of his troops would take them away, he washed and dressed in a fresh shirt and trousers, and then looked at his board and tried to ignore the ghosts beneath it.

The board was mounted on his wall and contained all the information they had gleaned at the fires that had spread across Hell these past weeks. It wasn't much, a disparate collection of words and thoughts, lists of ideas, of suppositions, of guesses and things crossed out as they were disproved or dismissed. Fool used threads to link resemblances between the various fires, but the only constant was that each fire was man-made; there were more differences than similarities. Some were near water and easily doused, some were miles from the nearest stream or pond. Several of the burned buildings had contained the dead in their seared rooms, others were empty or contained only the things that Hell stored, food or machinery or other, more obscure, items. Some of the information he had discovered or surmised himself, some he had taken from the reports written by Marianne. Recently, she had become his regular companion on the investigations, acting as sounding board but also revealing a useful talent for writing detailed précis of the scenes before them and the stories he drew out of the scenes. She also had a memory, could recite back to him the things he said as he wandered about the burned spaces, had become a repository for his mutterings and thoughts.

Stepping back and looking at his board, with its crossing threads and pinned pieces of paper, Fool was struck again by the depth of his ignorance while in the gathering shadows below it the ghosts of Summer and Gordie looked on. Summer smiled encouragingly but Gordie merely shook his head slightly, as though disappointed.

Gordie and Summer, his colleagues, his dead colleagues, the last of the Information Men to die before this new Information Office had been set up, before the Information House had had its derelict upper floors opened up as barracks so that demons and humans now coexisted uneasily, sleeping in quarters that stretched the length of the building. Gordie and Summer, his friends, returned to him these last weeks as these pale and silent ghosts standing in the room's shadows, as these pallid reflections of the people he had known and still missed.

Gordie was looking at Fool's notice board, peering at the ever-expanding diagram detailing the fires. So much information, and so little *fact;* the number of crossing threads and handwritten notes growing every day, more and more ideas being laid out among the sketches and thoughts, pushing off the corners of the board and spreading across Fool's walls like some creeping fungus.

"Can you see something I'm missing?" asked Fool, going to stand by Gordie. When the ghosts, or spirits, or whatever they were, had first appeared, or Fool had first started to imagine them, he had been frightened. Frightened of what they might represent. Now he was almost glad to see them.

Gordie did not reply, simply carried on looking at the board, his pale eyes darting along lines of thread and then returning, trying another tack. His lips were moving soundlessly as he read the board. Fool tried to follow the same lines that Gordie was traveling, tried to watch the man's face as well as the board, to see the routes the little ghost followed, but he couldn't keep up and in the end he simply stood and looked for himself. It was like looking into the water of a pool that was filled with floating, whirling debris, trying to see what lay in its muddy depths. Sometimes, Fool would think he was almost grasping the outlines of something and then it would shift, twist, break apart, and he would be looking at meaningless patterns again. It made his head ache and he turned away and went to Summer.

She was sitting at the small desk by Fool's bed and was writing despite the fact that she held no pen. Black marks were appearing across the surface of the scarred wood, meaningless marks that faded after a few seconds. Fool watched them closely, hoping to see something recognizable, a word or a sketch of some place or person or thing he could identify, but no; Summer's scrawls were as shifting and arbitrary as everything else in this fucking investigation.

Sighing, Fool turned away. Alive, Summer and Gordie had been his friends and his allies; as ghosts, they were just pictures given movement, dumb images without sense or opinion, and he had work to do.

The Information Office, although still housed only in this one building, expanded seemingly every day, and he had to try to keep track of it. Already there were troops whose names he knew he would never know appearing in the ranks, inventories of equipment to submit and sign off on, lower-ranking officers he had never met sending him reports on crimes he did not know had taken place, and above or below them all the Evidence, a thing under its own control snapping at their heels. Turning to the first of the reports, Fool began to read.

3

Hand was on duty.

"Fool," Hand said as he walked into the Questioning House's foyer, "we don't see you as much as we used to. Are you too important to talk to us now that you hold such a lofty position?"

Hand and Tidyman were now Hell's only two Questioners, although Fool suspected that more Questioning Houses would soon be opened to match the increased number of Information Men; more officers meant more crimes being investigated, after all. Neither man liked Fool much. Partly it was, he thought, the reverse of why the demonkind Information Men disliked him; whereas they had to take orders from a mere human, Hand and Tidyman saw him apparently consorting with the demons as though he was their equal or they his. It made him, for them, something other than human, a traitor or a half-breed thing with a foot in both camps but belonging to neither.

It was more than that, though. The ghost of Morgan stood between them and Fool, the knowledge that Tidyman and Hand had done nothing to help the man when he had been attacked and murdered in the Questioning House, and they knew Fool knew it and that he felt disgust toward them for their inaction.

"Hand," he said, uncomfortably aware of the uniform he now wore, its quality compared to the drab smock that Hand wore under the blood-spattered apron. It fit him properly, for one thing, the trousers long enough and the jacket comfortably tight around his chest and belly rather than flapping wide and loose.

"My, you sent us a lot yesterday," said Hand, looking over Fool's shoulder at the bodies lying wrapped in tarpaulins that the porters were laying along the foyer wall. "You've been a busy boy! It's good to see that Hell is using its favorite son well."

"I want this one questioned first," said Fool, ignoring Hand's jibe and pointing to the dead man at his feet. He had opened several of the tarpaulins, peeling them back like loose skin to reveal the savaged flesh beneath, before finding the man the Evidence had killed.

"Is he the most important man, like you?" asked Hand. "The first of the victims, the first among the lost and damned? Do you want to know how he died? Or perhaps the question today is who killed him, so that you can hunt the murderer down and slaughter them like the good servant you are?"

"I know who killed him and how he died," said Fool. "What I want from you, Hand, is to know if before he died he was a murderer."

Hand opened his mouth to speak, but before he could Fool stepped forward, face close to the other man's, and said, "Think carefully before you say another word, Hand. If I'm so important, perhaps I could shoot you where you stand, don't you think, without fear of punishment? Or maybe I could speak to my colleague Mr. Tap about you. Even you, Hand, hiding away in the House, must have heard of it, yes? All the rumors, all the terrible little things people are saying? How would you like it if it came to visit you, if the Evidence came calling? Are you so perfect, Hand, that you might be allowed to walk away from Mr. Tap's men without mark or harm? Shall I call him so that he can join us for these interviews?"

"No," said Hand quietly. He looked down at the floor, shuffled his feet, and then spoke without raising his eyes. "There's no need to be like that. I was simply going to say that I have a new technique that I think will work with this flesh. There's no need to threaten me."

Fool didn't reply, stepping back and letting Hand walk away. After a moment, he gestured for the porters to pick up the body and he followed, thinking, *What have I become?*

Hand had the body placed on the table in the center of the Questioning Room and then wheeled a smaller table over to its side. Instead of setting out the usual paraphernalia that accompanied questionings, the knives and scales and slides and liquids in stoppered bottles, he placed three plain bowls on the table and then filled two of them to their brims with water. Then he took two bottles from one of the cupboards that lined the walls, carrying them to the table carefully. The first he opened very slowly, never letting it tilt or spill, and poured a few drops of its contents, a clear liquid that steamed slightly, into the first bowl. From the second, which he handled with more confidence, he poured a string of thick, brown fluid into the next bowl. The smell of it was awful, shit and dirt and corruption contained in a bottle. Seeing Fool watching, Hand said, "Holy water and diluted excrement. Purity and filth."

"The extremes of Heaven and Hell," said Fool, remembering something that Morgan had once said to him. He glanced to his side as he spoke, half expecting to see Morgan's ghost nodding at him the way he saw Gordie's and Summer's. The room was empty.

"Yes," said Hand, a note of grudging, surprised respect in his voice. "I'll lift the corpse's hand over the bowls. Make a simple statement and I'll let the hand fall; if it lands in the clear water, the statement is true, if in the filth it's false, and if it lands in the empty one it either doesn't understand what you've said or it's irrelevant."

Fool waited until Hand had raised the corpse's arm and then said, "You did not kill the people in the Seamstress House."

The hand splashed into the clear water. Where it spilled out onto the table, the liquid steamed more violently for a moment before evaporating away to nothing.

True. Hand lifted the arm again.

Remembering Orobas's comment about hiring someone, Fool said, "You did nothing to help arrange the deaths."

True.

"You knew nothing about the deaths at all."

True.

"The Evidence killed you without cause."

True, and the last of the bowl's water was gone now and there was only the bowl of filth left, the bowl to confirm falsehoods. Fool wondered if he could try to question the corpse by making only false statements, but the thought of arriving at truth through untruth made his head ache and he decided against it. He stepped back from the table, from the corpse.

Hand said, "No more? Probably sensible, I think you've had all you're going to get. What do you want from the other bodies?"

"What do I want? The same as always, Hand; I want the truth."

Hand looked at Fool for a long moment and then turned away, muttering. Although Fool couldn't hear him properly, he thought the man might have said, "Some hope."

They were on a train.

The journey back to the Information House was slow and uncomfortable, and Fool felt, despite the apparent confirmation that he had acted correctly, exposed and raw, uncertain. *I've been stupid,* he thought, *little stupid Fool, thinking that things are different, that I'm important, that I'm protected. But Mr. Tap's right, I'm* not *important, I'm no one. I keep forgetting, and I can't, I* daren't. *I'm a human, in Hell, and I'm no one.* Out loud, he said, "I'm a fool."

"Sir?" Marianne, sitting across from him, head down and arms loose over her knees. The rest of the humans had seated themselves in the other bench seats, away from Fool and Marianne, opening a gap between them, telling Hell and those who watched them that, look, they weren't a part of what Fool and Marianne had done the day before, desperate not to be noticed. The demons were clustered together at the end of the carriage, and although none had said anything directly, he knew they were muttering about him, the resentment clear. What Hand had told Fool had made no difference to them.

"Thank you," Fool said quietly.

"What for?"

"For yesterday," he said. "For—" and then stopped, not wanting to say it. Saying it felt as though it might free it, somehow, send the truth of it onward and outward, to the eyes and ears of the Bureaucracy.

"It was nothing," she said, and he could almost hear the hope in her voice, *Let it be nothing, let it be unimportant.*

"It wasn't nothing, you did the right thing," he said. "It was interfering in our investigation, had just committed murder."

"Do you think they'll see it like that?" *They,* the demons they worked with and the demons above them and the Archdeacons above them and finally Elderflower, small and delicate and foul. Was Elderflower watching them still? Taking an interest? Were they still being watched by the thing that might or might not be Satan himself, or had it lost interest in them now?

"I don't know," he said honestly, unsure whose question he was answering, his own or hers, "but I'll try to make sure they do. You're a good Information Man, Marianne, or will be if you're given the time." It was the first time he'd spoken her name out loud, and the word felt smooth and full in his mouth.

"Thank you," she said, and lowered her head farther, the curve of her scalp and the solidity of the skull beneath showing through the soft down of her hair. She had kept the bag she had used the day before, reached for it and pulled it onto her knee and brushed it where it had hit the Evidence Man. "I knew the man hadn't done it, and I was so scared and I didn't think. I couldn't get to my gun in time and just grabbed at the nearest thing to use."

"You did the right thing," said Fool. "It'll be okay."

"Will it?"

"Yes," he said, and she did not reply but let the lie merge with the rest of the noise in the carriage.

The train was full, lumbering along the road back toward the Bureaucratic district and the residences beyond with stolid patience, but for once the Information Men had a carriage to themselves. They had cleared the space when they got on, pushing the other travelers out of it, the demons enjoying the chance to work out a little of their aggression. Fool wouldn't usually allow his troops to use their authority to gain favor this way, but that morning he needed to think without the clamor of workers returning or going to their employment, of Genevieves and Marys, Hell's whores, traveling in and out of the Houska, of people staring at him while trying not to stare and talking about him with ill-disguised interest. The demons were now sitting around the doorway into the carriage, and whenever anyone peered in through the grimy window in the door or tried to open it, they pushed it shut or banged clawed hands on the glass.

Fool thought.

Or rather, he tried to; there was too much going on in his head to gain any real clarity. He tried to compartmentalize the various strands, hoping to see his mind as an extension of the board in his room, with its connecting strings and clues and ideas. He sometimes thought that Gordie might have had a brain that saw things that way, everything touching everything else in some way or other, linked by fact and suggestion and inspiration.

Gordie. Fool missed Gordie, and missed Summer, and their ghosts were perhaps the closest things he had to friends now, shades inhabiting his room, ever silent and insubstantial. He looked again at Marianne, wondering if she could be molded into an officer like Gordie or Summer had been, thought that maybe she could be, and then returned to the bigger subjects that were crashing and swirling in his head.

Fires were springing up across Hell without any obvious connection besides the fact that they had happened and that they made the Bureaucracy nervous in some way; it wasn't something that had been said to him directly, nothing they would admit, but it was there in the spaces between the words and lines on the parchments in the canisters. Instead of the usual blunt information the canisters contained, *Murder of a person in the Houska* or *Battery of workers on the train*, the information given to him about the fires was warier, less clear. It contained words such as "unexplained," "purposeless," and "unacceptable." They were messages with no surety, tentative, asking for Fool's help rather than simply demanding his action.

The problem was, he had come to few conclusions. All he was sure of was that the fires were being started using human interventions rather than demonic, and each had grown like some glittering, monstrous flower, consuming everything from that one point. The question was, who was doing it? And why?

And then there were yesterday's murders. They bothered him, more than Hell's usual violence did; it was rare for such an organized slaughter to occur, and rarer still for it to be so clinical, so passionless. He could think of no other incidents like this. Violence in Hell was personal, individual, handed down from demon to human, and when more than one demon was involved it was as a mob, not in a planned attack as this one had been. Was this simply another indicator of how Hell was changing, along with the new *Guide* and emergence of the Evidence and the other tiny things that he saw shifting and altering every day?

It was all around him, when he thought about it, the new Hell emerging from the flesh of the old like a bug burrowing out from a long-dead corpse; the new rules, the disappearances, curfews that the Bureaucracy had started to place on certain areas and certain groups, the new uniforms that he and the rest of the Information Men had been given and the better food and drink they now had to eat. It set them apart from the rest of Hell, made Hell's human inhabitants jealous and demon inhabitants angry. *We're becoming a thing apart,* he thought, *little Fool and his Information House and the troops of the Information Office, accepted by neither the humans nor the demons.* It was too much to think about, and when he tried his mind couldn't hold the sheer size of what was happening.

And then there was the other thing.

In truth, everything else was a mere distraction from what had happened at the crime scene. Fool had shot an Evidence Man, one of Hell's appointed; true, the shooting might be justified given that the demon had been attacking someone who had since been proven innocent, but when did that ever count as a defense? As though justice in Hell was based on right or wrong? Fool had killed demons before, yes, but never ones that were in the direct employ of the Bureaucracy.

Never ones under the control of Mr. Tap.

Had he really started believing in his own unassailability? Forgotten the way things used to be, the way it felt to be frightened all the time that you would be noticed, even if the notice was only being glimpsed at the edge of something's vision, not knowing if the glimpse would become something more? "Fool," he murmured and had no idea if he was chastising himself or saying his name simply to keep himself real, to try to ward off an impending, unknowable disaster.

There was a clinking sound behind him, a choked rattle, and something rolled out from under Fool's seat. It knocked against one of his feet so that it turned, its direction shifting, and ended up against the train's wall. It was a canister, and an orange thread was wrapped around it.

Fool looked around, startled; several of the Information Men, seeing his reaction, looked around as well. There was no tube in the corner of the train, nowhere for the canister to have come from, and yet there it was, jolting slightly and rocking back and forth in rhythm with the train, tapping against the wall. Fool reached for it and even the demonkind Information Men stopped their surly head-bowed talking and watched him as he unscrewed the end and let the paper scroll inside it drop out. He unfurled it against his knee, smoothing it with the palm of one hand while holding it with the other. A single word, *NOW*, and an address. An address that, the orange ribbon told him, was burning.

Fool recognized the address, knew where it was; it was a boarding-house in Eve's Harbor, one inhabited by Marys. He looked out the train's window, trying to calculate where they were and where the train would take them. Nowhere near where they needed to be. Turning back to the carriage, he said, "Get organized."

The train wouldn't stop, had no driver, so they had to open the door and jump, one by one, landing on the street and stumbling or rolling clear of the vehicle's great, grinding metal wheels. Before he leaped, Fool looked at the muddied ground rolling past him. It looked unreal, like a fake surface, something without solidity, and he felt, for the strangest moment, that he would hit it and fall through, tear a hole in it and fall somewhere else, and then he stepped out and the shock of the landing tore up through his legs and he was staggering and one of his human Men caught him and held him upright.

"Let's go," Fool said, and they started walking.

Walking no longer seemed fast enough; they ran.

Despite the daylight the glow of the fire was visible over the tops of the buildings from a distance away, a glimmering orange scour that stretched over the intervening roofs like moss. Closer to, they heard the sounds of the fire, a low grumble as the flames ate at the wood, and the screams of the people trapped within the building as it burned.

The conflagration came into view as they emerged from between two buildings, and even from a hundred yards Fool could feel the heat of it, feel it pressing against his face and digging its fingers under his clothing and clasping at his chest and belly. A crowd had gathered in front of the building, small and restless and helpless. Some of them were crying, others screaming, and the sound of them was another layer to the day's cacophony, the music of Hell ringing out clear and loud. There was no water nearby, no stream or river to tap, and nothing to be done for the people trapped inside.

As Fool and the Information Men arrived at the boardinghouse, someone fell from an upper window. She was burning already and left a trail of smoke as she descended, striking the ground with a noise like a sack of grain dropping. Sparks and flames danced out from the impact, spiraling away into the air. Screams rose and someone ran out from the crowd, trying to reach the burning person, but they were driven back by the heat, choking and moaning.

Another dying Mary fell, or leaped, from a window and spiraled to the ground, coming to rest with a dark and final thud.

"Are any of you demons of flame?" Fool asked his troops. "Any of you?"

The demons among his Men looked at him. None replied. Orobas turned its back, ears twitching.

"Can any of you withstand flame?" asked Fool, desperate. How many Marys, how many *people,* were gathering in the windows of the building? There seemed to be hundreds, all imploring him to do something, to rescue them somehow. Some of the glass panes still had not broken, and faces were pressed up against the glass, distorted by the sheer mass of them, eyes weeping, mouths open, screams eaten by the fires. In other windows the glass had gone and the Marys were leaning out, arms outstretched and glass-torn, and their screams Fool heard, heard as though they were becoming the only sound in Hell, screaming, crying for help. One woman, hair on fire, leaned too far and she, too, fell. The sound of her scream cutting off as she hit the ground was like a blade across Fool's ears.

"None of you?" he asked, and again there was no response. He turned to the building, looking around to see if there was something, *anything,* that might help, but no, nothing. Fool stepped toward the building, pushing his way between the crowd, coughing as the heat dried the air in his mouth, but had to stop. It was too hot, the heat too solid for him to move any farther forward. Another Mary fell, this time from a lower-floor window. She flipped over as she dropped to the ground, naked and alight, leaving greasy strings of smoke behind her in the air. She carried on burning after she landed, the fall not enough to kill her, a triangle of flame flickering between the cleft of her legs, scalp raging with violent orange fires. She rolled over and managed to crawl three or four uneven feet and then collapsed sideways, arms outstretched, and the smell of burning hair and roasting, bubbling fat that reached Fool made him turn away and swallow down a mouthful of bile. He bent forward in the hope that he could keep the retch inside him, swallowing the sourness in his mouth as hot and bitter saliva spurted against the inside of his cheeks. Behind him, the sound of bodies hitting the earth was a constant tattoo, as though a heavy storm was brewing.

In the end, Fool sent his troops back to the House and watched the boardinghouse burn without them; there was nothing else he could do.

It took hours. The flames blackened the wood as the Marys inside screamed, most choosing to try to jump from the windows in the hope of escape. Several made it far enough from the flames to be gathered into the crowd's embrace, but their wounds were terrible, huge weeping blisters that burst as their skin continued cooking and shrinking, blackened scabs flaking away from their flesh to reveal raw fat and muscle below, and they died not long after their falls. At one point several members of the crowd tried to get close enough to catch the falling women, holding a blanket out between them, but the heat drove them back as the edge of the blanket singed its way to blackness and they had to abandon the attempt and simply watch as the fires raged and grew and swallowed.

Finally, the building's roof collapsed, sending a huge tongue of flame and grand swirls of burning debris into the air, and not long after one of its walls fell in and then there was nothing but fire and heat and the smell of scorched air and death, and Fool walked away.

He had gone perhaps half a mile when he needed to sit down at the side of the road, putting his head in his hands and resting them on his knees and weeping. His tears fell to the dust, dark pearls between his feet growing opaque as they rolled in the dirt before vanishing. People moved past him, uncaring, none of them stopping or acknowledging him. He wept, alone, and was glad of his solitude.

When he looked up, two of Mr. Tap's Evidence Men were staring at him from across the street, and he wondered what rule he might be breaking. Something to do with sitting still? With crying? With simply existing? As they approached him Fool rose, still crying, brushing the dirt from his uniform, and walked away.

He walked without thinking, occasionally glancing over his shoulder. The Evidence Men followed him for several minutes, seemingly undecided about what to do, and then they got bored or found someone else to focus their attentions on and left him alone. He walked on, trying to tread his thoughts into order, moving out into the farmland beyond the residential areas, passing fields in which scrawny beasts grazed, fattening themselves for slaughter. He walked, and gradually his tears slowed.

Eventually, the heat of the day became oppressive, and Fool looked for shade, seeing a copse of trees ahead of him. Where was he? he wondered as he approached them. Somewhere in the center of Hell, he thought; if he carried on walking, he would eventually reach the Flame Garden, east would bring him back around to the Houska, and if he turned west he would reach the Mount and the tunnel that led to Heaven. Thinking of Heaven made him look up, but the city in the sky was obscured by the daylight. He saw a pale glimmer that might have been towers or spires hiding behind the light and then he was under the trees and in the shade.

It was cooler here, the fragmented shade lying across the ground in an uneven pattern of light and dark, and Fool sat down and let his head fall to his drawn-up knees, no longer crying but tired, so very tired. He took a deep breath, smelling baked earth and rotten leaves, and thought. Ultimately, he supposed, there was little he could do but return to the Information House and carry on, to try to find whatever threads there were to be found, to try to do his duty until Hell decided upon his fate.

"Fool."

Fool jerked his head up off his knees and looked around; there was no one there.

"Fool," again, and the voice was almost familiar, as though someone whom Fool had known years earlier and miles away but had mostly forgotten was speaking. It was soft, as though made from two pieces of leather being carefully rubbed together, his name drawn out in a long, careful syllable. It made him think of the time of the Fallen, made images jumble in his mind, of something tilting out from a wall and collapsing down, of things being eaten or taken from the air, of a wide and toothed mouth opening by his hand and removing the feather from him.

Of something dead, of something alive.

"Fool," a third time, and this time Fool replied.

"Who is this?"

"Don't you remember me? Fool, I'm disappointed," said the voice, and then Fool *did* recognize the voice, the memory crashing back in.

The Man of Plants and Flowers.

Fool stood quickly, hand going to his gun; the Man was dangerous and not to be trusted, despite the help he had given Fool in the past. The ground at his feet rippled as something moved under the cover of dead leaves and then they were tumbling aside as the grass struggled free, weaving upward, knocking aside the mulch. Above him, the branches of the trees began to twist, bending with the creak of straining wood, coming down in front of him and wrapping around each other, forming a face made of stem and leaf.

"Fool," said the Man for a fourth time. "It's good to finally speak to you again."

"You're dead," said Fool but knew he wasn't. That last time he and the Man had spoken had the gloss of a dream now, something half remembered and disjointed. Had the Man really spoken to him after the death of the Fallen? Yes, yes he had, and yet Fool had then forgotten him and he didn't know why.

"I'm impossible to kill, Fool," said the Man, "but I have let myself recede into the background for a while, yes."

"You told me you weren't dead," said Fool, "but I didn't remember after. Why not?"

The branches shifted and there was a noise like tearing cloth. *He's laughing,* thought Fool, *laughing at me, laughing at the little dense Fool.* He drew his gun, raised it, lowered it again, feeling foolish. There was no one to point it at.

"Fool, you've done better than most in Hell, but you still don't understand it, do you? The whole of the Hierarchies think I'm dead, the Bureaucracy thinks I'm dead, thanks to you and your investigation and the intervention of that glorious angel, and if they think I'm dead then I'm *dead*. You forgot me because if the Bureaucracy doesn't acknowledge me then I have no reality here, and it has suited me to leave it that way. I'm still here, though, I've been here all the time, still the Man of Plants and Flowers, and I'm still *everywhere*."

The Man's voice sounded weak, the words not fully formed by the branches. *He's lying*, thought Fool, *or at least not telling me the full truth. Whatever he was, he's different now from what he used to be, and whatever the angel did to him has taken him time to get over, weakened him in a way I don't think he expected.* Aloud, he asked, "What have you been doing?"

"Nothing, Fool," replied the Man, and he was laughing again now, a raspy wooden chortle that filled the glade about Fool. "I found a secluded place, a little island of solitude, and had a rest and simply considered my options. I've enjoyed being nowhere, Fool. It's been fun."

"But now you're back?"

"I'm back, and thought I'd say hello."

"Why say hello? To me, I mean. Why not keep being dead?"

"Why do I do anything, Fool? Because it amuses me, because *you* amuse me. I enjoyed our chats, and hope to rekindle them one day if circumstances permit. Besides, you helped me die, so I decided I owed you a favor. Something is coming, Fool, coming for you."

"What's coming?"

The grass writhed, tangling over Fool's shoes and sending slimy strands up inside his trouser legs to caress his ankles. The branches hanging in front of his face shook as they formed the words, "Something big, Fool, big and terrible and dangerous. Watch out, little Fool, for where you are going even I cannot help you."

The branches had untangled, springing back up into the canopy above him, and the grass had fallen back from his feet. The Man had gone.

"Fool."

"Yes?" Thinking it was the Man back for one last utterance, hoping that it was, panic gathering in his chest, and wanting to run.

"You are wanted," said Mr. Tap, yanking Fool off his feet in a violent, startling jerk, and Fool knew that he had missed his chance and that if there had ever been a time for running, that time was past.

4

Fool's head was in a bag that smelled of blood and vomit.

He had tried to lift his gun, still in his hand from his time with the Man, but Mr. Tap was quicker, or Fool too slow, and the demon had wrapped Fool's fist in its bony hand and squeezed until Fool felt his fingers would be cracked against the gun's stock. When he yelped in pain, the sound escaping from between clenched teeth that wanted to give Mr. Tap no satisfaction, Mr. Tap loosened its grip and said in a strangely conversational tone, "Drop it." Fool dropped it.

Mr. Tap spun Fool about, tying his hands behind his back and pulling the bag down over his head; Fool's last view of Hell was of the farmlands beyond the copse, the dry fields stretching out and the ragged lines of workers moving across them. Then he was lost in a bitter darkness and was lifted, draped over Mr. Tap's bony shoulder, the edge digging into his belly, and then they were running. He was jolted, bouncing, the smell of the bag in his nostrils, dust tickling at his eyes when he opened them until he eventually left them closed; there was nothing to see anyway, just blackness and the fears that his mind wrote in the bag around his head.

He didn't know how long it took, in the end. Ten minutes? An hour? Fool's sense of time had deserted him, somehow closed out of that terrible bag along with the light; he knew only that the journey was ongoing, and he waited and itched and imagined the worms from the cracks in Mr. Tap's skin wriggling between the folds of his clothes and burrowing into his skin, writhing and burning, and then it was over. Mr. Tap suddenly halted and Fool was flung down, crashing hard onto a stone floor. He was flipped over onto his front, face pressing against the rough burlap of the sack and the foul odor was deep in his nose and mouth like muddy water, and then his wrists were untied and the blood was rushing back into his hands in a painful wave.

"Good-bye, Fool," said Mr. Tap in that same conversational voice. There was a sharp clatter by Fool's head and then the sound of footsteps as Mr. Tap left.

Fool sat up, reaching cautiously for the bag over his head. *What will I see when I remove it?* he wondered. *All the disappeared, hundreds of us heaped together, Hell's forgotten left together in some vast cell? Marianne, gathered from the streets as well, bagged and broken? Will they be dead? Will I be? Or am I alone, a man in the darkness?* He tugged at the rough material, the bag came away, and the space about him was revealed.

Fool was in a small, anonymous room. It was mostly bare except for a long table at one end and a door behind the table, with high windows set in one wall. The panes in the windows were grimy, cataracted with dirt and showing nothing through themselves except a gray that might have been sky or the ceiling of a corridor.

When Fool looked back at the table, Rhakshasas was sitting behind it.

"So, we find ourselves here again, Thomas Fool, Commander of the Information Office of Hell," Rhakshasas said, and the entrails around its torso squirmed and tightened and loosened as it spoke. The demon was huge, filling the end of the room, its arms lying on the table. When it moved, it left brown and red smears behind it that glistened before drying to silvery flakes. After several long moments of silence, it spoke again.

"Yet again, you challenge Hell and we have to decide what to do with you. Is it true, what Mr. Tap says?"

"I don't know, what does he say?" asked Fool and immediately regretted it. *I am the Commander of the Information Men of Hell, Rhakshasas itself has just used my full title, which must mean something, something I can't see, can't work out, don't antagonize him, little insolent Fool.*

"That you killed a bauta?"

"A bauta?"

"An Evidence Man, Fool, going about the lawful carrying out of its duty."

I thought so. "No."

"No?"

"It was not going about lawful duty, it was killing an innocent man."

"Innocent, Fool? Here?"

"You know what I mean."

"Do I?" asked Rhakshasas, leaning forward, its tone if anything even colder. The entrails swelled around it, pumping themselves up, making the demon seem even larger. Were they a part of Rhakshasas, or some separate creature living on it like a parasite? Fool wasn't sure, watched fascinated as they wriggled, moving like snakes around the demon's shoulders and torso. "The bauta believed him to be guilty at the time of the incident, Fool. That makes you a murderer."

"No. It had been told that the man's guilt was impossible but chose to ignore the evidence presented to it by more experienced officers."

"'More experienced officers'? You, Thomas Fool, most important of the Information Men in Hell?"

"Yes. No. Yes, it came from me, but no, I'm not the most important."

"I'm glad you recognize that, at least. And you have made no progress on the fires?"

"No."

"And are there other things you may tell the Archdeacons, Fool? Things we need to know, which may mitigate your actions?"

The Man lives. "No."

"Then we have a problem, Fool. The bauta may have been impetuous, but it has the right to act according to how it sees fit. Mr. Tap and the Evidence Men may do as they like to reach the truth, Fool, and the bauta's consumption of the man's fears and pain would have revealed to it the truth of his innocence. You prevented this truth from being revealed, got in the way of justice, simply because you did not like the methods being used, and yet who are you to make that choice? You interrupted the Evidence Man in the course of his duty, Fool, and the Archdeacons cannot ignore it."

Fool looked down, dropping his eyes from Rhakshasas's constantly moving skin of gut and slime, away from the smell of it and the face that sat atop the moving body, grim and with eyes that were bloody and dark. His gun was on the floor by his feet.

"Would you pick it up, Fool, try to shoot me?" said Rhakshasas, seeing Fool's gaze pick up the weapon.

"If I'm to die," said Fool, bending and deliberately retrieving the gun, turning it in his hands slowly, "then I may as well take my chances."

"Die, Fool? Who said anything about dying? No, Fool, you misunderstand. We're sending you to Heaven."

Heaven.

The word looped lazily out of Rhakshasas's mouth and caught Fool in the side like a punch. It rocked him, sending his balance tilting, and he stepped sideways and dropped to one knee. His gun fell from his hand, skittering away across a floor that seemed to yaw and pitch beneath him.

Heaven.

Did this mean he was saved? To be Elevated? Had he atoned for his sins, whatever they were? Did it? Fool raised his head to look at Rhakshasas, who was leaning back in its chair and looking at Fool intently.

"Heaven?" It was hard to even speak the word. Had he ever spoken it out loud before? He wasn't sure, but didn't think so. Most people in Hell kept it inside themselves, like some secret talisman that would tarnish if they let it out, their emblem of hope, hope that this time they would be picked, that this time they would be raised to the place above them that gleamed in the clouds, that this time was their time. Hope, always hope.

Rhakshasas was smiling now, still watching Fool, mouth split into a wide grin revealing teeth that were little more than black stubs.

"That was fun," it said at last.

"It was a lie?" said Fool, cursing the tiny, fragmented dreams that had birthed themselves in him, that had risen in his head and filled his vision. Did he really think he'd been picked for an Elevation? Rewarded for his service to Hell's Bureaucracy? Did he really still believe it might happen?

Yes. Yes, the worm was still turning in his belly, sending waves of nausea through his body, wasted adrenaline souring in his muscles and the taste of fire in his mouth.

"A lie? No, of course not. I rarely lie, Thomas Fool. I'm angelic stock, after all, and lying has little part of an angel's makeup. You are going to Heaven, Commander of the Information Office of Hell, you are simply not being Elevated."

Fool reached out and picked his weapon up. The hard floor had stopped moving now, was steadier, balance returning as the waves of sickness ebbed within him. He turned the gun around and peered into its black barrel, trying to see if he could discern the tip of the bullet in its narrow throat.

He was crying, again. Fool squeezed his eyes shut, felt tears break loose and make their way down his cheeks, opened his eyes again and stared once more into the darkness. What would happen if he pulled the trigger? Blew his brains out behind him, stopped this terrible cycle of fear and misery and hope and disappointment and violence? Simply ceased to be, unmade himself?

"It won't fire," said Rhakshasas. "You should realize that. We won't give you such a simple escape, it's far better to see you toil and toil and still fail. This is Hell, after all. Now, we have business. Stand, please, and we can begin."

Fool didn't move. Heaven—it dangled before him, almost visible in the room's air, a gleam somewhere in the gun's barrel, Heaven but no Elevation. He took a last look into the darkness of the weapon, bringing it close to his eye, and then flipped it around and dropped it into his holster. When he stood, he was pleased to find he felt steady, although his vision was still fogged with tears.

"Good," said Rhakshasas, also standing. The demon filled the end of the room, the intestines around it moving constantly, the bulk of it drawing in the light and creating dark, foul-smelling shadows. It moved around the table and came to stand before Fool, the smell of it thick, warm, oozing, and reached out clawed hands, taking hold of Fool's shoulders.

"You are the Commander of Hell's Information Office and all Information Men," it said, leaning forward so that its face was close to Fool's, filling his vision. "Tears are a luxury, and there is no space for luxuries in Hell."

A tongue covered in ragged spikes emerged from Rhakshasas's mouth, pushing past the rotted teeth, and licked Fool's cheeks. Its touch was surprisingly delicate, almost a caress, but the smell of it was grotesque, a reek of old feces and food gone to waste and bodies gone to rot. Rhakshasas pushed its face closer to Fool's, tilting its head slightly, and then its mouth opened wider and the tongue clamped on to him, wrapped around his head. The demon let out a long, slow sigh as it suckled at his tears, yanking Fool forward as he tried to jerk back, lifting him from his feet, moaning.

Finally, the demon let its head fall away, gasping aloud. It dropped Fool and shook itself, swallowing loudly. Its tongue pulled back, wiping slowly across the demon's face in lazy swirls before retreating into the mouth. Rhakshasas's coiled guts clenched, glistening, and then they, too, relaxed. "Delicious," the demon said. "Now, shall we get on?"

5

There were three of them, two older demons and one scurrying thing that Fool assumed would be little more than scribe and general servant.

"This is the Delegation," said Rhakshasas, "and you will serve them during your time in Heaven."

They were in one of the smaller rooms in Assemblies House, the central hub of the Bureaucracy's functioning in Hell. The first of the demons was apparently made entirely of larvae, a human-shaped figure that constantly writhed, maggots falling from it and crawling back into the mass in an ongoing stream. It had no face, but there were impressions where mouth and eyes should be in the thing that might have been a head atop its boiling, wriggling shoulders. It was, disconcertingly, wearing a cape that flapped and a hat that even when it was still rocked because of the movement of its maggot flesh.

The other was worse.

It was as though someone had stitched together the remains of hundreds of dead animals, all rotten, so that the flesh dripped and slithered and bones showed through the mess of it. Its head might have once been a dog's, its chest the remains of a bird, ribs exposed and covered in ragged feathers, arms long and spindly but ending in pads from which claws extended and retracted. It had no eyeballs, only weeping sockets that contained glittering red sparks in their depths, and its lips were torn and hanging, revealing teeth that were uneven and yellow. It wore an old suit, dusty where it wasn't wet with slime and filth, buttoned closed beneath the collapsing rib cage but too small, so that in the gap between trousers and jacket more rotten flesh was visible. Its feet were bird's feet, long-toed, mostly bone and leather. Neither was introduced to him by name.

They're sending the worst of Hell, thought Fool, *the most grotesque. This is about the look of things as much as the content. This is about the face we show in the trades, in the making of deals between Heaven and Hell, the appearance we decide upon and the way it makes those that look upon us feel. This is about how we make ourselves appear fearsome and fierce and* hellish *so we can get the things we want. This is the business of Bureaucracy.*

He glanced down at the new uniform Rhakshasas had given him, a black suit and shirt that fit him well and soft leather boots, the first footwear in Hell that Fool had possessed that was comfortable. They had dressed him up, too, a doll to make the Delegation look good; the jacket was long so that it moved when he did, swirling like wings, and the suit and shirt were made of soft material that seemed to absorb the light. Wearing it made him feel like a shadow.

Fool the shade, he thought, *little foolish shade.* They had made him into something new, something to present to Heaven, not an Elevated soul but a servant one, a part of Hell sent forth to barter and deal. He fingered the edge of the jacket, hand pale against the dark fabric, and felt even more like a ghost, not the Thomas Fool he had come to know over these last weeks and months but something new and unknown.

"We are almost ready," said Rhakshasas, "are we not?"

"Yes," said the stitch demon, its voice bubbling and wet. This was the Delegation's leader, the one through whom the trades would be finalized. Discolored saliva fell from its mouth as it spoke, dripping to its chest and adding to the stains that covered its suit. It inclined its head toward Fool and said, "Does it know its position?"

"Behind you," said Fool. "Serving you. Doing your bidding."

"Good," said the thing, more foul liquid spattering out as it spoke. The other watched silently, pieces of it falling, hitting the floor, and crawling eagerly back to their host.

"Thomas is an obedient servant," said Rhakshasas, coming close to Fool. "He is the first of Hell's humans to be sent to Heaven without being Elevated, the first and possibly the last. He will serve us without question, won't you, Thomas Fool?"

Fool opened his mouth to reply, and that's when Rhakshasas's coat of entrails leaped off the demon and swarmed around him.

The stench was terrible, thick and sour and rich and foul, but the feel of their touch was worse. They slithered, wet and warm, around his head and neck, burrowing under his new uniform, forcing it away from his body and ripping it, wrapping around his torso and legs and arms, tightening, leaving him naked.

Burning.

Fool tried to shriek but the thick ropes of gut were clamped around his face, pulsing, blocking his mouth and, oh God, things moving within the tubes. He could *feel* chunks beneath the skin of the intestines, churning and shifting, the pressure of them warm against him. A loop of it pushed into his mouth, flattening his tongue against his teeth, pushing his jaws apart, the taste of it foul. He retched, the vomit gathering in his mouth, backing up his nose, and he couldn't breathe and he was gagging and it didn't matter because he was burning, he was *burning*, the coils tightening and digging in and burning and burning and burning. Fool began to choke on the vomit, managed to spit some of it around the blockage in his mouth. Breathing in was impossible, breathing out impossible, there was just the taste and the smell and the burning. His jaws ached, mouth full of gut and slime, and a grimy blackness was crashing in on him and *Is this it, is this the end?* Fool wondered and then the moving entrails were gone and he was on the floor and coughing and vomiting and screaming.

He didn't know how long he lay there. He retched until his stomach ached, drawing in vast breaths between each spasm, spraying out bile and trying to get the smell of shit from his nostrils and the taste and texture of Rhakshasas's gut from his mouth. Waves of something that was like fever rolled through him, shivering him alternately hot and then cold, shaking his limbs in a palsy. He tried to get a hand underneath him to lever himself up but could not, managed to rise perhaps three or four inches, and then collapsed back down. Another wave of sickness gripped his stomach, but he only dry-heaved, unable to produce anything but long, winded groans that eventually died away to jagged, pained exhalations.

Finally, Fool felt able to move and rolled gingerly over onto his back and away from the pool of vomit. After a moment of swaying, uneasy dizziness, he felt confident enough to sit, arms propped behind him, legs still weak. He let his head loll back, taking deep breaths, sucking the saliva from his teeth and spitting it out to try to clear the last of the taste from his mouth.

In spitting, Fool had turned his head, and as he did so something danced in the corner of his eye. He looked back around, unsure of what had caught his attention, the raging burn across his skin throbbing but fading, and looked to see what he'd seen.

He was tattooed.

Rhakshasas's guts had left their mark across him, all across him, black swirls and lines and shapes inked across his legs and arms and belly. There were circles surrounding ragged triangles, ellipses joined end to end in an untidy chain, something that might have been a thorned branch or splintered bone, dots, a series of wavy lines laid over each other, a series of apparently unconnected letters and runes, a blot with uneven edges. He reached out, hand unmarked and shaking, and rubbed the skin of his thigh. The marks there, a complex interlocking pattern of ovals and rectangles, stung when he touched them, and did not vanish no matter how vigorously he rubbed. It was the same on his calves, his stomach, his cheeks, his forearms and shoulder, the same everywhere; his body was covered from his ankles up to his chest and down his arms to mid-forearm. There were even lines disappearing into the depths of his crotch and delicate new traceries across his scrotum and penis.

He'd been fucking tattooed.

"Get up and clean yourself," said Rhakshasas, its outer layer of entrails now coiled back around it, moving silkily over its shoulders and in tightening, breathing loops around its chest.

"What did you do to me?" asked Fool, climbing unsteadily to his feet.

"Branded you," said Rhakshasas, its tone unconcerned. "You go to Heaven as our man, as the Commander of the Information Office of Hell. The marks on your skin will remind you of a simple fact that you may wish to forget when you reach the place of gleaming spires and glittering perfections. You, Thomas Fool, are Hell's. You belong to the Bureaucracy, to Mr. Tap or any other demon that wishes to possess you, to *me,* and not to anyone or anything else, not even to yourself."

Fool stared at Rhakshasas, at the two demons of the Delegation, at the scurrying thing, and then looked around for his gun. He shivered, cold rather than sick, and saw his clothes lying crumpled on the floor in an untidy heap. They were covered in streaks of slime that dried as he watched, crinkling and flaking to a series of decaying silver trails. When he picked them up, he discovered that the shirt was torn and the trousers split down the center, legs held together only by a few threads of the waist. Another lost uniform.

His gun was under the dead clothes and he went to pull it from his holster. As it came free, however, a hand clamped itself over Fool's and Mr. Tap said, "We find ourselves in this position for a third time, Fool. There will not be a fourth."

Fool hadn't heard it come in, was half bent and unsteady, tried to turn, but Mr. Tap pushed him, sending him easily to the floor. From Fool's low vantage point, Mr. Tap seemed to tower, gaunt body a collection of angles and shadows against the ceiling.

"You have a regrettable habit of attempting to draw your gun against your owners," said the demon. "Control your temper and remember your place, human. The next time you reach for your weapon in my presence, you will lose your hand. Are we clear?"

"Yes," said Fool. His body ached, his head ached, his stomach muscles clenched when he moved, and his skin had been decorated, no longer felt like his own. He rose to his feet, *little always falling-down Fool,* wincing as he did so.

"You are leaving us, Fool," said Mr. Tap, "but do not worry, I will look after your Information Men as though they were my own troops in your absence. I'm sure they and my bauta will get on wonderfully and will work together seamlessly."

Fool didn't reply. What could he say? He was caught, again, in one of Hell's displays of power over its human inhabitants. *I got noticed,* he thought, *and now we all suffer.*

"Another uniform," said Mr. Tap, nodding at a neat pile of clothing on the table next to Fool. They hadn't been there before the attack by the intestines, but then, neither had Mr. Tap. Fool dressed slowly, each movement sending sharp pains through him. As his tattooed skin disappeared into the uniform, Fool thought about being branded, about being owned.

About being chattel.

"All clothed? Good!" said Rhakshasas. "Tell me, Fool, are you ready?"

"Yes," said Fool, meaning no, biting down on the hope, on the fear, on the pain, feeling his newly inked scars rub against the fabric of his uniform, feeling small and helpless. "I'm ready."

The Delegation left to go to Heaven.

They were taken to the courtyard of Assemblies House, where a transport, old and small and cramped, was waiting for them. Its driver was a demon with no arms but a host of tentacles, its face a moon surrounded by shaggy hair. It was wearing a peaked chauffeur's cap that showed signs of having been burned, brought in through the Flame Garden. It gestured at them, opened the front and rear doors, backed away bowing and scraping its face across the rough ground until it reached its own seat and climbed into the vehicle.

Fool squeezed in the back between the rotting demon and the one he'd assumed was the scribe, having deliberately kept himself away from the larvae demon. Even so, the bugs that constantly fell from it crawled across the transport's floor and seat, wriggling around his new boots, ripples surging along their fat, segmented bodies as they quested. Rhakshasas and Mr. Tap were in the front section of the transport, which was larger and roomier; Mr. Tap peered back at Fool through a glass panel in the dividing wall between the two sections for the entire length of the journey, its melted face split by a grin in which its teeth waggled back and forth as though gesturing greetings to him. Fool tried to ignore it.

Fool saw the glow before he saw the flames themselves, a red heartbeat reaching into Hell's sky. Closer to and the movement became more discordant, fingers of flame leaping from the pits and clutching upward, falling back only to reemerge in a new shape. The transport drew to a halt and they climbed out, Fool shaking bugs from his feet, finding them in the creases of his trousers and knocking them out and to the ground. The demon, who had still not spoken, reached down and, surprisingly tenderly, picked up the bugs with fingers made of long sticks of tightly bunched, shifting creatures, and placed them back into itself.

Fool didn't know whether to apologize, and then did so anyway; it certainly wouldn't hurt. The demon ignored him.

Rhakshasas and Mr. Tap joined them at the entrance to the Garden and began to converse with the stitched demon, listing things it needed to discuss and listening as it told them what it intended to do. Fool moved away, enjoying the heat of flames and the way the warmth drifted around him. Ash fell slowly from the sky in great lazy spirals, making the earth around the Garden dark and soft. Already, his boots and trouser cuffs were coated in the stuff, leaving gray streaks, and it was settling on his shoulders like flaked skin.

Beyond the gates at the Garden's entrance a concrete path snaked through the flames, wide enough so that, if a human stayed at its center, the flames that curled around the path's edges wouldn't reach them and they would remain unburned. He watched, fascinated, remembering the burning buildings, enjoying seeing flames without wood and glass and human at their heart. They seemed free, somehow, unfettered, leaping and rolling, curling back across themselves, lifting up and then dropping down like the waves of some huge, simmering ocean.

"Fool," hissed a voice. "Fool, come here."

Fool looked around. The demons were still deep in conversation and ignoring him, although as he watched, Mr. Tap glanced at him and grinned again, licking its lips before turning its attention back to Rhakshasas.

"Fool!"

Still he could see no one, but now he recognized the voice. "Hello," he said to the Man of Plants and Flowers.

"Come out of there," said the Man, "off the path."

"Why?"

"Fool, come here, I have a deal to offer you," said the Man. "Quickly. We haven't much time."

Fool remained where he was. The Man's voice was different, weaker, less confident. Why? Rhakshasas's presence? Mr. Tap's? The demons, senior in Hell's hierarchy, thought the Man was dead, and presumably he wanted it to stay that way?

"Fool, come now before our chance is lost!" said the Man urgently, and this time Fool responded, walking back along the path and out of the Garden. The Garden was separated from the farmlands by a swath of earth in which only discolored grass and twisted, low bushes grew. Close to Fool, two bushes were tangled together, bobbing in a breeze that he could not feel.

"Fool," said the Man in a voice made of the sound of branches and twigs rubbing together. "Fool, come here."

Fool went to the bushes, standing by them but not crouching, staring out over the farmland. If Mr. Tap or one of the others looked, he was simply looking out over the landscapes of Hell before he went on to Heaven, or up to Heaven, or however this worked.

"Fool, you're going to where I have no hold," said the Man. "I can't make it to Heaven, but you going there gives me a chance that I simply cannot allow to go unused."

"Yes?" Fool already knew.

"Tell me about it, Fool, interest me with the details of Heaven. What's it like? How are the angels like demons? How are they different? What does it look like and smell like and taste like? How does Heaven *feel*?"

"How to get there?"

"Of course, Fool, of course! You're learning! Imagine: parts of me in both worlds!"

"Yes, imagine the fun you'd have," said Fool. "Imagine how interested you'd be."

"Yes! Yes! Find it for me, Fool? Find me a way?"

Find the Man an entrance to Heaven? Something rolled over in Fool's belly, a tension that didn't sit easy, refused to leave. "I don't know what I'll be able to tell you, or how," he said, backing away from any kind of agreement. "Besides, what would be in it for me?"

"Ah, spoken like a true Information Man, Fool. Information, of course. I won't stay dead forever, Fool. Soon enough, I'll be back in Hell, different but the same, all over, hearing things, knowing things. You could use a friend, I think. Even now, Mr. Tap and his Evidence Men are taking over, and with you out of the way? It'll get worse. You can do nothing, Fool, and when you get back they'll be even stronger. You need me, Fool, need what I can offer. Information is leverage, Fool, information is strength."

"And I'm an Information Man."

"The Commander of the Information Office, Fool, the chief Information Man. I can help you stay safe, keep your men safe, keep the Bureaucracy from growing bored or tired with you."

"Fool." Not the Man but Rhakshasas, calling from the entrance to the Garden.

"I'll tell you what I can when I get back," said Fool, finally looking down at the twisting shrubs.

"No," said the Man, "before then."

"How?"

"Find a way, Fool, find a way."

"I'll try."

"I have your word? Your promise?"

"Yes. I'll try."

"Good. And you have my word I'll help you, try to keep your people safe while you aren't here."

A single branch emerged from the tangle, curled around into a shape approximating a smile, and then the shrub shivered and collapsed slightly. The Man was gone.

"Fool." Again from Rhakshasas, this time louder and less patient.

"Yes," said Fool and obeyed his master's voice, *little obedient Fool,* and went to the demon.

"Fool, while you are in Heaven you will communicate with Mr. Tap to tell him how the Delegation is performing, and to answer any question he may have," said Rhakshasas when Fool was standing back with the Delegation.

"How will I know how the Delegation is performing?" asked Fool, thinking of the complex and arcane discussions he had been party to between Elderflower and the representatives of Heaven in other meetings, thinking about how little of it he had understood.

"Simply give him your impressions. You will also give Mr. Tap instructions to pass on to the Information Men and he will deliver these instructions if he can."

"No," said Fool immediately, before conscious thought could inform his mouth.

"No?" asked Rhakshasas.

"No," repeated Fool. "Mr. Tap may be in charge of the Evidence but he is not in charge of the Information Office, and I will discuss the business of the Information Office only with another Information Man."

"You refuse a direct order?"

"No," said Fool, and stopped because, of course, he had. Rhakshasas's intestines were bulging, lifting from its chest likes snakes, swaying, beginning to move toward him in sinuous, aggressive waves.

"I will say it one more time," said Rhakshasas.

"No," said Fool, "the *New Information Man's Guide to the Rules and Offices of Hell* states clearly that 'no order may be given to an Information Man except by their senior officer, and no case discussed except with other Information Men and Information Officers.' I will not discuss Information Office business with Mr. Tap because I am forbidden to do so by the rules of my office, as set out by the Bureaucracy."

Rhakshasas paused, gestured back the approaching Mr. Tap, and then said, "If not Mr. Tap, then who?"

"Marianne," said Fool without pause. "She's the only one I trust to know what's happening and to be able to do what I tell her to."

"Very well, then," said the demon, "have her keep investigating the fires. All canisters will be sent to her, and you will have regular contact with her."

"Thank you," said Fool, without letting his relief show on his face. The new *Guide* might well say something like that, but if it did he certainly didn't know about it. It had been a gamble, an attempt to keep something back from Mr. Tap, banking on the guesses that Rhakshasas had not read the new *Guide* and that, although it was head of the Archdeacons, or at least the thing that spoke on their behalf, it was not properly senior in Hell. It was old, yes, had responsibility for the day-to-day Bureaucracy, lived in Crow Heights, but there were still older powers above it, and it wouldn't risk going against their orders. *Even you can be noticed, Rhakshasas,* Fool realized. *Even you don't want Elderflower's gaze turning upon you, do you?*

"We're done," said Rhakshasas. Its voice was, if anything, colder than before, despite the Flame Garden's heat. *It didn't like being reminded of its lack of total authority, and I've made another enemy,* thought Fool, although he was unsure whether Rhakshasas had ever really been anything other than a threat, a risk to be managed. *Little hated Fool. Maybe Heaven will be easier than this.*

The Delegation went into the Garden, walking out along the path, the black demon ostentatiously walking along the stone ledge, letting the flames lick at its legs without apparent injury.

"How do we get to Heaven? Do we go to the Mount? Are we here to collect something?" asked Fool.

"Only the Elevated and the angelic host use the Mount to ascend to Heaven. We use the Garden."

"The Garden?"

"The Flame Garden is the link between all worlds, Fool," said Rhakshasas. "Heaven prefers to use light and brilliance to travel, but we in Hell are content with the movement of flames and heat."

They had come to a platform sticking out into the flames. They were dotted at regular intervals along the path, were used as the tipping-off point for the flesh that died in Hell's brawls and murders and accidents and rapes. The Delegation made its way to the far end of the platform, and the rotting demon, without pause, stepped off and dropped into the flames. After a moment, without looking back, the thing of larvae stepped out and dropped away as well, followed by the scribe.

That left only Fool and Rhakshasas and Mr. Tap.

Rhakshasas stepped close to Fool, hunched over him, pressed its face close to his, and said, "I have my orders much as you do, but know this, Fool: If you can, die in Heaven. If you return to Hell, the Evidence Men will take you from the street one night or one day and deliver you to Mr. Tap, Mr. Tap will bring you to me, and you will never be seen again."

"Yes," said Fool. Another threat, another promise, another thing to fear. *Noticed Fool, put on notice.*

"Now get out of my sight, little human," said Rhakshasas. "Go. Fuck off to Heaven."

Fool turned his back on the two demons and went to the edge of the platform. Here, the heat was terrible, sweat weeping from his pores and plastering his clothes to him, the flames moving the air around like a grumbling, toothless mouth. He could feel the skin of his face tingle, tighten, and start to burn.

"How do I do it?" he called back over his shoulder.

"Step in," said Rhakshasas.

"Won't it burn me?"

"You're the first human to travel this way, we don't know what it'll do," replied Rhakshasas, and then a hand that Fool somehow knew was Mr. Tap's jammed into the middle of his back and thrust him forward. He tried to back away, instinct driving him back from the heat, but the push was inexorable. His feet crunched over the grit of the ground, met the lip, and felt space beneath his soles, and then he was over and falling, flailing down into the flames.

It was agony, and then it wasn't.

The flames were all around him, so thick he could see nothing but the heated wall of them, and even as he was falling it felt as though they were carrying him aloft on waves of burning. He tried to breathe but the air scorched his mouth and lungs closed. He felt his hair spark and flame, his clothes catch fire, his skin shrivel back from muscles that were already contracting and thickening. He thought of the bodies in the buildings he'd investigated, thought about those tautened poses they had in death, fists held before their faces as though to protect them-selves from their ongoing fate, felt his eyes burst and spray out and then dry, wondered how long before he became a hunched and blackened thing. Would they find him on the ground of the Flame Garden among the things that appeared there, ready to be harvested by the workers in their thick suits? Or would he simply be left to burn away to nothing? There was no air, just heat and burning and a thing that was beyond pain, and then he crashed into something hard.

A last, sharp bolt of pain, like the memory of his last few days, and then it was gone. Fool lay still for a second or two before risking open-ing his eyes, eyes that he found were not burst and dried to pits.

Above him, a huge creature with myriad eyes and long, insectile legs was hanging in the sky, mouth full of fangs, biting at him.

He didn't have the energy to scream or move. He was too tired, his entire body ached, his head ached, his violated skin prickled against his clothes, and he could still taste Rhakshasas in his mouth, smell it in his nostrils. If this was it, if this was where he died, then so be it. Let it kill him.

The thing, whatever it was, scuttled sideways, and the multi-jointed claws at the end of its legs scrabbled against a barrier between it and him, invisible yet apparently unbreakable. The more he looked at it, the more the creature looked *wrong* somehow. Not simply ugly or dangerous, Fool was used to that; he saw grotesqueries every day in Hell, demonic flesh twisted away from human and into shapes and functions that were terrifying and lethal. No, the creature looked insubstantial somehow, as though it was not so much real as a projection on the inside of some vast curved surface above him. And yet, it was solid, had weight and form. Fool could hear the sound of its feet as they skittered, hear the scrape of its claws on something he could not see. It was made of angles and shapes that his eye couldn't quite hold, that seemed distorted and warped in the corner of his eye. For a moment, he'd almost have it, could hold the shape of it in his mind, and then it would flip away, be impossible to visualize, as though it was shifting between a shape and the imprint of the same shape, both coming toward him and retreating at the same time. It was like seeing a picture from one angle and then seeing it in reverse in a mirror.

Fool closed his eyes, opened them again. He'd thought the thing was close at first, that it was a similar size to him and only a few feet above his head but he realized it wasn't, it was distant. *Huge.* The space around the thing was filled with other creatures, some smaller versions of itself, some made of tentacles and beaks and claws, some feathered, some with scales, some with leathern skin, all of them shifting and testing the same invisible barrier. There were no gaps between the creatures, they fit to each other's edges, moving in tight formations so that the sky above him was a tapestry of them with neither space nor hole between the creatures. They were the color of oil spilled on water, green and gray and blue, constantly mutating and flowing, and still his perspective on them would not hold, could not grip them. The creatures were there and then not there, solid and then flat, close to him and then vastly far away. They were all around him, dropping to the horizon on either side of him, before him, and behind him. They were the sky.

Fool looked to his side, not liking the way that staring at the things was making him feel.

"Ignore them," said the demon of pieces and parts. "They don't exist."

"Don't exist?" asked Fool, climbing slowly to his feet.

"No. They are the creatures that inhabit the places outside of worlds."

"They're not real?"

"They're outside and therefore unimportant. Come. We have to go."

"I don't understand. Where are we? What are they doing?"

"How surprising, a human that doesn't understand. Very well, seeing as you appear to be part of this Delegation, I will endeavor to explain. We are on the road between worlds and those are the things that inhabit the space outside of us, the places outside of everywhere. They are eternally trying to enter these worlds, this world and every other, and if they are successful, they will become real."

"And if that happens?"

"We do not know, seeing as it has never happened. I don't imagine it would be good, judging by the look of them. Now, we need to travel."

They were on a path, Fool realized, thin and snaking, heading toward a horizon that swirled and chomped and flexed. The demon of larvae and the scribe were already walking along it, and Fool and the tainted demon followed.

"What do I call you?" asked Fool as they walked. He kept his eyes down to the ground, concentrating on his feet rather than the dizzying, disorienting sight of the creatures from outside.

"You don't," said the demon. "You speak to me only if I speak to you first. My name is Catarinch, but I do not give you permission to use it."

"And the other one?"

"Wambwark," said Catarinch, "and you do not have permission to use its name either."

"And the third has no name?"

"Not that I know."

"And now, Catarinch," said Fool, raising his voice so that the other could hear him, "and Wambwark and the third of you, remember this, that I am the Commander of the Information Office of Hell, and I will use your name if I choose to. My name is Thomas Fool, and you may use that freely."

Ahead of them, Wambwark stopped. Catarinch turned to look at Fool, who met its gaze. Catarinch flexed its rotten arms, lips pulling back from doglike teeth. "I am a part of this Delegation," said Fool, "with a function to fulfill and a role designated by Hell to play, do you think Mr. Tap won't know if you harm me?"

"Mr. Tap?"

"You know who I mean," said Fool, "but in case you've forgotten, I will endeavor to explain. Tall, lots of teeth, runs the Evidence. Even you're frightened of them, Catarinch, and you, Wambwark. They'd disappear you and judge you if you got in their way as easily as they'd disappear me or any other human; you know this to be true."

Catarinch paused, caught between anger and the realization that Fool was right. *Brave Fool*, thought Fool, *little brave Fool, taking another chance, another gamble.*

"Rhakshasas hates you," said Catarinch finally, "as does Mr. Tap. Wambwark and I will leave you alone and do our jobs here, and you can do yours. You're dead when we return to Hell anyway. Enjoy your last few days of existence, human Thomas Fool."

"I'll try," said Fool and then, looking down at his feet again, followed the now-moving Catarinch along the path.

He didn't know how long they walked for. It felt like hours, but it may have been less or it may have been more. On the few occasions that Fool risked lifting his view, the horizon seemed to be getting closer, as though it was a fixed point that they were approaching, the space around them shrinking, bearing down on them. The creatures on the outside became more frantic, moving ever faster across the surface of whatever it was that stopped them from entering, limbs constantly seeking and prying and testing, mouths biting, teeth grinding. There was still no space between the creatures, just a single vast movement that was all longing and fury and desperation. The sound of them was as fragmented and unnatural as the sight of them, a cacophony that came from everywhere and yet had no recognizable noises in it. Was that a breath? A roar? The sound of a scream? No, it was none of those things and yet all of them, sound turned on its side and torn inside out and made alien and distorted and grating. Fool walked on.

An hour or a minute or a day later, they stopped.

The Delegation had arrived at a doorway. It was tall, high enough for a demon the size of Rhakshasas to walk through without ducking, and its frame was on fire, the wood of the door blackened and smoking. Wambwark reached out and knocked once, hard. The door swung open slowly, bright white light falling through the entrance and onto the path; where it hit, the path steamed, the earth sizzling and contracting. Wambwark reached into the light, holding its arm there for a second and looking; the illumination dripped across the mass of maggots, doing no apparent harm. As though decided, Wambwark flapped its cape over one shoulder, pushed its hat back, and stood taller and stepped through, into the light.

The demon grew brighter and then it was gone.

Catarinch stepped to the doorway, paused, then walked into the light. After a few seconds, the scribe followed. Fool was glad to see that the small demon, a scruffy thing with loping arms that reached nearly to the floor and a ruff of torn and broken feathers around its neck, looked nervous before it went through.

Fool took a deep breath, stood as straight as his aching body would allow, and went after the demons. The light glared, dazzling him, forcing him to close his eyes. He smelled something sweet and fresh, unlike anything he could remember. Something unspoiled that made him think of fields in which there were no demons and in which the grass grew green and strong, and then a huge, gentle voice spoke.

"Thomas Fool," it said, "welcome to Heaven."

6

The field below them was filled with humans.

Fool and the Delegation were standing at the top of a gentle slope whose grassed surface was a smooth, dark green. The doorway was behind them, a patch of wavering, shifting darkness through which Fool could still see the distant writhing of the creatures from outside. All around them were humans.

There were more people in one place than Fool had seen before; even the great crowds of the Sorrowful, those poor bastards waiting in vain for Elevation from Hell to Heaven, couldn't come close in number to the mass of people below him. They weren't packed tightly; the field was vast, its edges distant lines marked by simple wooden fences. Beyond the fence was another field, also full of people.

The crowd was not entirely still; people within it moved. Watching them was like watching the shadows of sunlight in water, a constant gentle swirl as they ambled along, slow and apparently without aim. It made streams in the crowd, flows and trickles that moved along then oxbowed back, curling on themselves. Some of the people turned as they walked, constantly revolving, arms out to their sides and heads bobbing; others didn't move at all, or simply swayed as they stood, heads back and faces to the light of Heaven's sun.

Fool looked up, half expecting to see the burning darkness of Hell above them, a reflection of the view of Heaven that was available to Hell's inhabitants, but the sky above him was a blue he had never seen before, light and deep and endless. It was broken here and there by clouds, white and puffed, unlike the black and swollen things that gathered above Hell and periodically burst in vicious downpours. Heaven smelled of flowers and clean earth and something fresh and subtly sharp, like the breath of healthy trees. It was warm, the air gentle on Fool's skin, and he sighed, feeling himself relax, feeling clean, trying not to think of the foulness he accompanied and the ugliness painted and scored across his skin.

"So this is Heaven," said Catarinch, its voice contemptuous.

"Of course," said an angel, stepping alongside them and looking down on the crowd, smiling. "You have reached your destination after a journey that I have no doubt was hard and unpleasant."

"It was fine." Catarinch again. "It was a simple journey, that's all. Now, can we get on?"

Catarinch's voice made Fool look around, peer closely at the demons of the Delegation. He had been too busy watching the crowd, experiencing Heaven, to pay them any attention before. The scribe had hunched down, wrapping its long arms around its legs and making itself small, Wambwark was standing and dripping maggots onto the clean earth, and Catarinch was standing tall, shoulders back and chin jutting forward in a pose Fool recognized from all the humans in Hell: if you can't be small, if you *have* to be seen, be seen as large as possible, be intimidatingly large.

The demon was looking around, eyes leaping rapidly about it, taking in the movement and the people and the angel, and Fool suddenly understood: *It's never been to Heaven before, it's never seen an angel before! It's scared.*

It made Fool smile. The angel saw the smile and returned it, broadening his own. Catarinch saw it, too, and scowled, brows knitting low over eyes that glowed a dark, burning red. Trouble, he supposed; Catarinch would have noted his amusement, and would make him pay for it later. *Foolish Fool*, he thought, *silly foolish Fool forgetting to keep low, keep unnoticed.*

"I'm Benjamin," said the angel, "and you are all most welcome. Heaven is grateful for your presence and extends its hospitality. Thomas Fool, you are in particular a welcome guest. Heaven remembers the service you performed for it and the kindnesses you have shown."

Fool didn't know how to respond, so said nothing. He had known two angels previously, Adam and Balthazar, and Benjamin was both like and unlike them. He was as pure and beautiful as they had been, his face handsome, his eyes smiling as much as his mouth. His hair was long, swept back from his unlined face, wings folded but stretching up above him, their upper edges curved in so that they formed a shade above his head. He was shorter than either of the other angels had been, and his only clothing was a tight loincloth. No, not a loincloth, Fool realized, feathers; the angel had a thick growth of white feathers around his groin covering his genitals. Did they have genitals? he wondered. Fool couldn't remember, wasn't sure he'd ever known. The skin of Benjamin's chest and legs and arms was hairless, as smooth as planed wood or marble, his color a deep brown.

When Benjamin moved, it was with a grace that made Fool feel clumsy and half formed, as though his angles were wrong and the angel's were absolute, and absolutely perfect. There seemed to be no effort in his movement, just a *flow* from one place to another, and it made the angel alien in his beauty.

"Excuse me," Benjamin said, "I have to close the door and then I'll take you to your quarters."

Benjamin left them and returned to the doorway. As Fool watched, the black space started to crumple in on itself, the edges rippling and blurring. The angel pushed and stroked the edges of the frame, narrowing the gap farther and diminishing Fool's view of the creatures. The angel's hands were swift and careful, his fingers pinching and pulling, describing intricate arcs and movements around the doorway, making it smaller and smaller until it was little more than a circle of black.

It was almost gone when the angel spoke again, a note of surprise in his voice. "Hello," he said, peering into the darkness. He reached through the gap, hand disappearing into the black, and took hold of something, pulling as though he was hauling on ropes despite the fact that Fool could see nothing.

"Can we go?" said Catarinch. Wambwark made a low rumbling, a fissure opening in its face and a foul smell emerging with the noise. Bugs fell from the fissure, landing in its chest and tumbling to the ground, where they rolled and started back toward it. Its cape flapped, hat rippling, as it waited.

"As my colleague says, we have work to do. We do not wish to be here any longer than we have to be," said Catarinch. The scribe, hunched beside it, tucked itself tighter down, made itself something even smaller.

"I apologize for the delay," said Benjamin, "but I will be a moment longer." He pulled in the invisible thing again, making hand-over-hand movements. Whatever it was, it took a few seconds longer to draw in through the opening, and then it was done and Benjamin stroked and moved and the doorway shrank to nothing and was gone.

"Welcome to Heaven," said Benjamin.

"Your greetings have already been acknowledged," said Catarinch. "Angel, we have no desire to exchange more pleasantries."

Benjamin stood, straight, still smiling, and said simply, "Of course. Let us go."

Benjamin led them down the slope, away from the crowd, toward a path upon which an open-topped transport was waiting. The five of them climbed into it, the seats thick and accommodating, and it moved off without sound and without an apparent driver. It did not move fast but meandered, the road they were on changing direction frequently, first this way and then that, doubling back and bending as though it had no real destination, was a thing created for travel rather than arrival.

During the journey they passed some of what Fool assumed were Heaven's equivalents to the boardinghouses, the Orphanages, the Houska—a huge fairground filled with carousels and rides, more fields, this time filled with crops as well as people, buildings that Fool couldn't identify, and others that made him feel like he knew them even if he could not quite place them or their function. He had never seen them before, they had no true equivalent in Hell, yet still he felt he should recognize them. He rubbed his head, closed his eyes, and tried to remember, but nothing came.

In the darkness behind his eyelids, Fool heard music. It was distant, impossible to recognize, sounded like singing one moment and hundreds of instruments without voices the next, from the beating tattoo of drumming to the rising lilt of flutes to the throaty roar of trumpets and horns.

I've never heard flutes, he thought, *so how do I know they're flutes? Or trumpets or horns?* There was no music in Hell, except for the occasional songs that the workers sang, the rhythms providing a beat for the workers to carry out their tasks to. Fool didn't know what flutes sounded like, yet he did, the information there in his head, growing like some tiny bud, opening, knowledge expanding. He groaned, unable to help himself, heard the music again, this time strings, guitars, and lutes, and then voices again. Thousands of them, thousands of voices, layered and singing different things yet somehow complementing each other, song after song after song, each voice carrying its own tune, creating its own themes, the sound of Heaven.

It was beautiful.

Fool opened his eyes and found Benjamin watching him. The angel smiled more broadly, but didn't speak. The music stopped, or at least fell away to something that almost disappeared past the cusp of his hearing.

Looking around, Fool found that the landscape had changed. Now the road was running alongside the edge of a gray and moving sea, waves rolling in and out against a sandy beach with a distant hissing. People were standing on the beach, not moving or swaying, heads back. Those closest to the water were getting wet but didn't seem to care, simply standing as the water washed around their ankles and calves and thighs, not moving. No one touched each other or spoke to each other as far as Fool could see. The smell of the sea came to him, a salt tang that caught in his throat, made him think of cool waters and, for some reason, the feel of fresh wind in his face. He'd never felt fresh wind in his face, only ever been in waters in Hell that were filthy and dank.

Fool breathed, deep, drawing Heaven into himself and feeling its cleanness fill his insides. It made him feel lighter, less grimy, yet strangely sad. He wasn't Elevated, hadn't earned the right to enjoy the cleanness, knew that it was finite and that soon he'd have to relinquish it and return to the place of filth and pain and heat and fear, yet enjoyed it anyway, holding it to him, not knowing how long he'd be allowed to experience it for.

"Will we be arriving soon?" demanded Catarinch.

"Soon, yes," replied Benjamin. "The journey is a useful one, allowing you to acclimatize yourself to Heaven. Please do not worry, Catarinch, we will arrive at our destination soon enough and the work can proceed then." Fool wondered if Catarinch would complain at the use of its name, saw the demon lean forward and then back, obviously thinking the better of it. Benjamin was smooth, felt curiously unassailable, and Fool suddenly understood; this was another power play. The journey didn't need to be this long, it was being made deliberately so to keep Catarinch and Wambwark and, presumably, him and the scribe, unsettled. As if to confirm it, he glanced ahead in time to see the road *move*, curving away from the sea, changing its shape, stretching and rippling and creating new loops for them to travel. Wambwark, facing the road, saw it as well and spat out maggots in a spray of foul odor to express its displeasure.

Benjamin simply smiled and the transport carried on its unhurried way.

Beyond the sea was a city, but not the city in the sky that Fool saw from his lowly place in Hell. Where that was all gleaming spires and towers that pierced the clouds above them, their feet lost in Hell's own atmosphere, the cityscape they now approached consisted of smaller buildings, low and made of simple brick. Nothing in it appeared to be over two stories tall except a central hall that had four layers of windows. The transport threaded through streets whose pavements contained yet more near-motionless humans, heads down or up, sometimes swaying, occasionally walking. Were they going anywhere? No, Fool saw. Now that they were closer to the humans, hemmed in by the narrowness of the streets, he saw that all of them had their eyes closed. Wherever they walked to, it was a movement led by instinct or dream rather than sight and intention.

What was this place? It wasn't the Heaven that Fool had imagined; that place had been filled with the sounds of fun and enjoyment, of conversation and interaction and friendship and laughter, but this place was silent except when he closed his eyes and heard the music, and the people looked as distant from each other as they were in Hell.

Above them, angels flew in great swoops and whirls, back against the sheet of the sky.

"We have arrived," said Benjamin as the transport came to a halt in front of the larger building.

"Good," said Catarinch. "At last. To work."

The meeting had been long, and Fool had understood little of it.

It had taken place in a room on the top floor of the large building, which Benjamin had told them was called the Anbidstow, with Cata-rinch and Wambwark and two angels who had not been introduced to Fool. Just as he had in almost every Elevation meeting in Hell, Fool stood by the room's windows and looked out, keeping an ear half open for the sounds of the meeting behind him in case they called upon him. Benjamin stood beside Fool by the window, silent and smiling continu-ously.

The view was of a vast tract of farmland, with no sign of the sea they had traveled past earlier. The space was split by thin green lines that he thought might be hedges or fences, creating a patchwork effect that fell back into the distance.

"Why does it change?" Fool eventually asked Benjamin. "Heaven, I mean. There was a sea before, we passed it, but it's not there now."

"Isn't it?"

"No. I can't see it, anyway."

"Then it must be gone, or at least, moved away. Heaven changes according to what its residents dream about. Before they were dream-ing about the sea. Now they dream about something else."

"I don't understand."

"No. Do you need to?"

"Yes." *Yes, because that's my job, that's what I have to do, I have to under-stand.*

Benjamin turned to face Fool, and for the first time, he wasn't smil-ing. "Heaven is of the dreams of its inhabitants and the places they feel safest and happiest. Before, people dreamed of the sea, and some still do, but many have moved on and they think of other things." He gestured at the view beyond the window.

"Now they dream of rolling fields and warm summers."

Fool closed his eyes again, trying to understand, and immediately his head was filled with music.

"Can you hear it?" asked Benjamin.

"Yes," said Fool, and opened his eyes. The music stopped. "What is it?"

"The sound of Heaven," said Benjamin simply. "It jolts you because you are not of Heaven."

"How do I stop it?"

Benjamin reached forward, and stroked Fool's cheeks with both hands; his touch was soft and cool. "If it bothers you, I can ease it."

"Please," said Fool, thinking that if he heard the sound every time he shut his eyes, he'd never sleep, might eventually go mad. Even when he blinked, he caught slivers of it, tiny sliced fragments of the sound, pure and delicate and maddening.

Benjamin removed his hands from Fool's face and licked the tips of his forefingers. He then pushed the spittled fingers into Fool's ears, rubbing the warm liquid around the edges of his ear canals.

"Close your eyes," said Benjamin. Fool did so; the sound was gone.

"Thank you."

"It was my pleasure, Thomas Fool. It is an honor to assist you. If you wish to hear the music again, simply rub away the barrier I have placed in your ears."

They turned back to the window. The view was still farmland, but Fool was sure that the arrangement of the lines, the edges, had shifted, creating a new patchwork. *I've held a feather from an angel's back, watched one fall and burn, and now I have one's spittle in my ears protecting me from music that I should find beautiful, that I do find beautiful but that's also oppressive. It's Heaven,* he thought, *how did I ever think I would understand it? Concentrate on the thing you can understand, on being Fool, and on the job. Concentrate on the Delegation.*

Catarinch was doing most of the talking, although Wambwark was making occasional injections in a low rumble, the smell of which reached Fool at the window a second or two later. The angels seemed to understand Wambwark well enough and replied to whatever it had said or asked. The discussion ranged around, but concentrated most on something that Fool thought might have been a border dispute, about the edges of Hell and the edges of Heaven, rather than souls taken or given. Both the angels and demons had concerns and raised them.

None of the four referred to Fool except to tell him when the meeting was finished, and the angels didn't come for him until later, when he was alone in his room.

7

Fool's room was little more than a large cell, containing a bed with soft cotton sheets and a woolen blanket, a desk, and a chair. A globe of glass was mounted to the wall on a bracket, and it grew brighter as the day outside the small window grew darker. When Fool touched it, he found it was not hot, and he could make it dimmer or brighter by stroking it up or down.

In the globe's light, Fool stripped and looked down at the tattoos that now snaked across his skin. Were they changed? Different from the designs that he had first seen? Hadn't there been a spiral under his left nipple, where now there was a thing that might have been an ear? Hadn't that stretch that looked like a branch been a series of linked circles? He ran his finger along some of the thicker lines, feeling them as a set of ridges under his skin, pushing out the scarring in a raised set of whorls and loops. They hurt when he pressed down, not terribly but enough so that the pain left its ghosts when he raised his finger and released the pressure. He sat on the edge of the bed, looking at the lines that wound around his legs and knotted across his thighs and hips, and wondered if he would ever truly recognize himself again. He was born an adult, fished from Limbo, and given flesh and a role in Hell little more than five years ago, and although he had been scarred during his time as an Information Man, his flesh had always been his own when he looked at it before.

Now it was marked with something else's design. He was owned, defined, and branded by Rhakshasas. He clenched his fists, tightened his tendons, and gritted his teeth. *Owned Fool*, he thought, *little owned Fool, like cattle.*

There was nothing he could do; that was always the endpoint in Hell. He was as helpless as ever, as controlled as ever, a man whose purpose and actions seemed always to be dictated by others. Best to try not to worry about it, he supposed, to carve out what little freedoms he could from the defined patterns of his life. Best to be Fool, his Fool, whenever he could rather than theirs.

He sat on the bed, the mattress relaxing under him, and wondered if he might be about to have a good night's sleep in sheets that were clean and thick and soft. He reached out and turned the glass lamp until the room was a warm and dark cocoon around him. He lay back, feeling every ache from the last few days work its way out into his muscles, feeling his heart finally settle into a slower beat as he tried to put his thoughts in order.

The shadows spoke his name.

As the words emerged from the darkness, a mouth formed in the air above Fool's head, the gloom shifting and twisting, creating a pair of lips several feet long. They reddened, taking on a cherry gleam, and then drew back, split to reveal a tongue and teeth that were white and smooth. They spoke again in a voice that rumbled and crashed, made Fool reach for his ears in pain. It was so loud, so heavy, and it pierced his covering hands and stabbed into his ears, through his ears and into his head.

"Thomas Fool, we apologize for the intrusion, but we have need of your skills."

Fool rolled off the bed, reaching out for his gun but unable to find it in the darkness. His skin tightened, prickles rising across it as a pale, ghostly blue light flickered around the room.

"Do not be afraid, Thomas Fool. We are the Malakim, the messengers of Heaven, and we must ask a boon."

Fool scuttled back, feeling behind him until he found the wall, and then pressed himself back against it. The mouthed darkness moved with him, hovering above him.

"My ears," he managed to gasp. "Please."

"Another apology, Thomas Fool," said the voice, volume lowering, still loud but less painful now. "We sometimes forget ourselves.

"There have been . . ." and the voice paused, the mouth pursing before continuing, "incidents that we do not understand but that you may. We have been told of your skills. We asked for your presence in this Delegation specifically, Thomas Fool. We need your help."

The voice filled the room and surely everyone in the building could hear it, surely the walls themselves had to be shaking at its crashing and roaring, even now, even at this lower level. Fool clamped his hands over his ears, spoke even though he couldn't properly hear himself.

"You asked for me?"

"Indeed. We asked for Thomas Fool, the Information Man, and Hell obliged, for which we are grateful. There will be a price to pay in future dealings with the Delegations from the Great Enemy, we are sure, but we considered that the price was worth paying."

"What do you want? How can I help you? I don't understand," Fool said, still scrabbling for the gun, knowing it would be of no use but wanting the security of it. Still it eluded his grasp.

"For you to be yourself," said the voice, the mouth in the air coming lower, shrinking, its volume finally dropping to something like a normal pitch, becoming almost conspiratorial. The blue glow shimmered around them, painting the walls with ripples and darts of light.

"To be myself?"

"To be an investigator, Thomas Fool, to ask the questions that investigators ask."

"Why?"

"There's an irregularity in Heaven, Thomas Fool, the first of its type in an age, maybe the first of its type ever."

"Surely you have someone who can investigate it for you?"

"We have soldiers, Thomas Fool, angels that guard against the return of the rebellious and the mistaken, but we have no investigators. Until now, we have had no need of them. This is a thing beyond our understanding, and we have need of you. We can learn, but it takes time. Please, Thomas Fool, assist us?"

He was being asked, not ordered. Did that mean he could say no, return to his soft bed and to sleep? Tell them to ask God, the all-seeing deity with a hundred hidden names, for the solution? Tell them that it wasn't his problem, his problem was staying safe, returning to Hell, and trying to stay safe there as well?

No.

No, of course not, because he was an Information Man, once Hell's only Information Man but now Commander of the Information Office, and it was what he did and what he was. He stood, watching the mouth, still several feet away, as it drifted across the room and came to a halt above his bed, the flickering glow shivering around the room creating shadows that swayed and turned.

"What do you want me to do?"

"You will help?"

"Yes," he said.

"We are told that you had a feather once, Thomas Fool, a feather from an angel who served Heaven? That you held his feather and assisted him?"

"Yes," said Fool, remembering the feather burning, the smoke of it greasy yet somehow clean.

"Then please, take this as a mark of our thanks and as a token of our respect."

A feather fell from the ceiling above Fool, drifting down to land at his feet. It was long and nearly white, curved gently, and glowed with a light that came from within it, tiny streaks of gleam drifting from it like sparks. Crouching, he picked it up, and where its light fell on his arm his skin instantly felt soothed and calm.

"You have our gratitude. Your guide will arrive any moment," said the Malakim, and the mouth dwindled, the shadows untwisting, becoming simply shadows again. Fool raised the light in the room again by touching the globe, not letting go of the feather, feeling its clarity, feeling its purity, and dressed rapidly. He was just strapping his holster on when there was a knock at his door.

Thomas Fool, Commander of the Information Office of Hell, went to investigate a mystery in Heaven.

PART TWO
FLOWERS

8

The dead man was lying on the carousel platform at the foot of a wooden horse, calliope music filling the air around him.

Fool stepped up onto the slowly revolving platform, looking around at the other horses gently rising and falling on their brightly painted poles in a constant wave, and at the humans on the horses' backs. A single angel moved among the riders, walking silently, occasionally repositioning a rider who had slipped or patting one of the horses' wooden necks.

The angel had arrived at Fool's door minutes after the Malakim had vanished, knocking on the door and waiting until Fool opened it before speaking. The angel was almost as tall as Mr. Tap, and it was burning. Its entire body was encased in bright fires, although no heat came from the flames, and at the center of the conflagration was the first female angel that Fool had met.

"Thomas Fool," she said, and bowed her head. "I am Israfil, and I am sent by the Bureaucracy of Heaven." Her long hair was hanging down, and the flames glittered and danced across it and played across her skin. The flames reminded Fool of the buildings in Hell, burning and glowing, the light of them a rich and moving thing. Israfil's glow spread along the corridor outside his room and, as he stepped out, showed him Benjamin waiting, wings still hooked over his head, face still partially shadowed. The angel nodded at him but did not speak.

Fool put the feather into his jacket pocket, pushing it deep in to ensure he didn't lose it, and said, "Shall we go? You can tell me about the mystery on the way."

"Mystery?"

"I've been asked to investigate a mystery."

"We know nothing about a mystery," said Benjamin. "We have simply been asked to act as your guides."

"We do not need him," said Israfil quietly. "There is nothing for the human to see."

"Israfil," said Benjamin, equally quietly. "We have our orders." *Dissent, little Fool, you're already the cause of angelic dissent.* Curiously, Fool found the notion oddly pleasing.

The angels hadn't been told that there was a mystery to solve. Why? Fool wondered. Because the mystery was shameful? Because they weren't senior enough? It was intriguing and Fool felt a first flicker of curiosity in his stomach. *This,* he thought, *is going to be interesting.*

The two angels led Fool through the corridors of the Anbidstow, down a flight of stairs at the rear of the building, and out into a small courtyard in which a transport waited. The vehicle was black, smaller than the one that had brought the Delegation to the building had been. It had no driver, and was roofed over with matte-black metal.

"I will not travel with him," said Israfil.

"Very well," said Benjamin, "meet us there."

The angel and Fool climbed into the rear of the transport and, as Israfil unfolded her wings and flapped them, rising into the air, they started moving. The journey to the fairground was quick, the transport finding or creating a straight road down which to travel, moving faster than the one that had brought him from the gate to the Anbidstow. It made him think again that their first journey through Heaven had been one intended to make a point; much as Hell had put Heaven's Delegation in the oldest and smallest transport it had, so Heaven had deliberately moved the demons and Fool slowly and through as many places as possible, showing them the sights, giving them comfortable traveling conditions, to prove who was in charge. He thought about it as they traveled, Benjamin silent beside him. *Heaven is as capable as Hell of pettiness and one-upmanship,* he decided. *It's all games.*

Games, and another journey that ended in a body.

The dead man was dressed in a simple robe; most of Heaven's inhabitants were, Fool saw. The robe was torn at the man's shoulder and the flesh beneath the tear was sliced open, the cut not deep but long, reaching from the center of the man's shoulder blade right around to just above his armpit. Fingering the edge of the cloth, he found that it was thick and soft, unlike the thin and scratchy material used to make the clothing given to Hell's inhabitants; he didn't look at his own new uniform as he made the comparison, simply carried on looking at the body, having his silent conversation with the corpse.

The cut hadn't bled much, which meant something, didn't it? But what?

The man had died, Fool thought, from a broken neck. His head was twisted too far around, looking back over his shoulder, and drool had spilled from his mouth to the carousel's wooden-deck floor. The spittle was pink with strings of blood and was stretched out in a long line, the man's eyes open and staring but clouded as though a film had grown over them.

He was dead before he was cut, Fool realized. Dead bodies didn't bleed, so the injury to the neck occurred first, followed by the one to the shoulder. Experimentally, he placed his hand against the man's shoulder, lining up the cuts in robe and flesh. The cut and rents matched, and when he looked more closely, he saw pale threads driven into the wound and a line of blood along the inner surface of the torn robe.

Something had slashed across the man, tearing from rear to front, pressing the robe into the cut and fraying its edge slightly, but only after he had died.

Fool stood again, moved away from the body, and went to the nearest horse and rider.

"Did you see anything?" he asked. The woman on the horse did not answer. Her eyes were closed, and behind the pale lids was a constant flicker of movement. She was asleep.

"None of them will have seen anything," said the carousel angel, coming up to Fool. This one appeared older, its hair short and gray, its wings folding away into a robe similar to that which the humans wore.

"Are they all asleep?" asked Fool. "None of them are awake?"

"It is not sleep," said the angel. "They are in Heaven."

"I know," said Fool, "but surely some must be awake?"

"None are asleep," repeated the angel. "They are in Heaven."

"He doesn't understand your confusion," said Benjamin from behind

Fool. Both he and Israfil were standing close to the carousel watching him as he worked. Beyond them were other carousels, rides in which people traveled in cars along rails, and stalls at which clusters of people stood motionless or making that odd swaying, dreamlike movement.

"He is of a lower order of angel," continued Benjamin. "His job is menial, simply to mind our residents as they move through the fairground."

"How can they all be asleep?"

"They are not. Heaven is unlike Hell, Thomas Fool. In Hell, pain can be shared, can be seen in others, fear can travel from one person to the next, infecting, like a contagion. Rumors and lies can expand, yes? But joy is individual, and can only be experienced alone. Hell is communal, but Heaven is personal. Heaven is individual." Benjamin came up the steps to the carousel's platform floor and stood by the woman Fool had tried to speak to. "This one, for example, her Heaven is different from everyone else's."

Benjamin leaned in toward the woman, and as he did so, something beneath the skin of his face flexed, his bones seeming to shift and re-form, his cheeks stretching down as his mouth opened and opened and opened, bottom jaw unhinging and dropping away to reveal a maw that was huge and black. Before Fool could stop him, Benjamin had clamped his mouth across the back of the woman's head and taken her in his arms, wings shivering and expanding, curling around the two of them like a feathered cage.

Before Fool had managed to draw his gun, Benjamin had broken his hold of the woman and placed her carefully back on the horse, making sure she was stable and balanced. His mouth closed, jaw moving from side to side as it folded back up into a semblance of a human face.

"This one is with her husband and children," he said after a moment. "Her memories, the place she feels safest and happiest, are a day they spent in a park near her home. They ate food and played together. The sun was shining and they were all happy, so she's created her Heaven there. Everyone here has a different Heaven, the place they create for themselves from the lives they lived or wanted to live. They cannot mix, these Heavens, are often at odds with each other, because people's joys are not as people's pains. They do not often sit comfortably next to each other. One may like noise, another peace, one crowds and another solitude, and these cannot easily exist alongside one another, so Heaven is created in each of them and we merely caretake the bodies and see them to the next stage of their journeys."

"They're all in separate Heavens?"

"Yes."

"And all this?" Fool asked, waving his hand around at the carousel and the fairground, at the fields he'd seen yesterday, at the sun and the breeze and the air.

"Places that make them feel safe, places from their childhood, or places they imagined being at in their childhood. When enough of them think about a type of place, Heaven forms it around them, a beach or a field or a town. Other times, like this, Heaven creates itself from their childhoods, from the books they read and loved, from memories and ideas, and it simply becomes a place where people are happy, are secure. There was no carousel in this woman's past, but there was a park and enjoyment and her memories of that and her memories of the stories she read as a child, of fairgrounds and adventures, merge to create this place."

"And they're all like this? All the time?"

"Yes," said Benjamin, and then, seeing Fool still staring at him, intently asked, "What I did disturbs you?"

"Yes."

"We must eat, Thomas Fool. No one here is unhappy, everyone is in the place they love the most, often with the people they love and who love them. Angels must eat, and we feed on happiness and love and joy. We do not harm those we feed off, and we take only a little."

As if to prove Benjamin right, the carousel angel wandered over to another rider, mouth opening, jaw lowering, and latched onto the back of her head, remaining attached for only a few seconds before backing off. The person on the horse did not react to the angel's touch, stayed in her own private place, eyes closed and arms around the horse's neck.

Fool lifted his head and sniffed, liking the smell, of burned sugar and sweetness, the faint waft of oil and grease, liking the music that hung in the air, a constantly looping calliope tune. He looked at all the humans sitting on rides and the angels on the carousels and platforms who tended them. *They're the opposite of the Sorrowful, they're the Joyful,* he thought, *and they're replete with all that happiness, stuffed full and just waiting to be harvested.*

"Heaven is vast and filled with joy, Thomas Fool," said Benjamin. "It is a place of safety."

Fool, looking down at the body, said, "Tell that to this poor bastard."

"It was an accident," said Israfil, speaking for the first time since arriving at the fairground.

Fool climbed down from the carousel and began to walk around it, looking at the ground. He wasn't sure what he was looking for, whether he was looking for anything, but something about the man's death wasn't right. "Do accidents happen here often?"

"No," said Israfil, "but what else can it be? The attendant was careless and did not watch his charges properly, and this man fell and died."

Fool looked down at the corpse, its torn flesh, thinking of death and lies and truths hidden and not seen, and wondered. After a moment, he said, "How can he die? He's already died and come to Heaven, surely?"

"How do people die in Hell, Thomas Fool? Their bodies become damaged, their souls released. Heaven and Hell are just part of the greater journeys everyone takes."

Fool didn't reply. "And what about you?" he called to the carousel angel. "Did you see anything?"

"No," the angel replied. "I came across the body and reported it."

Fool looked around. The carousel was at the edge of the fairground, close to a fence constructed of ropes and brightly colored pennants, triangles of material fluttering gently in the soft wind. Beyond the fence was a field filled with some kind of crop, high and moving in rhythm with the dancing air, the sound of it a long sloughing sigh under the fairground's music. He walked to the fence and turned. Anyone coming to the fairground through the field would see and be able to easily get to the carousel upon which the dead man now lay and to two other rides, each equidistant from the field.

Turning back, Fool studied the crops. Ducking under the fence, he walked to the edge of the planting, finding several areas where the stems were broken or bent. The earth was churned but there were no recognizable prints on its surface, and the damage could easily have been done by farmhands tending the plants.

Fool circled back to the fair and went to a smaller ride close to the fence. It consisted of a set of the oversize cups that each held four people, spinning around as they traveled on a circular track. The ride was slowing as Fool approached it, the cups spinning slower and slower until they stopped. No one got out; each inhabitant simply sat there until the ride started over again, gradually building up speed until the riders' hair was whipping about their faces, and trying to keep track of individuals made Fool feel dizzy.

One of the cups was empty.

Fool went to the ride on the other side of the carousel, a simple arrangement of cars, linked together and each holding two people traveling along a set of rails, traveling up small slopes and dropping into low dips as they went. It, too, had an empty car. Intrigued now, he went deeper into the fairground, looking at each ride and carousel as he went; none had empty cars except the three near the fence.

Back to the fence and looking at the ground again. Was there a trail leading from the crops to the fairground? Faint and not well traveled, but yes, maybe so. There were definitely marks in the grass, trampled areas, a point where something had dug through the surface of the earth to reveal a thin streak of mud below. Here and there in the damaged grass, tiny blue flowers grew. He picked one idly, thinking; the plant smelled unpleasant and he dropped it, straightening, still wondering. Broken crops and grass that may have been trodden down?

It wasn't conclusive, but it was the start of a trail.

Fool went back to the carousel, intending to study the body more, but found it gone.

"Where is it?" he asked. "Where's the body gone?"

"To the Garden, where the dead go," said Israfil.

"Why?"

"Because the journey carries on," said the angel.

"Bring him back," said Fool.

"No," said Israfil. "His journey must be uninterrupted, and what happened here was an accident."

"I'm not sure it was—" said Fool, but the angel interrupted him before he could go on.

"The man fell because the attendant was not looking after him correctly. He caught himself on the way down and cut himself before hitting his head on the floor. It was an accident. We do not need the interference of a human from Hell to tell us this."

Fool looked at Benjamin, who nodded. "It is a tragedy," said the shorter angel, "but they can start their journey again."

"Can I at least speak to the attendant again?" asked Fool, looking around, unable to see the other angel. "He may have seen or heard something and not realized it was important."

"The attendant has been removed," said Israfil calmly. "His replacement will arrive soon. You may talk to him if you wish."

"No," said Fool, "that's pointless, he wasn't here to see anything."

"There is nothing wrong here, so there was nothing to see," said Israfil. Around them, the rides were all drawing to a stop and this time their inhabitants were moving, standing up, exiting the cars and cups, climbing off the horses. Soon they were surrounded, a crowd of people wandering past them one way as new riders came from somewhere else, took up residence on the rides, and mounted the horses. None were awake, all their eyes closed, feeling their way with their feet and guided by the angels that moved among them, pale and delicate against the heavier human flesh.

"Can I see the body at the Garden, before it's burned?"

"Our Garden is not one of flames, Thomas Fool," said Benjamin. "It is one of earth and air, a hilltop where the dead are released, and you are already too late to see them. They are gone."

Fool muttered angrily, turning on the spot and looking around, trying to see if he had missed anything. He lifted his face, let the sun warm it, and then looked out across the field again.

The scribe was crouched at the edge of the field, almost hidden by the crops, watching back as Fool stared at it.

Fool took a step in the direction of the scribe, struggling to keep it in view as he stepped off the carousel and descended into a moving sea of humanity. He glimpsed it as a dark shape, fragmented between fluttering white robes, and then it was gone.

Fool broke into a run, weaving between people with difficulty before coming to the edge of the fairground. He ducked under the rope fence, hearing the crackle of the flapping pennants as he passed below them, and then he was at the edge of the crop. The scribe had been farther along the field, away from the trampled earth and bent plants, and its prints were clear in the damp soil. Fool crouched, trying to make sense of it.

Had the scribe injured the man? Murdered him?

It was swimming in his head, the images of the dead body and the carousel and the scribe jumbling, refusing to separate. Fool wavered, putting out a hand to steady himself, liking the feel of the warm, soft dirt against his fingers. *Even Heaven's dirt feels clean,* he thought. *Clean dirt, little Fool, clean and healthy dirt.*

"It's late," said Benjamin from behind him. "You need sleep, Thomas Fool. We will escort you back to your room."

"No," said Fool but then realized that yes, he was tired, was *exhausted,* that Benjamin telling him had shown him the truth of this. He'd carry this on tomorrow if they allowed him. Now, he suddenly understood, he had to rest. He stood, rubbed his eyes to clear them, and let them take him away.

When he got back to his room, Fool found that someone had put a bottle of ink on his desk along with lengths of string and a sheaf of plain paper, thick and creamy and entirely unlike the thin, near-transparent sheets he used in Hell. Paper and ink, and it was easy to understand the meaning in the items, so he sat at the desk despite his tiredness and tried to set his thoughts in order. He was required to make his report, and to make it now. *Information about this mystery must be delivered, little knowledgeable Fool,* he thought, and then realized that whoever had left the ink and paper hadn't left a pen. Fool wondered how he was going to write before remembering the feather.

It was smaller than the feather he had owned previously but it glowed as brightly, and when he waved it, it left trails in the air that sparkled even as they faded and vanished. Its calamus was bone-white and curved, the delicate spine darker and the barbs soft to the touch. Its pale glow made his hand look like marble, a ghost in the darkness. Sighing, he unscrewed the top of the ink bottle, dipped the feather in the ink, and began to write.

It took him an hour or so to write up everything he had seen, to note the things that concerned him and the few conclusions he had drawn.

He did not mention the scribe in the report, for reasons he was unclear about but had to do with wondering where his loyalty lay, and wanting to find out what the scribe had been doing before reporting it. When he had finished, he rolled the paper into a small scroll and tied it with a piece of the string and looked around for a tube in which to place the scroll. It was in the corner, where no tube had been before. Beneath the tube was a canister, and Fool put the scroll in the canister, was about to insert it into the tube, when he stopped. After a moment, he opened the canister and tipped the scroll back onto his desk. Untying it, he smoothed the paper and took the feather and, in large letters, wrote beneath his report:

THIS WAS NO ACCIDENT.

He was asleep and then he was awake and screaming.

The pain was similar to when Rhakshasas's guts had wrapped themselves around him but somehow reversed, not something burning in but something clawing out. Fool threw back the blankets and tried to sit to reach the lamp, but the pain that wrenched at him from his belly was terrible, made him collapse back. He was naked, sweating, riding a wave of cramping agony and then lurching up again and this time his fingers hit the globe and brought it to weak life.

The tattoos on his body were twisting and moving across his skin. The lines across his belly and chest had formed themselves into a single large eye and a wide, grinning mouth, and both were opening. The eye was across the skin of his lower stomach and the mouth just below his ribs, both upside down so that he faced them and they him. His flesh was tearing along the line of the eyelid, the skin splitting with a sound like ripping linen, and the pain roared through him and he screamed, and then the lip of the mouth curled back at one side to reveal red and gleaming muscle beneath. Fool screamed again, the noise cut short by a bolt of pain so terrible, so *loud*, it tightened his throat to a clenched pipe, and then both eye and mouth were open fully.

The eye blinked, opened wide to show a spread of red and fatty muscle, then blinked again, and when it opened a second time, Fool's raw musculature was gone and a dark, slitted pupil had replaced it. Inside the mouth, which was opening and closing as though to bring the new lips to life, his flesh had disappeared and there was instead a blackness that held in its depths, impossibly deep so that it appeared to be coming from a place below both Fool and the bed he lay on, something that rippled. The pain was ridged now, coming in waves and peaks, making him gasp and cry. The eye and the mouth, disproportionate, eye larger than the mouth, opened and closed a few more times, as though testing their newfound existence, and then the mouth spoke.

"Hello, Fool."

The voice came from inside his stomach, the vibrations of it running along his torso and arms and legs, making his teeth clench. The voice was different yet familiar, the mouth something he recognized, the pain still crashing over him but slower now, receding. The eye blinked again, rolled, slit pupil widening and then narrowing as it took in the room around Fool.

"They treat you well, I see."

Mr. Tap. Mr. Tap's voice, coming from Fool's belly, Mr. Tap's eye staring out at him from his own flesh. He tried to cry out, reached for the eye, not knowing if he was hoping to close it and hold it together or poke at it, fight it off. The mouth snapped at his hand, the edges of his stomach pulsing as the teeth forced themselves forward, sending another yelp of pain through him and out of his own mouth. He pulled his hand back, weeping, and waited.

"That's better, Fool. Try to remember, you were told that we would need to communicate, and this is our chosen way of doing it. This way, Fool, Heaven has no part of our little chats, and cannot listen in. I can be honest with you and you can be honest with me, yes?"

"Yes," said Fool, lying back, partly through sheer pained exhaustion and partly so he didn't have to see the edges of his stomach move and flap, forming Mr. Tap's words. The sound of them, and the feel of them, were bad enough, but seeing them was somehow worse, his own body manipulated and torn, his skin curled under itself to create lips, warped and distorted like putty.

"So, Fool, what news?"

If Fool lay still, the pain was almost gone, almost a memory, except for the throbbing around the edges of Mr. Tap's eye and mouth and an itch that crawled across the rest of his skin. Were the rest of the tattoos moving, forming into new shapes that could open, talk? *Little talking Fool,* he thought fleetingly, trying to keep his tears at bay, and said aloud, "About what?"

"The Delegation, of course. How does it fare?"

"We got here safely," he replied. "I didn't burn up in the Flame Garden. We didn't get eaten by the things from the place outside of everywhere."

"And the discussions?" asked Mr. Tap. Fool risked another look at his chest. The eye blinked at him, the pupil inside the eyelids slicked with pale blood, the mouth an open tube with teeth, Mr. Tap's teeth, impossible yet real, clicking and clacking together.

"I didn't understand them, but they seemed to go well," replied Fool. Talking was wearying and he collapsed and closed his eyes.

"Good," said Mr. Tap, sounding uninterested. "And now, tell me about Heaven. What have you seen? What have you heard?"

"Nothing," said Fool, and immediately a fresh wave of pain bloomed within him. He jerked up, looked at himself, and saw that the mouth had started to gnaw at its lower lip, was pulling on the skin of Fool's upper chest. The skin stretched, was pulled toward the mouth, one nipple coming close to the teeth, and he screamed again, hearing his own hopelessness in the sound, and said, "Stop! I don't understand what you want to know!"

"Everything," said Mr. Tap, letting go of Fool's skin. Blood welled and trickled, rolling down his lower rib to the edge of the mouth. From inside him, a tongue emerged and licked at the blood, slurping it. The mouth grinned, the edges of the grin disappearing into Fool's flanks.

"You taste good, Fool," said Mr. Tap. "You taste *wonderful.* I must eat you again sometime."

"Heaven is in people's heads," said Fool, trying to sort through the dense fog of his pain for what the demon using his skin wanted to know. What could he tell Mr. Tap?

What *should* he tell it?

"We know that," said Mr. Tap. "They don't share like we do in Hell. More."

"It changes. They . . . dream, or remember or think, I'm not sure, but they bring places into existence, when enough of them are thinking about something similar. I think that's how it works."

"Interesting," said Mr. Tap. "That may prove useful one day. And what about you, Fool?"

"What about me?"

"You know by now that the Bureaucracy of Heaven requested that you be sent with the Delegation, requested you specifically?"

"Yes," said Fool.

"Good. We'd like to know why, Rhakshasas and I."

"I don't know."

Pain, just a tiny wave of it, as the mouth took an edge of skin and pulled on it, nibbling. "Come now, Fool," said Mr. Tap, said Fool's *torso,* the words slightly muffled as the mouth clenched a morsel of skin between its front teeth.

"I think it was to thank me," said Fool, thinking fast. For some reason, he didn't want to tell Mr. Tap or the Archdeacons, in the shape of Rhakshasas, about the mystery, the accident, the whatever it was. This was Heaven, and Hell would use any weakness to infiltrate, to attack, to gain advantage. "Because of what happened, I mean. The angel who greeted me mentioned it, as did the Malakim later."

"The Malakim?" asked Mr. Tap, voice suddenly serious, darker, colder. "You've spoken to the Malakim?"

"Yes," replied Fool. *That was a mistake, little Fool,* he thought. He was struggling to concentrate, struggling not to simply tell Mr. Tap everything, just to stop the pain, make it go away.

"Why? Why did the Malakim speak to you?"

"For the same reason. They came to my room, appeared in it, actually, scared me, then told me I had their gratitude." *Almost truthful Fool, little lying Fool.*

"Gratitude? That may be useful, Fool. See that you don't lose it."

"No."

"Is there anything else, any other snippet you can give me?"

"No. Yes, wait, there's one more thing. Catarinch, it's scared of the angels here. It's rude to them."

Why had he added that? Why make trouble? *Because my skin is being abused, and because Catarinch is a problem for me, even if I'm not sure how yet.*

"And Wambwark?"

"It doesn't say much. It seems calmer, less afraid."

"Your comments are noted, Fool," said Mr. Tap. "You've been useful tonight. We shall speak again tomorrow. Have something else to tell me or I may decide to eat you again and this time simply not stop."

Fool didn't speak, just lay there as the mouth and the eye closed and the flesh knitted back together. It itched, a maddening burn below the surface of his skin, and when he touched the area tentatively after it was sealed it hurt, was bruised, but at least the sharp, slicing pain had gone. Even as he looked, the tattoos were swirling apart, the eye and mouth now irregular patterns that contained only faint hints of the things they had just been.

There was now a clearly drawn mouth and a pair of eyes on his inner left forearm that hadn't been there earlier, and Fool had only a brief moment to steel himself before they, too, ripped apart and opened.

The pain wasn't as bad as Mr. Tap had been, the holes created smaller, but it still knocked him back. He let his arm fall across his bruised stomach, waiting for the mouth to speak. The eyes blinked, bloody tears weeping from them and dribbling down onto his navel, and then the mouth opened, wide. For a second it was silent, and then a voice he recognized said, "Mr. Fool? Sir?"

"Marianne?" he asked, startled beyond pain. "Is that you?"

"Yes. Where are you?"

"Heaven. Where are you?"

"In your room in the Information House. In Hell. Are you really in Heaven? They said to expect a contact from you, but not like this."

"How am I talking to you?" asked Fool, suddenly worried that Marianne's flesh had split as his own had, that she was feeling the same kind of roiling pain he was.

"There's a drawing of you," said Marianne. "It's moving, speaking. I can hear your voice."

Fool closed his eyes, concentrated. He could feel the link to Hell, some great chain he couldn't understand but at whose end was a throb unlike anything else he'd experienced, this link to the place of his birth, the place he hated. He let it fill him, the throb of fires and pain and fear, and then he could *see* Marianne. She was blurry, as though he was looking at her from behind a thin curtain of greasy material. *Or from within a thin sheet of paper,* he thought, but it was her, Marianne with her soft face and short hair.

"They tell me you picked me to act as your liaison with the Information Office while you're away? I got a canister telling me. Why me?"

"Because I trust you," Fool said, "and you're about the only one of my troops I can say that about."

There was a moment's silence. Fool looked at Marianne, and wondered what expression was on his face in the picture. The same as his face in reality? Or had they given him a different one, twisting him into what they wanted him to be?

Was it a picture of him that Summer had drawn, saved by the Bureaucracy for a purpose like this?

"What's been happening?"

"There've been more fires, arson," said Marianne. "Another warehouse, not empty. It had had workers in it. They were all dead by the time we got there."

"Did you look at the scene, look at it the way I showed you?"

"Yes. It was another set fire, started in the corner near the entrance so that the workers couldn't get out. We found some of them huddled together at the back, all dead. They hadn't burned, they'd suffocated on the smoke. There was vomit and they'd tried to shield each other, made masks but it hadn't worked. Their faces were black and purple and their eyes were bugged out." She stopped, swallowed. Fool's image of her faded as she moved away, and then she was back, leaning over him, close, whispering. "We're being told to investigate, but no one knows how to do it, and we found something, sir."

"Something?"

"A pincer, a huge pincer or claw."

"Have you got it?" Thinking that, perhaps, Marianne could hold it up in front of his paper self so that he could see it.

"No. The Evidence have taken it, but they're not letting us near it. They're all over everything. They try to look like they're investigating but they're not, not really. They're useless, they don't know anything."

"No, they won't, not anything real anyway," said Fool, thinking. "Describe the claw."

"It's big, and solid. We found it on the edge of the fire. I think whatever it was that left it got burned, it's charred around the edges. No one I asked when I still had it remembered seeing anything like it before. It's strange."

"'Strange?'"

"I can't explain it," said Marianne, "but it feels like it isn't really made of bone or flesh exactly. It feels wrong."

Did that help? No, not really, not without seeing it. Some of the older demons had claws, was this something old turned arsonist? He thought for another second and then said, "Have there been any more murders like the one we were at before—" He paused. What could he call this?

"Before this?" he finished, eventually.

Marianne shook her head, then, thinking he couldn't see her, said, "No."

"I can see you," he said. Experimentally, he opened his eyes in Heaven and Marianne vanished; there was simply his arm and its tattoo. He closed his eyes again, Marianne filling his view.

"No, no murders . . ." she said, one hand appearing and scratching at her head, brushing at her hair.

"There's a 'but' there," he said. It was obvious in the way she'd paused, the way she drew the words out longer than they needed to be. Even through the blear of the paper, he could see that she was thinking, struggling to work out how to say something, or whether she should even say it at all.

"Just say it," he said, wincing as his arm-eyes blinked, squeezed shut as she thought, and then gasping a little as she spoke again.

"We've had reports of people seeing things in the distance."

"'Things'?"

"Things dancing," she said. "The man, the supervisor, he said something about them dancing, didn't he?"

"He did," said Fool. "Where have the dancers been seen?"

"All over," said Marianne. "There's no logic to it, as far as I can tell. They've been in alleys on the outskirts of Eve's Harbor, at the back of a boardinghouse, once in the middle of a farm. It doesn't make any sense."

"No," said Fool again, and let out a short, ragged breath. His arm was throbbing, the pain a sleeve that stretched from wrist to shoulder.

"Are you okay?" asked Marianne. In his vision, she looked concerned.

"I'm fine," he said. "Keep an eye open for any more reports of dancers. Try to plot them on a map if you can get one, see if there are any common elements or obviously central points."

"I will."

"And Marianne?"

"Yes?"

"Be careful. Watch out for the bauta. Mr. Tap is dangerous and his Evidence Men aren't to be trusted. Stay away from them if you can, give them what they ask for only if you have no other choice."

"Yes," she said and yawned. The mouth in Fool's arm stretched and he groaned. He was a single ball of pain now, limbs heavy, eyes clenched against more agonies.

"Are you sure you're okay?" Marianne said.

I'm talking to you through my arm, through a tattoo that was burned into me and is now using my flesh to create a moving mouth and eyes—no, I'm not okay. "Yes. Marianne, I need to go. I'll be in touch again. Be careful, Marianne, please. You're my eyes in Hell now, the only ones I have."

"I will. Good-bye, sir, and you take care, too."

"I'm in Heaven, Marianne, what could possibly happen to me here?" he said and concentrated, broke the connection between him and her apart. Even before the mouth and eyes in his arms had sealed themselves, Fool had fainted and dropped into a sleep that was blacker than any he'd known before.

9

Fool noticed the pictures the following morning, on the walk from their rooms to the next Delegation meeting. They lined the walls of the Anbidstow, all near-identical, dark-framed paintings of hooded figures. The pictures were large, filling the walls from floor to near the top of the ceiling, and the figure in every painting was facing away from Fool, the broad expanse of its back the central element of each picture. The backgrounds were dark, unclear, although there were sometimes hints of landscape, twisted bushes or stunted trees, grasslands or expanses of heath or moorland. The figures were wearing robes, dark and plain, and they seemed somehow sad, their shoulders slumped. None had wings, or if they did, they were hidden beneath their robes. The air of the pictures and the people they contained was somber.

Fool stepped close to one of the pictures, looking for a plaque or mark to tell him who or what it might portray. The glass was dusty and he reached to rub at it, but Benjamin caught his hand, gently, and stopped him.

"No," said the angel. "They should rest uninterrupted."

"Who are they? Are they all one person?"

"No," said Benjamin. "These are the saddest of God's angels. They are the Estedea."

"Estedea?"

"Do not ask about them, Thomas Fool," said Benjamin, still smiling that smile, delicate and slight, a curl to the edges of his lips and a crinkle in the perfect skin around his eyes. "To ask about them might attract their attention."

"And that's bad, I assume?"

"It would increase their sadness," said Benjamin. "They are created to carry the sadness of the worst days, and they come only when they are most needed and least wanted. They are the Estedea, Thomas Fool. Pray their sadness never reaches you."

They carried on walking, kept passing the pictures, and Fool couldn't stop himself from asking, "How many of them are there?"

"As many as are needed," said Benjamin, and the kindness in his voice had become chill, the absoluteness of knowing what Fool needed to do even if Fool himself did not. "Now let them be. Let them rest and hold their sadness." *He doesn't like them,* thought Fool, *doesn't like them at all. It's not their attention on me he's bothered about, it's their attention falling on* him *that worries him.* He did not mention the figures in the pictures again.

They had arrived at the room, Benjamin opening the door for them. Wambwark, now without its cloak and hat, and Catarinch, still rotting and dripping, took their places at the table, where they were joined by the same angels from the day before.

"So. Day two," said the first angel, and gestured behind it. Its scribe came forward and pulled a piece of parchment from the air, began reading a report of the previous day's agreements.

"Do you agree with the record?" asked the angel when the scribe had finished reading.

"Yes," said Catarinch, "with one exception." Fool tuned them out and moved across to his usual space when attending Delegation meetings, by the window. Benjamin, as before, joined him.

The view from the window had changed. Gone was the patchwork of fields and dark green hedges or fences, and where they had been was now a rolling swath of gorse-scattered lowland fields that dropped to a gently undulating ocean. Was it the same ocean Fool had seen on the journey here from the gate? He couldn't tell. It was shaped into a sickle bay that was lined with a fat strip of sandy beach, and at its far edge it pressed against tall gray cliffs topped with woodland. Had the ocean yesterday come up against cliffs? A beach, certainly, that he remembered, but the cliffs he was less sure about.

"How do you know where things are?" he asked Benjamin, quietly. Behind him, Wambwark, Catarinch, and the two angels were talking again about borders, the scribe standing at Catarinch's shoulder, its equivalent standing behind Heaven's representatives. Both scribes were now holding books, writing notes; presumably the dispute about the record had been solved. Neither scribe had, as far as Fool could tell, spoken apart from the initial reading.

"We don't need to," said Benjamin. "We simply go where we are required."

"But it's all changed," said Fool.

"Yes."

"So how do you find places? How do you know where places are? What if a place you want to go has moved or vanished? Are there maps?"

"There are no maps," said Benjamin, "but nowhere vanishes. Places simply move. The roads we use find them, the paths through the air lead to them. It simply is."

"This is how God wants it? With everything shifting and moving, I mean?" *God. The great enemy of Hell,* Fool thought. *Why have I brought Him up. Or Her?*

"God? We have no contact with God, and I would not presume to know my Lord's business or plans." For the first time, the smile dropped completely from Benjamin's face. "We are not meant to understand God's design of Heaven. Ours is simply to carry out God's will."

How do you know God's will? Fool wondered, but didn't ask. The smile, he thought, Benjamin's missing smile, it told him so much. God was as distant and remote to the angels as the Devil was to the human and demonkind inhabitants of Hell. Had Fool ever seen Hell's Devil, its grandest demon? He wasn't sure even now, though he suspected he may have, but he knew from Benjamin's reaction that neither he nor, Fool thought, any of the other angels he'd met had ever been graced with the presence of God. *We're all workers toiling at the face of something we cannot grasp,* he thought. *Poor Fools all.*

Wambwark said something behind him, voice raised. Fool glanced over in time to see it stand, crash one larval fist on the table between it and the angels in a spray of maggots, and shout again. The two angels simply looked at it until Catarinch placed a hand on its fellow demon's arm; the torn and dripping demon's clawed hand sank slightly into the mess of writhing bugs, pallid white shapes falling over the rotten wrist and onto the table. Wambwark remained standing for a few seconds, angels and Catarinch looking at it, and then sat back down. The parts of it that had fallen to the table wriggled back toward its arm, questing snouts burrowing between the other bugs, and rejoined the mass of flesh.

Fool looked back at Benjamin. The smile had returned to the angel's face, although it seemed, to Fool's eyes at least, a little less sure than before. *It's not good when someone shakes the foundations of your world, makes you question, is it?* he thought. *Those little uncertainties, that little worm of concern and doubt?* Aloud, he said, "Does the fairground we were at yesterday still exist?"

"Of course," replied Benjamin, "although it may have changed. Everywhere exists in Heaven, the spaces themselves simply appear in different places, that is all."

That is all, as though shifting geography was something usual, something normal. It is normal here, he realized, all perfectly normal, to be in a place where geography could not, apparently, be trusted. Fool thought of Hell, of the burning buildings, and of how much harder it would be to investigate if they were constantly moving, if they were constantly changing where they sat in relation to the things around them.

On the beach, visible more as dots than as individuals, people were standing, moving around slowly, clustering and separating. Some were in the sea or at its edge, white curls of breaking foam clinging to them as the water parted and came back together around thighs and waists. Angels, easier to make out because of their color and the speed at which they moved, arced through the crowd, sometimes stopping behind one of the human dots, never for long, then moving on. *Feeding,* he thought. *Feeding on happiness and joy like bugs, like parasites.* He looked again at Benjamin, who smiled more widely, and Fool couldn't help but see that mouth yawing open, the throat dark and empty.

"May I ask you a question?" asked Benjamin.

"Yes," said Fool, startled. It was, apart from the angel's initial greeting to Fool, the first time he had sought interaction instead of simply responding to queries.

"Do you know the two who follow?"

"'The two who follow'?" Fool repeated, confused.

"You do not know they are there?"

"No." He looked back over his shoulder, uneasy. The room contained nothing unexpected.

"They are clearly yours, Thomas Fool, tied to you by threads that are thin but strong."

"I don't know," said Fool, still looking around. His hand, without him telling it to, had drifted to the butt of his gun, was rubbing at it as though unsure of whether to grasp it.

"If you will allow me, I can show them to you later?"

Fool hesitated. He had followers? He remembered being followed by a crowd of the Sorrowful, remembered them staring at him in helpless, terrible, cloying *hope*. Were they like that? "I don't know," he said. His hand was still toying with his gun.

"They are yours, Thomas Fool, you should know about them and own them," said Benjamin. "Give me permission to bring them to your sight?"

"I—" said Fool and interrupted himself with his own silence. Then, "I don't know."

"You are fearful," said Benjamin, a statement. "Do not be. This is Heaven, and no harm can befall you here." Fool, thinking of bodies on carousels and his own splitting flesh, still bruised and sore, did not reply.

"Fool," said Catarinch from behind him. "We're finished."

Fool followed Catarinch to the door, falling in behind Wambwark, walking alongside the scribe. As Benjamin passed him, the angel said softly, "Later, Thomas Fool."

They exited the room and started down the corridor, Benjamin leading, as ever. At the end of the corridor, at a T-junction, the members of the Delegation turned right, and as they did so, Fool saw Israfil standing just to the left of the intersection. The angel, head wreathed in flame, nodded recognition at Fool, the expression on her face stern in the fire.

Wambwark, seeing the nod, reached back and cuffed Fool on the side of the head, knocking him into an ungainly stumble that ended with him kneeling against the corridor wall. Wambwark might look soft, pliable, but its fist was hot and its blow had been as hard as if he'd been hit by stone. Fool's vision shimmied, blackness creeping in at its edges, and then a hand was on his shoulder and another was under his arm and he was being helped to his feet.

Israfil's hands were as wrapped in flames as her head and body, but the flames did not burn Fool or his clothes. She turned him, still unsteady on his feet, to face her and then placed one burning palm at the place where Wambwark's blow had landed. The pain immediately subsided, its sharpness reduced to a dull throb and then a mild ache. "Thank you," he said. Israfil merely inclined her head so that her forehead was above Fool's, her hair hanging down around their faces like a caul.

"We do not need you or want you here, but you are still our guest," she said, and then stepped back and was gone. Fool rubbed at the spot she had touched; it was warm, and did not hurt. From behind him came a shriek and a sizzling sound, and then Catarinch cried out in fury. Fool turned, hand automatically going for his gun, to see Benjamin in the center of the corridor, ropes of fire dancing from his hand.

Wambwark was in pieces on the floor under him.

The demon was thrashing, struggling toward a detached arm, which was already collapsing, the shape of it becoming simply an elongated mound of white bugs. One leg was also gone, severed and flung away, a pool of maggots spreading behind the demon, dripping from its thigh stump like blood in which each droplet had a will of its own, was crawling to safety.

"Angel!" shouted Catarinch, and grasped at Benjamin's shoulder. Benjamin shrugged off the grip, sending Catarinch staggering back.

"All of you are the guests of Heaven," Benjamin said, "including Thomas Fool. Aggression against him is aggression against Heaven, and cannot be left unmarked." His fire dipped, encircled Wambwark's other arm at the wrist, and then tightened, snipping it off in a sizzle of foul-smelling steam.

"We are the members of the Delegation of Hell," said Catarinch, trying to regain its composure, "and aggression against a member of the Delegation is an act of aggression against Hell." The demon's voice was uneven, fearful.

"Then Wambwark is itself guilty of aggression against Hell," said Benjamin, without looking around. His fire curled lazily away from the cauterized wrist and wound around Wambwark's neck, tightening slowly. The air filled with the sound of popping and crackling as bugs cooked and exploded in the heat, smoke drifting up in loose wraiths. "By striking another member of the Delegation, Wambwark became the aggressor and this is a just retribution."

What to do? Fool wondered but knew that he had little choice in the matter. He was here as a representative of Hell, as Hell's Commander of the Information Office, he was Thomas Fool of Hell, and Wambwark and Catarinch and the scribe were, like it or not, his colleagues and his masters and his responsibility and his peers.

"Benjamin," he said, stepping forward. "I appreciate your intervention, yours and Israfil's both, but please don't carry on with this or I'll end up regretting what I have to do next."

"And what will you have to do that could cause you regret?" asked Benjamin, still without turning around or looking up from the straining Wambwark. Benjamin's color had, for the first time, darkened to a dull red, the glow coruscating within him, throwing off light that was almost a shadow, so dark was it. His wings had opened slightly, the whiteness of the feathers shaded pink by his glow.

"Draw my weapon and point it at you," Fool said, "and try to get you to leave my colleague alone, which would make us enemies and probably get me killed. Please." Catarinch opened its mouth to speak; Fool saw the movement from the corner of his eye and shook his head, mouthing an angry *No*. Catarinch, surprisingly, did as it was told and closed its mouth without sound.

"You'd side with a demon against me?" asked Benjamin, finally looking around.

"No," said Fool. "I'd protect the members of the Delegation of which I am a part against injury or death. I have no choice."

"Yes. It is your duty, and possibly your curse, I see that. Very well, Thomas Fool," said Benjamin after a long moment. His fire whipped away from the fallen demon and disappeared, his glow softening but not entirely vanishing, and he stepped back. As Wambwark rolled and sat up, waiting for the bugs now scattered across the floor to return to it and remake its leg and arm and hand, the angel spoke again.

"You are guests here, not free souls, none of you, and you need to remember that. The next time you are violent without permission, the next time you attack Thomas Fool or any other person here, I will take my pleasure in separating each part of you from every other part, and this time I will not stop, I will rid Heaven of the evil you represent. Do you understand?"

Wambwark, still remaking itself on the floor, made a noise that could have been assent, and although it was hard to tell, Fool thought it might have been glaring at him; Catarinch merely nodded, short and sharp, and when it carried on walking, it knocked Fool aside with its seeping elbow as it passed. *Even when I help, they hate me,* he thought, and then, *Fuck it, next time I'll let Benjamin slice them to nothing.*

The envelope was on the desk in Fool's room, and the invitation to see Mayall was contained within it.

The path to Mayall's home started at a large fence, its bars topped with elaborate metal fleur-de-lis, its gate already open. Benjamin left him at the head of the path and gestured along it.

"He's in the building and he'll meet you there," was all Benjamin said.

"You're not coming?" asked Fool, suddenly nervous. Benjamin and to some extent Israfil had been the only constants during his time in Heaven, and he found that walking away from the angel was oddly difficult, as though he was stepping out onto brittle mud that might break and let him fall through at any moment.

"I have not been invited, Thomas Fool," said Benjamin. "No one sees Mayall without an invitation, and no angel is ever invited."

"Never?"

"Never. Mayall is a solitary thing, apart from his own kind, surrounded by the resting inhabitants of Heaven and by his own thoughts. I must stay, Thomas Fool, and you must go. I will meet you here after you and Mayall have finished."

Fool went. The path was long and threaded its way between fields of neatly mown grass, lined by tall trees whose caps of green leaves blocked his view of the sky as he walked under them. The path turned gently and his feet made soft sounds on the stone roadway as Fool went among the trees. It was cooler in the shade, the smells of earth and grass thick and clean in his nostrils, and the undergrowth rustled about him. The noise was curiously reassuring. Finally, the path turned back on itself in a gentle sweep before emerging from its ranks of accompanying trees to reveal Mayall's home.

The building was facing Fool, the path designed to bring the visitor out of the trees and to be looked at directly by the structure. It was, for the most part, long and low, two wings stretching out on either side of a taller central section like arms open in welcome. It was made of red stone or brick, had ivy creeping across it, the plants verdant green capillaries that shifted slightly in the breeze. The wings were two stories high and topped by a neatly tiled roof, but the central section was at least four or five stories tall, visible before it disappeared into banks of very low cloud, a white puffball mass that crept around the upper windows and cast its shadows on the ground about him. The underside of the cloud was stitched with darker gray patches that made it look heavy and deep, a ceiling above him that was claustrophobic in its proximity.

Fool approached the building across a graveled forecourt, his footsteps louder here, crunching, and came to a set of doors that were already open. There was a person standing by the doors, head down behind a curtain of long hair, beckoning him, one arm waving slowly at Fool as though the waver was underwater. When Fool got closer, he saw through the hair that it was a man, and his eyes were closed.

There was a sign on the wall by the doors, weathered wood attached to the stonework by rivets whose heads dripped rust, and although there was writing on the sign, words across the center of some kind of crest, Fool could not read it. It wasn't that he didn't understand it because it was in some other language, but the words themselves seemed to shift and slip whenever he tried to focus on them. When he looked away, the words slithered across the sign's face in his peripheral vision, always retaining their basic shape, almost making some kind of sense but never forming into anything he could properly recognize. The crest also blurred and twisted, refusing to hold any form, simply hinting and suggesting. Was that a lion? A dog? A shield? Fool couldn't tell. When he looked at the sign directly, everything in it broke apart, became a flurry of gray and brown shapes that held no meaning he could recognize.

"Thomas Fool," called a voice from beyond the doors, "enter, please. I am so looking forward to meeting you!"

The sleeping man beckoned Fool forward again, this time actually going as far as taking a light hold on his elbow and simultaneously pulling and ushering him up the steps toward the doors. Fool allowed himself to be led to the doors, hands nervously brushing down his neat black uniform but feeling the smooth lines of the fabric as a rough and clumsy thing under his fingers, and then he was through them and into the space beyond.

Fool was in a long corridor with a tiled floor and walls lined up either side by regularly spaced doorways and, between the doorways, rows of wooden cupboards and metal lockers. From the ceiling above hung light fittings, long bars of illumination held by two chains. Dust hung in the air in the thick skeins, caught by the light and curling slowly, chasing themselves around in languid twists. The corridor smelled of wood and chalk and, more faintly, of sweat and old paper and something that Fool could only think of as concentration or intense attention; this was a place where people *thought*.

Above the lockers and cupboards strung out along the exposed faces of the walls were posters and pennants, but like the sign outside the words on them were impossible to read and kept rippling, changing whenever Fool looked at them, attaining only a half-formed reality at the edges of his sight.

Except for the man who had ushered him inside and who was now standing inside the doors with his head bowed and his shoulders slumped, arms hanging loosely, the corridor appeared empty. At its far end was a staircase that rose, widening as it did so to open out into the long horns of two upper corridors. A banner hung across the wide space in front of the staircase, covered in the now-familiar shifting words and shapes.

Fool, for want of anything else to do, began to walk toward the staircase, glancing at the cupboards and open lockers as he went. Some of the cupboards were glass-fronted and contained shelves on which stood small statuettes in gold or silver, set on plinths with tiny plaques on them; others were wooden-doored, closed and locked. The lockers were in sets, blocks four across and three high, all of them a dull green, most dented and battered. In one or two open lockers, he saw books haphazardly stuffed into the narrow spaces, piled on each other. The books looked old, well worn. Unable to help himself, he took one out and let it fall open in his hands. The pages were crumpled, some torn, covered in yet more of the shifting text as well as diagrams, lines, and angles that blurred and moved constantly. He put the book back, stepped again into the center of the corridor, and then saw them.

The nearest door had glass panels in its top half, and through them Fool could see rows of people sitting at desks. None were moving but each appeared to be concentrating on something hidden from his view. He moved closer to the door, peering in through the glass, seeing more of the room beyond.

There were perhaps forty of them, sleeping humans, seated at plain wooden desks. Some had paper in front of them on the desk surfaces and were writing, or at least pretending to write; their hands held pens or pencils and moved across the pages, but the marks they made were simply scrawled lines as far as Fool could see. Others merely stared at the far end of the room where an angel was standing motionless beside a large blackboard, across which white chalk lines were appearing and then vanishing; Fool could dimly hear the faint scratch of the lines being made and the low slosh of them being unmade.

"They're in school," said a voice from behind Fool, the breath of the words brushing across his ear. He started, jumped, and banged into the door, his forehead knocking against the glass panel sharply. Whoever it was behind him laughed, loud and delighted, and clapped its hands. Fool turned, rubbing his forehead, and found himself looking at an angel who was grinning more widely than anyone Fool had seen before.

"Thomas Fool," the angel said, "welcome, welcome! I'm Mayall, and this is my home, and you are welcome to roam its corridors at will!"

Before Fool could speak, Mayall reached forward and grasped his hand, shaking it furiously. The shake became almost frenzied, Fool's arm being yanked up and down until Mayall suddenly let it go and spun away, turning the rhythm of the shake into a kind of loose caper, his feet beating a jig on the floor. He laughed as he spun, the sounds echoing along the corridor and layering so that for a moment it sounded as though the corridor was filled with hundreds of laughing creatures rather than simply one. Mayall finally came to an uneven halt, gasping and still laughing, facing Fool and wobbling slightly as though he was dizzy. He panted, his tongue hanging from his mouth, a pink worm wriggling delightedly around his chin.

Mayall was unlike any angel Fool had seen before. He was dressed differently, clothed neither in flame nor feather, and not in robes but in trousers and an old shirt that was stained and wrinkled. His hair was long and so thick it looked almost greasy, swept back from his head, bouncing manically as he moved and dropping in lank strings that he continually had to brush back. His feet were bare and filthy, dirt in black swathes between his toes and disappearing up under the trouser cuffs, and his eyes were huge in a face that was handsome but not perfect in the way that other angels' were. He had lines across his forehead, although whether of frown or laughter Fool couldn't tell, and his mouth had an odd set to it, almost a pout of petulant humor.

He looked human.

At least, human apart from the wings that beat the air behind him, outstretched and constantly flapping, although even they looked some-how less than angelic, the feathers not aligned perfectly, noisy as they moved. Mayall had little of the stillness of the other angels Fool had met and none of the calmness; he *jittered*, constantly moving, his hands rising and falling as he spoke, his eyes darting around, taking every-thing in.

"It's such a pleasure," said Mayall, "such a pleasure. Thomas Fool, the investigator from Hell, here in Heaven. We are honored."

"Israfil doesn't think so," said Fool without thinking.

"Israfil's a fool," said Mayall and then roared with laughter again. "A fool! No offense intended, Fool, you're your own fool, as Israfil is hers! Both fools but different fools, Heaven's fool and Hell's Fool! Perhaps you should be friends, yes? Do you see?"

"Yes," said Fool, not doing so, trying to keep up. "You wanted to see me?"

"See you, meet you, touch you, smell you!" said Mayall. "I told the Malakim we needed you, and I was right. We need your help, Fool, we've lost the skills that you have so recently gained." Mayall suddenly spun and launched himself down the corridor, leaping up into the space and roaring with laughter and swooping through the air in front of the staircase, cycling around the banner before crashing back to the floor in front of Fool. His landing was clumsy and he staggered, arms flailing, into the wall, knocking a set of lockers down and sending their contents across the corridor in a scatter of paper and dust.

"Damage," shouted Mayall, "there's damage in Heaven! Heavenly damage!" He began to dance again, spreading the paper more widely. Fool watched, utterly confused, as the angel kicked and slapped at the mess, tearing and ripping at the books and throwing small pieces of paper into the air to float above them, wavering in the updrafts of his wings.

"Paper in the air, paper on the floor," the angel said as he danced among the chaos, "paper in the lockers and paper by the door!" He carried on chanting lines of doggerel and poetry as he kicked and leaped, all interspersed with laughter and hand claps and snatches of hummed tunes. The paper snowstormed around him, the air filled with torn pieces and battered dust, never allowed to rest because of the angel's dervish movements and agitations. He went on for maybe two or three minutes before finally coming to a halt, panting, letting the fragments of page fall to the floor in drifts around him.

"This is the only place in Heaven where things get damaged," he said, his voice suddenly low, serious. "We're frightened of it, of damage, we've become too perfect, we've forgotten how to face imperfection."

"I don't understand," said Fool. Being with Mayall was exhausting; even after the scant minutes of his visit, he was tired.

"Come with me," said Mayall and set off down the corridor. He walked rapidly, speaking in a constant stream as he went.

"Heaven is a place of joys, Fool, that's the point of it. We gather them together, the people who have earned their place here, we fish them out of Limbo after their lives of toil and we let them experience the places of their most private dreams, the places they were happiest. Those places become real around them, and so Heaven mirrors their loves and *becomes* their loves, and they stay until they're ready to move on. Look at them here, in school. They remember school as a place of safety, enough of them, so Heaven creates a school for them to be safe in while they dream their own Heavens into existence."

"I'm not sure I understand," said Fool.

"No," replied Mayall, leaping and turning with another roar of that manic laughter, "you don't, because what I've told you isn't true. It's maybe half true, or a quarter, or a fraction or even mostly true, but it's not the actual truth. Nothing in Heaven is *actually* true."

"'Actually'?" Mayall's emphasis was odd, and Fool thought it was deliberate, a test to see if he was listening properly.

"Every person here has a truth that they can see but no one else can. Even the angels, Benjamin and Israfil and all the others, only see the Heaven they believe should exist, the Heaven they have walked every day of their existence. They see the everyday, Fool, but none of them sees things *actually*, none of them sees truthfully, no one sees the *actual* truth of things. Israfil and Benjamin and all their angelic kin cannot see that Heaven has a need for you, cannot accept that Heaven has imperfections, that things are going wrong, that there are mysteries! The Malakim see a need for you because their view has the breadth of vision that most angels do not possess, but even they cannot see the danger of letting you loose in Heaven because they see this as a mere clerical exercise. There's the everyday, and then there's the actual."

"I'm a danger?"

"Of course. You aren't fettered by the shackles Israfil and the others wear, so you have no reason to avoid seeing the actual Heaven around us."

"But if I'm a danger, why ask for me? Why bring me here?"

They had reached the staircase but they didn't start up it. "Why?" repeated Mayall, his voice quiet now, almost reflective. He reached out and touched Fool's cheek, just a brush of his fingertips, gentle. "Why? Because we need you, Fool, even if we don't wish to admit it. We need you."

Mayall shook himself suddenly, as though shaking off a mood, and started to dance again, twirling on the spot and making little gavotte steps up and then back down the first few risers. His shirttails came free from his pants and flapped, revealing a belly that was smooth and hairless but stretched by a small paunch. After several increasingly fast ascents and descents, each time getting farther up the staircase before coming back down, Mayall practically bounced up to just past half-way but turned too fast and slipped, falling and rolling down the steps toward Fool. His wings wrapped around him, protecting his head and upper body as he fell, but when he reached the bottom of the stair-case they whipped open to reveal that the angel was still grinning, still exposing teeth that were huge and white and even.

"Ta-daaaaa!" Mayall said loudly, rolling and somehow coming up onto one knee and throwing his arms wide in a sweeping, grandiloquent gesture. Fool took a step back.

"Why ask for you? Haven't you realized? Because I *like* the risk you pose, Fool. I *like* the danger you represent. I *like* the chaos of you, Fool, and I like what you'll do when you see what you're supposed to see."

"Supposed to see? What am I supposed to be seeing?"

"The truth," said Mayall. He strode purposefully to the nearest locker and removed three books from it, began juggling them, head back as he flung them faster and faster through the air. Once he had them moving in a swift, easy arc above him, he started to remove more books from the locker, snatching them with sharp, darting gestures and adding them to the juggle. Four books, five, six, eight, now ten and still he added, panting and laughing, starting to dance as he threw, legs kicking out in a rhythm that counterpointed the books' movement. Finally, one of the books went too high and hit a hanging light, setting it swinging, then fell back and hit Mayall on the forehead. The angel made a show of shrieking and collapsing, rolling exaggeratedly on the floor as the books fell around him, and then suddenly springing up again with a roar of laughter. He landed and dropped to one knee again, making the same open-armed gesture and shouting "Ta-DAAAAAA!" louder and longer than before.

"What truth?" Fool asked, trying to ignore the angel's antics, wonder-ing if it was somehow mad, an insane thing.

"Any truth you care to find," said Mayall. "Any truth that Benjamin or Israfil or any of the others cannot or will not see."

"'Any of the others'?" repeated Fool. "You aren't one of them?"

"Of course not," said Mayall, his tone indignant. "Haven't they told you? Haven't you guessed? I'm Mayall, and I am the only clown angel, the one and only. I am the thing that dances as the worlds collapse. I am the thing that throws the worlds up to see where they fall. I am the thing that finds the joke in the hurt and the hurt in the joke. I am the only one of the Host prepared to see the truth, the whole truth, the whole ugly and breaking truth."

"Then why do you need me? If you can see the truth?"

"Because no one listens to clowns, Fool," said Mayall, finally stilling, looking at Fool again. He smiled, a sad little moue that pulled at the corners of his mouth and tugged at the tips of his eyes. "Clowns are ever the most truthful and honest but the most ignored of all creatures, even angelic ones. We fall and get hit, we laugh and point, we show where the absurdities and the truths are but are dismissed as fools. Fools, Fool, we're all fools but you more so than most!" Mayall leaped forward and into the air, wings flapping. One wingtip clipped a cupboard and it sent the angel yawing, crashing over, closely followed by the cupboard, which split open and spilled hundreds of old notebooks across the floor. Prone, wings splayed across the corridor, the angel said, "I am the only angel of accidental destruction, Fool, I am the slip and trip, the drop and crash, the mistake and the groan, and they prefer me to stay in here for fear I might cause damage out there, but I see things, Fool, I see *everything.*"

"How?"

"That's the wrong question, Fool," said Mayall, climbing to his feet, and in standing he underwent another of those dizzying shifts, became serious, and when he spoke his voice was quiet and slow and the expression on his face was calm. He looked into the nearest room, seemed to be concentrating on something, and then said, "You have to go, there's something I have seen that you need to see also. Word has been sent and Benjamin has gone on ahead. Israfil is waiting outside to take you. Quickly, Fool, quickly now, think about the very wrongest question you could ask, and then ask the very rightest one."

Fool thought for a minute, sure that asking Mayall *how* he saw things wasn't wrong at all but playing along because he had little choice, and then said, "All right, if not how then what. *What* do you see?"

"Better, Fool, so much better. I knew you were the right one to bring," said Mayall, clapping again, feet already beginning to shuffle into another dance. "What do I see, Fool? I see stains, Fool, I see corruptions. You found the blue flowers? They're the blooms of corruption, growing here, growing in Heaven, where such things should be impossible, little buds of foulness growing in the purest earth there is. Heaven is being invaded, Fool, just skirmishes on the borders so far, but it will get worse, so much worse, and I see it happening now and I see it happening in the future but I cannot see *who*, Fool, I cannot see the *who* of it. Make no mistake, though, Fool, be clear; in the most perfect place of all, I can see the one thing that should not exist.

"I see imperfection."

10

Israfil was, as promised, waiting for Fool outside Mayall's house by a small, gleaming transport.

They journeyed in silence, Israfil looking out of the small vehicle's window at the landscape beyond the glass and Fool thinking about Mayall. Being in the angel's presence had made him feel dizzy, as though his cycle of frenzy and seriousness was somehow contagious, a hysterical whirl communicated by proximity and only now slowly fading. Fool found that he was tired, not physically but mentally, his thoughts slipping and unable to stay on one thing, refusing to focus. He felt drained, weary inside himself in a way he'd never felt before. *Has Mayall fed off me somehow?* he wondered. *Without touching me, without me realizing? Yes. Yes, I think he has.*

Fool sat back in the seat and let the rhythm of the road, seeping up through the vehicle's wheels, lull him into something that wasn't a sleep but wasn't wakefulness either, something in between where his body felt heavy and colors splashed across the inside of his closed eyes in sinuous waves. His limbs felt stiff, leaden, and his head bobbed down and lolled to the side despite his efforts to keep it up. *What's wrong with me?* he thought. *What's the angel done?* He thought of the sleeping humans and wondered if he was becoming like them, forced his eyes open and tried to focus on the landscape passing outside the window.

Instead of land, Fool saw only mist that held, in its depth, dark shadows that might have been hills and fields that might instead have been forests and buildings. Was this the truth, hidden behind the façade?

Was this Heaven?

Fool's eyes dropped closed again despite his struggles to keep them open; they felt like rough balls of lead in his head, his eyelids weighted blinds that pulled ever downward. He dozed, dreaming of carousel horses ridden by grinning, laughing angels, and was woken only by the change of rhythm as the transport came to a halt.

Their journey ended at the edge of a beach, where the transport had pulled off the road and onto a long stretch of coarse sand fringed by dunes and scattered with patches of sea grass. It took Fool a moment to pull himself back from the place he had collapsed to, dragging himself out of the fairground in his dreams and back into the transport, back to what Mayall had called "the everyday," and even then he felt dislocated and slow. When he moved, it was draggy and clumsy, his fingers feeling thick and senseless. It took him three tries to open the vehicle's door, and when he climbed out he had to hold the top of the door to steady himself.

"Are you unwell?" asked Benjamin from ahead of them, where he waited with the usual smile on his face, now tempered by a moue of concern.

"Mayall," said Israfil simply, emerging from the transport behind Fool.

"Ah, of course," said Benjamin, understanding flitting across his face. "I should have realized. You spent time with the capering one, and now you feel the weight of your visit with him?"

Fool realized that the question was being addressed to him, brought his eyes around and tried to focus on the angel. "Yes," he said, and Heaven blurred and then came back into sharpness before him. He felt himself grow heavier, fell to his knees and then onto all fours. The thought that Benjamin didn't like Mayall, didn't like that Fool had been invited to see the clown angel, flashed briefly across his mind and was then gone, replaced by a wave of tiredness and the image of books being juggled, circling higher and higher above him while something vast and grinning danced just out of reach. Was he going insane?

Was he dying?

"It'll be fine, Thomas Fool," Benjamin said, but it didn't feel fine, not at all. Fool slumped, the strength gone from his arms and legs completely now, leaving him prostrate on the beach. He inhaled grains of sand and the smell of brine, coughed but couldn't seem to clear his throat of the obstruction. *I'm dying,* he thought, *dying in Heaven and not in Hell,* and found he was strangely disappointed by the realization. *Marianne,* he thought. *Marianne, be safe,* and then Israfil yanked him up and poured a cupped handful of seawater on his face.

It was cold, bitterly cold, and it snapped through the feelings of lethargy like a falling icicle. Fool gasped, his throat shockingly, suddenly open and his lungs remembering how to breathe. Some of the liquid went into his mouth and he tasted the rich, uneven tang of salt. Blinking, he focused his eyes on the burning angel that held him. Her face was expressionless behind the caul of flames, and when she saw that he was alert again, she let him go.

"Pull yourself back together, Information Man," Israfil said. "There's a task that needs your attention."

Fool stood, unsteady but feeling stronger, more awake. He saw Israfil's disdainful look and said, "Mayall said there was something I should see," emphasizing the angel's name, wearing it like armor. "Perhaps you can take me to it?"

Whereas the first body had, possibly, fallen from the carousel horse and snapped its neck when it hit the floor, this one was floating facedown in the water several feet out from the shore. It bobbed with the waves, rising up as they crested and then dropping into the troughs as the ocean washed over it. Fool waded out and grasped this body and rolled it, the body's shoulder breaking the water like the fin of some undersea creature before the corpse settled to float on its back.

It was a woman, her hair drifting in the water and framing her pale, bloating face. Her eyes were open, the sclera bloodshot, the pupils huge. Fool pulled her toward the shore, watched by Benjamin and Israfil, both surrounded by the usual crowd of swaying, slowly moving sleepers. An unnamed angel, another one of the caretakers Fool assumed, was huddled into itself and standing farther back from the shore, looking on. For the first time since his arrival, he saw an expression on an angelic face that was less than happy. This angel was worried.

"Another accident?" he asked as he brought the woman's body up onto the sand and laid her carefully down. Water spilled from the dead woman's mouth, foamy and blood-streaked, and her robes clung to her body. She was older, her stomach and thighs fat, wobbling as Fool moved her. He pulled at the material, trying to lift it from her flesh and give her some dignity, but as soon as he let it go it fell back and molded again to her shape, exposing her.

"What else?" asked Israfil. "She was not being watched carefully enough and she slipped under the water."

"Let me ask you," said Fool, remembering what Mayall had said. "In all your time in Heaven, both of you, how many accidents like this have there been?"

"None," said Benjamin. "Heaven is perfect."

"And yet here we are. Two accidents, two imperfections, in two days." No, more, he realized; hadn't the Malakim said he'd been requested specifically, Mayall had told the Malakim that he, Fool, was needed, meaning that there must have been at least one earlier incident, an earlier mystery, an earlier truth to be uncovered. A death? More than one?

How many?

"I repeat, these are clearly accidents. If they have happened, then they have happened for a reason. They are part of the Plan," said Israfil, and Fool heard the capital letter that "Plan" began with in Israfil's voice in the way she emphasized its plosive opening. A wave washed up past her, covering her feet, and Fool was fascinated by the way she still burned even underwater, the flames orange and distorted through the liquid. The sea steamed slightly where the water touched her.

"What if they aren't?"

"They are, and to question further is to question the perfection of Heaven," she replied, "and you cannot. The only imperfect thing here is you, and your degraded colleagues, those things of worm and rottenness. If there is foulness here, you have brought it, you *are* it, and it will leave with you. Out here, there is only that which is supposed to be, which is designed by God."

It's hopeless, he thought. *Mayall's right, they can't see it, can't or won't allow themselves to.* Instead of replying, Fool moved away from the body, going first to the huddled angel. "What about you? Did you see anything?"

"No, sir," it said.

Sir?

"Nothing?"

"No, sir, I was tending my flock as always and when I came to tend here, I found her like this."

"How big is your flock? I mean, how long were you away from the people here, from her?"

"From here to away," said the angel, waving one perfect hand along the beach in the direction that led away from the cliffs.

"Did you feed?" asked Benjamin. "Were you feeding?"

The angel looked down. "Yes."

There was a moment then, a tiny space in which it felt to Fool like Heaven paused, that everything froze, and then the angel stood straight, nodded at Benjamin and Israfil, lowered its head so that its chin was resting on its chest, and broke to pieces.

Cracks appeared across its face and hands, light spilling from them, and then light was swelling under robes that were billowing out and a great halo of illumination surrounded the angel. It brightened, intensified to a violent glare, and then a sharp zephyr of dust that burned with yellow flames rose from where the angel had been standing, and it was gone.

"Where is he?" Fool asked, knowing the answer.

"He was negligent," said Israfil. "And negligence has to be punished. Feeding is permitted only when Heaven's lives are secure."

"You said it was part of the Plan," replied Fool. "It was punished for being a part of the Plan?"

"We have our rules, and we adhere to them. That, too, is part of the Plan."

"Rules," said Fool. "Of course. There are always rules, aren't there? I hadn't finished talking to him; he might still have had something to say that would have been useful."

"No," said Israfil. "There is nothing here of use to you. You are a human, a damned human, and there is nothing for you to hear and nothing useful you can tell us."

"Really? That's not what the fucking Malakim think, nor Mayall," snapped Fool, irritation bubbling through for a moment.

"You will keep a civil tongue in your head," said Israfil, and her flames brightened for a second before flickering back to their usual hue.

Fool ignored Israfil's comment, instead turning where he stood and looking around, *really* looking. The sound of the sea washing in and out was a low susurrus like the sleeping breath of some great creature, oddly calming. He tried to clear his mind, remove the irritation he felt toward Benjamin and Israfil and toward their insistence that the two deaths were accidents, remove his own insistence that these were not accidents, remove the memories of pain that still crawled over his skin and the tiredness following the visit to Mayall, remove everything but the scene before him. What could he see? *Really* see? What was the scene telling him?

There were no other bodies, but there were gaps on the beach where people had been standing.

Fool could tell where people had been because there were indentations in the sand, sometimes surrounded by arcs dug into furrows. *They stood, and sometimes they turned around,* he thought, looking at the massed crowd. Yes, there; someone turning on the spot, head tilted back to the sun, eyes still closed. *The Joyful, I once called them, but they don't look Joyful, they look asleep. They look fucking half* dead!

He walked rapidly around in an expanding spiral, weaving between what he now knew he would always consider the Joyful, counting. Nine spaces, nine gaps, nine pieces of churned sand, the beach's dark and wet underbelly exposed.

Nine missing people?

Nine missing, and one dead.

Each space in the crowd was connected by a set of trails in the sand. The trails all led in one direction, closing in on each other, so that by the time Fool was fifty yards from where the gaps were there was a single thick and tangled track. He crouched by it, looking for anything in the mess of sand and wetness that he could use. Was that something? A partial print?

Whatever had left the print had claws that had dug into the sand; the rear of the indentation had collapsed, the sand there too dry to hold its shape. Slightly farther on was something that looked like a wheel print, the thickness uneven, the line of it not straight, a continuous furrow through the grains. The track went on for around six feet through a wetter part of the beach, and in the deepest parts of the furrow were occasional more delicate imprints, distorted hexagons and pentagons. Scales?

Claws? And scales? The longer print, was it some kind of tentacle? It was too consistent, unbroken, to be feet, so something like a snake?

What the fuck was going on here?

Fool followed the trail farther, then turned back. The gaps in the ranks of the Joyful occurred at the edge of the huge crowd of them, in the first people you'd meet if you were walking along the beach from the cliffs. He looked down at the trail again, and then called Israfil and Benjamin to come to him.

When they arrived next to him, Fool told them to stand still and went to look at the tracks they had just left. Both left essentially human footprints, although Israfil's sometimes had brush marks alongside them. Fool peered at the angel's legs and saw that her lowest wings, the tiny ones that curled out from her ankles, were not as tightly wrapped around her skin as Benjamin's were, that they continually flexed in and out in time with the rhythm of the sea.

"Are all angels' footprints like this?" he asked.

"Why do you want to know?" asked Israfil.

"Because I'm interested," snapped Fool, "and you uncreated the only other angel that I could have asked, so now I have to bother you. So I ask again, are all your tracks like this?"

"Yes," said Benjamin. "We are all alike, or at least, all similar enough to leave similar tracks."

The trail wasn't made by angels, then. Fool went back to it, crouching again. Sand stuck to the hems of his trousers and scratched the leather of his boots, crunching underfoot. What was that? He reached forward, then thought better of it and unstrapped his gun. Using the barrel, he dug into the sand and worked out what he had seen: a small blue string of plant material. He lifted it and it came free with a sucking sound, pale and thin white roots hanging from its end, stem and tiny flower bud hanging loose. It smelled, reminding him of the plant he'd found at the fairground the day before. *The blue growth of corruption*, he thought. *Imperfection in a perfect place.*

"What's this?" he asked, holding it out toward Benjamin and Israfil.

"A sea plant," said Israfil, uninterestedly.

"That's all?"

"Yes."

Fool dropped it and went on. More of the long fronds grew in the trail, here and there topped by closed flower buds.

"Have you seen this plant before?" he called over to the angels.

"No," said Benjamin, "but I rarely attend the beach. My role in Heaven is at the Anbidstow, as is Israfil's."

Fool found more prints and elongated tracks within the trail the farther he went along it, and soon came to the conclusion that this was actually two trails, one overlaid across the other. Some of the clawed prints faced the Joyful, some of them the cliffs, and at one place he found a print facing the cliffs pressed over a similar print facing the crowds.

"They came from the cliffs to the crowd," he said aloud. He had a sudden thought and went rapidly back to where the body was still lying on the beach. Here were his tracks and gradually soaking-away splashes of water he'd made as he brought the dead woman from the water. He looked at the sea, saw that it was flowing slightly along the coast as well as washing in and out, and moved along the surf against the flow. Several yards farther away, he found what he was looking for.

A set of footprints in the sand, leading from a space on the beach to the ocean.

The woman had walked from where she had been standing into the water, a distance of about forty feet. The spaces between the prints grew longer as they approached the water, becoming blurred and oddly wide, irregular. Experimentally, Fool walked a few steps, then turned. His prints were evenly spaced. Why the difference between the way his tracks looked and the way the woman's looked?

Wondering, Fool started to run, accelerated over thirty feet or so, and then stopped and turned back to look at his tracks. The spaces between individual prints grew larger the farther he had run.

She started running, he thought, *but why? And why do her prints get wider toward the water's edge?*

Fool went back to the body, glancing down again at his tracks as he did so. The last of his prints, the ones he'd made as he surveyed the marks he'd pressed into the sand while running, were wider, similar to the woman's prints near the water's edge. What had he done?

I turned, he thought. *I turned to look at where I'd come from, turned to see behind me. She turned, she was turning as she ran, trying to see behind her.*

Trying to see what *was behind her?*

Fool retraced his steps, looking at the tracks the dead woman had made. He walked along, imagining a woman starting to run, turning as she did so, and then? Then? What happened to her? How did she go from running and living to dead and floating?

Just under the edge of the surf was a rock, jutting up from the sand like a stumped tooth. He judged the distance between her last prints, at the edge of the surf. It was the right distance, assuming that there hadn't been more prints nearer to the rock that the water had washed away, a body's length. Was that it? If so, there would be a mark on her. Fool started back to her corpse.

There were six tiny black naked angels around the woman's body, holding her, wings fluttering so fast they were little more than blurs, and lifting the woman into the air.

"No!" shouted Fool, starting to run, aware he'd just run over the woman's tracks, obliterating them, confusedly aware that his own tracks would show greater distance between each print as he accelerated and knowing that it wasn't important, still shouting.

"Put her down!"

The angels carried on raising the woman, wings frenzied, air beating and swirling, sand lifting from the beach in the downdrafts, and then he was at the corpse and grabbing it, trying to pull it back to the earth.

Fool was lifted from the ground. He tried to concentrate his weight downward but it was hopeless; the angels simply continued to rise, carrying him as though he wasn't there. He wrapped one arm over the woman's belly, gripping hold of her flesh, dangling below her, and tried to pull again. The body shifted in the angels' grasp but continued to be borne aloft with Fool its unwilling passenger. "Stop," he cried again, but his voice sounded weaker, thinner, even to him.

"Do you wish to stop this poor soul from moving along her rightful path?" asked Benjamin. The angel was flapping his wings gently, rising alongside Fool and the woman, one arm reaching out and stroking the head of the nearest black angel.

"Yes," said Fool, not looking down, breath coming in ragged looping swallows.

"Why? She has surely earned her peace?"

"I need to examine her corpse, to check something. I need to see what the woman can tell me," said Fool. How high up were they now? How high, and how hard would he hit if he fell? His arm slipped, his grip loose, not wanting to dig into the woman's dead thigh but having no choice.

"The dead cannot speak, Thomas Fool."

"Yes, they can," said Fool, and then he had no more words, had a band of fear running around him, tightening so that he couldn't speak. His grip slipped again, the wet material of the woman's robe slithering, his fingers unable to keep a solid grasp of her. He looked down, saw the beach and the Joyful below him, too far below, and then the ground was lifting toward him.

He wasn't falling. The little black angels were descending, bringing the woman back to earth, Benjamin taking hold of Fool and support-ing him, lowering him. As his feet touched the ground, Fool let out a tangled sigh and, as soon as Benjamin let him go, dropped to his knees. He swayed, dizzy, breathing deep, and then managed to lift his head.

"Thank you," he said.

"I cannot pretend to understand," said Benjamin, "but my instruc-tions are clear. She is yours until you need her no longer. But please, the angels of the dead should have her flesh as quickly as possible."

"The angels of the dead?"

Benjamin inclined his head, gesturing slightly at the black angels that were now hovering over their heads. "They have the sacred duty of caring for the flesh as it slips away. They are the kindliest ones, the most revered of the angelic host of Heaven."

"It should only take a moment," said Fool, feeling carefully around the woman's head. He probed her scalp and neck, running his fingers through her still-wet hair, pressing and pulling.

There.

Carefully, Fool rolled her over and parted her hair. There was a long gash, washed clean by the sea, its edges pale, across the rear of her head. The bone below the cut felt loose, shifted in a way that a skull should not. When Fool pulled free some of the strands of hair that had pressed into the gash, they brought tiny flecks of dark stone with them.

"She woke up and ran. She was running," he said, "turning to see something behind her as she ran. She fell as she turned and hit her head on the rock. I would think that the impact knocked her out and she drowned." He pressed her chest. Foamy water bubbled up from her lungs and spilled down her face, threaded with pink streaks.

"Her lungs are full of water," he said, watching as the strings of water soaked into the sand.

"Impossible," said Israfil. "While they inhabit their personal Heavens their bodies sleep here, but it is not the simple sleep of rest, it is the sleep of joy and reward. They cannot wake up."

"Really?" said Fool. He went to the closest person, a young black man with a beard and short hair, and stood in front of him. He thought about the first body, about the slash across its shoulder, and took hold of the man's upper arms. *If I had claws, long claws, they'd be over his shoulder blades,* he thought, *and if I pulled forward but lost my grip, I'd cut him from rear to front.*

Experimentally, he shook the man.

"Don't," said Israfil, but Fool ignored her and shook again, harder. The man's head wobbled loosely on his neck, rocking back and forth. Fool shook even harder, and then pushed the man, who stumbled back and fell. His head hit the sand with a crunch.

"Fool, stop this now," said Benjamin, and then the man's eyes flickered open.

"What?" he said, his voice sounding as though it came from far away, from a place of wooziness and deep, drowning sleep. "What's this?"

"Where are you?"

"Fool, *stop,*" said Israfil, and her fire was blazing now, throwing leaping yellow and orange shadows around them, the color at her center darkening to a grim, crackling red.

"Where's Richard?" said the man, looking around, eyes darting back and forth. "He was just here. Where's Richard, where's my boy?"

"Human, I command you to *stop,*" Israfil said, but Fool ignored the angel, took the man's hands, and helped him to his feet, guided him back to his space. By the time the man's feet were planted back in the marks they had made earlier, his eyes were closed again and his head was rotating slowly, rolling on his neck until his face was pointing at the sky. Fool stepped away from the man, letting him return to his Heaven, wherever that was, and whomever he was sharing it with. Richard, presumably. His son? Lover? Fool would never know.

"Don't ever do that again," said Israfil, stepping toward Fool. "These people are souls who have earned their place here, they are those who do not need to experience Hell's touch, and they should be able to enjoy their reward uninterrupted." Her features were almost lost in the fires about her now, tongues of it snaking out from her hands and mouth as she spoke, curling about each other.

"I apologize," said Fool, "but it proves something, doesn't it?"

"What?"

"The Joyful can be woken," he said. "Something woke that woman and she ran, she ran and fell and died."

"What woke her? Why run?" asked Benjamin.

"I don't know," said Fool. "Shall we try to find out?"

The trail in the sand led back along the beach toward the cliffs. This time, Fool didn't stop to inspect it; he already knew what it would show him, and the blue growths rarely looked different from one another. He walked along the side of it, followed by Israfil and Benjamin, leaving the Joyful behind and approaching the rock walls ahead of him.

Close to, it became clear the cliffs were not an unbroken line of rock but were split by gullies and gorges. The trail beetled across the sand, meeting the rocks and turning, following the base of the cliff, staying parallel to the lower edge of rocky outcrops. The sand was coarser here, crunching under Fool's feet but not, he noticed, the angels', the trail less defined. The blue growths were stronger, as though more rooted, and the track became covered with them. They smelled foul, the odor thick in Fool's nose.

Eventually, the trail turned toward a valley formed by a deep cleft in the rock. A narrow stream trickled out of the valley's opening, and thick vegetation grew on its banks, choking the space in greens and browns and humidity. The trail stopped at the valley's entrance, and Fool stopped with it, peering up into the narrow throat. He looked around, *little constantly-turning-around Fool, little always-looking-behind-him Fool,* and took his weapon from his holster.

"There is no danger here," said Israfil, seeing the gun in Fool's hand.

"No?" asked Fool. "Then what was the woman running from?"

Holding the gun out before him, he walked into the valley.

11

It was warmer in the valley, claustrophobic, the greenery pressing in on him, dripping water on his head and down the back of his neck. Thick trunks and twisted vines blocked Fool's way, forcing him to constantly step sideways and to backtrack to find alternative ways past. *How do I know I'm going the right way?* he thought, and the answer came to him almost immediately.

Because of the blue flowers.

There were more here, budding on the vines, rooted into the trunks. They were larger, seemed somehow older, as though they had been growing longer. Around the places where the flowers had burrowed into the wood, the trees' flesh had become pulpy and wet, rotten. In several places, he found plants so thick with the blue flowers that they were crumbling and bent, strangled by the growths. The blue flowers stank, a smell that Fool recognized but had almost forgotten in his couple of days in Heaven—the smell of death and things decaying.

The ground rose as Fool progressed, the valley climbing the farther he went. Would it eventually come out on top of the cliffs, or narrow so far that it closed away to nothing? What was he looking for? He wasn't sure.

No, that's wrong, I am sure, he thought. *I want information. I'm an Information Man, the Commander of the Information Office of Hell, and I'm looking for information, for the answers in the information.*

I want the truth.

And the truth was, Fool wasn't alone. Something was moving alongside him in the undergrowth.

Fool heard it first, the crack of a branch breaking underfoot, the rustle of plant material being pushed aside as something passed by it. He stopped. The sounds stopped. Carefully, he moved forward; the sound of something also moving forward started again, stopped when he did.

Was it the angels?

No. Turning, he found that he could see them through the tangles of growth, perhaps fifty yards behind him, Israfil's fire gleaming and moving in the fractured view through the branches.

Something dark shifted to Fool's side, darting ahead of him.

It was a fast movement, small, keeping its distance but moving around him so that it was now slightly farther up the valley than he was. It stopped again as Fool turned back toward it, whipping his gun around. He crouched slightly, looking through the framework of leaves and branch ends. Whatever it was had remained still, hidden in the patchwork of color and shadow.

Had he imagined it? Disturbed some creature, startled it into running?

Fool carried on up the valley, slower now, listening. After a moment the noise of something moving, now just ahead of him, started again. The sound was somehow *cautious,* as though whatever or whoever it was, was being deliberately quiet. There was a definite sense of observation and concealment to the noise. Fool reached out to push aside a heavy tangle of branches and blue flowers that left streaks of dankness across his hands and clothes. The thing in front of him moved again, coming no closer but keeping the distance between them steady. Reaching out had pulled his sleeve back, and the tattoo of Marianne's face on Fool's forearm was exposed, as though she, too, was looking out into the foliage.

Was it the scribe? In the excitement of the morning, with the Delegation meeting and Benjamin's attack on the demons after, he had forgotten to try to talk to the little demon. Had it come out here, scared the woman somehow, caused her death?

If it was the scribe, what was it still doing here?

Fool stepped on something loose. His foot rolled and he stumbled slightly, attention drawn momentarily away from the movement ahead of him. He steadied himself, looked again, gun wavering.

It was closer.

Fool didn't know how he knew, nothing had changed, nothing to say that it was nearer, but it was. His instincts, grown and sharpened in a place where to stop paying attention was to be killed or taken or lost, told him that the thing had used his momentary distraction to move closer in. How far away was it now? Ten yards? Fifteen? Five?

What was it?

Fool took another step. Another. The soft sound of shifting air alongside him, the itch of branch against branch, and then a gentle pressure of wet leaves being trodden upon. A hiss.

Fool pointed his gun to where he thought the hiss had come from. Was that a shape, lurking behind a thick fringe of hanging vines and wet leaves? An eye, peering at him, the pupil slitted and dark. He pushed forward, stretching his arm out.

"Come out," he said. "Come where I can see you."

Nothing, no movement.

Another step, closing in on the dark shape, gun barrel waving, trying to pierce the shadows. His foot came down on something that rolled and he stumbled again, crashing into the tree next to him, and as he did so the thing moved. It darted, away this time, putting distance between him and it.

Was it there at all? Was this all in his imagination? Another step, another, another, and the undergrowth was thinning, opening out now, and the thing had slipped behind the tree trunk, thick enough to hide it completely.

Fool pressed himself against the trunk, trying to listen. The air was filled with the rustle and patter of water rolling down leaves and spilling to the floor, with the sounds of tiny creatures skittering through the mulch at his feet, with his own breath a hollow rattling in his ears. Which way around the trunk? Widdershins, or righthandwise?

Widdershins.

Fool took a step to his left, hugging against the trunk, careful to keep his gun low so that it could not be taken from him.

A hoarse inhalation, from ahead of him.

Fool took two rapid steps and came around the trunk, and a clawed hand slashed at him.

Instinctively he jerked away, the back of his head cracking against the tree, hard, and then the claws were at him, digging into his cheek and curling through his flesh. There was an audible grind as they collided with his cheekbone and then they were yanked forward and Fool felt them peel open his face. He screamed, gun jerking up and firing without thought. The percussion of it was terrible, the flash huge even through his closed eyes. He slipped down the trunk, legs uneven and weak, raising a hand to his cheek and feeling blood run fast and warm over his fingers, feeling something flap against his palm. His legs sprawled out and then he was sitting on the ground, back against the trunk, and he opened his eyes.

His vision was blurred, pain and blood stretching it and twisting it, making the thing running from him look distorted and warped, its motion uneven and ragged. It pitched, first to one side and then seemed to tilt farther the same way, before almost rolling back the other way. The angles of its legs seemed wrong, although maybe that was his vision, which was rippling at the edges. Was it the scribe? Something else? Pain flared and died, flared and died in his cheek as he tried to bring the gun up. He heard Israfil shout, then Benjamin, and then he fired again.

The echo of the shot rolled around the valley, broken and splintered by the plants, a channel tearing open through the leaves as the shot went wide and missed the running figure.

"Stop," he shouted, feeling his cheek flap open, feeling air spill into his mouth through the hole, air that hadn't been drawn in over his lips. "Stop," he shouted again, the word oddly elongated and breathy. Fool pulled his legs under him, stood, unsteady but at least upright. He could hear Benjamin and Israfil, close but not close enough to help, and started after the thing that had run.

Fool's run was a stagger, and he wondered if he appeared as uneven as the thing he was chasing. He banged, hard, into a trunk, and bounced away from it with blood spilling out from him in hard-edged droplets, slipped to his knees, and then rose, ungainly, and carried on. Ahead of him, the dark shape, scribe of the Delegation or whatever it was, ducked under a fallen trunk, and Fool raised his gun again and fired a third time. The trunk above the space the thing had disappeared into exploded in a spray of splinters and pulp.

"Thomas Fool, do not fire your weapon again!" came Benjamin's voice, booming, from up above him. Fool glanced up, seeing the two angels as tiny shapes against the sky now, specks flying above him. A stream of fire leaped from Israfil and crashed down into the valley somewhere behind him, causing a violent explosion and a plume of flame and black smoke to rise into the sky, buffeting the angels.

Were they trying to kill him?

It didn't matter. Fool pressed forward, following the figure as it shifted through the growth, still ahead of him, still moving with an uneven, collapsing gait. Fool pursued it, face throbbing, feeling his skin fold down, hanging and open. Another bolt of fire curled down into the trees, closer now, ahead of him and to his right, the glow of flame crackling through the gaps in the trees, the sound of it loud, the smell of it raw and sharp.

"Thomas Fool, stop!" cried Benjamin again, and again Fool ignored him. The valley was untangling a little now, more grass appearing on the ground, the gaps between the trunks and twists of vine wider. Blue flowers grew in abundance, the stink of them heavy and thick, mixing with the fires' scents, creating something new and cloying. He saw the running thing again, fired and missed, the shot tearing a steaming path through the damp air.

"Human, do not fire your gun again," boomed Israfil. "Damned creature, foulest thing, you will stop it now!"

The figure disappeared between two clumps of growth ahead of him, its run now a clumsy, hopping set of leaps, leaving the branches disturbed by its passing, the tree limbs still swaying, dripping water, and then Fool was pushing through the same gap and emerging into a clearing. It was roughly circular, hemmed in by trees and bushes, and at its center was a hole. There was no sign of the figure. What looked like a tangle of black vines slipped over the edge of the hole as Fool stood, and then nothing moved.

Fool waited. Benjamin called him again, and in the sky above the clearing he watched as the two angels swooped and rose, Israfil's fires a bright sunspot against the blue. Another long thread of flame dropped from the angel, striking the earth somewhere back down the valley. If he walked out to the hole, into the clearing, would they look down and see him?

Burn him?

His face was sticky, still dense and hot with pain. Fool lifted a hand to his ruined cheek but couldn't bring himself to touch it, not wanting his fingers to poke through the holes and into his mouth. The figure had entered the clearing and vanished from it, either into the hole or into the foliage on its far side—likely the hole, dragging the vines Fool had seen with it. He had been asked to investigate, and the hole and beyond was where his investigation had led. He had to check, it was what he did. *Little Information Man Fool,* he thought, *little target* and walked out across the clearing.

The hole was about a man's length across, the edge crumbled and uneven, and Fool stopped several feet away from it and approached slowly. The speed at which the thing had been moving meant it was unlikely to have made it to the far side of the clearing without being seen, so he was assuming that it was at the bottom of the hole, ready to spring on him as he appeared at the edge, but when he looked in, he found that in this assumption he was wrong.

The hole was the opening to a shaft.

Above him Benjamin called his name again but Fool paid little attention, looking instead into the space in front of him. It dropped away, a gullet that descended through the earth, its sides the metallic and roiling colors of oil spreading on the surface of turbulent waters, its bottom too distant to make out. Roots poked from the earth at its upper edge, dangling white and wormlike into the opening.

In the sides of the tunnel the swirls were coming together and parting, creating shapes that fit against each other without gaps. "The things outside of everywhere," Fool whispered, watching as the patches resolved themselves into claws and many-jointed legs and the hint of tooth and rough-edged carapace and then the clearing exploded into fire as Israfil's flame struck the earth on the other side of the shaft.

The pressure wave lifted Fool and dashed him backward, a huge warm hand that slammed him hard against a trunk and spun him violently. The breath was driven from his lungs, something new tore in his face, and his gun was bounced from his hand. He glanced away from the tree and collapsed hard onto the ground, his face striking the earth with a jolt, undamaged cheek down, damaged one facing the sky. He tried to roll, managed to struggle perhaps halfway over, staring into a sky almost obscured by burning, and watching as the angels dropped through the flames.

Benjamin landed in a cloud of swirling, burning dirt in front of him, Israfil a second behind, and both angels were glowing with heat, redness washing across Fool as he lay stunned.

"You discharged your weapon," said Benjamin, voice calm but face still pulled into an expression of fury.

"Yes," said Fool, and the word seemed to escape from his mouth and through his cheek at the same time. "I was chasing something."

"Something?"

"Something," agreed Fool. "It attacked me, slashed my cheek, ran. I think it might have jumped into the hole, into the tunnel, I'm not sure." Speaking was hard; the voice he heard seemed layered, lazy, and spreading out sideways, not his own. His tongue kept darting to his teeth and past them, finding the holes in his cheek, the spaces where flesh used to be. The taste of blood, metallic and sour, filled his mouth and he spat, trying to clear the thickness.

"What tunnel, human? What lie is this that you've brought here?" asked Israfil. Fool managed to roll onto his front and then pulled himself up onto his knees. More blood spattered down onto his shoulder, soaking into the fabric of his jacket. Benjamin held a hand out and Fool took it, grateful for the support. He managed to get to his feet, dizzy, and saw that the clearing behind the two angels was empty, the ground burned and smoking but smooth, the earth flat.

The tunnel had vanished.

12

Fool opened his eyes. Was he floating, facing down at a floor of rough, white-painted plaster? He reached out, trying to grasp the surface, trying to anchor himself, but instead he spun, dizzy, dislocated, and getting farther and farther out, and then the pain in his face reached out and took hold of him and he crashed down and he was lying in his bed staring at the ceiling of his room.

The flesh of his cheek felt huge, burning inside and puffy, and he raised a hand to it only to have his wrist grasped. "Don't," said a voice, the grip soft yet firm, the word gentle. Fool tensed, pushing against the hold, wanting to reach his face, to press against it and push away the blanket of aching that was wrapped around his head, but could not bring his hand any closer. Finally, he gave up and let his arm fall back to the bed. He turned his head to look around, his left eye too swollen to see out of, and found Benjamin sitting in a chair next to his bed.

"We apologize on Israfil's behalf for the damage to your face," said Benjamin. "We have no excuse, except to say that we had to prevent you from discharging your weapon again. Heaven is a place of peace, Thomas Fool, and the weaponry of Hell has no place here. Violence has no place here."

Fool, remembering Israfil's fury, remembering Wambwark lying in the corridor being neatly separated into pieces by Benjamin's flame, didn't contradict Benjamin and instead said only, "Apologize for Israfil?"

"You were damaged when Israfil's fire lifted you and threw you across the clearing," said Benjamin. "For this, you have the apologies of Heaven."

Perhaps he'll give me another feather, Fool thought, *and if I get enough apologies and thanks I'll have enough feathers for a set of wings and I can fly the fuck away from here and never look back.* Out loud he said, "No, I told you, there was a thing, it attacked me, sliced my face. There was a tunnel."

Something in his face cracked as he spoke and fresh blood spilled down him, rolling down his neck. Pain radiated out from the injury, sharp and bright.

"A thing?" asked Benjamin, reaching forward and pressing a hand against Fool's wound. His touch was warm, solid, and yet somehow smooth, as though it was a hand of sun-warmed glass rather than flesh. Fool felt the edges of the split knit together, the blood flow slowing and stopping. The pain remained, however, and he realized that Benjamin hadn't healed him completely but only started the process. A punishment, he wondered, for firing his gun?

"A thing," agreed Fool. What had it been? The scribe? Another demon? No, he couldn't be sure but he didn't think so; it hadn't moved like a demon; its run had been uneven, tilting one way and then another like a ship in a gale, like a creature running on pitching floors. It had reminded him of something, hadn't it? No, not reminded exactly; rather, it had made him think of something but he couldn't remember or grasp what. Every time he tried, the thought of it slipped away, lubricated by the grease of pain and tiredness.

"It was in the valley, hiding from me. It tracked me, trying to see where I was going. It was watching me," said Fool. Was that what it had been doing? Yes, yes, it had been tracking him, spying on him. If it had wanted to attack him, it could have done so far earlier. Its eventual violence was, he was sure, only a means of effecting its escape.

"Nothing in Heaven would attack you, Thomas Fool," said Benjamin, removing his hand from Fool's cheek. Relieved of the angel's touch, the damaged cheek throbbed, feeling cold. This time when Fool raised his hand to it, Benjamin did not stop him. Cautiously Fool placed his fingertips to his cheek and let them walk over the surface of his face. It felt alien to his touch, its topography altered and foreign. Three lines of scabs, roughly parallel, started from a point just in front of his ear and ran down, parallel to his jawline, finishing just under his cheekbone.

They throbbed, feeling warm and knotted and fragile, furrows torn through his face and inexpertly fixed. He let his hand fall away again.

"We have no physicians in Heaven," said Benjamin, "as we have no need of them. Israfil is asking the Gardens of Fire if they can provide something for your treatment."

Fool lay back, relaxing into his pillow. "Does the Delegation know what happened to me?"

"Yes," said Benjamin. "The demon Catarinch is using it as an excuse to complain and levy further concessions from Heaven. Wambwark merely laughed."

Fool grinned, felt one of the slashes flash a warning at him, and stopped grinning. "What time is it?"

"Evening, Thomas Fool. You have been asleep for several hours. Are you hungry?"

"No." Fool was surprised to find that he hadn't even thought of food since he arrived in Heaven. How long was it since he'd eaten? Three days? Four?

"You will need to force yourself to eat, Thomas Fool," said Benjamin. "Heaven is not a place of physical appetites, only ones of the mind, so it is easy to forget and become ill. We are not used to catering for humans who are not one of the flock."

"The Joyful."

"You called them that earlier. Is that the name you have for them? The Joyful? Well, I suppose they are, so it's as accurate a name for them as any other."

There was a soft knock at the door. Benjamin rose from the chair, wings flapping slowly and expansively before returning to their usual position, cowled behind and over his head. The globe on the wall was dark and Fool realized that the light in the room was coming from the angel, his pale glow suffusing the space around him, painting it in shades of ivory and yellow.

"Fool," said Benjamin, his voice coming to Fool over the angel's shoulder, "it is time for me to show you your followers."

In the frenzy of the day, Fool had completely forgotten about the two who followed him. *Another thing forgotten, you're getting sloppy,* he thought and sat, too quickly, feeling a wave of dizziness and pain wash across him. He managed to get his arms behind him, propping himself on his elbows and looking around the room. It was empty apart from him and Benjamin.

"They're here," said Benjamin without looking around. "They're with you every moment. They have no choice."

The angel opened the room door, revealing a second angel, a female, dressed in a sleeveless shift dress. "I do not have the skills or power to reveal your followers, Thomas Fool. I'm an angel of fire and war and conflict on the borders, but I have friends. I have taken a liberty and asked Bal Koth to act on my behalf."

The angel Bal Koth entered the room, head down, blond hair hooked behind her ears, arms crossed in front of her.

"Your service to Heaven is remembered," she said and bowed to Fool. She walked to the center of the room and looked around and then raised her head, sniffing. Her skin was flawless, her expression one of fierce pride. For a moment she looked masculine rather than feminine, her face hard planes and lines, and then she was female again.

"If I am permitted, I'll begin," said Bal Koth, the angel who might or might not be female.

Fool nodded and she knelt and began to feel across the floor of the room, finally wrapping her hand around something that he could not see. Benjamin had gone to stand in the corner of the room, was watching, motionless. Bal Koth began to pull gently on the thing that she held, following the line of it toward Fool. She came to him, still holding the thing he could not see, and delicately pushed him forward, tilting him so that his face was close to his knees under the covering sheet, and then her hand was tickling up and down his back. Finally, she took hold of something high up, the pressure of her grasp between his shoulder blades, and she *yanked*.

It was as though a tooth Fool didn't know he had was being twisted. Something not a part of him but connected nonetheless tugged against not his flesh but the thing inside his flesh, the thing that made his flesh Fool, and then she yanked again and it came loose. Fool gasped, feeling a hollow space open in his back and close again just as quickly, and then Bal Koth cried out, a wordless song, and was tugging and it was as though she was pulling the shadows and shades up from the edges of the room.

Darkness crept out from the room, where the floor met the walls, sheets of it slipping out, spilling and bubbling into the open. It pooled around Bal Koth's ankles, puddling in greasy waves around the feet of Fool's bed, a darkness moving like oil and lapping hungrily at the furniture and swallowing the floor, and still she pulled, hand over hand, her teeth gritted and strain showing on her perfect forehead. The light in the room clenched in, balling at the center of the space, forming a tight sphere around Bal Koth and the thing she pulled.

Bal Koth's arms were carved alabaster, the musculature sculpted in perfect curves and angles. She pulled, and pulled, and pulled.

Something pulled back.

Bal Koth staggered. Her hands tightened, veins rippling around her pale wrists, and she leaned back, straining. She swept her wings open, spreading them wide and beating them once, the air washing over Fool. The pressure lifted her, moving her back, and she was still pulling, hauling now, and the thing in her hand was becoming visible. It was a cable, no, two cables, twisted hanks of yarn or rope, stretched and taut. One end of the cables, Fool was astonished to see, disappeared under the sheets of his bed, the other submerged below the surface of the roiling darkness and somehow connected to the darkness, dragging it with it as the angel tugged and the blackness fought back. The other, close to Bal Koth's hand, was torn, ending in frayed strands that glistened and twitched.

Bal Koth pulled, harder and harder, and the cords spooled back through her hands, more and more of the lengths emerging from the blackness, and now the momentum was with the angel, the cords falling and tangling by her feet. The blackness rose up faster now, soupy, filling the room.

"They are rooted in darkness and pain," the angel said as the cords tugged back against her again, her voice a hard flint in the room. She set her feet into the swirling, eddying blackness that now entirely covered the floor and had reached to above her knees, was rippling just below the edges of Fool's mattress, and leaned back and gave a final, savage yank. There was a sound like a bubble rising through thick mud and the ends of the cords burst from the darkness, flailing violently, something flapping at their ends.

The darkness bucked and crashed and strained, sloshing farther up the walls, slapping against the edges of the ceiling, leaving a space around Benjamin that the angel filled with his pale, penumbral light. The black surged, its surface a gleaming rainbow of roiling colors, and fell back toward Bal Koth. She knelt and gathered herself together, wings curving around her, dress pulled taut across her thighs, and hissed at the encroaching shadows. They flopped around her and then, finally, collapsed away, leaving fragments of themselves clinging to the surfaces that slowly dripped, fading and vanishing.

The blackness that spread across the floor bubbled, surface broken and pitching, and then it, too, shrank down. In seconds it had drained away, lost in a great dark swirl, and the room was normal again. The globe on the wall popped noisily and light sprang out, expanded into the room's corners and edges, revealed Benjamin still standing and watching. He flicked one hand out and a thin wrinkle of fire leaped around the room, burning away the last scraps of darkness in a series of unpleasant, earthy sizzles.

At first, Fool thought old clothes were tied to the cords, and then he realized that it was skin.

Fool wasn't sure the skins were real, not exactly; they seemed too thin, almost translucent, the impressions of floorboards visible through them. They were pale, shining with damp and cold, glittering with frost, and they faded and came back as though attached to the breathing of some distant lung. Bal Koth pulled them to her, crouching lower and lifting the skins tenderly onto her now-bent knees. She ran one hand along them, trailing the backs of her fingers across the now-here, now-gone thinness, and then made a motion in the air. The cords fell away from the two skins, severed, and then disappeared in a spray of glittering silver sparks.

"Ah, so, so beautiful," Bal Koth said, still stroking. Where her fingers touched them, the skins began to color, pinks and traceries of blue veins appearing, solidifying. The colors spread, giving the skins a reality that they had previously lacked, turning them into something approximating human. Fool thought of demons without skin, of muscles exposed and ropey with oily blood, and wondered if this was some kind of opposite creature, a thing of skin and little else, sent to keep track of him, seeking him out for reasons of revenge or malice or observance.

The skins shifted on Bal Koth's knees, pinkly unpleasant in the angel's glow. "So beautiful," she said again and then leaned over and kissed the nearest of them.

The skin swelled as Bal Koth kissed it, unfurling, expanding. Its arms flopped back, its legs unrolling across the floor. Its feet and hands were abandoned socks and gloves suddenly filling, flexing as they did. The skin made a noise as Bal Koth kissed, or maybe it was Bal Koth herself, a low exhalation that was halfway between a groan and a sigh.

Bal Koth stood and draped the skin, still filling, across her arms. She stopped kissing it but it still grew, tiny pops coming from it as the skin smoothed and fitted around whatever was filling it. *She's kissing it to life,* Fool thought, *an angel's kiss,* and looked at his jacket hanging on the back of the chair in front of the desk. The feather was in his pocket, he remembered, another thing forgotten in the chaos of the day, and he felt a pang of jealousy that he clamped down on as best he could. An angel's feather given to mark a possession lost or being created by an angel's kiss, who was to say which was worth more?

Bal Koth was kissing the other skin now, her lips clamped onto it, her cheeks puffing out. The skin flopped back, crumpled arms and legs collapsing out, and then it was expanding, and then there were two groaning sighs in the air, two competing sets of pops and soft rustles as of thin leather being manipulated and caressed. The second expanding skin seemed smaller than the first, the tones different, the colors of it fractionally darker.

"They need to grow," Bal Koth said after breaking the kiss with the second skin. She watched them for a few seconds, the expression on her face unreadable, breathing heavily. She looked tired. Had he ever seen a tired angel before? No, he didn't think so; even at the height of the battles in Hell, the angels had always looked fiercely joyous, fiercely *alive* and vibrant.

"Whoever they are, I'll tend them tonight and send them back to you tomorrow morning. Is that acceptable to you?"

"Yes," said Fool. The farther away the skins were, the better. The thought of whatever they were having followed him from Hell was threatening, unsettling.

Bal Koth picked up the still-growing skins, carrying them carefully, and went to the door. Before she opened it, she turned and faced Fool. "This has been my honor, Thomas Fool," she said and looked, for a brief glimpse, male again before her face seemed to shift and change, becoming female once more. She left, taking the skins and shutting the door behind her.

"How do you feel?" asked Benjamin, finally leaving the room's corner.

"I'm tired," said Fool. "I hurt."

"Yes. Israfil should be here soon."

As if in response to Benjamin's statement, there was another knock at the door and, without waiting for an answer, Israfil pushed it open and entered. Her flames made the room shift and glimmer around them, the walls suddenly a moving kaleidoscope of light and gleam and shadow. In her hand, the angel held a bottle and a glass, both black with earth and silver with melting frost.

"The Gardens of Earth and Air have provided," she said, opening the bottle and pouring out a splash of the liquid within it into the glass. Fool took it and smelled it, unsure of what he was being offered. There was a label on the bottle but it was stained to a brown illegibility, and any writing that had been on there was long gone. What was the liquid? It smelled sharp, moved like thick mud in the bottom of the glass, shards of ice glinting in it. What would it do?

Fuck it, he thought and drank, too tired to ultimately care what it was or what it did. It was cold in his mouth, tasted vaguely of mint and something else loosely herbal, and it left his throat feeling pleasantly warm after he swallowed. Within a few minutes, as the two angels watched him, the throbbing in his face drifted away to a distant mumble and his vision blurred. Despite himself, despite wanting to talk to the angels about the thing in the valley and the tunnel and the dead bodies and Bal Koth, Fool collapsed back into a thick and curdled sleep.

And then a timeless period later his flesh tore open and Fool was screaming again.

"Fool, Fool, be quiet," said Mr. Tap, and Fool felt the muscles of his belly ripple and shift to form lips around the words. He threw back the sheet that covered him, finding that he was naked underneath it, and revealed the grinning tattoo again.

"I'm thinking of the longest words I know," said Mr. Tap conversationally, "and I'm thinking of saying them one after another to make you scream, and each time you scream I'm going to take a bite from you."

Fool didn't reply. He clenched his lips, hoping that he would somehow get used to the pain, but clenching pulled his cheek and a savage bolt of new agony pulsed across him.

"So, Fool, what's to tell?" asked Mr. Tap, asked his stomach wearing Mr. Tap's face. When Fool didn't reply immediately, Mr. Tap opened its mouth and then clamped down on the tattooed lip, on Fool's skin, and bit, those surging teeth tearing into him. Fool screamed again.

"You taste as good today as yesterday, Fool, but you are a limited supply and if I continue to eat there will be nothing of you left, will there?" said Mr. Tap. "Perhaps, instead, I should speak the names of all the demons I know, most of them have names that twist and writhe as you say them. They can cause you lots of pain, Fool. Perhaps I could say my real name, the name given to me by my father. My name is long and painful but I'm sure you'd enjoy me speaking it through you. Shall I begin?"

"No," said Fool, and started to talk. He began with the Delegation meeting and the incident in the corridor after, which now felt like a day and a lifetime ago, and then went through the rest of his day. He told Mr. Tap about the body and the valley, and about the thing that had spied on him and the tunnel into which it had vanished. As he spoke, he was reminded again of something, although he still wasn't sure what; when he described his injury, Mr. Tap laughed, the guffaws ripping through Fool like spasms. Finally, he told the demon about Benjamin's comments and the way the hole had vanished, to which Mr. Tap said, "Typical angels, only seeing what they want to see.

"So. Is there anything else?"

"No," said Fool, and the lie was smooth in his throat as he swallowed it down. What he had told Mr. Tap was true as far as it went, but he had omitted so much—the way the thing in the valley ran, the waking up of the member of the crowd, the ease with which Benjamin had hurt Wambwark, Mayall and his house, the shifting, interlocking colors on the walls of the tunnel seen in the moments before the clearing was lit to flame by Israfil, his followers and Bal Koth's retrieval of them. Anything he thought he could leave out, he did, for reasons that weren't entirely clear even to him. *I'm lying about Heaven to Hell, while Hell demands a truth about Heaven,* he thought abstractly, *little confused Fool.* He was lying because he didn't trust Hell, lying because he wanted to keep some of Heaven's secrets, although why he wasn't sure, as he couldn't see how Hell could damage Heaven by knowing the things he hadn't told Mr. Tap. His job, his *loyalty,* was supposed to be toward Hell, yet he felt a need to . . . what? Protect Heaven? From what? Hell? They must already have protections in place; the accord, the truce between the two places, had existed for generations, for millennia. No, it wasn't that, not exactly. *It's information,* he thought, *the currency of trade and power and truth and lie and rumor, information. They want it, I have it, so the more I keep the more power I may have.*

May have.

"So, Fool," said Mr. Tap, "have you enjoyed our little chat?" The tattooed split in his belly grinned at him, showing teeth in that impossibly deep throat, and the eye widened, revealing the wetness at its center.

"No," said Fool. His face was stiffening now, less mobile as the slashes gummed together and dried. His belly hurt, a deep and grimy throb.

"Perhaps you'll enjoy tomorrow evening's conversation more," said Mr. Tap, its voice muffled as the tattoo sealed shut. "Perhaps that's the night I'll speak my name aloud. It's been so long since I've heard it spoken, after all." The mouth grinned and then closed completely, the skin knitting back together; the eye closed and for a few seconds his flesh burned with the itch of it sealing and then Mr. Tap was gone.

Fool collapsed back on the bed. "Being in Heaven's more painful than being in Hell," he said aloud, feeling the sweat roll across his newly smooth chest, feeling the tautness of his cheek as he spoke. Already the tattoo on his stomach had changed, no longer a mouth and an eye but a random pattern of lines and dots and blocks.

"Pardon?" Marianne's voice, roaring in on a second wave of pain, this time from his arm. He jerked, sitting upright.

"Nothing. Hello, Marianne," he said. "How are things?"

"Fine," she said, and he knew from her voice that they weren't fine, not at all.

"Report," he said, becoming formal, giving her a framework into which she could fit, a structure in which to shore up her fears and uncertainties, giving her the support of information.

"There've been more fires, and another slaughter," she said.

"Tell me."

"A group of Genevieves this time," she said. He looked at the tattoo, seeing the brow above her eyes furrow as she tried to put the facts into order and tell him. "We were called to a boardinghouse."

"Which one?"

"It doesn't have a name, one of the smaller ones, on the outskirts of Eve's Harbor. It was the same as the Seamstress House, they'd come in through the windows, attacked everyone at once."

"They?"

"They," she said firmly, the word vibrating its resolution up his arm. Her mouth, the mouth in his skin, pursed, and then she said, "Multiple attack points, and no one inside had a chance to run."

"Tell me about the scene."

"Lots of footprints in the blood, but nothing recognizable. We took the dead to the Questioning House but Hand didn't get much from them. The poor bastards were asleep when they got attacked, so the most they saw was some fucking claw or sets of teeth coming at them, waking them up in time to kill them."

A claw. He blinked, thinking about claws, about the pincer. There was something there. "Go on. There's more." A statement not a question, he could hear it in her voice, feel it in the pent-up energy that trembled along his arm from Marianne's painted, split mouth.

"There was a crowd, Marys and Genevieves, all watching as we carried the bodies out. I thought it was odd, the size of it, so I asked a few questions. Everyone was talking about the deaths, everyone had heard a rumor about them, most of them exaggerated and untrue. It was like someone wanted the crowd to gather, wanted them to see us bring the dead out."

"Why?"

"I'm not sure. The Evidence arrived, started to arrest people, question them on the street. Before long they said they'd got the murderers, but they'd not, they'd just arrested a couple of Genevieves too stupid to get out of their way. It was like the crowd had been gathered to show them the dead, to present them to the Evidence, to let them see the Evidence being their usual brutal selves. To give the rumors somewhere to grow."

Clever, Marianne, he thought. *You're seeing things that aren't on the surface, you're finding the threads, you're listening to the rumors that form inside your own head, the guesses and theories, and you're working out which are real. You're an Information Man.*

"Did they do anything to you or the other Information Men?"

"No. They seem to be giving us a wide berth."

"Good. And the fires?"

"Three since yesterday, scattered all over." She listed the places that had burned, and there it was again, the hint of something, a pattern that was rising up through the murk, but it wasn't clear yet, not enough to see, not enough to *read.*

"Anything else?"

"No." There was.

"Marianne," he said. "Whatever it is, you have to tell me."

"It's nothing," she said after a long pause, during which he rubbed his forearm around the tattoo, hoping to ease the dull ache of their conversation. "But, well, the canisters. The Bureaucracy, they're almost panicking. They're demanding we find who's setting the fires and not even pretending to be confused from them now. Here, let me read one of them to you." There was a pause, the tattoo motionless, and then it blinked again and the mouth opened.

"'Find the person making the burning.' Here's another: 'The burnings must be stopped.' They've never been so demanding but so vague before. Do you see?"

"No." What was the pattern, what *was* it? Warehouses, workers' houses, abandoned shacks, a boardinghouse holding however many Marys who had died, now factories making Hell's furniture, farm tools, or parts for the trains and other buildings scattered across Hell, but there was a link, there *had* to be.

A field behind the first place that had burned. The thick forest covering the hills behind the Seamstress House.

Wait. Wait a minute, not the places that burned maybe, but the places around them. "Marianne, can you get together all the sites of the fires before we talk tomorrow night?"

"I have them in front of me now," she said, and there was a hint of pride in her voice, a recognition that she was getting the work done, getting ahead of her orders and doing the job well.

"No, it has to be tomorrow, I need time to do something. Wait there a minute."

Fool looked at the tattoo across his stomach. Mr. Tap's face was still no longer visible, lost in lines that shifted, distorting him. Still, nothing ventured nothing gained, he thought, and then spoke.

"Mr. Tap," said Fool and prodded the tattoo.

"Mr. Tap," again, louder, and another prod, hard into the bruised muscle. After a moment, the tattoo eye tore open and the mouth split into existence.

"I don't appreciate being summoned, Fool," said Mr. Tap.

"I'm still the Commander of the Information Office of Hell," said Fool as coldly as his pain and fear would allow. "As Hell's representative in Heaven, I need something from you, something to assist me in the investigations you tasked me with continuing despite my absence from Hell."

"From me?" said Mr. Tap, and the mouth curled back into a vast, humorless grin, stretching the skin farther than it had been before, revealing a red and raw expanse of fat-flecked meat at its edges.

"Yes," said Fool, trying to breathe, trying to stay awake, trying not to faint. "I need a map of Hell, as accurate as you've got, as detailed as you can get me."

"Why should I get you a map?" asked Mr. Tap, and already the mouth was nipping at the edges of him, tearing strings of skin away and spitting them out, sucking on the blood.

"Because I'm working to make Hell safe," said Fool.

"Safe? I think you misunderstand Hell and its purpose," said Mr. Tap.

"No, I don't," said Fool, "but perhaps you do. Now, get me a map before we talk tomorrow and I may be able to tell you and your masters something about the fires."

Mr. Tap paused, then the tattoo nodded without speaking. Fool's muscles rippled to make the nod, bulging and falling away in a nausea-inducing wave. The eye closed, the mouth resealed, and Mr. Tap was gone.

"Marianne, are you still there?"

"Yes?"

"Can you do me a favor?"

"I'll try," she said. "What do you want?"

"Can you go out into the courtyard? Without being seen?"

"I can try. Why?"

"Because," said Fool, remembering a promise made to a thing of fern and leaf, "I need to talk to the Man of Plants and Flowers."

How long had it been since Fool was in the courtyard? He used to come here regularly, enjoying its peace and relative calm, but recently he'd not been able to get out of his rooms as much. There was always some administrative function that needed addressing within the Information Office, some crime to investigate, some internal grievance to rule upon. As Marianne and he went into the courtyard he felt an unexpected thing—a swell of emotion that it took a moment to recognize as pleasure. He genuinely liked it out here, and was glad to be back.

Only, he wasn't there, not really; rather, he was lying on his bed in Heaven, eyes closed, as Marianne carried the piece of paper with the sketch of his face on it, and only through those open and pencil-sketched eyes could he see a slightly distorted view of the place he used to know well.

It was like looking at the world through a lens of glass that had fogged at the edges and warped, and which made things off-kilter, uneven and distant. It was also a view out of his control, moving when he did not want it to, focusing on things he wasn't interested in, and gliding over those things he wanted to spend time looking at, a view dictated by whatever the paper was facing.

The statues around the courtyard's edges were the same, Fool

thought, when he managed to catch sight of them. A little more weath-
erworn, maybe, their coats of moss and lichens a little thicker, but they
were standing in the same places, old friends waiting to welcome him.
The flagged floor was covered in a shroud of old leaves that Fool heard
crackle under Marianne's feet, and the sky above them was filled with
stars that were cold and remote. He heard Marianne's teeth chatter, felt
the chatter in the movement of the tattoo, realized it must be cold but
did not feel the chill. In Heaven, Fool was warm.

"What do we do now?" asked Marianne, having seated herself on one
of the stone benches that lined the courtyard. She had placed his paper
faceup on her knee and his view was suddenly of the underside of her
chin, upside down, and the skies above her.

"Hold me out," he said.

"What? Oh, yes, I'm sorry," she said, fumbling the paper upright and
holding it out so that Fool could see the area in front of him. "I didn't
mean to put you like that, I wasn't thinking. I'm not used to speaking to
someone like this."

"It's okay," said Fool, smiling and grimacing at the way it stretched
his healing cheek. "I don't mind seeing you upside down. The bottom
of your chin is very pleasant."

She spun the paper toward her, a wary expression of amused surprise
on her face. Was she blushing? he wondered. There was a faint tinge to
her cheeks, difficult to make out but definitely there.

"I'd thank you, but you're only paper," Marianne said finally. "I don't
suppose the opinion of a paper person matters."

"I don't suppose it does," he agreed, and the two of them started
laughing at the absurdity of it all, Fool wincing as he did so.

"Well, this is very cozy," said a sibilant voice, and Marianne jerked
back, snapping the paper around so hard that she folded it, and for a
moment Fool had a view of the world that was bent, doubling back in
on itself so that he could see his own penciled chin and had to open his
eyes in Heaven to block the view of Hell. It was dizzying, this jumping
between places, between views. He swallowed, aching, and then closed
his eyes again.

He was looking at an empty courtyard. The shrubs in the borders
around the courtyard twisted, tangling around each other, and then the

Man was there in front of him. More of the plants were pulled into the mass being created by the continual twisting of the stems and branches so that it formed a growing bulk with a vaguely human shape. At its top, a knot of thorns and flower heads had clustered together to form a full head, the first time the Man had done so in front of Fool.

"Hello," said Fool, talking through the picture.

"Hello, Fool," said the Man. "You look different."

13

Talking to the Man was easier than talking to Marianne. With his real eyes closed and his paper eyes open, he could see relatively clearly the moving plants that the Man had created himself from, despite the vision having a slightly blurred, sepia hue, and hear him through the sketch Fool's ears; only when the real Marianne spoke did the tattoo Marianne split his skin, and for most of his conversation with a thing made of growth and leaf she stayed quiet. She was, he thought, wary; it was a sensible approach to the Man.

"How's Heaven?" asked the Man.

"Cleaner than Hell," said Fool, truthfully. He still wasn't sure how much, or what, he was going to tell the Man. He didn't trust him, was cautious of him in the way that he had learned to be cautious of distant demons, where safety was only temporary and delicate because they could come closer at any time and he was unsure of what would attract them, start them moving in his direction.

"Oh, Fool, you have to tell me more than that!" said the Man, his eagerness showing in the way his fronds twisted and curled around each other, the urgent edge his voice had taken on.

"I have another feather," said Fool, still avoiding.

"Fool, really? Is it as beautiful as the one you had before?" asked the Man, and Fool could practically hear the wanting in his voice. "Will you be bringing it back with you?"

"If I can." What to tell?

"And what of the angel it came from?"

"I don't know," said Fool. "It was given to me to replace the one I lost. They said it was in thanks for my services to them. To the angels, I mean."

"Fool, you mean to say you're well known in both Heaven and Hell? You may be the first human ever who's managed that trick. Think about it, we all know of the Devil himself, black and afire in Crow Heights, and we know of God creating the Heavens and the rest of existence, but tell me, do you think the Hosts of Heaven cared about the names of the demons in Hell, or of the people in Hell? Except as part of the trading missions?"

"No."

"So there's the Devil himself, the summoner of fires and terrors, the thing of flies and sin, and there's God, the nameless goodness above, that all of us know."

"Yes."

"And now there's you, and you are *known*, Fool, part of an elite triumvirate known in both worlds. Thomas Fool, equal of God and the Great Enemy! It's too rich, Fool, too interesting for words! Now, what else have you got for me?"

I'm a little paper Fool, talking to the Man of Plants and Flowers, thought Fool as he started. *I'm in Heaven and in Hell, and in pain and the equal of God and the Devil, and I'm nothing, all at the same time. No wonder I'm confused, little damaged, helpless Fool that I am.*

So Fool talked. He told the Man about the places outside of everywhere and the creatures they contained, those multi-limbed things that cleaved to each other with such accuracy, about the way angels ate happiness like demons ate fear, about the changing landscapes that all still existed, about the Joyful standing and swaying and spinning. He did not mention Mayall or dead people or tunnels, and the Man did not ask about his slashed face. *My paper mask is protecting me,* he realized, *showing the Man a flat and unmarked version of me. I'm a lie.* In Heaven, eyes still closed, he raised a hand to his cheek to feel the crusted lines of damage, and then dropped it again.

At the end of the conversation, the Man said, "And you, Fool? Are you enjoying your time in God's realm? Are you making friends, brokering deals?"

"No."

"Why not, Fool, why not? There are riches to be had there in among the carousels and in the seas you tell me about, grand secrets hidden in the school buildings and the caves, Fool, and if you reach out and take them, you could be the most powerful man in Heaven or Hell."

"I don't want to be," said Fool and realized, as he said it, that it was the truth. "I want to do my job, that's all."

"Really?" The Man sounded disappointed in Fool, and Fool felt, for the shortest moment, oddly ashamed before remembering that the Man wasn't his friend, was only friends with the Man himself. "Then go, Fool, solve your crime and talk to me again."

"Yes."

"And Information Man Marianne?"

"Yes," she said, and Fool heard her voice simultaneously in his ears in Hell and through the tearing and ripping of his arm as the tattoo moved.

"I thank you for your assistance in this matter. If you ever need help, simply come out here and ask for me. After all, Fool isn't likely to be here forever. None of us are, are we? His star is clearly in the ascendant, and if he leaves us all behind you may find you need a friend in the future."

"Thank you, but I have faith in Commander Fool," said Marianne.

"Faith? Faith, in Hell?" asked the Man, and started laughing and did not stop until the cluster of plants in front of Fool had collapsed down and was lying still on the damp earth.

They came for him in the morning. Fool didn't remember falling asleep, didn't remember saying good-bye to Marianne, just knew that suddenly it was light in his room and that someone was knocking on the door. It wasn't a demon's knock, it was too polite, so he hadn't missed the start of a Delegation meeting, which meant it had to be the angels. Dressing in his stained and torn uniform, every part of him groaning with aches and discomforts, he made sure the feather was still in his pocket. He hadn't written his report last night, he realized; he'd have to do it tonight. If he was right, there would be more to add anyway.

He was right.

The building was long and low, its ceiling glass reflecting the sun in painful darts.

"Why are we here?" asked Fool, suspecting he knew before the angels answered and confirmed his suspicion.

"We are told here is something you should see," said Benjamin.

"'Something'?"

"Yes," replied the angel.

"Fine," he said, "let's go then." Fool walked to the building, passing through a gate set in a fence of metal posts and crossing a grassy field whose surface was marked with regular white lines. Crowds of the Joyful were standing on the field, spinning or still, heads back or down, arms outstretched or down at their sides. Fool ignored them. The building's door was open and Fool stopped, taking out his weapon, looking into the space ahead of him. The interior had marbled floors and tiled walls, the light from the glass ceilings coating the surfaces in buttery yellow smears and filling the air with dust motes that swirled gently. There was even a desk on the far side of what he assumed was a foyer, paneled in dark wood, gleaming with a patina of age and use, although no one was near it now. It reminded Fool of the Questioning House.

As Fool stepped through the doorway, Summer and Gordie appeared at his side and started walking with him.

14

Summer and Gordie.

For a second time in as many days his vision doubled on itself, looped around, and for the briefest moment Fool was watching Summer and Gordie walk alongside him down the Houska when they were alive, the streets filled with demons and the stench of blood all around them and they were here next to him in Heaven with angels behind them and the smell of cleanness and freshness against their skin. The two images overlapped and he could see both Heaven and Hell behind them, gaudy brothels and the crowds of the Joyful crashing in a dizzying wash of color and emotion and odor. He tried to speak, only to have his voice crack, the words lost in a popping blister of sound, and then the image of Hell collapsed and he was back, back in Heaven, and Summer and Gordie were here alongside him, walking at his pace.

Summer and Gordie were at his side—his friends, his colleagues, back to where they belonged, back where he remembered them being.

Fool looked behind them; they cast shadows, the same length and thickness and shade of darkness as his own. He could hear their feet, hear the impact of them against the smooth floor, hear the gentle swish of their clothes, hear their breathing. He reached out, went to touch Gordie, but pulled back at the last minute. He was used to their ghosts appearing in the corner of his room, had persuaded himself that the apparitions were either not real or only-just-real, but the figures beside him now were different, looked here and solid and *actual*. He stopped walking, felt faint, and leaned against the sun-warmed desk, steadying himself. Its solidity was reassuring, an anchor in a world that seemed to be constantly pitching and yawing around him.

"Summer? Gordie?"

"Bal Koth sends her regards," said Benjamin from the doorway. "These are those who follow, returned to you."

"They followed me?"

"They are tied to you, or at least were. Bal Koth has split those ties and brought them in from the darkness."

"Are they real?" Gordie was looking at Fool, smiling and nodding. Summer was in Gordie's shadow, her face showing more concern. That was how it had always been, Gordie approaching things with the freedom of innocence, Summer with a cynical caution.

"Everything in Heaven is real," said Benjamin. "Everything here exists."

"But are they people? Or ghosts?"

"Is there a difference?" asked Benjamin. "They are there. Were they your friends? They were tied to you with strong links, perhaps forged because of their deaths alongside you, deaths caused by the Fallen. They care about you, and you about them."

"They were colleagues, yes. And friends. They were together."

"When they died? Bal Koth imagined so. They're linked to each other as well as to you, and they're returned now. Enjoy them."

"They weren't together at their deaths, they were together in their lives. You make them sound as though I own them," said Fool, looking again at his dead friends. "Are they alive?"

"You own them as much as they own you," said Benjamin, holding one elegant hand out toward a set of double doors on the far side of the room. "Now, the thing Mayall wishes you to see is that way. He says he will see you afterward, all three of you. I assume he'll find you when he wants the meeting to take place. To your task, Thomas Fool."

"Are you coming?"

"No. You have your own companions now. Israfil and I will wait for you here." And then the angel was gone and the doorway was empty and the sun was falling in through the space and dancing across Summer and Gordie, and Fool was left trying to work out what the fuck was going on.

This time, he managed to touch Gordie's arm. It was solid, the material of the plain suit he wore coarse but well made, the flesh underneath firm. The skin of his face was smooth and unmarked, no trace of his death written on that pink surface. His hair was long, longer than it had been when he had been alive in Hell, and fell in waves around his face. His eyes were blue, brilliant blue, and they crinkled in greeting, the man's smile growing, if anything, even wider.

Fool reached past him and placed a hand on Summer's shoulder. She was dressed in clothes made of the same material as Gordie's and her body was solid under them, and he marveled at the feeling of her *thereness* in his hand. He found it impossible to remove his touch from her, just holding her and looking at her, until she reached up and placed one hand over his, curling her fingers around his and finally smiling at him. Her touch was warm, the fingers soft. His eyes dropped unconsciously to her belly, looking past the clothes and skin to the guts within her that he had last seen stretched out and pinned to columns in a warehouse, and then back to her face. She shook her head, other arm moving protectively to cover her stomach, but didn't stop smiling.

"Are you real?" he asked. "Are you really here?"

Neither replied.

"What are you?" he tried again, but again both stayed silent. Gordie shook his head, raising a hand and covering his mouth.

"You can't speak?" Nods.

"Ever?" Shakes, a shrug. They might be able to? They weren't sure? Fool looked up, looked through the glass ceiling at Heaven's perfect sky with its acreage of deep blue, the distant marks of flying angels written across it, and let his breath out. One more question, then.

"Do you still have to stay with me?" Shakes, then nods. Still no sense. He let out a long breath, feeling tears prickle at the back of his eyes. "*Will* you stay with me?"

Nods; emphatic and clear.

"Good. Good," Fool said, and then added more quietly, "I've missed you." Then, gathering himself, he nodded in the direction Benjamin had pointed.

"Shall we go?"

Fool led Gordie and Summer to the doors in the far wall that Benjamin had gestured toward. They were wooden, old like the wood of the counter, and their handles were mounted against brass scratch plates that had been rubbed to a rich golden luster by however many hands had pushed against them in the past. When Fool touched them, they were warm.

Pushing open the doors, Fool felt a soft wall of air fall out, drifting over the three of them, humid and thick. It carried on its breath gently lifting wreaths of thin mist that curled around them like the tongues of some ghostly creature that wanted to taste their skin. The mist smelled slightly sharp, as though it was laced with some extra ingredient, not just water and air but water and air and something else, some seasoning that made it tang in Fool's nose. It was cloying, coated his face and left silver trails across his jacket.

Beyond the doors was a pool that filled almost the entirety of the room that contained it. The room itself was huge, the ceiling vaulted above them and the floors that ran to its edges laid with flags that were rough-surfaced yet carefully fitted so that they formed an intricate lattice. The walls around them were clad in veined marble tiles that sweated in the heat, water forming a skin over them and then collapsing into trickles that ran swiftly down and puddled in the narrow channels between the floor tiles. The floor was at an angle, Fool saw, a very slight decline so that the water on the walls and floor ran back into the pool.

The pool itself was filled with the Joyful. Some were standing, others moving slowly about, eyes closed, arms carving out slow arcs ahead of them as though using the water to pull themselves forward. Still others were floating on their backs, robes drifting about them, hair untethered and loose and creating halo patterns around their heads. The light played across the water, breaking and reforming as the surface moved, reflections from it shifting in constant movement across the rest of the room. Across the ceiling, shadow Joyful moved in slow, steady patterns.

A breeze hit Fool, colder, and he looked up over the water and its inhabitants to the far wall. Here the steam that rose did so in fast loops, curling around clear tongues of colder air coming in from a broken window. A motionless Joyful was slumped below the window, its face a mask of drying blood, its eyes open.

Here it was, then. The thing they had come to see.

Fool walked around the pool to the body, seeing as he came closer to it that it was a man, his skin a dark coffee brown. He was lying against the wall, half propped up against the tiles, arm loose at his sides, and his palms turned up so that he appeared to be asking a silent question. There was a piece of glass, presumably from the broken pane, sticking up from behind the man's collarbone, angled so that it had pushed into the meat at the base of his neck. The robe around it was soaked with blood and there were a series of smaller scratches across his face and scalp. His right ear, on the left as Fool looked at him, had been neatly half severed from the top and was flapping down like a bitter tongue to reveal a wet, red hole in the side of the man's head.

Fool crouched in front of the body, hand automatically reaching for the feather in his pocket. It had been a habit, since lost and now found again, to hold the piece of an angel's wing while he looked at the dead, studied the places they had been strewn, using it to shore himself against the horrors he was forced to see. It was cool against his fingers, the light of it a faint glow within his pocket.

So, what was he looking at?

The man was wet, not just with blood but with water, his robes soaked. The water that spilled out from them and was slowly trickling back toward the pool was tinged pink near his upper body but clear lower down, meaning what?

"He was dragged from the water and over to the window, which is where his injuries occurred," Fool said aloud, wishing he had Marianne here, anyone to provide another pair of eyes. *But I do,* he remembered, *the ghosts that may be real, those who follow.*

"Can you see anything?" he asked, turning to Summer and Gordie. The two were standing several feet away, holding hands. Gordie looked at Fool, the expression on his face one of incomprehension, but Summer was staring at the body, eyes darting up and down. Finally, she raised a hand to the window and made a gesture that Fool didn't understand. She made it again, pointing at the window, the floor, the pool, and then the man. He looked back around, staring again at the scene before him. The glass from the window lay across the floor, some of it small and jagged, other pieces larger, wicked curves glinting. The dead man was sitting on one of the larger pieces, its sickle edge protruding from under his thigh. Had it cut him? No. So?

The glass was on the floor when the man was dragged here, meaning it was broken from the outside in. Something came in through the window, dragged the man from the pool, and slaughtered him.

No, no, that wasn't right. There was a single thick streak of blood seeping down from the window to the man, starting by the bottom frame and angling toward the man's injured shoulder. Smaller streaks ran alongside it. He looked again at the wound in the man's shoulder and the smaller ones across his head, leaned in close to see the smooth, even edges of the slice to the man's ear, and then leaned back on his haunches.

"If they were going to kill him, why not simply kill him in the pool, or just pull him onto the side and attack him there?" he said, looking again at Summer, only to find that her expression had softened again, was similar to Gordie's. Whatever clarity she'd had, it was, for the moment, gone.

So they didn't simply attack him, he thought. *But what did happen? They took him from the water and dragged him to the window but he got, what, caught on the glass? Impaled on it as they tried to push him through?* Fool stood, reaching onto tiptoe and looking through the window, careful to avoid the glass teeth that still grew from the frame's wooden jawbone. Outside, down the wall, another long, thick spray of blood was visible. Below it were prints, the earth churned and muddied.

He turned back, facing into the room. A pool full of the Joyful, the spacing of them appearing random but, he knew, having an order that he simply couldn't see or recognize.

Only that wasn't true, not now. The longer he spent in Heaven, the more he saw the massed Joyful, the easier the patterns grew to spot. Even in the pool, there were areas for the floaters, areas for the standing, areas for the moving. It was easier to see where the man had been from the space he had left, and the closer he looked the more gaps Fool saw. The Joyful, even the floating ones, tended to stay away from each other and move in regular patterns, and now that he was looking for them he could see the holes in this delicately choreographed movement. How many holes? It was difficult to tell, but certainly six or seven, perhaps as many as ten. When he inspected more closely, he discovered more puddles of water on the side of the pool, trails leading from them to the window. By one puddle were a few strands of long blond hair, still attached to a scrap of skin, sticking to the edge of a tile. He lifted the skin by the hairs, pulling it free to reveal a moist, dark surface underneath. It was, he guessed, a piece of someone's scalp.

One or more people or things came in, dragged some of the Joyful from the pool, knocking one of the poor bastard's heads on the side as they did so. They took him to the window and thrust him through, dropping him to the outside, until this one messed things up. He got stuck, injured, started to bleed out in front of them. Did he make a noise? Were they worried they'd attract attention? Or maybe he was simply the last one anyway and his being injured was an inconvenience, so they left him to die. I'm sure there weren't any taken after this one. There are no tracks in the blood, only in the water. Nothing walked over him or around him, no one moved him or saw him until I got here. He was the last one.

What next? Fool crouched again, stroking the feather and looking at the body, hoping for its clarity, but nothing came. Someone, he had forgotten who, had told him that the feathers made him think more clearly because they were a part of a thing that was entirely truthful, that holding it made the truth seem simpler and easier to see and speak.

"It's not working," he said aloud. Maybe he'd seen all the truth there was to see here? He looked up, watching the reflected ripples swirl across the ceiling, the shadows and lines of light moving around each other in a gentle gavotte. It was beautiful, made him think of the slow roll of clouds or the way the grasses in the fields full of the Joyful had moved in unfelt breezes. The patterns drifted down the walls around the pool, their shifting edges sliding over the tiles, the movement constant around him. The shapes of the Joyful were sometimes visible in the reflections as black spaces, their robes swaying out from their arms like angels' wings, flying in the water.

What were the Joyful being pushed out of the window for? Who was waiting to receive them outside the pool?

Just what were they being pushed out to?

"Wake up," he called, loud, standing and moving to the pool's edge. "Wake up. Did anyone see what happened here?"

For a second, none of the Joyful moved, and then one of them closest to him, a younger girl who was standing still rather than spinning or floating, opened her eyes. She wore the bleary expression of a drunk or someone who'd been hit on the head and just regained consciousness, her eyelids flickering up and then dropping as she tried to open them.

"What did you see?" asked Fool.

The girl didn't reply, then her shoulders tensed up and her head jerked back, flicking her hair back off her face, eyes suddenly wide, suddenly *open*. "No, no," she screamed, backing away, arms flailing, "no! They're coming! They're coming! The leaping things!" She took another ungainly step, the water slowing her, and then tripped and disappeared in a splash of swirl and wave. The surface roiled, bucked, and then she reemerged several feet from where she had gone under.

"Tell me," Fool said, but the girl merely stood, and her eyes were closed again. Her chin dropped toward her chest, shoulders slumped low, and she walked with vague steps back to her original place in the pool. Her robes were wet, clinging to her, but she didn't appear to notice as she settled back to motionless, and nothing Fool said could rouse her again.

"Hopeless," he said, and let out a long sigh. What next?

What had the Joyful been pushed out *to*?

"Come with me," said Fool. He went quickly past the body, past Summer and Gordie, their hands still intertwined, and went back to the door. When he looked behind him, his two followers had begun to walk after him, still holding on to each other. Good. *Let them keep each other,* he thought. *Let them be each other's follower.*

Israfil and Benjamin were waiting in the foyer, if that's what it was, looking at him expectantly. "What do you know about what's happened here?" asked Fool.

"Nothing, we are simply sent the message from Mayall," said Israfil, and her tone was like the crash of stone doors slamming shut.

"There's a body in there," said Fool, pointing back to the pool. "Can it be questioned?"

"Another accident?" said Benjamin, and the pity in his voice was absolute, was total.

"No," said Fool. "Murder, or at least, someone accidentally killed while something else was going on."

"There can be no body," said Israfil.

"It's right in the other fucking room!" Fool shouted, patience finally snapping. All the pain, all the fear, all the uncertainty, all of it crashed out of him as he screamed at the two angels. "It's dead, *he's* dead, some poor bastard who was punctured with glass from the window as someone or something tried to shove him through it. He's in there now!"

"No." Israfil again. "There is no body."

"Go and look."

"No. There can be no body in the state you describe, because this is Heaven and events like this do not occur, little lying human."

"Why would I lie?"

"Who knows, Commander of Hell's Information Office, consorter with demons and ghosts, who knows why you might lie in Heaven." Israfil's voice dripped sarcasm and dislike. *Fuck her.*

Fool looked at Benjamin, who smiled at him. "Perhaps you're mistaken?" asked the angel.

"No," said Fool, "I'm not." There was no help there, no information to be found.

Behind him, Fool heard the flap of wings but did not turn around. The black angels, the kindliest ones, the ones that looked like infants, would be taking the body away but he did nothing to stop them. There was no way to talk to the body, and instinct told him he had learned all he could from it; without Hand or Tidyman or Morgan, the poor dead man's flesh would remain mute and secretive. Instead, ignoring the angels, he crossed the foyer and went outside.

Heaven's day was still warm, still sunny, and Fool's shadow stretched ahead of him as he walked along the side of the building. It was joined by the shades of Summer and Gordie, heads at his shadow's waist, walking behind him. He stopped, waiting until they caught up with him, and then the three went around the building's corner together.

There was a field along the side of the building that housed the pool, its grass short, covered with white painted marks over which another crowd of the Joyful swayed and stood and walked. There were differences here, though; some of the Joyful seemed to be moving together, not simply around each other. There was a definite sense of them moving in packs, the packs sometimes almost meeting as they moved, never touching but flowing against and through and around each other. Fool stopped and watched, fascinated, Summer and Gordie standing next to him, watching without understanding. *More patterns,* he thought. *I know there are patterns there, just like there are patterns to the movements and spacing in the pool, but I can't see them properly. I can see the outline of them but not the content. There must be* reasons *why they move like that, why they move around the pool like they do, but I can't understand them.*

Fool carried on walking, going to the next corner and then around to the rear of the building and to the outside of the broken window.

From inside, it had been hard to see the ground, and Fool had under-estimated the number of prints and tracks. The ground was churned and thick with them, with indentations and scars, with tears and rips. Standing by the window, Fool looked along the lines of marks, the track they formed, following it back until it disappeared into a thick copse of trees. His hand rose without thinking to his face, touching the wounds that in the heat of the investigation he had been able to forget for a few minutes. Now they reacted angrily, as though to remind him of his presence, and he saw again a set of claws at the end of an arm that was dark and spindly rising toward him. He flinched, stepping back, and bumped into Summer. She placed a hand on his shoulder, both stopping him from taking another step and squeezing reassuringly. She smiled at him.

"I wish you could talk," Fool said.

Summer made a sound that might have been a word, half formed and shallow, and then smiled again, shaking her head. He turned to the window.

There were scratches under the frame, long striations cut into the wooden side of the building that reminded him of something. He tried to find the memory but it was just out of reach and he let it go; it would come back soon enough, he was sure. Instead of pushing, he turned again, looking back at the tracks. He crouched, looking closely at the torn earth.

The tracks were similar to the ones that he had seen on the beach. There were some that might have been made by clawed feet, others that were unbroken irregular lines that, when he got on his hands and knees, had the impressions of scales or some other kind of segmented skin at the base. Familiar blue flowers had started to bud in the rich, dark earth; as he watched, one of the tiny flowers opened, the petals angling toward the sun and trembling slightly. The smell of it reached his nostrils. Without thinking, Fool reached forward and crushed the open flower head between his finger and thumb. It popped unpleasantly, leaving a greasy, foul-smelling residue across his fingers, which he wiped on the clean earth by the churned trail.

Following the prints back to the trees, Fool came to the same conclusion as he had come to on the beach: that the trail was in fact two trails, one lying over the top of the other, leading from the trees and then back to them. The returning trail had additional marks, a series of twin parallel lines cutting all around the track. Heel marks, from the dragged Joyful? Fool thought so. Here and there, blood puddled along the trail. Not much, but enough to let him know that at least one of the vanished Joyful was injured. Another glass cut from the window? Again, he thought yes, although when he thought about the dead woman on the beach and remembered the slash around her shoulder, he realized that it could equally be an injury from the snatch itself.

He stopped to think, let his head fall back and his vision fill with Heaven's sky. In the distance, a shape that he thought might be the dead body being carried by six small angels floated across the blue, growing smaller and smaller. Another silent, vanished corpse, another thing that couldn't exist but did, and where was he?

Nowhere. Worse than nowhere; each step he took made things more confusing. In Hell, at least, the lines of cause and effect were clear-cut, but here he had no one even to acknowledge the deaths, let alone help him see the bigger pictures that the dead formed.

No one? No, that wasn't true, there was one thing that knew more about what was happening here than they were telling, Fool was sure. There was one person who knew about the trails and the Joyful and the dead.

Mayall. Mayall saw things. Mayall would know about the dead.

"You cannot demand to see Mayall."

Israfil was standing outside the pool house, her silent flames flickering a thick, curdled orange. She was angry—angrier than usual, looking down at Fool through her face of fire and scowl.

"Why?"

"Because we are not bound to obey your requests, Fool, because you are not our master and we do not have to jump to the call of a human."

"That's not good enough. I need to see Mayall, and I need to see him now. He has information. If he sees things, he may be able to tell me what's going on here."

"Little human, you aren't listening. You cannot see Mayall simply because you wish to, because Mayall does not see anyone. Mayall stays in his house and never leaves, Mayall summons, Mayall is the one who *sees*, not the one seen. He sends us messages telling us where to look and what to think. Mayall is the angel in hiding. He has already indicated he will come to you soon; wait for him and be patient. Better yet, take your stain of corruption and leave. Leave this, Fool. Leave this, join your Delegation, and go back to Hell."

Fool sighed, letting the breath out in a long, weary roll. Even in Hell, where obstructions were common, he rarely came across anyone as objectionable as Israfil. "What," he asked slowly, "is your fucking problem?"

The swearing this time was deliberate, baiting the angel, and probably unwise. For a second, she simply stared at him and then, very slowly, she reached out and with a casual flick of her hand slapped his uninjured cheek. His head snapped sideways, the neck wrenching, the gashes on his other cheek splitting, starting to weep.

"Israfil," said Benjamin quietly. "That is not the way."

"'Not the way'?" asked the angel. "Then what is? This thing, this *monkey*, dares to challenge me? It comes to Heaven not even one of the raised, not even one of the beloved of God, yet thinks to question us, to order us?"

"Monkey?" asked Fool, grinning but unable to help himself. "I'm a monkey?"

"Of course," said Israfil. "You and all the other inhabitants of Hell, nothing but monkeys, foul things flinging their excrement at each other."

"We're monkeys," said Fool, looking around at Summer and Gordie, still grinning. Both of them smiled, although neither appeared to understand what they were hearing, assuming they were hearing anything at all. They were still holding hands, he saw. Fool turned back to Israfil, still grinning.

"This monkey is investigating deaths in Heaven, Israfil, investigating *mysteries*."

"Accidents."

"Deaths, angel, mysterious deaths. I do so at the request of the Malakim and at the specific instruction of Mayall, and I expect your help. Now, take me to Mayall."

"We cannot," said Benjamin, sounding, at least, apologetic. "The clown angel does not see anyone except at his own request. His home moves, and we cannot know where he is unless he allows us to know. I'm sorry, Thomas Fool, but it cannot be permitted. He will find you soon, that is the best we can offer."

"Can you ask him?"

"No. No one speaks to Mayall, no one asks Mayall, Mayall is the asker and the speaker."

"But if Mayall sees things, surely he can tell me what he saw and this whole situation can be sorted out?"

"There is no situation, Fool; there are simply accidents, a series of coincidences." Israfil again, chipping in, voice disdainful.

"One of the Joyful did the impossible and woke up, accidentally climbed out of the pool, broke the window from the fucking outside, tried to climb through, and stabbed himself to death."

"Assuming the body was there, then perhaps that's what happened." Airy, uninterested.

"And what of the things before?"

"Before?"

"Before I came to Heaven. There were things before, incidents, things that can't be explained. That's why I'm here, after all."

"No," said Israfil, but Fool saw her eyes dart away from his as she spoke, recognized the sign of a truth avoided.

"Then why am I here?" he asked. "Why did Mayall and the Malakim ask for me?"

"I don't know," said Israfil, eyes back on Fool now, glow rippling and raging, and that was the truth; she didn't know and it *burned* her, caustic and bitter and scalding. "Possibly they felt it amusing to see a monkey from Hell perform tricks and scurry after its own tail?"

It's pointless, Fool thought. *They're worse than the demons in Hell, so blind and determined that this place is perfect. And it should be perfect, shouldn't it? This is Heaven, the place of perfection, so why isn't it?*

Why isn't it perfect?

Fool didn't know, but he saw one thing clearly: whatever was happening in Heaven was getting worse. He turned away from the angels, facing away from the building, and saw movement at the edge of the far fields. Something stepped back, drawing itself into the tall grass that grew there, becoming part of the shadows, but not before Fool had seen it clearly.

The scribe. The scribe, watching him again.

15

Before Fool's head gave the command, his feet were moving.

He covered the space between the building and the edge of the grassy area quickly, accelerating as he went, muscles unused to this kind of action and beginning already to protest. From the corner of his eye he saw Summer and Gordie follow, saw the crowds of the Joyful fall away from them as they ran, felt the heat of the sun above him, and this was good, this was right, this was action after all the uncertainty and inactivity, this was movement both literal and figurative, and he ran.

He hit the grass and pushed in among the high stalks, stepping into a place of shadow and fractures. Something snagged at the healing lines of pain across his cheek and tugged and he jerked back, fearing an attack, but it was simply the stalks reaching for him, their high tips above his head, their edges stiff and sharp. It dragged against him as he pushed farther in, rough and stiff across his body, grass with tiny serrations along its edges. Fool raised his gun hand and used it to shield his face, trying to work out where the scribe had gone.

"Stand still," he said to the still-moving Summer and Gordie, and then waited until the sound of them had settled to nothing. At first, there was only the sound of the grass rubbing against itself, a low hiss like the distant exhalations of some slumbering creature, and the near silence was like a living thing curling around him and caressing his skin. Then, on the edge of his hearing, Fool heard the faint sound of feet hitting the earth and a body crashing through the grass somewhere ahead, stumbling. Ahead? No, not quite. He listened again.

Ahead and to his right.

Fool turned slowly in that direction, moving forward and peering through waving stems that were now above his head. It was impossible to move quietly; the grass stems tugged against his clothes as he passed them and brushed together, making a surprisingly harsh, bitter sound. To his rear, Fool heard Summer and Gordie following and he motioned for them to stay behind him.

Was the scribe still running? He couldn't hear it anymore, but surely it hadn't gotten so far ahead of him that it was out of earshot? No, there it was again, the sound of something driving itself forward, crashing and breaking thick stems as it went. It sounded clumsy, desperate but slow, hampered by the vegetation, thrashing.

Fool followed.

Farther into the field the grass was denser, harder than ever to push through, but the denseness worked in Fool's favor. He could see the scribe's trail now, a path marked in broken plants and churned earth below. Why was it running from him? It should know he posed no threat.

Only he did, didn't he? He had killed demons, killed them fairly regularly, in fact. He was Fool, the killer of demons, and it probably feared for its life and whatever soul it possessed. Should he call to it, reassure it that he meant it no harm, he simply needed to talk? No, he didn't know the thing's name, or if it even had one, and simply calling out "scribe" would feel wrong. He pushed on, following the trail the small demon had left for him.

Something was standing in the grass to his side, watching him.

Fool froze. He could see the figure in his peripheral vision, motionless, a thing of shade, feet back from him in the stems and made into an abstraction by an interlocking crosshatch pattern created by the grass stems and their shadows. Fool cautiously dropped a hand to his gun, withdrawing it slowly. As he did a breeze blew, ruffling Fool's hair, and the figure shifted slightly, a fractional spinning movement. Fool jerked back, bringing the gun up fully but not firing.

There was another figure behind the first one, and more behind that one, ranks of them standing in pools of shade, hidden by the thick growths. The grass was course here, old, the stems knotted and tangled, dense clusters of it twisting together to form shapes that looked almost like stunted trees. All the figures were still, seeming to watch him, a forest of them, arms outstretched and hands dangling like the scarecrows he had sometimes seen in Hell's fields, although what purpose they served he had never been able to ascertain.

The scribe forgotten for a moment, Fool approached the first figure. Still it didn't move, resolving out of the patterns of light and dark first into a human rather than angel or demon, and then into a woman, another of the sleeping Joyful. Her hair was wild, standing out from her head in knotted tangles and twists, and her skin was a rich ocher color. She was older, her face lined, her eyes closed, and she was dressed in a loose smock. It was baggy around her outstretched wrists, and her feet, emerging from below the hem, were bare and sunk several inches into the soil.

She was being lost to the plants.

Grasses had pushed up between her legs and had grown up under her clothing, the tops of one or two of the stems emerging from the neck of the dress and tangling into her hair. More stems emerged from the open expanse of her sleeves, green tips tickling around the woman's wrists. Fool could track the growth and travel of them by the way the material of the dress bulged over the woman's shoulders as the grass was forced to turn by the material barrier, some toward the neck, some pushing along her arms. The seam of the dress had split in one place and small tendrils of greenery had pushed their way out of the opening, the questing face of the plants turned up to the sun.

How long had this woman been standing here?

Fool went past her, seeing that all the other figures were the same, men and women standing in the field, sleeping and dreaming or being somewhere else or whatever it was that Heaven allowed the Joyful to do, and the grasses had grown up through their clothes and their feet had sunk into the earth. The farther back Fool went, the older he thought the Joyful were. Or, at least, the longer they had been there; the deeper he went, the less of the human he could see and the more they were festooned with growths. One of the figures' faces was completely lost behind a thick mass of plant material, the fronds covering him and burrowing into the hair of his head like some twisting green crown. Fool let his gun hand drop as he walked among the Joyful, and put the gun in its holster. Whatever was happening here, he didn't think these people were a threat.

They looked different from the others he had seen, their skin tanned by the sun and somehow thicker, rougher. Where their hands were visible and not lost, the growths were gnarled and callused, fingers thick with skin pads, nails squared and chipped. Here, their clothes were often splitting away entirely, forced into torn rags by the pressures of the plants growing between cloth and skin. One or two of the figures were entirely naked except for the growths, and Fool was reminded uncomfortably of the Man, sitting in the corner of his room and gradually becoming lost to another form. *Was this how he started?* wondered Fool. *By simply staying in one place too long and dreaming? But of what? Of change? Of the earth? Do these Joyful love the earth so much they want to be a part of it?*

Finally, Fool found himself standing in the middle of a group of Joyful, all almost gone beneath the growths now. They were cruciform masses of green and brown, tangling stems and vines smothering the humans at their core. Insects buzzed around them and the air was warm and smelled sweet, of honey and healthy wood and the rich musk of soil and growth and light.

Fool saw movement to his side. At first, he thought it was one of the Joyful turning again, making one of those tiny, shivering rotations, but it was not. Something pale was approaching from deeper in the field, glimmering light emerging from the shadows. He stepped behind one of the motionless people, using them as cover and peering around them to watch what was happening. Was it the scribe? No, not the demon, it was small and dark and this was definitely light, and there were two of them, delicate shapes coming toward him through the forest of grass and people. He wondered then if it might be Summer and Gordie, but quickly dismissed the idea. They were still somewhere behind him; he could hear them moving through the crowd of the Joyful, the noise of them the harsh rustle of disturbed stems and of careful, crackling footsteps.

The figures were pallid, twinkling in the shadow, moving slowly but not, he thought, furtively, and as he watched, the shapes came closer and then he saw them for what they were and two angels stepped out from between the grass.

They were smaller angels, the sort that Fool had seen at the beach and outside the pool and at the fairground, the kind he had come to think of as caretakers. They moved silently, managing to pass among the grass without disturbing it, apparently slipping without difficulty through spaces that were far narrower than they appeared to be. Silently, they walked around several of the Joyful before finally coming to a halt in front of a figure who Fool could tell was male only by the fact that a part of a bearded chin was still visible between the growths, and whose clothes were little more than fragments of cloth discarded to the ground and whose presumed nudity was covered from view by thick growths of green and brown grass.

Fool carefully stepped back from the figure he was hiding behind, retreating as silently as possible to hide behind another shape. If the angels heard him, they gave no sign. One of them began to sniff at the Joyful, starting at his head and then descending, sliding across the man's belly and then down his legs before coming back up the man's rear, taking constant stretching inhalations as it went. The other began to run its hands over the man's body, delving into the grass to touch the skin beneath, stroking and pulling and tweaking as it did so. There was no aggression in either's actions; both were gentle and slow. Eventually, the sniffing angel unhinged its face, expanding itself and taking the rear of the man's head, grass and all, into its mouth. The angel's eyes closed in pleasure as it fed, its throat working as it swallowed and its light pulsing to a rhythm Fool couldn't feel.

Finally, the angel broke the contact. Looking at its companion, still without speaking, it nodded and as it did so its face drew back in. Fool watched, fascinated, as the mouth collapsed back to something approaching normality, the throat rippling as it smoothed and narrowed, becoming a normal neck again. Light flickered in its open mouth, tiny sparkles of yellow and blue, and then it swallowed a last time and they were gone. A flush bloomed over its skin, a roseate glow that shone briefly and then was gone. While it lasted, it sent warm shadows into the space around it that turned the Joyful into delicate pink statues.

In response to the nod, and the end of the feeding, the second angel stopped running its hands over the man and produced a long, curved blade from the air, the knife appearing from nothing. It began to cut at the grasses by the man's feet, tugging away the plants as it did so. As the grass was removed, the man's body became visible, a pale and wasted thing that seemed to be all skin and joints with little flesh around the skeletal frame. Without the supporting strength of the plants to anchor it upward, the man collapsed back, unable to bear his own weight, and fell into the first angel's arms. The angel laid the man on the ground gently, folding his arms over his chest and straightening his legs, brushing fragments of grass from his face and his hair back from off his forehead so that his closed eyes and mouth were exposed. The man did not move and the two angels stood over him for a moment, heads bowed. It was impossible to tell whether the angels were male or female, they were sexless and smooth in their grace, and then they moved on.

The two went to the next Joyful and repeated the process.

Soon, as Fool watched, the angels had gathered four of the Joyful, each laid alongside the others as though they were crops being harvested, stopping when the fifth person the angel fed from was obviously different and it shook its head after it detached. The two then stood and waited until eventually, after what could have been minutes or could have been a few seconds, a flurry of smaller angels drifted down from the sky and surrounded the four prostrate figures.

These weren't the blackest angels Fool had seen at the beach but were similar, small cherublike things that reminded him of the Orphans, but Orphans remade into perfect beings. They were a pale brown, their skin gleaming in the sunlight, and they hovered on wings that weren't feathered but were gossamer, thin membranes that reflected the sun in a rainbow of flashing colors. They had pudgy fingers, fat little bellies that jounced as they flew, and their eyes were entirely white, without pupil or iris.

These new angels clutched at the Joyful and then, when each of the tiny figures had a solid grip, beat their delicate wings and lifted the men and women into the air. Fool watched as they rose, spiraling upward and away until they vanished. The two caretaker angels stepped silently back into the grass, merging with the shadows until they, too, were gone. Fool let out his breath, kept trapped inside until then to avoid detection, and stepped out into the small clearing that had been created in the field. He placed his feet where the feet of a Joyful had been until only recently and looked back into the now-clear and flawless sky.

What had he just watched?

Beside Fool, Summer stepped out into the clearing and looked into the sky. She was crying but didn't appear to be upset, her face turning to follow the path that the angels and the Joyful had taken, the tears that streaked her cheeks glinting. Behind her, Gordie was crouching and looking at the ground, moving the cut grass about with a hand as though stirring a pot of stew. What was he looking for, or looking at? Fool wondered. Was he trying to become an Information Man again, or remembering what he had been before his death, looking for clues? Clues to what? How could anything explain the things they had seen? Heaven was proving more unknowable than Hell had ever been.

Of course it is, he thought. *We're from Hell, all three of us, what chance have we got of understanding?*

As Fool watched Gordie, he remembered that he had been chasing the scribe before this oblique distraction had occurred, and he turned back to the trail left by the small demon. How far had he let the thing get by forgetting about it? He cocked his head, listening, but heard nothing. Was it so far away that he would be unable to pick up the sound of it again? Fool took several slow steps along the broken path, still listening.

Nothing.

He had the physical trail, at least. He'd follow that as far as he could and hope either that he caught up with the demon or that he found something to explain what the scribe had been doing. He started walking, pushing his way through the already broken grass, forcing his way through clumps that had twisted around each other and whose tops were above his own head. It was hot in among the plants and Fool was soon sweating, the salt stinging his eyes and making his ears and mouth and nose warm and slippery. He wiped at his forehead, felt the scratch of chaff against his skin, and then something ahead of him screamed.

The sound rose into the air like a flock of ragged birds from somewhere down the trail where the scribe had run, and Fool knew instinctively that the scream was coming from the demon. The noise had no human elements, had a pitch and tone that could be made only by the throat of one of the demonkind. It was distorted, rough, had no cadence of humanity in it. It sounded not just lost but *damned*, giving shape to a misery that Fool could only imagine in his nightmares. He started to run, pushing through the tough stems, feeling them tear at his clothes, and another scream sounded, this one closer and, if anything, more hopeless.

Ahead of Fool, the field's growths were finally thinning, the spaces opening out so that movement became easier, and then he was into a larger clearing, and the fleeting image of a huge pile of harvested Joyful cut down and lying stacked like cordwood flickered in his mind and then he saw the scribe.

The demon was lying in the center of the clearing, grass trampled beneath it, old and broken stems jutting up from the ground while motes of dust and fragments of chaff floated in the air, catching the sun in yellow flickers. Mayall was standing over the fallen demon.

The clown angel was still, his feet not jigging that clumsy dance, but motionless in the dry, rolling dust. He was dressed in the same brown trousers and white shirt but this time had a baggy coat on, its tails flapping, his hair hanging in loose strings over his face.

"It's not where it's supposed to be," said Mayall in a somber voice as Fool came to a halt, confused. "Hello, Fool. Have you come along to watch? Watch the judgment for the thing that's somewhere out and about but that's where it isn't supposed to be? Shall we judge together?" As the angel said "judge," he leaned forward and calmly slapped the recumbent demon, straightening again afterward so that his shadow fell across the fallen thing.

"No," said Fool, walking slowly across the space toward the angel and the demon. The scribe looked terrible, sprawled on the ground with its limbs outstretched. The ruff of feathers that wrapped the demon's neck had peeled away and stretched out into wings that were sticking up from its back, and Fool wondered if it had been attempting to fly; now it would have no chance. One wing's thin, feather-dotted leather membrane was torn and bleeding and the other wing had been broken halfway along its length and was hanging lopsidedly down. Fresh blood oozed from the broken section of wing, thick and dark, and the smell of it reached Fool as a burning, corrupted stench. Where it spilled to the earth, tiny blue flowers were already emerging, buds opening and turning toward the sun. The scribe raised its head and looked at Fool and its eyes were alien and haunted and lost.

The clown angel leaned down and cuffed the demon's head, hard. The movement was shocking in its simplicity, the blow meticulous, graceful, using the minimum of movement to effect a maximum of force. The scribe's head jerked to the side and smacked against the ground, and Fool heard a crack as something in its neck wrenched. Blood and drool spilled from the scribe's mouth and it groaned as it tried to raise its head again, the liquid spattering to the dry earth beneath it, more flowers struggling and growing up from the dank liquid. After a second, it gave up and let its head flop down, helpless and broken.

"Stop," said Fool.

"No," said Mayall, stepping around the figure in front of him, voice chill. "It's out and about instead of hidden and closed in where it is supposed to be, so it is a thing without rights and without chances." There was no humor in the angel's voice now, none of the manic capering, only a low menace. He clapped his hands once, arms darting forward like snakes, simultaneously striking either side of the demon's head with flat palms, then moved back and howled as though he were the one in pain. Mayall's head rocked back, exposing a neck that worked as he howled, spitting out each ululation with greater and greater volume.

"Have mercy?" asked Fool.

"Mercy?" He turned to Fool, looking at him for the first time since he had arrived. "No, Fool, this thing has broken the rules and deserves nothing but condemnation and punishment."

Another blow, followed by another howl. Mayall turned on the spot again, letting his arms drop to his sides, tilting his face to the sun and howling again.

"Mayall, it doesn't deserve this," said Fool quietly, trying to inject calm into the situation with just his voice. He stayed still, hands out from his side, head down, deferential and small.

Mayall came back around, slowing, and peered at the demon in front of him as though he'd never seen it before. "Everything in Heaven is deserved, Fool; every last thing is needed and required and deserved. Ah, the thing is broken," the angel said, and shoved his hands into the pockets of his coat, bringing them up and angling his arms so that they mimicked the scribe's broken wings. The action was strangely humorless and sad. "Poor, broken thing. Poor, foolish thing."

After a moment, the angel removed his hands from his coat and reached out, plucking feathers from the demon's wings. They were unlike angel's feathers, not long and elegantly pale but gnarled and black, looking like burned twists of wood. Mayall began to drop them, letting them scatter around him like charcoal tears. When there were no feathers left in the scribe's wings, the angel stood and trod on each where it had come to rest against the earth. Even from where he was standing, Fool heard the tiny things crack under the angel's feet. The scribe winced at each sound, the battered face jerking, and Fool wondered if it could still feel, if it was still linked to those parts of itself despite their separation from it.

"Let it be," said Fool, not demanding but not exactly pleading either.

"No," said Mayall, walking around the demon.

"Please," said Fool. "The scribe may have broken the rules, but it may also have seen something that will help me in the task you've asked me to complete and I need to speak to it."

That brought up Mayall short. He stopped moving and looked at Fool for a long moment.

"You're not alone," the angel said eventually. Fool glanced behind him to see Summer and Gordie standing on the edge of the clearing, now holding hands again.

"No, I'm not. And the scribe is part of my Delegation and I need to talk to it and I am responsible for it. It is Hell's."

Mayall seemed to give this some thought, stepping over the crumpled demon and walking toward Fool. When he was close enough, he leaned in so that his face was mere inches from Fool's and said, "Do you know the difference between a demon and a rock?"

"What?" asked Fool, startled. "A demon and a rock? Now what? I don't understand."

"A rock cannot be redeemed," said Mayall and then walked away, turning and crouching in one simple movement, grasping the scribe in arms that looked, suddenly, huge. The coat flapped away from his back and became wings, vast and brown, and then he was circling up into the sky holding the demon and his laughter was filling the sky, becoming a cloud of sound like thunder. "But," Mayall's voice rumbled from above them, "they both fall so very, very well!"

And then the demon was falling.

The scribe screamed as it dropped, a scream that lasted for seconds and a lifetime before stopping abruptly as it hit the ground with a solid, shuddering crunch. Blood and dirt sprayed up in equal measure, a crown forming in the air above the mangled thing, before it, too, fell. A blue streak, small and crumpled, rose from the dead demon and expanded into the sky above it until it was so dissipated that it vanished.

Mayall floated down and hovered above the body, his face serious, his expression calm.

"I have redeemed it, set it free," he said, "but no black angels will come for this. It is all alone."

Alone, thought Fool. *We're all alone at the end, aren't we? Really?*

Ignoring Mayall, Fool went to the scribe's body and sat beside it. It was already rotting, crumping in on itself in a pool of slime and heat, a haze rising from it. The smell was terrible and the rapidly blooming blue flowers were adding to the odor, more and more of them growing where the demon's blood had hit the earth, petals shivering as they peeled back from stamens that looked like long, thin phalluses. They opened wide, grasping at the sun, twisting on their delicate, foul stalks so that their faces were fully exposed.

"Why did you kill it?" asked Fool when Mayall finally stopped spinning and flying. "I told you I needed to talk to it. You asked me to investigate, you *told* me to find out what was happening, yet you block me when I try to do what you've asked."

Mayall sat cross-legged in front of Fool, leaning forward, oddly conspiratorial. "Because I decided it was the just thing to do," said the angel. "You were given permission to leave your rooms, but it was not. It was a wrong thing in a wrong place, and I dealt with it."

"You murdered it!"

"I redeemed it," said Mayall. "I released it from its sin, from the body of evil it inhabited. It is free now, Thomas Fool. Surely I did it a service, performed a mercy?"

How could you argue with it, this merciful blindness? "I needed to speak to it," Fool repeated. "It could have helped."

"No," said Mayall, and his tone was gentle. "Ask your Delegation colleagues what it was doing out of their rooms, the explanation lies there."

"You know?"

"Of course."

"Then tell me."

"No. You and Elderflower spoke about this, Thomas Fool, you should understand. Elderflower and I, we may see but know that we cannot tell or the plan falls sundered. This is Heaven, the glory that Hell is a red and burning reflection of, and things are necessarily this way for reasons you will never be told and would never understand even if you were. What we may know, you may not. This is the role you have been assigned, Thomas Fool. You are the question in the absolute, you are the chaos in the order, the hunchback in the line of soldiers, you are the joke in the seriousness. You are the Fool in the line of the sensible, and I cherish you for it."

"Help me," said Fool, head sagging. He was tired, his face hurt and felt thick with dried blood and new scabs, and his brain hurt. Dead Joyful, angels that wouldn't or couldn't see, the hectic and confusing and violent Mayall, it was all mustering in his head, mixing and crashing and bitter.

"Yes, you deserve something," said Mayall, and that light was in his eyes again, that glitter of the approaching storm of movement and noise. He sprang to his feet, the mania returning, his feet starting to prance, and gestured to Summer and Gordie. Fool felt his hand move toward his gun and forced it to stop, move away. Whatever would happen here, there was nothing he could do to stop it.

"Come here," said Mayall. His voice was rising again, crackling with laughter, bubbling with a barely restrained hysteria. Already, his feet were kicking up, starting to palsy into a ragged dance that set his whole body into rhythm. Fool nodded at his companions when they stayed still, wary but knowing there was no more choice for any of them here than there was in Hell.

Summer moved first, Gordie following her, never letting go of her hand. By the time they reached Mayall, the angel was practically jittering, the dance lifting him from the ground in long, slow risings that were almost flight but not quite. Each time he came down, he did so on the flowers that grew from the scribe's decaying flesh, trampling them into the ground, and Fool did not suppose it was an accident. The smell rose around them, thick and heady and corpulent.

"Bal Koth did such a good job, didn't she?" asked Mayall when Summer and Gordie reached him. "She has pulled them from the darkness and created them in the light so wonderfully. They are growing, so close to perfect, so very close, the perfection of humans made in the image of the brightest being in all of Heaven or Hell, but they have not quite achieved it, have they?"

"I don't know," said Fool. Even to himself, his voice sounded dead and toneless.

"Don't *sulk*, Thomas Fool, it's a lazy man's way of letting his feelings be known! Be angry or be happy or be sad, don't be this turgid middle ground of pointed silences and wearying frowns. Turn that frown inside out, turn it into a smile, Thomas Fool, I'm about to help you!"

Fool didn't move, head bowed, suddenly too tired to care.

"I'm waiting," said Mayall, that singsong voice now sharper, breaking in its upper regions to a harsh and strident demand. Fool looked up and saw that Mayall was staring at him, a pointed expression on his face, an exaggerated glare of attention. His lips were pursed, his brow furrowed, eyes wide, hands on his hips. "This is you, Thomas Fool, Mr. Grumpy-Face Information Man. Now, smile!"

Fool smiled. It felt like a scream without sound.

"That's better, so much better. Now, shall I begin?"

Without waiting for a reply, Mayall turned back toward Summer and Gordie. Some of his mania fell away and his movement slowed even if it didn't stop entirely.

"Such a beautiful pair," he said quietly, as though to himself. He reached out, ignoring the flinches his touch generated, and placed his hands on Summer's and Gordie's necks. "So nearly perfect, but Bal Koth didn't have all the power, did she? No, not enough, but clowns do, clowns have a piece of the power that the serious do not.

"Tell me, Thomas Fool," said Mayall, calling back over his shoulder without looking around, "what do jokes need?"

"I don't fucking know," said Fool, angry and sad and hurt and confused. "I don't know anything."

"Jokes need voices to be told," said Mayall, either not hearing or ignoring Fool's anger and the swearing. "Jokes need sound. Tell me a joke, Thomas Fool."

"I don't know any," said Fool. "I've told you, I don't know anything. I know less than nothing."

"Nonsense, Thomas," replied Mayall, still holding the throats of Summer and Gordie. His grip didn't look tight but it did look firm, unyielding. "Everyone knows a joke or two. Everyone except my companion angels, that is. Tell me a joke."

"I don't even know what a joke is," said Fool.

"Something funny, Thomas, something to make us laugh or see the absurdity of the situations we find ourselves in. Something witty, something stupid, something that makes us roar."

Fool thought for a minute and then said, "Me. I'm your joke, the little Fool you expect to investigate but who knows less than nothing and who even the angels think is a monkey, investigating things that the same angels do not see. I'm the joke."

"Bitter, but good enough," said Mayall, "although you underestimate yourself, Thomas Fool. You may be a joke, but it is not one of idiocy or ignorance. You may not know it, but yours is the humor of the unexpected, of the sudden jump and shock. You are the thing that keeps everything else spinning, the joke that makes us see the changes needed and the changes too far and the changes lost and missed. Have faith, Thomas, have faith in yourself. Now, your reward."

Mayall let go of Summer and Gordie and stepped back. Already, his dance was picking up, as though once he was not touching anything else he became untethered, was set loose. He opened his wings and flapped, lifting himself into the air and spinning. "Good-bye, Thomas Fool. I'll no doubt be in touch soon. Enjoy your rewards."

"Rewards?"

"Perfection, Thomas, the perfections of completion," and then he was gone, there and then suddenly not there.

"Rewards?" asked Fool, speaking to himself. He rose to his feet, feeling the weariness of old and souring energy ripple through him, the weariness of frustrations and not understanding. He felt hungry and wondered when he had last eaten. Today? Yesterday? Did days even mean anything when his time was so fractured?

"Rewards," he said again. "There's nothing, Mayall. What is there?"

"Hello, Fool," said a voice, and it took a moment to recognize the voice as Summer's.

16

"Summer?" Fool asked, feeling slow and stupid. "You can talk?"

"Yes," she replied. "I can talk." She smiled as she spoke and it was good to hear her again, it was fucking *wonderful* to hear her again, hear that voice that he had last heard in a scream.

"I can, too," said Gordie, sounding surprised, and he was laughing and then Fool was across the clearing and holding them both, arms around them and neck buried against their shoulders, pulling them into a clasp that he never wanted to release. Mayall had made them complete, given them their voices back, and it was so good, it was perfect, and Fool was crying, the first time he had ever cried tears of joy rather than pain or fear or sorrow.

"It's okay," said Summer, stroking the back of Fool's head, her touch gentle. "It's okay, we're here, we're with you."

"Yes," said Fool and could say no more. Gordie's hand clasped Fool's shoulder and for another long, warm instant they hugged before breaking apart. Fool wiped at his face, the wipe triggering a flash of pain from his cheek.

"It's really you," said Fool. "Really?"

"Of course," said Gordie, as though there was no question, that it couldn't be anyone else.

"It's us," confirmed Summer. Fool saw her hand clasp Gordie's tighter for a brief moment, their fingers whitening as they gripped.

"Where—" said Fool, and stopped. How could he ask it?

"Where were we? I don't know," said Summer. "I remember darkness. I remember pain and then nothing."

"I remember fire," said Gordie, his face creasing slightly. "Then nothing until I woke up here. In Heaven, I mean."

"I remember losing you," said Summer to Gordie and there was pain there, and loss. She leaned in to kiss him and after a slight resistance, Gordie returned the kiss. They stayed connected for seconds, lips touching, eyes closed, before breaking apart.

"Never again," she said. "Never again."

"Why didn't you go on, or out, or wherever?" asked Fool, unable to stop himself. He felt light, like he could burst into laughter for no reason. Was this how Mayall felt, this euphoria, this sheer *joy*, this need to somehow explode, to show the amazement of it all?

"Because of you," said Gordie. "Because we were tied to you. I don't know why, but we were. I couldn't move on because of you."

"Me either," said Summer.

"I'm sorry," Fool said.

"Don't be," Summer replied. Her voice sounded light, lilting, like a song that Fool had never heard before but had known all his life. It sounded as though it could lift him, create wings for him. "You didn't do it, we know that. Maybe it was Hell, or maybe it was Heaven planning to move us to this point."

"You know what happened after . . ." *After you died*, Fool almost said but stopped himself.

"No," said Gordie. "I just know I'm back."

"I know we're here to help you, that we're linked, everything's linked, you and us and the murders."

That brought Fool back. "Murders," he repeated. "You agree with me? They're not accidents?"

"Of course they're not," said Gordie.

"Israfil thinks they are," said Fool, pushing against Gordie's certainty to test his own.

"Israfil thinks we're monkeys," said Summer, grinning. "I couldn't speak but I could hear. Fuck her. Now, should we see what we've got?"

"'What we've got'?"

"What we've got," repeated Summer. "Let's investigate. There are crimes to solve."

"Yes," said Gordie, and Fool nodded without speaking and went with his friends to investigate murders in Heaven.

Fool had forgotten that he'd demanded Mr. Tap find him a map of Hell.

He found it on his desk when the three of them returned to his room later that day, tired and despondent and elated all at the same time. They had spent the preceding hours simply walking and talking, going over what they knew and thought they knew and needed to know, throwing ideas out and then pulling them back in when they proved unworkable or leaving them out there to see if they could gain a coating of fact as the investigation proceeded. It was, perhaps, the happiest Fool could remember being, because although there was urgency within the investigation, for the first time he felt the urgency had been diluted and that he could share it with someone.

Part of the problem was, of course, that they were out of the places they knew and understood. At least in Hell they could predict and delineate some, if not all, of the parameters they were supposed to function within, but here? Everything was confusing, from the geography that shifted to the angels that refused to see the evidence in front of their eyes to the Joyful who were apparently asleep and dreaming of Heavens inside themselves even as they stood in Heaven itself. He didn't know whether to turn or stand still, felt like they were spinning without moving, like the trails they might follow all eventually turned back in on themselves to become looped and endless things.

Why had he wanted the map?

It was drawn on old parchment and scrolled tight, tied with a thick hank of cord. When he cut the cord, the map unfurled slowly, spreading its tired arms across his desk, letting loose a faint aroma of dirt and burning. Its face was covered in dense black drawings, notations, indicators of scale and direction and inhabitants. Gordie was immediately fascinated and started poring over the document in excitement, pointing out things with comments like "I knew it!" or "There! See?" At one point, he looked at a vast black patch in the center of the map, finger hovering above a series of white spots, and said, "Look, there are islands in Solomon Water. Little ones, all connected by spits of land. I kept hearing rumors about them, but I could never prove it."

Summer stroked Gordie's back as he leaned over the map, the expression on her face somewhere between pride and interest. Fool tried to remember, and then did. He had asked for the map because of the places that burned, hadn't he?

"Gordie, Summer," he said. "I need you to sit away from the map and just watch for a while. Don't worry, and don't interfere."

"Interfere with what?"

"You'll see. It's fine, though. Just sit and listen and watch and let me talk, yes?"

"Okay," said Gordie and withdrew from the map, clearly reluctant to do so.

Fool had no choice in what he did next; rolling up his sleeve, he rubbed the skin around the tattoo of Marianne's face and said, "Marianne."

There was no reply. He spoke her name again, louder as though it would make a difference; perhaps it would. Still nothing.

"Marianne," again. What time was it in Hell? As far as he knew it was the same time as it was in Heaven, late evening but not yet night, so she was unlikely to be asleep. Was she busy, in a place where she couldn't hear him?

Had something happened to her?

Fool looked at the tattoo, wondering. Unlike Mr. Tap's shifting, angular illustration on his skin that broke apart after their conversations, Marianne's image seemed permanently etched upon him. Did that mean something? Over these past days, the art of the tattoo seemed to have refined itself so that what had originally been a blocky version of Marianne, almost a caricature, was now an accurate, carefully drawn representation of how she looked, or at least how he remembered her looking. Her face, outlined and shaded on his forearm, was a delicate tracery of line and shadow that caught how she was in his mind—hair short, jaw firm but not square, eyes sharp and intelligent. *Where are you, Marianne?* he thought, and then the skin under the marks itched violently and the eyes blinked and the mouth opened.

The pain was as startling and sharp as it ever was; Fool had hoped that it would lessen, or he would somehow become used to it over time, but no. It was agony, the skin tearing open along fault lines created by a demon's entrails burning into him, dribbling blood as the eyes flickered and the mouth formed itself into the shape of the black-drawn lips.

"Thomas?" Marianne's voice, wafting out from his arm on a breeze of misted blood and an exhalation that should not exist. "Sorry, sir. Sir."

"Thomas is fine. Marianne, are you okay?"

A pause, then, "I think so."

"You think so?"

"There's been another fire, Thomas, another slaughter." Another pause, longer this time, and then, "The Evidence are here. Mr. Tap is here."

Fool's belly clenched, the skin preparing itself for the ripping, as though the mere sound of the demon's name would summon him, give him a voice to talk, but thankfully nothing happened.

"In the building?"

"Yes."

"What's he doing?"

"Nothing. The Evidence Men are going through all the offices looking at the paperwork but I don't think they understand it, it's like they're playing at being proper Information Officers, pretending to read and talk to each other about what they've read without actually understanding any of it. Mr. Tap is sitting in the mess taking their reports, but most of the reports seem to be nonsense, more of the game they're playing. He gathered us all together and told us their presence was merely to support us, but it feels more permanent. It feels like we're being removed, pushed out."

"It would, and I suspect you are," said Fool. "He's taking over. Are you safe?"

A third pause, the longest of all. "Yes. I think so, I mean. For now. I'm in your room. So far, they haven't been in any of the bedrooms or your office but it won't take them long, I don't think."

"Then we need to work quickly. Look at my board, tell me where all the fires have occurred."

For the next few minutes, Fool plotted the positions of the fires on the map of Hell, using an angel's feather dipped in ink. When the end of the feather's calamus touched the map, the thick paper wrinkled and tiny scorch marks appeared within the ink, but it did not burn through and the damage was light enough for him to still use the document as he wanted to. When he had finished, the map had more than twenty new marks, twenty places where fire had eaten its way through wood and flesh and drywall. The pattern of them seemed random, the scatter to have no real order that he could discern. There was a cluster here but only individual fires there, a smaller group here, one out on its own there, a larger grouping there. He sighed, frustrated.

What had this shown him? Nothing. Why had he wanted this? He'd thought of something last night, something about how the fires had been started.

No, not about how they were started, he already knew that, about how the sites for the fires might have been chosen.

Fool looked at the map again, staring at the marks, looking at the things around them marked out in old, faded colors. At first it wasn't clear, and then it came into focus as though someone had twisted his view around and brought it to the right angle for him to see it clearly.

The site of each of the fires was close to an area of old growth, forest or farmland allowed to go fallow or simply abandoned.

Fool tried to think about it from the perspective of the arsonist. *You want to set something on fire,* he thought, *but you don't want to be caught. So you . . . what? Hide in the forests and farmlands where the undergrowth is at its thickest, you come through it, and when you emerge, you go to the nearest building and you set your fire, then you escape back into the shadows and you watch it burn from a distance.*

Yes. Yes, that sounds right.

"Marianne?"

"Yes?"

"Where did the slaughters take place?"

She gave him three more areas, which Fool plotted, and saw that they were the same. Each backed onto or was close to an area of wilderness. Were they carried out by the same creatures? Creatures growing in confidence, moving between fires and murders and the wholesale slaughter of workers, depending on how their whim took them?

"Thomas?"

"Yes?"

"About the fires and the murders?"

"Yes?"

"There were more of the crowds around them today. Remember I said that it felt as though the crowds had been brought together somehow? Deliberately, so that they could see the fire and be encouraged to make things up about it?"

"Yes?"

"It was the same today. It was as though someone had set the fire, and murdered people, as an act, as a way of getting people to talk about it, to be scared. Even today, I heard three or four stories about who was doing it, from old demons to mysterious black assassins to creatures that haven't got a name but that even the Devil himself is frightened of, creatures from nowhere in Hell or Heaven or any other world. It's like a coordinated campaign designed to cause uncertainty."

"Uncertainty? In Hell?"

"You know what I mean," she said, his arm said, the flesh rippling and shifting on waves of pain. He closed his real eyes, seeing through the sketch again, the view a bleary section of his room and Marianne herself, face concerned and attractive.

"No. Tell me," he said.

"There are rules, even here," she said, "and what's happening here is outside of those rules. The Bureaucracy doesn't know what's happening, and I think that whoever's doing it is deliberately feeding into the confusion. The stories I heard today felt fully formed somehow, not things that were growing the way rumors and gossip usually do. They were dropped into the crowd as entire creations, designed to make people frightened, to confuse them. They were *detailed*. Does that make sense?"

"Yes," he said. She was smart, he thought. She listens, and she guesses in the right directions and hears the things that aren't said, and she makes the links between them all.

"There's another thing."

"Yes?" Wincing again at the pain, wiping at the blood that trickled down his arm. Summer bundled one of the sheets off the bed and held it to his arm, soaking up his dripping blood, but it muffled what Marianne said next and he pushed it away, grateful but insistent.

"There was another rumor, the most common of all the ones I got told. I heard it three or four times, the most of any of the stories. The things that carried out the slaughters, that lit the fires, they moved oddly."

"'Oddly'?" But already thinking he might know what Marianne was going to say.

"Oddly, as though they weren't usual, weren't normal. Not like demons or humans, I mean. Not like the things that live in Hell."

"Like they danced?"

"Maybe. Pale things, I heard. Pale things like angels."

Angels. Angels, dancing angels attacking the inhabitants of Hell, setting Hell aflame?

No. No, it couldn't be.

Couldn't it? Mayall was an angel, and he danced.

It was too big to consider now, he needed to focus again on the specifics, on the things he could hold and feel and sense the shape of.

"If the attackers came in through the overgrowth, then there's someone who can maybe help us," Fool said.

"The thing we spoke to the other night?"

"The Man of Plants and Flowers," Fool confirmed.

"I don't know what he is, but he's not a man," said Marianne. Fool did not reply.

The garden was empty of humans, demons, and bauta, but getting there took a long few minutes. The corridors of the Information House bustled with Evidence Men and Information Men, human and demon, the two groups clearly avoiding each other. Even viewed through the hazy vision of the sketch as Marianne carried it and him to meet with the Man, the divisions were clear; the Evidence Men strutted and preened as they made their way about the building, the Information Men made themselves small and kept to the sides of the walls and scuttled from doorway to doorway. At one point, Fool thought he saw Mr. Tap, or at least its angular, twisted back as it stooped to enter a room, but the glance was fleeting and it was difficult to tell. When they finally came to the rear entrance of the Information House and Marianne took them outside, Fool relaxed a little, but only a little. The risks of Hell were too easy to forget in the confusions of Heaven, but even the short journey with Marianne had reminded him: to be in Hell was to be in danger.

"What's Heaven like?" asked Marianne as they waited. She had seated herself on one of the old stone benches, the picture held in front of her so that they were face to face. Fool, in Heaven, closed his eyes so that he might see her and what was around her as clearly as possible.

"It's nothing like I expected," replied Fool truthfully. "There're no spires, at least not that I've seen. It's like the Heaven you can see from Hell is an image they want you to see, to aspire to, or maybe just to show you what you're missing. The real Heaven isn't as bright, it doesn't glow. Oh, it's beautiful and clean and smells good, but it's still earth and air and rock and trees and people, just like Hell."

"Is it filled with love?"

"I don't know. I don't know what being filled with love is, not really. I know that the parts I've seen, some of them at least, are wonderful."

"Only parts of it?"

"Yes," said Fool, thinking about the dead body on the side of the pool, its blood mingling with the water from its robes and spilling slowly back toward the body of water, thinking about the Joyful wrapped in grass being cut down by angels after they had taken their fill.

"What are the people like? The Elevated ones?"

"Not like us," replied Fool. "They're asleep, or in some other place. No one talks."

"No one?" asked Marianne. "That's sad. I like talking. Heaven for me would be to be able to talk to people all the time without being frightened I'd say the wrong thing, without worrying that what I said would lead to them judging me, and people would say what they liked back."

"Yes," said Fool.

"I like talking to you," said Marianne. "You listen to me. You never make me feel scared or stupid when I talk."

Fool didn't know what to say so simply said, "Thank you. You aren't stupid, and I like talking to you as well. I'll be happier when we can do it properly, though, rather than this way."

Marianne didn't answer. Instead, Fool's vision began to shake as the paper she held trembled in her previously steady hands. Slowly, she turned it around so that Fool's view slid sideways, moving over the thick, brambled foliage before ending up facing the gate in the far wall.

There was an Evidence Man staring at them through the metal lattice.

It had pressed itself against the bars, hands clenched around two of the struts, face jammed into the gap. Its tusks ground against the metal, making a wretched wail of noise as dribble spattered down its chin. In the gathering gloom its eyes gleamed, pale yellow glitters almost lost in the depths below its heavy brow, but not lost enough that Fool and presumably Marianne didn't realize it was staring at her.

"Don't move," said Fool as quietly as he could.

The bauta slowly began to rattle the gate, shaking it back and forth in its frame as though to test its strength. It hissed, long tongue emerging from its mouth and lips, the sound coming to Fool through his paper ears and sounding dusty and dry. It shook the gate harder, and even at this distance Fool could see the rust flake away around the hinges, see the masonry grind and begin to crack. *Those little fuckers are strong,* he thought abstractly as the thing shook the gate more furiously.

"What do you want?" called Marianne, her voice steadier than Fool thought his might have been in the circumstances. The bauta carried on grunting and shaking the gate.

"I am an Information Man of Hell, part of the Information Office, carrying out my duties," Marianne continued, "and you have no authority to interfere. This garden belongs to the Information Office. Now, leave me be."

As they watched and waited, Fool heard the sound of other Evidence Men walking on the other side of the wall, approaching the bauta at the gate. They were grunting at each other, their language guttural and hoarse, and their feet rasped against the ground. Marianne hunched down as the voices and footsteps came closer; looking at her from below, now held forgotten at waist height, Fool watched as she trembled and her eyes closed; whatever bravery she'd had to challenge the Evidence Man at the gate had been almost used up. *We still try not to be noticed,* thought Fool, *all of us, but we can't manage it, not really. Marianne creeps down here but gets seen anyway, challenges that little thing, hoping to face it down, and suddenly there are more and that's it, she's in their view. And what about me? What about little Heaven's Fool? Everyone and everything in Heaven and Hell seems to be watching me.*

The new Evidence Men joined the first at the gate. There were four of them now, clustered in the space and staring through the bars at Marianne and the paper Fool she held, faces piglike and coarse. Although she was holding Fool down and sideways, he could see the bauta in his peripheral vision; in Heaven, eyes closed, he turned his head to where they were in Hell, but it didn't help and the movement of his flesh without the parallel movement of his view was slickly nauseating. He stilled himself and waited.

The four bauta seemed confused by Marianne's refusal to back down. Instead, she sat as still as she could and opened her eyes again, staring at them without looking down. Fool could see the effort it was costing her, could see the muscles in her jaw clench, see the sweat trickle around her hairline at her temples, and was glad that the bauta were far enough away to miss those details. If they saw them, they would know, and in the knowing Marianne would be doomed.

The four began to speak, their grunts curiously whispered, interspersed with things that might have been words made guttural and torn, and squeals that they kept muted. They seemed to be arguing, the original one still occasionally rattling the gate, making the hinges grate, drool and blood slicking its tusks, shiny in the light of distant lamps. The others split their attention between Marianne and the first at the gate, glances jumping back and forth until, at last, they pulled the creature away. Gesturing, they left it peering through the bars into the garden before it gave the gate a last shake, snarled, and then turned and left. Fool's last sight of them was their shaggy hair catching the light and the rear of their filthy breachclouts disappearing into the shadows.

Only when they had been gone for a minute or so did Marianne let out her breath.

"Well done," said Fool as she raised the paper, let him look at her clearly again. She was breathing deeply, was still trembling, and for the first time he wished he could reach out and hold her, feel her the way he had felt Summer and Gordie today, tell her it was okay, she had survived. He wanted to embrace her and tell her there was no point in being frightened of what hadn't happened or what could have happened; there was too much else that still could happen to worry about.

"Yes," said a voice that could only be the Man's, "very well done, Information Man Marianne. You did marvelously."

Marianne didn't reply. Instead, she spent another few moments bringing her breathing back under control, steadying herself, and then she turned Fool so that he was facing the knotted undergrowth. Already, the plants had hunched themselves into a mass that might have been a body, a growth that might have been a head. Its mouth was exaggerated, created by two branches that fluttered and bent in a wide parody of lips as the Man spoke.

"Two visits in two days, Fool. I'm honored. So then, what information do you have for me?"

"Nothing."

"Nothing? Then we have nothing to talk about."

"Yes we do. I've given you information, now I want my payment."

"Payment?"

"Payment, in information."

"Oh, Fool, you're getting better, you're learning!" said the Man, his tone that of a delighted teacher watching a favored pupil excel unexpectedly. "Fine, then. What information can I pay you with?"

Fool listed the places where the arsons had occurred, and the slaughters, and then said, "You live in the plants around those places?"

"Of course."

"Then you must have seen what came through them, came through *you* before they burned things or killed people?"

"No, but then, I wasn't looking for anything, Fool. I am still keeping a low profile, keeping my attention low so that the attention of others slides over me without catching."

"Can you look in those places now? See if there's anything there that shouldn't be? Anything that might tell me who's responsible?"

"And I get?"

"More information."

"Very well. Wait." The Man's shape slumped, as though wires that had been holding him had been cut, the branches bending back to their more usual position. He bobbed in the breeze, unmade, while Fool and Marianne waited. Marianne was, without thinking, turning the paper Fool so that he saw the whole of the courtyard as a slow, gyroscopic twist. Eventually, he said, "Marianne, can you hold me still?"

"I'm so sorry," she said, immediately holding the paper up, facing her, still. Was she blushing again?

"Don't worry," he said. "I was just getting dizzy." She grinned and then spun the paper again in wide, deliberately ornate loops so that he felt like he was flying, making him laugh. He stopped laughing when she slowed, stopping him, and spoke, his arm pained again.

"Do you trust the Man?"

"No, and you shouldn't either. It suits him to help us at the moment, but one day it won't and then he'll use you and leave you behind. Be careful of him."

"That's good advice," said the Man, rising up again from the growths, rising *into* the growths. "Information Man Marianne, Fool is a sensible man, and you'd do well to heed his advice.

"Now, to business. Fool, you were right. I found trails through the undergrowth. Someone's been trekking their way through me without asking, which is simply rude, walking through me like I'm some common forest, and all the trails lead to clearings."

"Clearings?"

"Yes. Clearings, natural ones. There's nothing there now, not obviously, but if you know what to look for, what things should be, it's obvious. The ground; it's wrong. It's been dug through, churned and disturbed and then put back together but not very well. It's something I've not felt before, as though the earth has been opened and then inexpertly closed. Does that help? Do you know who might have caused it?"

"No," said Fool, and wondered if that was true because he might, he thought he *might* know, "but I know what happened."

"Really? Tell."

"Tunnels," said Fool. "Whoever it is, they're making tunnels."

"And what might that mean, Fool?"

"I don't know, not yet. Let me think. I'll be in touch soon."

Later, after saying good-bye to Marianne and waiting until his skin had sealed itself again, Fool opened his eyes on his room. Blinking gave him some kind of focus, albeit a brittle and fragile one that showed him Summer and Gordie watching him with almost identical looks of concern on their faces.

"I'm fine," he said, and wondered if he was, really. No, he thought, he wasn't, not at all. He was tired, the kind of tired that seemed to be pulling him in different directions all at once, making his vision double and clash and his body ache and the pains magnify into sharp and stabbing things, but that was usual, wasn't it? He might be in Heaven but he was a thing of Hell, and pain was his birthright and his burden.

And yet, he still had work to do. What he had learned from the Man and from Marianne was a step onward, a new piece of a pattern he still had no real idea about, and now he had to start trying to piece it together, or at least, to make the pieces seem less jumbled.

Fool used the feather and began to write on the walls. Their plain white openness invited it, he thought as he made the first mark. Besides, he had to work this out, Heaven had instructed him to, and this was how he worked. *I'm writing on Heaven's walls,* he thought. *If I wasn't damned before, I fucking well am now.*

He didn't care. For the first time since the canisters with their gaudy orange ribbons had started dropping from the tubes carrying details of fires in Hell, Fool felt he had seen a break in the flatness, had a sense that he might have found a start of the trail that led back from the flames and blood to the creatures that were causing it all.

Carefully, he wrote his notes on the wall, speaking them aloud to Summer and Gordie, writing down the things they chipped in alongside his own thoughts. Ink dripped in rivulets from the words like tears, forming long streaks on the white walls like wounds. Then all three of them linked various words with arrows, each using the feather but always giving it back to Fool after they had finished, trying to re-create the information board Fool had in his room in Hell, trying to create a logical structure from the mess of thoughts and facts. They added in the slaughters, wrote what they knew about them, made their links, and then stopped.

"It's like a maze," said Gordie after a few seconds of peering at the information before them. "There's a path here, there has to be, but we're lost in the middle of it rather than seeing from above."

"No, not a maze," said Summer, "a storm. It's like everything's been thrown at us at once and we have to try to dodge most of it and work out which bits are needed and which bits are just damage and rubbish."

"None of it's rubbish," said Fool. "That's the point. The picture is drawn from everything, even the things we look at and then decide aren't part of the picture. We still have the information, we still have the rumor or the fact or the question, it's there but we choose not to include it. We can always go back, look at it again, sift it out and see if it fits the new picture we make, add it later."

"But now it's just chaos, all wind and spray and nothing we can see," said Gordie, and he sounded *just* as Fool had remembered him when things went like this, like a child disappointed with reality, unhappy that it had let him down. He saw Summer take Gordie's hand again and smile. Gordie saw the smile, returned it, and then leaned over to kiss Summer on the cheek. She, in turn, twisted so that his lips met hers and they kissed again properly. When they broke apart Gordie said, quietly, "It's nice to be able to do that without worrying."

Without worrying, thought Fool. *That's it, isn't it? That's the difference, really. Here, you can act without so much worry, without so much fear. There's judgment, yes, but it's distant and kinder, less random.* He wondered what Summer and Gordie would make of the thing Hell had become, and how it would be when they got back; he had told them about some of the changes but had not gone into detail, wanting them to focus on the investigation and not wanting to flood them with new information. *They'll find out soon enough,* he thought. *We all will.*

He turned his attention back to the information-painted wall. As he looked at what they'd written, Fool kept thinking about the thing that repeated, that kept coming up, a word that emerged again and again.

Dancers.

At least two people had described the murderers in Hell as "dancing," and he'd thought about the way the thing that attacked him in that choked valley had moved oddly. It had wavered and twitched as it ran, pitching one way and then another, its arms and legs continually jerking and twisting. Had it not attacked him, had he simply been watching it, might he have thought that its gait was less of a run and more of a spastic gambol?

Might he have thought it was almost dancing?

Yes, *yes*, because its rhythms had been as though it was responding to pulses, to some beat that only it could hear. Fool hadn't seen the things that attacked the workers in the Seamstress House, or the things that Marianne reported that people were talking about, but he had seen his own assailant, and the similarities, vague though they were, were clearly present.

Very carefully, he wrote the word "Heaven" on a blank space on the wall and studied it for a minute. What else? Then, equally carefully in the gap between their massed information and "Heaven," he wrote "tunnels." Finally, with slow deliberation, he drew a long line between the map of the incidents in Hell he was creating and the word "tunnels" and then on to the word "Heaven." There it was, there was the connection, it was finally revealing itself to him, fragment by fragment. There was where everything linked.

The dancers. The dancers were attacking both Heaven and Hell.

17

Fool expected to have a conversation with Mr. Tap after he sent Summer and Gordie to bed with instructions to rest, but the demon did not contact him that night. *It's probably busy,* Fool thought, *taking over the Information Office and sending its squat, ugly troops out across Hell to disappear people and demonkind alike.* How many had gone now? he wondered. How many shadows had swirled and merged, formed themselves into bauta, reached out and pulled someone back? And for what idiot crimes?

And what could he do?

Nothing. *I'm helpless,* he thought, *helpless little Fool, sitting here in his third night in Heaven and worrying about his Information Men.*

But that wasn't right, not really. Fool wasn't worrying about simply his Information Men, he was worrying about everyone in Hell and, despite the hubris it meant he was showing, about Hell itself. Mr. Tap, tall and warped and toothy, was somehow growing at Hell's heart. Its Evidence Men, little demons or ghosts or whatever the fuck they were, were creeping everywhere, were disappearing not just people but demons, were creating a new strain of fear. Before, Hell had been rumors and aggression and the hopeless feeling of lives worth nothing, but now? Now it was almost worse, it was accusation and punishment without justice, it was a binding of rules that were now applied so tightly you couldn't breathe, it was the fear of the very shadows themselves, that they might reach out and steal you away. *And we welcomed it,* he thought. *We thought it would mean Hell got better for us when the number of Information Officers went up, when there was more law, more order. We wanted it because we had the hope that things would improve, and now? Our hopes have been used against us to make us feel worse. Again. I wonder, are there people in Hell talking about how it used to be, saying that it used to be better?*

Yes, there are. I've not heard them, but they're there, they have to be because we're always looking, always wanting. We're damned whichever way we look, forward or backward. We're the Sorrowful, and we get taken or eaten or disappeared whenever something wants us. I thought I was making a change, but I'm not, not really. If anything, I've helped it get worse.

And why not let it? Why not simply keep his head down, keep himself and those few he cared about safe, and let it happen?

Because it's not theirs, the thought came immediately. *They weren't there in the fire and the riots, they have no right to come in late and take over.*

"Listen to me," he said aloud, "worrying about Hell, sitting in Heaven and worrying about Hell. Damned again, Fool, damned for a fool if nothing else. Hell is theirs, not yours." And even as he said it, he knew he didn't accept his own argument.

The problem was, What could he do? And the answer seemed to be: very little. All he had were thoughts and suspicions, fires and the slaughters forming a pattern that he could see but seemed to be the surface edge of something much deeper, but what thing was it? And why did the fires and the slaughters feel like they were something new, something dangerous, more dangerous than the usual crimes and violence? He didn't know, he just knew that this new Fool, the one that was still emerging, still being created, could see things differently, could see angles and segments that the old Fool would have missed, and in the seeing they became his responsibility.

If he could go all the way back to when he had held an angel's feather for the first time and it had sharpened him and allowed him to see that the corpse he found floating in the waters of Solomon Lake was so different from the countless bodies that came before it; go all the way back before he became this new thing, before he started down the path of murdered Genevieves and farmhands that would lead to him becoming the Commander of the Information Office of Hell and do something different, would he? Would he stay as he had been, head down and unnoticed and small?

No.

No, this was him now, and he couldn't imagine being any other way. If the price he had to pay for this sharpened vision was worry, was a more accurate sense of Hell and how it worked and his space and his insignificance within it, then so be it. This was his life now, and he had little choice but to do his best with it.

And the dancers? They danced in his mind, capering around claws and tunnels and dead Sorrowful and dead Joyful, and there was something there, something about, but he was too tired, too confused, and he let them dance away, knowing they'd dance back soon, knowing he couldn't escape them for long. And then, despite it all, despite the pain and the worry and the stress and the thoughts that whirled spindizzy in his mind, or maybe because of it all, Fool lay back on his bed and lost himself in the collapse of clean white sheets.

He slept well and dreamlessly, and woke to find food and hot coffee on his desk standing next to a bowl and a pitcher of steaming water. Although Fool's hunger had again receded, he forced himself to eat and drink, chewing carefully and slowly so as not to tear his healing cheek, filling his belly, and then washed himself with the water. There was a bar of soap by the bowl and he spread its lather across his skin and head, enjoying the scent and the feel of it. The heat of the water eased the itch that nestled under the tattoos and having clean hair felt good, so clean it squeaked when he ran his fingers through it. He couldn't remember the last time he'd ever felt this free of dirt; maybe he never had, not really. In Hell there was always a thin scurf of grime over everything, and even the water they used to wash with felt contaminated, dirty.

Sleeping, eating, and washing had eased some of Fool's aches, and dressing was easier than it had been the previous days. He sat on the bed to pull his boots on, enjoying the way the mattress gave under him, enjoying its softness. *Don't get comfortable, little soft Fool,* he reminded himself. *You're going back soon, and then you'll have to deal with Mr. Tap and Rhakshasas and the rest of Hell's terrors. You don't belong in Heaven, you're as alien and warped here as Wambwark or Catarinch, and this isn't your home.*

Strapping his gun on, then tying the holster against his leg, Fool wondered again about who was attacking both Heaven and Hell. There was a pattern, a structure beginning to be glimpsed among the fragments he and Marianne and Summer and Gordie had gathered and set out, but it was still so unclear and there was so much that didn't fit. Why fires in Hell but the theft of the Joyful from Heaven? Where did the slaughters in Hell fit?

Where did Mayall fit? What was he, orchestrator or observer or something less or something more?

Fool moved the bowl and pitcher from the desk, placing them carefully on the floor; even though they were plain porcelain, they felt delicate and old and precious and he didn't want to damage them. Sitting at the desk, he took one of the pieces of thick paper, dipped the end of the feather in the ink again, and wrote his second report. As before, he was honest but did not include everything; he left out the Man's information, presenting the idea of linked attacks on the two places as a thought based simply on a similarity of the crime scenes and the odd movement of the attackers. He formally requested that Summer and Gordie be included as official members of the Delegation, that they be seen as his equal colleagues. He also requested that they be armed, but had little confidence that this request would be granted. Finally, he dipped the end of the feather in the ink again and placed it on the parchment. Without thinking, letting his hand move without seeming to connect to his brain, he wrote in large letters, *THESE WERE NO ACCIDENTS*. He had just placed the rolled report up the tube in the corner of the room, when there was a knock on the door and Catarinch called, "Fool, come. You are needed."

18

The walk to the Delegation's meeting took them along the corridor with its pictures of the Estedea again, and Fool found himself looking at the turned figures as he went past them. Each one seemed to absorb light not only from the scenes around them but from the corridor itself, glowering in its own patch of darkness. Fool had the sense that each of the Estedea was tense, that under the shapeless robes were angelic bodies ready for movement.

Were the figures closer, taking up more space in the pictures?

Fool stopped, trying to remember. The day before, or whenever it was that he'd last looked at the paintings, the Estedea had been framed by images of Heaven's rolling fields and forests and hills, a thick collar of pleasantry around the cowled shoulders and heads, but now that scenery felt more cramped, reduced, compressed into ragged strips. Surely paintings couldn't change, painted figures couldn't back toward the viewer?

Could they?

Of course they can, silly Fool, Fool thought. *This is Heaven, anything can happen here.* He walked on down the corridor and tried not to imagine that, behind him, the Estedea were silently approaching, coming after him.

Fool could tell there was trouble as he came into the room. The angels of Heaven's Delegation were standing on the other side of the table, their stance formal. The lead angel, whose name Fool still did not know, held out a scroll to Catarinch, who took it without comment. There was a long pause in which no one moved or spoke and then, finally, Catarinch glanced down at the rolled parchment in his clawed hand, and the string tying it into a tight tube burst into greasy flames that sputtered and died as the scroll unfurled. It was a parlor trick, the kind of thing demons did to make themselves appear impressive. The angels did not look impressed.

"This is a formal complaint," said the angel. "Your scribe has extended the remit of his Delegation. We wish to have it on record that this is unacceptable, and may affect our ability to bring these discussions to a satisfactory conclusion."

"Where is the scribe?" asked Catarinch. "Bring it to us."

"It's dead," said Fool.

"Dead?" repeated Catarinch. Wambwark grumbled something, low and throaty, and Catarinch said, "Dead how?"

"It was killed by an angel," said one of the angels of the Delegation. "It was a just punishment for its transgressions."

"How dare you!" said Catarinch, its voice growing louder. "How dare you harm one of Hell's Delegation? There will be repercussions, you sinless bastards!"

"No," said the head angel, his voice still calm. "By the terms of the treaty, we can act to protect our sovereignty. Once it stepped out into Heaven, your scribe was stepping out past the terms of this Delegation and past the boundaries set out in the agreements reached over eons between our two kingdoms."

"It was Hell's," hissed Catarinch, and its rotten frame shook with fury, the stains on its coat and trousers glinting wetly in the light. Wambwark seemed to be swelling, the writhing mass of bugs churning angrily, cloak and hat dropped to free itself for movement. Once again, parts of it were falling to the floor and wriggling out, a growing mass of them. The angels began to separate, wings expanding, arms starting to come away from their sides, and Fool could almost see the lines of fire begin to snake from their hands. Things were escalating, tensions mounting, falling apart.

Fool remembered something Mayall had said, and suddenly he understood. *Ask the Delegation,* he had said. But why, unless they knew something? Why ask? Because the scribe hadn't been involved in the things Fool had been investigating; no, the scribe had been carrying out its own investigation, but not of its own accord.

"You set it to spy on me," said Fool to Catarinch and Wambwark both. "You didn't trust the human, you didn't trust the Bureaucracy or their equivalents in Heaven. I wonder, before you start this fight, have you thought how you'll explain this to Rhakshasas or Mr. Tap? I assume you did this with their permission?" Of course they hadn't, the answer was in Catarinch's sudden deflation, shoulders drawing in, and in Wambwark's low sound of confusion.

"You acted without the permission or knowledge of your elders?" asked the angel.

"I acted as head of Hell's Delegation in Heaven," said Catarinch, and even Fool could hear the fear in its voice. It was a little demon out of its depth, overstepping marks it didn't even know existed, and suddenly realizing it was as vulnerable as any human in Hell had ever been. Nothing and no one was safe, that was the point. For a long, drawn-out stretch of time the room was silent as various courses of action and outcomes were assessed, Fool could *feel* them unspooling around him, being considered and dismissed. The calculation reached a peak and suddenly the angel smiled and sat.

"An unwise move, but understandable," he said, his voice friendly but oddly hard. "Still, it can remain here and go no further. A reasonable explanation can be found, I am sure, once we have these negotiations suitably concluded."

"Yes," said Catarinch, its voice small. The demon sat as well, followed a moment later by Wambwark. Neither spoke as the angel began outlining a series of modifications to the agreements reached so far. *Poor demon*, thought Fool, *you have to accept them or explain where the scribe went, but then you have to tell the Bureaucracy why you didn't get the concessions or agreements they wanted. You're fucked.*

Tuning out the discussions now that the tension in the room was dropping, Fool went and stood in his usual place by the window. After a few seconds, Benjamin joined him and the two of them looked silently out at a landscape that was now a rambling village, the houses small and wooden. The Joyful were walking along its streets or standing in front of the houses, some seated on benches in front of the houses. In a small park, more of the Joyful seemed to be playing some kind of game that consisted of forming a huge ring and moving around and around. Behind Fool, Catarinch and Wambwark and the angels argued back and forth about minor boundary infractions in places Fool had never heard of, but Catarinch conceded almost every point after a few listless comments and Wambwark simply growled in a low punctuation.

There was a black speck in Heaven's perfect sky.

The speck grew rapidly as Fool watched, resolving itself into an irregular, shifting mass that approached the building at speed. It flew in over the village, its shadow moving in a long streak over the ground below, although none of the Joyful looked up at it. Fool glanced to his side and saw that Benjamin was looking at the shape, still smiling but with a quizzical look playing across his perfect face. As the shape came closer Fool expected it to become clearer, but it did not; instead, it continued to blur and collapse and re-create itself, one moment a sphere and the next an elongated cloud like the breath of the fires he had investigated in Hell. The only constant was its movement, an inexorable approach.

Beside Fool, Benjamin breathed out a word that Fool did not catch.

The shape reached the building and flattened itself against the room's windows, revealing itself to be not one thing but thousands. A swarm of pitch-black bees.

The creatures crawled across the panes, blocking the light so that the room became a thing of fractured, brittle shadows. The angels and demons at the table stopped talking and looked at the windows, at the bees.

"What's this?" asked Catarinch.

"A message," said the senior angel, the one who talked the most.

"A message? For whom? From whom?"

"Be quiet, demon," said Benjamin. The bees were crawling over most of the glass now, blotting out the light and filling the view with a bristling blackness.

"How can this be a message?" asked Fool.

"This is sometimes how he talks," said Benjamin.

"Who?"

"Mayall," said Benjamin, and then the bees spoke, the voice coming from all of them at once, metallic and bitter and loud, and it spoke Fool's name.

"Thomas Fool. We have need of you."

"Need of me? Where? I don't understand," said Fool.

"Fool is ours," said Catarinch loudly, to an accompanying rumble from Wambwark. "He is not yours to take whenever you want. He is Hell's."

"Thomas Fool is more important to us than he is to you," said the bees. "You are but a bad dream, without value. Fool is useful. Fool, you are needed at the Sleepers' Cave."

"I don't know where that is," said Fool, ignoring the furious splutterings of Catarinch.

"We can take you," said Benjamin. The bees had started to lift away from the windows, letting the light filter back in. For a moment, the room's walls were covered in heaving shadows, fat bodies and segmented legs cast large across the surfaces, and then the cloud of them was gone.

"You will not go," said Catarinch as Fool turned. Wambwark stood, stepped in front of Fool, blocking his passage to the door. Benjamin made to step in front of Fool but Fool stopped him.

"Wambwark, I have business here, business that my involvement in Hell has agreed to. Get out of my way."

"We have received no such instruction about help you may provide," said Catarinch, also standing and coming around the table. The demon's rotten flesh dripped and spattered, and Fool saw that it had left a series of long, oily smears on the seat when it stood. Bugs began to wriggle and fall from Wambwark again, the surface of the demon becoming a moving, constant fleshy wave.

"If the Bureaucracy has chosen not to inform you of its decisions, just like you don't inform them of yours, that's no concern of mine," said Fool. "Get out of my way."

"No." So, it came to this, the powers of Heaven and the representatives of Hell pulling in two directions again, and Fool himself now the stretching point in the center of them. *It's a question of loyalty*, he thought, *a question of who needs me the most.*

"Catarinch, this is work agreed to by Mr. Tap and Rhakshasas," said Fool, trying one last time to avoid the conflict he knew was inevitable.

Not exactly true, but one lie in the center of all this anger and death hardly mattered, did it? "I serve no purpose here in the meetings, but out there I can be useful."

"Why should we care about being useful to Heaven? We have a job to do here, and your job is solely to assist in that. You are Hell's man, Fool, nothing more or less."

"As are you, yet you chose to act without reference to those above," reminded Fool. "Ask Rhakshasas when we get back, or explain to him your refusal to let me go if you like. You can tell him at the same time as you tell him why you didn't achieve what you were told to in these discussions.

"My doing this puts Heaven in Hell's debt, a debt that might soften the disappointment of whatever agreements you eventually reach here."

Catarinch was silent. Fool could see the thoughts churning in that rotten skull, the need to show its authority set against the chance that it might anger demons older and more powerful than itself. The struggle danced for a few seconds and then, with a wave of a hand that was little more than leathery skin and exposed bone, it stepped aside and gestured Fool onward. Wambwark, after another moment, moved out of the way as well.

"My apologies for interrupting your discussions, but we should go," said Benjamin to the room. "Thomas Fool, please, I should escort you now. Mayall would send the bees only if what he wanted was urgent."

"That's fine," said Fool, "we're done." The two of them started for the door.

As they passed the table, Catarinch suddenly leaned forward and gripped Fool's upper arm. Its foul head came close to Fool's and lips that flapped and sprayed spittle brushed against his ear.

"Be careful, Fool," the demon hissed, the stench of it washing across Fool's face and making him gag. "You are not always going to be protected." Another rumble from Wambwark that might have been laughter, and then the two demons sat back at the table, and as Fool left the room he heard the meeting start up again.

Israfil was waiting for them outside the building, her flames pale in the light. She looked at Fool angrily as they emerged, then at Benjamin, who merely said, "Mayall requested him."

"Why?"

"I don't know, Israfil. He does not explain himself to me, or to you. Now, we should leave."

"Where are we going?"

"The Sleepers' Cave."

"What's the Sleepers' Cave?" asked Fool, seeing the expression of surprise and something else, something closer to fury, pass across Israfil's face.

"It is Heaven's holiest of places, and nowhere that you should be allowed entry to," said Israfil, her eyes becoming globes of pure red in a face that was wreathed in smokeless flame. "It is a place for the saved and those who serve them, and this does not, by my reckoning, include you, monkey."

"Nonetheless," said Benjamin, "that is where we go, and we take Thomas Fool with us. His companions will meet us there."

"Companions?" asked Fool, before realizing: Summer and Gordie.

"God's mercy, Benjamin," said Israfil. "Are we to allow hordes of monkeys, of the damned, into the caves? Are we to allow Hell itself to take root there, to corrupt it? It is where the sleepers are, Benjamin, the *sleepers*. Are we to disrupt their sleep?"

"If we are being sent there, then that's where we go," said Benjamin, resolute and calm. "Have faith, Israfil."

"You still haven't told me what the Sleepers' Cave is," reminded Fool.

"True. Well, Thomas Fool, the Sleepers' Cave is where the Joyful go to die."

There were thousands upon thousands of them.

The Joyful were motionless, lying on cots that had been placed into niches carved in the cave's walls. The cave itself was vast, a honeycomb of walls and tunnels, each itself honeycombed by the sleepers' spaces, lit by myriad globes of light mounted on sconces, and fixed at regular intervals along the walls. The niches had been carved into the stone in rows and columns so that the Joyful were lying alongside and on top of each other in ranks, all of them covered in thin blankets.

The cave was warm, and smaller caretaker angels walked its shadowed lengths constantly checking on their sleeping charges. Sometimes, the angels beat their wings to rise up the columns, stopping at this niche or that and checking the inhabitant before rising on or drifting back down.

The bee swarm had been waiting for Fool and the angels outside the cave's entrance along with Summer and Gordie, both of them looking into the impossibly blue and clean sky, heads tilted back so that their faces caught the sun. They were still holding hands, Fool saw, their fingers intertwined, anchored to each other.

"You'll grow into each other and never be able to separate," he said, smiling, when he saw the linked hands.

"Can't imagine anything better," said Gordie, grinning.

"Good," said Summer, and her voice was fierce. "We've been separated once but I won't let it happen again."

"Wonderful," said Israfil as they walked into the vast opening of the cave system. "Two more monkeys, monkeys in love with each other. They are not raised up, Benjamin. Whatever is happening, it is our business. I say again, this is Heaven, we do not need them or any help from the residents of Hell. They should not be here, Benjamin, we are enough authority."

"Mayall doesn't think so," replied Benjamin. "The Malakim don't think so. Whatever we think, we are bound by their wishes, Israfil. You know that. Complain to them if you feel strongly enough."

Israfil didn't reply but Fool recognized her body language, the way her fires suddenly pulled in and she made herself somehow smaller; like Catarinch, she was unsure of her place, he realized, and that made her uncertain. Her bluster and anger were not strong enough to stand against the thought of challenging the voice that came from lips formed from shadows or the mysterious Mayall. *There are hierarchies even here,* he thought, *even in the place of perfection there are those who are more powerful,* more *perfect. Patterns, repeated everywhere, little Fool, patterns if only you could see them.*

Fool looked at her, at the red glow of her flames, the sullen anger that coruscated across her flesh as fire, the look of disdain on her face as she stared at him and Summer and Gordie, and wondered, Was this how the original Fallings had started? An anger that had nowhere to earth itself, resolved itself into violence that was argued away as good, appropriate, that had a greater purpose? Israfil had a little power, a little authority, but around her things were happening that she could not control, could not understand or even acknowledge. Had she gone further than her position allowed? Was she the one?

Was it Israfil? Israfil, murdering the Joyful for some reason he had no concept of, becoming a Fallen before the Fall?

It could be, Fool supposed, but it didn't make sense, not really. If it was Israfil, why the curious setups of the deaths, why the tracks and the broken windows, why the complex schemes? Just to throw observers off track? It seemed overly elaborate, unwieldy in its execution when simpler methods would surely have presented themselves. And how did the dancers fit, and the attacks in Hell? Could it really all be Israfil, lashing out against a Heaven that had altered in ways she could not acccpt, fighting against things whose outlines she could not grasp?

The bees dipped and swung above them, agitated, communicating without speech that they needed to move. A single bee dropped from the group and landed lightly on his shoulder; he could feel the tiny whisper of its wings blow across his injured cheek, hear the near-silent buzz of it. A voice made of buzzes and metallic clicks but so quiet he was sure only he could hear it said, "Come, please," and then the bee rose and rejoined its companions. Fool nodded at the swarm, moved across the cavern, and Summer and Gordie and the two angels, after a moment, followed him.

As they crossed the space, Fool began to appreciate just how truly massive the place they'd come to was and how many sleeping Joyful it contained. Countless tunnels opened up from the atrium, and in the gentle light Fool saw row after row of the spaces carved into the rock and motionless people in the shadows. Apart from the caretaker angels, nothing moved and the only sound was that which Fool and the others made themselves.

The bees flew along at head height, leading them through the labyrinthine structure, buzzing somnolently ahead of them as they hurried along, waiting with an air of impatience whenever their followers didn't keep up. As they walked, the party passed the sleeping Joyful, recumbent and still. Some of the humans moved their mouths in their rest, and close to, their voices were wordless rustles like leaves of falling paper brushing together. It accentuated the silence rather than breaking it, and was strangely pleasant.

"I don't understand," said Fool as they walked. "I mean, I understand that the Joyful can die from accident or murder, that happens to the humans in Hell, but what's happening to these people?"

"Their time in Heaven is over," said Benjamin. "They've been here long enough, and they grow tired. Eventually they let go of the Heaven in their minds, their dreams, and embrace joys that are less defined, less easy to hold. For some it happens quickly, for others more slowly, but it happens to all of them eventually. They fall asleep, more deeply asleep, and are brought to the cave. We tend to them until eventually they let go completely."

"And then what?" No one in Hell died naturally; even the old man Fool had held as the life fled his body had done so as a result of fear, and he had no frame of reference for what Benjamin was telling him. Simply letting go? Falling asleep and drifting off, tended by angels? It sounded like a dream, like something that people in Hell hoped for knowing it would be impossible to ever attain.

It sounded wonderful.

"I don't know," said Benjamin simply. "That part of the plan is not for me to see. We minister to this part of these people's journeys and no more. Where they go from here is their business; theirs and God's."

Fool couldn't help but stop and look at the Joyful, despite the urgent buzzing from the insects above him. They were all old, lined, and pale. Their skin seemed thin, almost translucent, as though he might see their blood moving beneath its surface. Were they fading, he wondered, their flesh slowly vanishing as they let slip the grip on the Heavens they inhabited? Would they simply vanish, the life slipping from them and leaving a thin skin like a deflated bubble, the imprint of a person no longer there? And then? Was there a Heavenly version of Limbo the skin would return to until it was fished out and used to house another new soul? It was too big, too complicated for his head to hold, and he had to turn away, to look at Summer and Gordie and his own feet, at smaller things, things he understood or, at least, almost understood. Looking at the Joyful made him think of freedom and pleasure, of peace and stillness, of *joy*, and the thought of those things he would never truly have hurt him in ways he couldn't articulate; he only knew it *hurt*.

Fool started walking again, away from things beyond his grasp, focusing on putting one foot in front of the other and moving toward the thing ahead of him, toward the simpler mysteries of what he assumed would be another crime, toward something he could grasp and perhaps understand and maybe solve. Toward something he could give shape to.

Ahead of them, one of the caretaker angels leaned into one of the sleepers, brushing the hair from her face gently, and then kissed her. The angel's lips drifted against the sleeper's forehead and then it opened its mouth, the lips swelling and clamping onto the skin. The angel's jaw stretched, the bottom of its face writhing momentarily as the lips flexed against the sleeper's head, and then spread out and swallowed the whole face. The angel's neck worked, swallowing, its wings stretching out from its back and shivering slightly, feathers rattling, and then it detached.

The angel's face contracted back, the lips rippling and smoothing, the cheeks ballooning in until it was back to its smoother, more usual perfect visage, and then it walked away. Several beds along, it stopped and did the same thing, its face elongating as it leaned over the sleeping woman on the bed. When it had finished, it backed away and licked its lips. The angel had seemed insectile as it leaned over the Joyful, parasitic, something alien and dangerous like the demons that prowled the Houska in Hell's brutal evenings. He realized his hand had dropped to the butt of his gun, and he forced himself to relax, to let it go, to let his hand fall back to his side. What would he shoot at? *I'm out of my depth, as ever*, he thought, *and getting deeper.*

They walked on.

The bees swept along the caves, threading through the air ahead of them, a shifting cloud caught by the light from the lamps; at once a single mass and a thousand individual pieces moving around each other. Fool and the others followed, and as they did so they passed more of the silent angels moving slowly among the Joyful. Mostly they tended the sleepers, rearranging the bedding or wiping foreheads, repositioning them to make them more comfortable, but sometimes they fed off them like beautiful parasites. After a while, Fool had to stop watching.

In one gallery, the roof was covered in the smallest, blackest angels, clinging to spars with their toes, dangling with their eyes closed and their arms folded across their smooth, pudgy chests, wings neatly lined along their backs.

Still the bees led them on. The ground they walked along wasn't sloping down, so at first Fool assumed that the space was hollowed out into the rock behind the cliff, stretching back into the solid earth, but then he realized that this was Heaven, where the landscape seemed able to shift at will. Maybe they were actually deep in the earth moving down or padding happily through the sky. Maybe they were upside down and inside out and backward and forward all at once.

Eventually, they came to an open space, the walls of the cave tunnel falling away to either side to form a huge, roughly circular room. The bees circled up, losing themselves in the darkness above Fool and the angels, their buzzing fading to a distant drone before vanishing altogether. The room smelled of something rich and metallic and there was a different sound here, the distant drip of liquid hitting rock.

"Why has the clown angel brought us here?" asked Israfil, walking out into the center of the space, her flames growing larger again as she became more irritated. Fool didn't reply; in her expanding light, he could already see what the bees had led them to, what Mayall had wanted them to find.

One of the Joyful on the far side of the space was hanging from its alcove, head down, upside down and arms swinging out so that its upper body formed a pale cross against the rock. It was a man, his chest scrawny and covered in dark hair like the moss one of Hell's old trees, the shape of it also cruciform as if in a parody of the position of his body. The sheet covering the man's bottom half had tangled around his legs, shroudlike and pale in the shadows of the niche, and his shoulders were covered in scratches that were still bleeding. Blood dribbled down the wall below him, was dripping onto the sleeper below.

"Another accident?" Fool called as he walked over to the man. Neither Israfil nor Benjamin replied.

Close up, he knew he was too late. One of the scratches started at the man's nipple, ran up to the man's shoulder, and then curved into the side of his neck, exposing the meat of the man. In the depths of the slash, an open artery winked at Fool, and a spray of blood curled around the wall of the alcove. The bed below the man was soaked in blood, glinting and wet in the light from the wall lamps. The smell of it was rich, like metal heated over a cooking fire. He knelt, putting his face close to the dead man, trying to see everything at once.

Look, Fool thought, *really* look. *What's happened here, what's the* story? *What's this poor bastard's body telling me? I haven't got Morgan or Hand or Tidyman to question this dead flesh, so I'll have to do it myself.*

Footsteps from behind Fool, two sets in rhythm with each other. Gordie leaned over Fool's shoulder, his face furrowed in concentration. Summer came to the other side of him and also knelt, her leg brushing against Fool's, and even now he marveled at their presence, hers and Gordie's. They were here, really here, and even in the sight of death, Fool took a moment to enjoy their return. He was not, he remembered, totally alone.

"I think . . ." said Gordie, and then let his voice trail away. He held out both hands, fingers spread, over the slashes in the man's chest. Although the injuries were wider apart than Gordie's fingertips, their spacing was similar, and when he mimed pulling on the man, the shape his fingers traced in the air ran back along similar lines to the wounds. He looked at Fool, the question half answered in his frown.

"Yes," said Fool. "Someone grabbed him but didn't have a good hold and they cut him when they tried to pull him. They had claws, I assume." Gordie nodded and went to the alcove alone, leaning in and grasping at the sleeper it contained without actually touching him. His back bumped against the roof of the space and it was quickly clear he couldn't get his arm around the person without a struggle, leaning on the mattress on either side of him.

"That hurt," he said when he emerged. "I'm not that big, so I think we can assume that whatever killed this man was trying to pull him from the alcove but was struggling to get him out."

"I agree," said Summer. She rose and looked around. "Why this man? Why him and not the others?"

Fool looked around. The dead man's bed space was at chest height, which made sense; anyone trying to remove a Joyful from his bed would presumably do so by leaning into one at the easiest height, this level or the one below if it was an average-sized man like him or Gordie. *So,* he thought, *so* . . .

The wrong things were obvious when he looked for them, an empty bed several spaces along at the same height, and then more empty ones past that, both at the same level as the dead man's bunk but also higher and lower in the wall. Fool walked to the nearest niche, watched by Israfil and Benjamin, and leaned into it. The sheet within it was twisted and spotted with blood. The one below was entirely empty apart from the mattress, held neither sheet nor person.

Empty? No. Almost hidden under the thin sheet was a black shape, small and long and thin. Fool reached out and took hold of it gingerly, half expecting it to slash up at him. It didn't react to his touch and he pulled it free. It was a claw, curved and sharp, the root of it bloodied and with a tiny tendril of dark flesh still hanging from it. A claw here, a pincer in Hell.

A claw and a pincer.

"Something or someone has stolen the Joyful," he said, turning to the angels, holding up the claw.

"Stolen?"

"I don't know what else to call it. You've said they can't wake up?"

"That's right," said Israfil, apparently forgetting the sleeper at the beach that Fool had woken, however briefly.

"These Joyful are beyond sleep, at least as you might understand it," said Benjamin. "Even if the Joyful outside might be able to be roused for a moment or two, these are different. These people are in their last days, they are simply joy and memory and flesh without intellect or will, they cannot wake."

"If they can't wake, they didn't leave of their own accord. Assuming that they weren't taken by angels, and given that I don't think angels have claws like this, then someone else took them. Someone, or something. They were taken. Stolen."

"Perhaps the spaces were empty to begin with, Fool, have you considered that? That you may be wrong in this, as you are with the other things?" asked Israfil.

"I'm not wrong," said Fool.

"You are akin to God, then? Infallible?" Israfil's light blossomed, the rage in her growing again. Fool ignored the angel and walked back to the dead man. There had been the body at the pool, a damaged thing beyond the reach of life, a similar one here. What did it mean?

That the dead were of no use to whoever was taking them?

That they needed living Joyful?

Fool heard the dripping again. Thinking it was the man's blood spilling down, he moved the sheet under the dead flesh to catch the liquid, but even after doing so, he heard the slow, steady *tap tap tap* of droplets hitting stone. He sniffed. That smell, that rich smell. He had not expected to smell it in Heaven, thought it reserved for Hell, but he had been mistaken in that thought. It filled the space, the rich and dense aroma of blood coming not from one place, not from the dead body in front of him, but from many.

"Can I have some light?" he asked, walking back toward the center of the space, suspicion growing in him, but keeping his voice calm. "To fill the whole room, brighter than it is now, I mean?"

"Why?" asked Israfil, but Fool again ignored her. She was becoming a chore, and he had no time for her. Let her be blind, let her be angry, he had work to do. There was information here, and he and Summer and Gordie needed to find it.

"Of course," said Benjamin, ever the calming diplomat. He raised a hand and the globes around the room began to brighten, exposing more of the space around them. It revealed a huge space, domed at its upper reaches, the walls curving gently around and filled with spaces to hold the sleeping, dying Joyful.

There was blood everywhere.

It seemed like hundreds of the niches had blood spilling from them, some decorated with huge red slashes that had sprayed out or up, had spattered across the faces of the walls and into the surrounding spaces, some with smaller trickles that rolled from the lips of the carved spaces. Not all the spaces were empty and many of the Joyful were still visible in their beds, some still sleeping peacefully, others twisted, tangled in ripped and stained bedding, but a significant minority of the Joyful were gone. Fool saw one or two hanging down from the gaps like the dead man, their robes and flesh torn and mangled. On the ground, crumpled at the base of the walls, were Joyful who had fallen, necks wrenched around, limbs splayed out or bent into angles that were not natural.

"Look around, fast," said Fool to Summer and Gordie. "Ignore the dead, look for things that shouldn't be here. More claws, marks, anything."

"Ignore the dead?" said Israfil, and her voice was hollow, whistled like faraway breezes.

"You see them now?" asked Fool angrily. "They're clear to you? Good, Israfil, good. Look at them, *remember* them, and then ignore them. They can't tell us anything that other poor murdered bastards haven't already told us. What we need to see now are the things that aren't right, the things that are here but shouldn't be, or aren't here that should be."

"'Aren't right,'" repeated Israfil, voice still disconnected somehow. Her angelic shoulders were slumped and the flame of her had burned low, revealing a skin that was, for the first time, the pale cream of warm alabaster. "Is anything here right?"

"Here," called Gordie, holding something up. "I've found something."

It was a scale, about two inches across and shaped like an irregular diamond, one corner, like the claw, still connected to small pieces of flesh that even as they watched curled up and dried, smoking slightly.

"What's it from?" asked Fool, immediately deferring to Gordie, who had always *known* things, had facts at the fingertips of his brain.

"I don't know," said Gordie. "It's not something I've seen before. I mean, demons sometimes have scales but this doesn't look like a demonic scale. It feels . . . odd."

Marianne said that the pincer was odd. Everything's *fucking odd,* thought Fool. Out loud, he asked, "Odd how?"

"I don't know. Let me think about it, leave it with me and I'll see if I can work it out."

"Hurry, Gordie. We haven't much time." That was true, he could feel it, things were closing in, the end was approaching, but what end? Where was this trail heading?

"Fool, what happened here?" asked Benjamin. Israfil had walked away, was making her way to the far side of the chamber, walking slowly, weaving as though drunk or stunned. A caretaker was flying slowly along the walls, stopping and hovering occasionally, appearing not to notice the blood or gaps. From the entrance behind them black angels started to emerge, their wings fluttering rapidly, making their way to the closest of the remaining dead.

"It was a slaughter," said Fool. "But the slaughter was an accident, I think, because this was worse, it was a mass stealing, I think. The ones left are just the Joyful they broke while they were trying to get them out or the ones they didn't get around to taking."

"Taking? Who took them?"

Fool looked at the claw in his hand, at the scale in Gordie's, thought about the pincer in Hell, and said, "I'm not sure. There's something happening here but it's not clear." *Outside,* he thought, and then, *outside everything, outside what we understand.*

Why outside?

One of the lights went out.

There was no sound accompanying the light going, there was simply a gap that appeared in the illumination, a dark patch at the upper reaches of the far wall. The gap moved like oil, shifting around to cover the niches, swallowing them whole. Was that something moving at the edge of the patch, darting back up the wall to the shade's far edge, disappearing into one of the Joyful's bed recesses?

There was a chittering sound.

Another light went out.

This one was lower, the circle of darkness spreading across the wall and creeping across the edge of the floor, touching the other patch of gloom at its highest edge. Another shape seemed to ripple in the shadows gathered above a slumbering person, several rows below earlier movement he thought he'd seen.

More chittering, like chitinous plates being rubbed together.

Another light gone, farther away, and this time Fool saw something at the globe just as the light vanished, a thing that might have been a tentacle or an arm reaching out to take the light in its grip and *twisting,* pulling it free and extinguishing it. The globe hit the floor with a sharp cracking sound.

Fool moved fast, going toward Israfil, his hand falling to the butt of his gun. As he approached her the angel turned to him and spoke, voice low and conversational.

"This is your fault, monkey. You brought this here."

"Oh, do fuck off, Israfil," said Fool, thinking briefly, *I wonder if Catarinch would applaud me for that?*

"Pardon?" said the angel, clearly startled.

"I told you to fuck off," said Fool, still looking at the far wall. "You're boring me and you're not helping things. Hold your peace or hold your tongue, but either way stop fucking bothering me." Was that another movement, a snake or cable or long, writhing limb connecting one bed to one above it?

A fourth light went out, the shadows spreading and pooling together in a thick black swathe that covered the far wall now. More chittering, louder, like the rubbing of a rough paper, like the clicking of beaks and the snapping of claws.

One of the caretaker angels drifted placidly to the place where the darkness now swelled. Flapping its wings, it rose in an elegant, lazy wave into the air.

Fool walked closer, still peering into the depths of the shadows, trying to see if anything was actually there. The pale shape of the angel rose into the gloom, visible as a slowly shifting blur of ivory, and then it was suddenly gone, extinguished as quickly as the lamps themselves.

"What?" said Fool aloud, breaking into a jog, lifting his gun, and then Israfil dropped in front of him, flames glaring, and grasped his wrist. The heat of her was terrible and Fool smelled burning hair, *his* hair, as a bracelet of pain wrapped his arm and he dropped his gun. It skittered across the floor, coming to rest a few feet away.

"You speak to me like that?" said Israfil.

"Israfil!" snapped Benjamin.

"Yes," said Fool. "You're getting in my way, Israfil, you're an obstacle, not a help to me. Now either help me or fuck *off*! There's something happening over on the other side of the cave."

She let go of his wrist and he pulled it back, already feeling the blisters rise and pop, wetness running down onto his hand. "What terrible thing can be happening in this place that has not already happened?"

Fool didn't answer. The other angel hadn't reappeared yet.

A fifth lamp went out. A sixth.

A seventh.

Gordie came to stand by Fool, head tilted. "Listen," he said, almost whispering.

Fool held his breath and listened, too. There was a faraway sound under the chittering, the rustle of something moving stealthily, feet crunching against grit, the leather slip of skin against wall.

An eighth light went out and now almost all of the far wall was black, the edge of the darkness creeping closer to them. The caretaker still had not reappeared.

"They're still here," said Fool.

"Israfil," said Benjamin again, "I think that perhaps Thomas Fool is correct. Perhaps we ought to assist him?"

"Never," said the burning angel, and then the shadows behind her moved and something reached out and took her in its arms and yanked her back and away.

19

Fool couldn't see the thing clearly, but he could tell that its arms were broad and muscular and seemed to have too many joints, that they ended in hands with curved, taloned fingers, and that the face beyond the arms was wrenched and warping and its eyes burned a bloody red. It clamped itself around Israfil, arms pinioning the angel's limbs and wings, and then swept back into the shadows, taking the startled angel with it.

For a stretching, fragmented second no one moved and then several things happened at once. Israfil, now being dragged rapidly toward the far side of the cave, burst into a vast sphere of flame, a beautiful angelic fireball that threw light around them in a bright, dizzying wave and drove the darkness back before fading as Benjamin rose into the air, wings emerging and flapping in one sweeping movement. Fool grabbed his gun from the floor, wincing as new pain fired in the exposed flesh of his wrist, and started to run. Another flare of light sprayed out from Israfil, and Fool had to clench his eyes against it, turning his head away and stumbling. Even through his closed eyelids the air *glowed*, blinding him. He took another couple of tentative steps, feeling with his feet to avoid obstacles, arm outstretched and gun wavering, and then Israfil screamed and the sound knocked him back, unbalanced him, and he fell.

There were no recognizable words in the sound, no expression except anger. Fool risked opening his eyes, found that Israfil was burning at a level that he could just about manage to look into, as though a sun had birthed and was now fading on the far side of the cave. What was happening? He could see little, merely a chiaroscuro of light and dark crashing together, sparks and flows battling each other in his sight.

He blinked, felt Summer take his hand and help him up, Gordie at his other side. "Keep back," he managed to say, "that's a fucking order. First chance you get, run, do you understand? Keep each other safe." His vision was returning in fractured, splintering waves, gradually resolving itself. His eyes were flowing with tears of pain, his cheeks wet as he continued blinking.

"What is it?" said Gordie.

Somewhere by the base of the wall there was a mass, black and writhing, a dark heart in the center of the angel's light, surrounding it. Consuming the light.

Israfil screamed again and her glare pulsed more violently and she rose, glowing, and tried to fly free before the blackness swelled up, reaching out and dragging her back down. A curling string of fire leaped up and circled the cave, stretching and stretching, crawling over the walls and sending snatches of smoke upward, where it scorched the flesh or bedding of the sleeping Joyful or hit the patches of still-wet blood. When it reached the roof of the cave, a curved dome lost above them, it clung to the rough rock, crackling like lightning, crawling between the ridges and juts, and then dropped away, dwindling as it fell.

More lamps were going out all around them, the shadows crowding down on Fool and his companions, swarming the struggle below.

The chittering grew, becoming as loud as Israfil's screams. Benjamin, now a blurred shape in the growing darkness, swept toward his companion, but in the confusion he came too close to the wall and something leaped from one of the niches and crashed into him, sending him spiraling away. He hit the ground heavily, rolled, and did not move. There was a great roar and then what looked like a great web emerged from dozens of niches all at once, black knots slithering out of the spaces, visible only as edges of light that caught on pincers and claws and tentacles and eyes and teeth.

Each shape was connected to the others by constantly moving strands that bisected and joined, twists of angular line that bent in sharp angles but did not curve.

"What?" Fool heard Summer say and he pushed her back, away from the thing.

"Go!" he shouted. "Both of you go, now!"

Was it one creature? It moved in all directions at once, some up, some down, some along, as though it was a hundred things, but there were the threads and the joins connecting every part of it and they never broke, never split, a living shadow flowing out of the wall and filling the far side of the cave. As it emerged, it dragged the Joyful with it, pale shapes emerging and then lost again. Parts of it were insectile, moved in ragged twitches and twists, irregular and tilted, a movement that Fool remembered from the thing he had chased and that had slashed his face.

The web of things moved down toward Israfil and the lower parts of itself, clustering together, thickening the gloom, giving it density and mass and shape, a bulging shifting thing. Israfil screamed again and her light blossomed, but less of it escaped now, the web coating her, covering her.

Swallowing her.

Fool raised his gun, but before he could fire, before he could decide what to fire *at*, there was a wet crack, loud and sullen, and another scream, torn and wretched. Benjamin snapped through the air, wings huge and swept back and gleaming like blades of ivory, and then he was sweeping down, arrowing toward the center of Israfil's now-guttering glare. A thick string of fire leaped from Benjamin's hand and crashed toward the failing gleam of his companion, hit the darkness, and burned with a sound of sizzling, scorching dampness.

Israfil was being dragged along the base of the wall of the cave, the creatures swarming her and pulling at her. No, not creatures, Fool reminded himself, still unsure where to fire; one creature, a thing of parts and segments connected by the threads and tangles, and all the pieces working as one to drag the angel away.

Fool followed, moving faster now but cautious, still unable to see properly because of the streaks that remained in his eyes, head down so that any sudden flare of light didn't dazzle what little vision he possessed away to nothing. His face ached along the lines of torn and healing skin and his heart was thundering in his chest, but he went because this was it, wasn't it? This was the job, this was a crime, *this* was the act of crime that led to the birth of information.

This, ultimately, was Fool's given purpose, as the Commander of the Information Office of Hell at work, and it didn't matter that he was in

Heaven, that the criminal was a being he'd never encountered before, that the victim was an angel. This was his job.

Behind him, he heard Summer and Gordie follow. Fool glanced over his shoulder and saw his friends running with him, no longer holding hands but still at his back, still by his side. He gestured back at them but they ignored him, keeping behind him but coming along nonetheless.

Israfil screamed again, the sound of it echoing and furious and agonizing in the cave. Her light tumbled across the cave walls, catching in pockets and illuminating those Joyful who slept on undisturbed. The glow of her was weaker now and Fool risked looking at the angel directly. She was still caught in the center of a struggling mass on the far edge of the cave, shifting inexorably along the wall, visible and then lost in the darkness and then visible again. Dark shapes moved around the angel, dragging at her and clambering over her. Benjamin sent another bolt of fire toward them, and between its light and Israfil's pulse, the attacker surrounding the struggling angel was more fully revealed.

It was made of a huge number of writhing shapes, the angles of them wrong somehow, as though they had extra limbs that they were waving as they moved. There were joints that were in the wrong places, limbs bending backward rather than forward, bending in three or four places rather than simply one, lashing the air. They moved oddly, capering even as they attacked the fallen angel, apparently unable to move in easy lines. It was as though some terrible spiderweb had come alive, huge and rippling, gathering into itself spiders and forcing them to work together in grotesque yet horribly, awfully efficient harmony.

One part of the whole turned and glared at Fool and then at Benjamin, its face a torn and bloody mess of mouth and teeth and weeping, crusted eyes. Seeing how close they were, it reached back into the mass and clasped at something, threw it up at Benjamin, the throw exposing its body to the light briefly. It was foul, a black mass made of fractured and jerking shadows and black lines that caged and punctured a body that was buckled and wrenched, skin peeling to reveal bones that showed a sickly yellow against that dark flesh. Whatever it had thrown arced up toward the flying angel above it and then fell away, white and spinning. Benjamin beat his wings and chased the falling thing, calling, "Fool! Fool, help me!"

Fool ran.

Despite their odd gait and the angel fighting them, the mass made fast progress, moving rapidly along the wall, its various parts working alongside each other in a disjointed rhythm. Fool chased it as, behind him, Benjamin howled, the sound even louder than Israfil's scream.

Some new part of the attacker broke away from Israfil, again throwing something into the air. The thrown thing jerked spastically up and out, hitting the cave wall high and slithering down, leaving a dark streak behind it. Benjamin flew to it, grasped the now-falling thing, and wailed, high and keening. A third curl of flame rippled out from him and snaked toward the part of the creature that had thrown whatever it was, but it dodged easily, leaping over the fire so that it passed harmlessly underneath. As it jumped, it flung a third thing out, and this time Fool realized what it was: a Joyful, naked, limbs flailing bonelessly. Benjamin swept toward the hurled sleeper but missed her, overshot as the still-sleeping woman reached the peak of her arc and then started falling, spinning toward the cave floor, where she landed with a deep, rich crunch.

There was an exit in the far wall of the cave and the mass had reached it now, was bunched around it, pulsing and feeding itself into the narrower space in surges. There was another cracking sound, ragged and dull, and the noise of something ripping, and then Israfil's light *bulged* at the center of the mass, sending out darts and shadows in equal measure. The angel shrieked, the clamor furious, the echoing yammers of something lost in agony, and then a white shape spun from the light. At first, Fool thought it was another Joyful, thrown to keep Benjamin busy, but it wasn't. It was a looping, graceful curve of white in the cave's darkness, and even at this distance Fool thought it looked smooth and clean except for one end, which tapered to an uneven red stump.

Israfil's wing, torn free and discarded, and then the second followed it.

The two wings landed apart, slithered across the cave floor in different directions before coming to rest, one in front of Fool and the other away to his side. Benjamin, above Fool, dropped toward the farthest wing, making a sound that Fool had not heard before, a yowling as though he had hooks in his throat that were stretching his vocal cords taut, stretching them beyond taut. The angel landed, dropped the battered Joyful he was still holding, and collapsed to his knees over the mutilated piece of Israfil. His own wings shook as they stretched away from his back, shivering violently.

Fool, still running, had little choice but to leap over the other wing, over the weeping stump and the perfect feathers that were now ruffled and torn, landing clumsily on the other side of it. The jolt of his landing sent waves of pain through his face and burned wrist and he cried out, stumbling then regaining his equilibrium. Israfil screamed again, the sound now ragged and lost and weak, the shape of her gone into the web creature now, the surges of it almost done, the bulk of it through the entrance and vanished from sight. The rearmost part of it, the part he had seen before, lingered a moment after the rest of it had vanished, throwing several more Joyful in different directions back into the cave. Benjamin, still keening, left Israfil's wing and launched himself into the air, trying to catch the hurled people. He managed to clasp the first of them to him but the rest, too far away to reach, fell like dropping clouds to the rocky ground and the sound of them hitting was like tomb doors thudding closed.

Fool chased the departing creature, reaching the exit a few seconds after the last piece of it had vanished. The tunnel that the exit gave on to was dark, the lamps, assuming there were any, were extinguished. Fool listened but could hear little over Benjamin's continual howls. "Go and tell him to be quiet," he said to Gordie, resigning himself to the fact that they weren't going to obey his instructions to leave. "Summer, you come with me."

Inside, the tunnel smelled of dirt and blood. Torn feathers were scattered across the floor, bloodied and mangled, their glow already almost nothing, little penumbras of light that were gathering in and fading even as he walked past them. He reached into his pocket, felt his own feather still safe, and pulled it out, holding it above him.

The glow revealed a long throat of stone, empty apart from more of Israfil's feathers and streaks of blood along both the walls and floor. Some of the streaks glittered and Fool thought they probably came from Israfil, the duller ones from injured Joyful. Summer tapped him on the shoulder, pointing at something without speaking. Ahead of them, just at the edge of Fool's feather's glow, was a white bundle, and Summer went to it and picked it up, holding it out to him. It was a sheet, filthy with dust and blood, from one of the Joyful's beds.

"Summer, come back here," said Fool quietly, but he was too late; the shadows behind her moved and something lunged forward and struck at her.

This time, *oh thank God oh thank fuck,* Fool was faster, lifting his gun, aiming and firing at the same time. The crash of the shot was huge in the tunnel, the sound shattering back against him, the explosion burning his eyes, illuminating the tunnel behind Summer.

The creature filled it, an interlocking mass of limbs and teeth and claws and hating eyes.

Summer dropped as the part of the thing behind her that had tried to take her jerked away, a spray of thick, viscous liquid bursting from it as the bullet tore through its flesh. It grunted, falling, and then it was on its knees and scuttling back toward her. She crabbed away, moving toward Fool, who felt the reassuring weight of the bullet formed in his gun and fired again.

This time, the bullet tore through the thing's face and exploded through the rear of its skull. Pieces of it spattered away, spraying up the tunnel wall, flesh and liquid clinging to the rough surface. The thing spun back and collapsed and the tendrils connecting it to the others pulled tight, dragged it back into the mass. Moving as one, the various parts of the creature gathered it in and carried on retreating, moving away from Fool and Summer. Deep inside it, he caught a glimpse of Israfil, still moving, flames burned to almost nothing, her beautiful face twisted in agony and fury.

"Let her go," said Fool, moving in front of Summer, gun still pointing at the creature. It shifted, drawing farther back along the tunnel. Some parts of it were clinging to the ceiling, some to the walls, all backing away and watching him carefully. Face after face peered at him from the mass. What was it? It looked like separate creatures but moved as one, although its movement was jumbled and twitching. The separate parts themselves were all different, some vaguely humanoid and others more insectile, but all were surrounded by the connecting tissues. Fool studied it as it moved back, trying to fix its details in his mind in the hope that afterward he might be able to identify it. Assuming he survived, of course.

The creature, or some part of it, snarled at Fool. He gestured with his gun, pointing it at the nearest thing he thought might be a face. There were eyes there, anyway, a mouth splitting back around the skull and filled with teeth. "Let the angel go," he said, but the thing merely snarled again. Its mass of connecting limbs twisted and rippled, surging forward and tangling together in front of the faces, forming a thick caul across the tunnel, the surface of it moving like thorned and bitter ink. Fool fired and, briefly, a hole tore open in the barrier, but it was filled quickly by more of those rapid, writhing limbs. The way it moved reminded Fool of something, although he couldn't think what it was. Something he'd seen recently, though, something constantly shifting and connecting and surging, filling spaces.

Outside, again outside.

Fool fired again, more out of frustration than the hope it would achieve anything. Again, a hole was torn in the thick skin that now filled the tunnel, and again it was filled almost instantly.

The tunnel narrowed as they moved down it, the creature shifting quickly, its makeshift shield protecting it from Fool's bullets. The ceiling was just above Fool's head now, scratching at his crown and hair. There was no light ahead of him, the illumination at his back coming from the cave but becoming fainter as he went farther from it. Behind the caul Fool could hear scuffling, the sound of claws clicking across stone, and then Israfil groaned again, low and weak like a candle about to gutter out.

I'm helpless, Fool thought, *a little helpless Fool listening as an angel is tortured.* He fired again, and again the hole his bullet created was filled within seconds by a ripple of angular, twisting strands.

"Get out of the way," said a voice from behind Fool—Benjamin, his tone low and dangerous. Fool, still holding his gun out ahead of him, still wary, moved to the side of the tunnel, flattening against the wall, hearing Summer do the same behind him.

"Thing, give the angel back," said Benjamin. The tunnel filled with a fierce, angry light as Benjamin came along it, this light the sullen red of fury. As he passed Fool he felt the angel's heat, his *rage,* felt the light wash over him and it stank, the sour tang of burning metal and distant ovens and righteous justice and loathing. The angel's hands, he saw, were dripping with blood, spots of it spattering across the floor as he walked.

"Thing," the angel said again, "let her go."

The caul shifted, the parts that created it moving, twisting more tightly around each other. It thickened, crackling as it filled the tunnel, forcing itself against the wall but still moving away from them steadily. Fool held his gun out front as the angel raised its blood-streaked hands and summoned his fire and then, suddenly, the barrier collapsed.

The pieces flopped to the floor, relaxing, and then were sharply dragged away. Benjamin launched himself forward but the tunnel's narrowness prevented him from opening his wings properly, made him slow, and the creature and the dying angel it carried managed to stay ahead of him as it burst from the tunnel's mouth and fled into Heaven's night.

20

Benjamin shrieked in anger and launched himself out of the tunnel and rose up into the sky as a dark and speeding shadow. Fool followed far below, running as fast as he could, Summer at his side, an angel's anger ringing in his ears.

They emerged onto a gently sloping area of grassland. Before them, the ground inclined away, dropping to a flat, smooth plain that reached out to surround a ramshackle building perhaps half a mile distant.

The creature carrying Israfil had already covered half the distance to the building, moving fast, visible in the moonlight as a black and flowing stain on the earth. Above them, Benjamin loosed twin bolts of flame that crashed into the ground near the creature. Despite its ungainly movement it dodged the attack with ease, moving more and more quickly, gathering itself into a thicker and smaller mass as it went. Benjamin let fly more fire but this, too, missed as the creature shifted and went around the blast as soil and grass were thrown into the air and then fell back like rain.

"Where's it going?" asked Summer.

"There," said Fool, pointing, starting to run again. Just before the building was an area that looked at first glance like a darker patch of shadow but that Fool recognized.

The creature was heading for another of the tunnels that burrowed into the ground.

Benjamin saw it as well and swooped low, flying ahead of the thing and sending his fire down to block its passage, but it again jerked sideways, never stopping, and darted around the explosion. The mass moved strangely, its edges jittering in an arrhythmic pulse. Benjamin circled as

Fool fired, knowing as he did so that the shot was pointless; the thing was too far away for him to hope to hit it. Benjamin came around in time to see another Joyful be flung from the creature, thrown behind it so that the angel had to launch himself past the creature, fires and attack forgotten, trying to save the sleeper. Fool ran for the tunnel as Benjamin crashed into the falling human, the two connecting just above the earth and then crashing into it, rolling in a spray of dirt and frustrated noises. Fool's breath was hot in his lungs, his wrist and face throbbing, chest burning, but still he ran, trying to close the gap.

As Benjamin untangled himself and rose once more into the air, the webbed creature reached the edge of the tunnel and, without hesitation, plunged over and vanished from sight. Benjamin shouted something that Fool didn't hear clearly as he reached the flat part of the ground. A low hedge ran across the ground in front of him and Fool vaulted it clumsily, falling into an uneven roll on the far side before coming up and starting to run again. At his side, Summer hurdled the hedge gracefully and landed still running, sprinting ahead of him. Benjamin came in low over the tunnel, fire curdling from him in loops that provided a guttering illumination. Beyond, darker shadows were filling the sky, the stars blotted by them.

Fool reached the lip of the tunnel just after Summer and found himself looking down into an endless thing, tapered in its depths to a tiny black point, its walls a swirling blur of colors and shimmering rainbow patterns. Benjamin shouted again and dived into the tunnel, his flame dwindling as he dropped into it, his voice fading.

"Benjamin," Fool shouted. "No!" He waited, helpless, expecting the tunnel to close as the one near the beach had done, vanishing to nothing and trapping the angel, but it did not. Instead, the tube began to grow dark, the colors in the walls fading and blackening like fires gradually slumbering to embers before being completely extinguished, the earthen sides becoming a cracked and ravaged skin. As Fool and Summer watched, Gordie arrived at their side, gasping.

"Where is it?" he managed to ask through his gasps.

"Gone," said Fool.

"Gone where?" said Gordie, peering into the now-dark tunnel.

"I don't know," said Fool.

"Isn't it obvious?" said Benjamin as he rose out of the tunnel, wings beating wearily. "It has gone home. It has returned to Hell."

The shapes in the sky were angels, hundreds of them. They flooded the plain, landing in ranks, wings beating the air raw and lifting clouds of dust that swirled and lined Fool's throat and made it dry and uncomfortable. The angels' gleam was like moonlight and it lay over the ground like gossamer, the shadows between them like threads of moving cotton.

Rising in the air above the angels, Benjamin began to bark out orders, sending some back to the cave and ordering others to surround the tunnel that descended through Heaven's earth. Still others he sent out on tasks that Fool didn't understand, to borders and places that he had never heard of.

As the angels went about their tasks, they sang, a low lament whose words Fool could not understand but whose meaning was clear enough; they were mourning Israfil. The missing angel's wings were brought from the cave onto the plain and laid down, one over another, and then more angels formed a circle around the wings and stood with their heads bowed until, eventually, the kindliest angels came and lifted the wings away to wherever their journey was bound to end.

In the chaos, Fool tried to look into the tunnel again, but there were no gaps he could slip through in the wall of angels guarding it. When Fool tried to explain that he needed to investigate, the angel he spoke to gave him the kind of brief look that Fool might give to an insect and then looked back at the tunnel's mouth, arms folded in front of it and wings bristling out to its rear.

With little else to do, Fool and the others walked to the building beyond the tunnel. The space in front of it seemed to have become a staging ground for whatever operation Benjamin was controlling. The angel would rise into the air, spinning and floating, and then descend to give out more instructions to angels who would then go back to the waiting ranks, presumably to gather troops and carry out the orders they had been given. Fool tried to get to Benjamin but was again blocked, and eventually the three Information Men found themselves leaning against the side of the building.

"What is this place?" asked Summer, looking up at the structure. It was small, only two stories tall, and its roof was sloped and incomplete; holes dotted it here and there, although in the pale light it was impossible to tell if they were the result of missing tiles or breaks in something more solid. The building was made of rough stone, carefully hewn into bricks, and its heavy wooden doors were locked and resisted Fool's experimental push.

"I think it's a chapel," said Gordie, gazing up at the building's roof. "Look, can you see the symbol?"

He pointed to one end of the roof, where a symbol was mounted on its highest point.

"I can," said Summer, "but I can't see what it is."

"It's everything," said Gordie. "It's changing, can you see?" It was, Fool saw. Like the writing in Mayall's home, the shape on the roof's edge was constantly shifting, appearing now as something that might have been a cross and then as a star before becoming a shape that might almost have been a dagger and then changing again into something unrecognizable.

"I read about it," said Gordie. "This is one of the places where all the religions meet. They used to have places like this in Hell, but there they were used for blasphemy, for corruption. Here, I suppose it's used for worship or just to . . ." He trailed off, unable to say what he thought.

"To acknowledge them," said Fool.

"Yes. We may not even be seeing the same things at the same time, it may be different for each of us depending on our background, on the people we were before we came into Hell."

They paused, looking at each other, not speaking.

"You read about it? In a book?" asked Summer finally, looking at Gordie, head tilted. "When?"

"Before," said Gordie, his voice short and tight. "Before now."

"You never cease to amaze me," said Summer lightly, reaching up to stroke the man's cheek. "We were born in Hell, we *died* in Hell, and yet you read books and you remember everything you read. How did you find books in Hell?"

"They're there, if you know where to look," replied Gordie, voice still tight. "I just looked."

"You just looked," said Fool. He had never seen books in Hell, except various volumes of the *New Information Man's Guide to the Rules and Offices of Hell* and a slim book called *Maps and Geographies*. Where had Gordie been, to find books?

Summer and Gordie carried on talking quietly and Fool moved along the wall a ways to give them a little privacy. He leaned against the stone, feeling it breathe out the warmth of the day into his back, unknotting muscles that he didn't know were tense. From where he stood, he could just see the symbol on the chapel's roof and he watched it for a few minutes, enjoying the way it changed constantly, never the same thing twice, lost in its blur and shift. What would Summer or Gordie see if they were looking at it with him now? What would Benjamin see? Or the Man? Would he see it not as a chapel but only as some kind of opportunity, something to be used and bled dry before being discarded?

What would Marianne see?

Thinking of Marianne made Fool turn and look, discreetly, at Summer and Gordie. They were standing close together, facing each other, and Gordie's head was bowed so that his forehead was resting on Summer's and they were talking quietly. Was that something he could have with Marianne? It was a dangerous thing to think, let alone hope for, but he could not help himself. *A chance,* he thought. *Just let me have a chance, that's all I ask.* Gordie and Summer started to kiss, gently, and Fool turned away again, giving them back their privacy.

Fool walked to where the shadows had caught in earth that had been recently trodden down and buckled beneath passing feet. Close to, he caught the faint whiff of corruption, a scent that grew stronger the closer he came, because they were tracks, fucking *tracks,* and how the fuck could the angels have missed them?

They weren't looking for them, he thought, following the tracks. *Because they aren't Information Men. They don't understand the unknown, they're things of absolute and absolution. You need a suspicious eye to see this, not a loving one, not one that sees everything as perfect and cannot even see the imperfect until it's thrust into your face on a wave of blood and screams.*

The trail led around the side of the chapel to its rear, where the ground was constrained by a low stone wall that created a long, trapped rectangle of grass. As Fool came around the corner he thought that the space was filled with birds, or maybe some kind of tiny angel that he had not seen before. Hundreds of small pale shapes were dancing up and down, flickering across the grass and swooping in tight circles. In the gathering night it was impossible to make out anything but the most basic of details of them, except that he could see that none of the shapes was more than a few inches across, their shapes irregular and ragged. Some seemed to be covered in lines of black or brown or etched shapes. Tattoos, he wondered, rubbing at his arms and at the designs that covered them beneath his clothes without thinking.

No, he saw as he came closer, not tattoos. Writing.

The shapes were pieces of paper, hundreds upon hundreds of pieces of paper fluttering and moving on the breeze, torn edges flapping, faces covered in writing or pictures. He reached out as one floated up past his face and managed to grasp it from the air. The paper was old, thin and worn, torn from some larger segment so that the words printed on it appeared to start and finish mid-word, "ot listen to m." Fool let the paper go and knelt, picking up another, larger piece. On this was printed, "the PRINCIPIA is just a ha-ha, go re." He let this go, too, and walked off the path, onto the grass, and immediately the ground beneath his feet was missing and he fell.

At first, he thought he'd fallen into one of the tunnels, that he would fall and fall until he either died or burst into Hell at the other end, where demons would eat his fear and leave him empty and dead, but just a moment after falling he hit a floor that gave slightly under him. The impact drove the breath from him, trapping one arm beneath him and jamming it into his ribs. His head jerked forward and struck something that felt initially soft but was hard underneath, like material wrapped around stone, and he smelled dust and something like linen or cotton left to age and rest.

It took Fool a second to move, rolling gingerly onto his back so that he could move his arm again. When he tried to reach for his gun, needles of pain ran along the limb, distorting the message between brain and hand, and he missed his grip, fingers thick and not seeming to bend properly. He reached with his other arm, the ground shifting beneath him, and rubbed at his upper arm and the lower, finally taking the damaged hand in his other and flexing the fingers back and forward carefully until he thought he had achieved some more usual level of mobility there.

Despite his expectations, nothing had attacked him. Reaching out not for his weapon but to his sides, he found walls carved into the earth. It was dry dirt that crumbled beneath his fingers, and as he leaned back more dirt spilled onto his shoulders and head. Above him, a rough square of the night showed, stars and a rich darkness framed by the blacker solidity of the walls. An angel, high, flew across the square, graceful even at this distance.

When he was sure that the wall wasn't going to collapse inward and bury him, Fool reached into his pocket and removed the feather. Its light, undimmed, showed him clearly where he was.

Fool had fallen into a grave. The hole was around six feet long, perhaps three wide, and, from what he could judge, about four feet deep. Had he landed on a coffin? He didn't think so, it didn't feel solid enough, was even now slipping beneath his buttocks, shifting him slightly. He lowered the feather, letting the light pool around his thighs and lower legs.

Books. This was a grave for books.

Fool picked up the nearest book. It was old, ancient, the pages slipping from the binding and scattering down over him like some patchwork sheet drawn up to keep his legs warm. On the worn leather cover of the book, embossed in gold, were the words *Lebor Gabála Érenn*. He put the book down, picked up another, and found this to be in a similar state. Its pages fell out to join the others and its cover was peeling, mock leather flapping back from old and damp cardboard. Printed on this were the words, barely readable, *Book of Common Worship*. When he opened the book farther, more pages drifted loose, leaving only a few leaves attached to the inner spine.

Using the wall, Fool pushed himself upright, still holding the book. His head and shoulders emerged and he found himself looking out across the space behind the chapel at almost ground level. From this angle, he could see evidence of more holes, disturbed ridges of earth, piles of soil and torn grass, and when he pulled himself free and stood up, stretching to his full height, he saw that the ground was extensively dotted with holes, was sick with them.

"Fool? Are you okay?" Gordie, coming around the chapel, Summer with him.

"I'm fine," said Fool, brushing the dirt from his arms and legs. "I fell, but it's okay."

"Fell where?" asked Gordie, coming closer.

"Into a grave for books," Fool replied and, seeing the confusion flit across both of his companions' faces, gestured at the hole beside him.

Gordie knelt on the edge of the hole and looked into its depths. "So many books," he breathed, seeing what the grave contained.

"But why bury books?" asked Fool.

"Can we get some light?" asked Summer, who had walked past the two men and started looking into the farther holes. "I can't see where I'm walking."

Fool raised his feather as high as he could and followed Summer, the feather's eldritch light allowing them to pick a delicate path between the open graves.

Gordie came with him, pointing to a grave whose inner walls had started to grow a cover of thin, scratchy grass. It was a deeper grave and its far wall had collapsed and the earth had covered the few books that remained in its depths. Here and there, a page or cover stuck up out of the dirt, but there were not many.

"It's empty," said Summer. "The one you fell in was still partly full, but not this one."

"Yes," said Fool, moving to the next one. This one, too, was empty. Fragments of torn pages blew across the ground, sometimes zephyring around their feet, sometimes colliding and dancing together before separating again.

"What fresh misery is this?" came a voice from behind them as the light picked up, fully illuminating what Fool had now come to realize was a graveyard. Turning, he watched as Benjamin came toward them walking under a phalanx of caretaker angels, a living set of lights casting their glow down on the churned earth.

"What's happened here, Thomas Fool?" asked Benjamin.

"I'm not sure, because I don't understand what this place was to begin with."

"It is where we send religious texts to their rest," said Benjamin.

"When they are old, when they can no longer serve the worshipers because their spines are cracked and their insides are falling loose, they are discarded above and come to us through the Garden of Earth and Air. We bury them with the respect due those that have provided long and faithful service to God."

"In graves?"

"This whole place is one huge grave, Thomas Fool. The chapel is built on foundations of buried texts from all the branches of the tree of faith."

"Would they ever be dug up? To move them somewhere else, or to make room for new burials?"

"No, except to carry out new interments. We gather them in the chapel, and when Mayall commands, we come and pay our respects and we bury them with the ceremony they deserve."

"Look around."

Benjamin walked under the hovering ceiling of the other angels, going silent among the graves, head bowed. His wings were folded back against him but occasionally they twitched and then stilled, as though the angel was controlling some great anger or shock.

"They are gone," Benjamin said after a few long minutes.

"Yes," said Fool. Now he could see clearly, he walked deep into the graveyard, finding more and more holes as he went. "And not recently. These holes are old, they collapsed, plants are growing in the collapsed sections."

"My God," said Benjamin, and Fool wasn't sure if it was an imprecation or a plea.

Fool went back to the grave he had fallen into and looked around it. The trail he had originally followed around the chapel led to it, and in its trodden face he found one or two of the blue flowers, crushed and dead. Had he done that in the darkness without realizing? Turning and crouching, he followed the trail with his eyes, watching as it split and split again, older parts of it leading back to the rear of the fields and the graves there.

"Holy books," he said to himself, "and the Joyful. They're being taken."

"Taken where?" asked Gordie, coming and crouching next to Fool.

"I'll bet we'll find this track leads from the graves to the tunnel opening," replied Fool. "Or it would if a thousand damned angels hadn't stepped on all of the ground around it."

"We are not the damned," said Benjamin from just behind the two men, his voice cold. "You are, Thomas Fool. You should never forget that."

"How could I?" asked Fool. "Israfil and you remind me of it often enough. I'm a monkey, a damned monkey. Wasn't that what she said?"

"And I have to wonder, was she right after all?" said Benjamin. "All this started when you and your demon brethren arrived."

"No, it started before that," said Fool. "That's why I'm here."

"We have only your word for that."

"Go and speak to the Malakim, or to Mayall, or believe what you will," said Fool, feeling the repetition in his mouth. "I don't really care. Now, if you'll please leave us alone, we have work to do."

Fool stood, Gordie doing the same, but Benjamin did not move. Instead, he placed one hand on Fool's shoulder and the other on Gordie's, the grip on Fool unyielding. Behind the angel Fool saw one of the caretakers drop out of the blanket of moving light and land behind Summer, who was watching them closely. Gordie opened his mouth, but Fool sent him a warning glance and the man closed it again without speaking.

"Benjamin, what are you doing? We need to investigate. I've been *asked* to investigate."

"There will be no more of this farce. Matters progress without you now, as they should have all along. Thomas Fool, you and your companions' presence is required."

"Where?"

"Where decisions are made, in the court of Heaven."

21

Fool was marched back around the chapel, Benjamin's grip firm on his shoulder but not painful. Summer and Gordie were allowed to walk ahead of the other angel. *If we ran now,* Fool thought, *would that fire leap from them and split us into pieces?*

Yes. Yes, I think they'd kill us.

Fool had assumed that they would find a transport in front of the chapel, waiting to take them back to the building in which the Delegation was housed, and was oddly cheered to find he was correct. The small black vehicle was idling beyond the wall on a road that had not been there when they emerged from the Sleepers' Cave, however long ago that had been. Its doors were open and it was empty. Behind it, the night was being gently split by the light of more caretaker angels, these hovering over the exit from the Sleepers' Cave. As they stopped to watch, shapes, dark and swift, were entering and leaving the cave in quick succession, moving around each other in a complicated, elegant aerial ballet. There was an urgency to their movement that Fool had not seen in Heaven before, a purpose in their arcs and dips that he could grasp even if he could not read its intent.

From the center of the cave's mouth a slower, heavier shape emerged and started into the sky. It was like a distant storm cloud, black and shifting as it rose, its edges sharp and then blurring and then making themselves again, and Fool realized it was the small, kindest angels carrying one of the dead onward. The tiny angels were clustered around the body, lifting it, moving around it. As it climbed into the sky another of them flew ponderously from the cave and started its slow journey upward. If he could have given that flesh to Morgan, or even to Tidyman or Hand, what would they find it saying? What horrors would it tell them about its last moments? Or would it lie mute on the table, its story done and told?

Where were they going? He supposed it didn't help to speculate, not now anyway.

"They're beautiful," said Summer, watching with Fool. "What are they?"

"They're the kindest angels," said Fool. "That's what I was told, anyway."

"They're the Sundô," said Gordie.

"Pardon?"

"Sundô," repeated Gordie. "The angels that carry the dead on, help them complete their journeys. Even Heaven has the dead, after all, and they need as much help as anyone else."

"'Sundô,'" said Fool. The word rolled around his mouth like oiled silk, soft and rich and gentle.

"How do you know these things?" asked Summer. "I mean, I can understand you knowing things about Hell, we lived there, but about Heaven?"

"There are Sundô in Hell," said Gordie, "haven't you see them? And you know how I know this stuff; I read books." Even in the darkness Fool could tell Gordie was smiling, and could tell that the smile was a sad one. He knew these things because of the life he'd lived before he died, before he and Summer both died.

"Are you sure?" asked Summer, her own voice balanced between disbelief and query.

"Of course," said Gordie. "Sundô: angels that move the dead on, the kindliest ones, the kindest ones. Always small and always black and always mute. Sundô."

Summer paused, still watching the retreating shape of another that had drifted out from the cave and was floating up, following its companions. "I'm glad they're not alone. At the end, I mean," she said eventually. "And we have them in Hell?"

"Yes."

"How? How are they in Hell, if they're angels?"

"Because all demons are angels that fell, or the descendants of angels that fell," said Fool.

"I'd like to see them," said Summer.

"I'll show you," said Gordie, and Fool knew the two were looking at each other, and he wondered, if they ever got back to Hell, how long those looks would be allowed to continue before the Bureaucracy took notice and moved against them.

"Enough," said Benjamin, cutting into Fool's reverie, and pushed them toward the transport. They climbed into its rear, Benjamin following them, and the four sat silently, Gordie and Summer on the rearmost seat and Benjamin next to Fool facing the other two with their backs to the front cabin. Close to, Benjamin smelled of smoke and blood and clean linen and flowers, and he glowed, the shimmer dancing in the delicate fronts of his feathers and rippling under his skin like lightning in the rain. The transport's doors closed without anyone touching them and then they were moving.

The vehicle jolted as it turned around, rolling over the uneven grass before rejoining the road, sending all its passengers besides Benjamin sliding along the seats, Gordie's and Summer's shoulders banging together. They gripped hands, as ever, sitting in silence, Summer's head down and her eyes closed and Gordie looking out of the window. Even now, the man looked fascinated, excited by what he was seeing, what he was taking in and storing.

Benjamin's light filled the compartment, dazzling Fool, and after a minute in which he had to keep his eyes squinted to half shut, he said, "Benjamin, could you please dim yourself? I'm sorry if that's rude, but I can't see and I suspect that Summer and Gordie can't either."

Benjamin shuffled in his seat, leaning forward, looming into the space, and Fool thought that he was going to attack, felt his hand drop to his gun in defense, but the angel merely folded his wings farther back, the tops of them curving over his head and casting his face into glimmering, deep-set shadow. His glow faded, leaving afterimages in Fool's vision, the angel's body becoming a pale shape in the carriage beside him.

"I apologize, Thomas Fool, Summer, and Gordie, for both my brightness and my shortness these last minutes."

"It's fine," said Fool. "I know it must have been difficult."

"Difficult? These things do not happen in Heaven, and we are, all of us, struggling to understand their meaning. It has unsettled us, which must seem strange to you who live in a place of horror and fear and pain, but this is Heaven and things here are normally good, normally perfect. Watching Israfil be taken was terrible, Thomas Fool, and it made me angry. I am not used to being angry, so please forgive me if I was unpleasant or unkind."

"You weren't," said Summer.

"Thank you," said Benjamin simply.

"You aren't used to being angry, but Israfil seemed angry all the time," said Fool, musing aloud more than anything else.

"Israfil is from different stock than me," said Benjamin, and then corrected himself. "She *was* of an order older than mine, one of the oldest. She was here during the great battle and the time of the original Falling. She was . . . protective . . . of what she believed Heaven is. Your coming here, the things we had to see accompanying you, it unsettled her and her old nature began to show."

"I'm sorry she's gone," said Summer, Fool and Gordie both adding their agreement to the statement.

"As am I," said Benjamin. "I know you and she did not agree, Thomas Fool, and that she was a beautiful thing that meant no offense."

"Yes," said Fool, noncommittal, remembering her rage and her fire and the slap she had placed on his cheek and still feeling the burned skin of his wrist. Her ire had made her careless and sloppy. Instead of seeing Heaven as it was, she had seen it through the lens of her own beliefs and experiences, and it had made her miss what was actually there and, ultimately, exposed her to the thing that came out of the darkness and made her unprepared for its attack.

Was it really the things from outside of everywhere? Had they broken in?

They rode in silence for a few minutes, the darkness outside splintered only by the starlight and the occasional distant glow of angelic activity, before Benjamin spoke again.

"We are almost at our destination. It has not been a pleasure watching you work, Thomas Fool, but I wish you all best for what comes next," the angel said and his voice was low, ended, and final. "I cannot wish you luck as there is no luck in Heaven."

"Just like there's no murder," said Fool. Benjamin looked at him curiously, peering from under his wings.

"Yes," he said finally. "Just like there's no murder. We have never had need of either."

"You still don't see?" asked Fool.

"I see the hand of the Great Beast, the Great Enemy," said Benjamin as the vehicle pulled up and stopped in front of the Anbidstow. "There is no murder, there is simply corruption and sickness that we will root out."

"How?"

"That is not for me to know," said Benjamin. "Now, we need to go."

The four of them left the vehicle and, led by an angel, went inside to where the courts of Heaven waited.

"What fucking travesty is this?" asked Catarinch.

The Delegation, without the scribe, was in the room that the previous meetings had taken place in, and the angels of Heaven's Delegation were standing on the other side of the table from them, simply watching. Mayall was sitting, cross-legged, on the table, bending and tearing at a piece of paper, showing uninterest in what was happening around him. Fool and Summer and Gordie had been led to the room by Benjamin, who now stood in his usual place by the window. When Fool had made to join him, he had been gestured to stand alongside Catarinch and Wambwark on Hell's side of the table, Gordie and Summer behind him. There were no seats.

"Travesty?" asked one of the angels, although Fool couldn't be sure which one.

"Being removed from our rooms and brought here, given no choice but to come, when no meeting is to take place."

"This is a meeting. It is taking place."

"It is not on the schedule!"

"It has been added. There is business to discuss."

"Business? More about the boundaries? We've settled that. Tomorrow—"

"Now," interrupted the angel, "we will discuss the business of Hell's attacks on Heaven. Now that we come to look, there is the business of hundreds of missing souls, of missing angels of the lower ranks, and of the angel Israfil, taken from her rightful place alongside God and dragged down to Hell."

Catarinch didn't reply. What was left of its throat worked convulsively for a few seconds before words finally emerged from it.

"We know nothing of this."

"Nonetheless, this is the business to discuss."

"Hell denies it," said Catarinch. Wambwark grumbled in support, standing straight and making itself swell slightly. The angels ignored it.

"Of course it does," replied the voice. "Hell denies all things."

Which isn't, Fool thought, *really true.* Hell had little need of denial; rather, it reveled in the truth of its brutalities and grotesqueries, and it enjoyed the hurt and shock and pain it caused, and on the heels of this, Fool thought: *Look at me, correcting angels, even if it is only in my mind. Little clever Fool.*

"We demand an apology," said Catarinch, drawing itself up, finding courage in its indignation. Its rotten flesh dripped, sending oily spatters to the floor around it.

"No apologies shall be given. We require the return of the angel Israfil, or whatever remains of her. We require the immediate cessation of your incursions into Heaven. We require reparation. Pass this on."

"I have no need to pass it on. We do not have the angel Israfil."

"Are you sure?" and the voice was colder now, its patience fraying.

"I would have been told," said Catarinch, but the demon's voice gave away its uncertainty.

"I repeat, are you sure?"

"Yes! I am Hell's representative here, and I am senior in this Delegation. You talk of incursions, yet it is Heaven who sends its angels into Hell, who sets fires, and who creeps across the borders. We demand it cease!" Catarinch was shouting now, its voice the shriek of metal grinding against metal, of something rattling and slipping, warping.

"We demand an apology," it said, angrier, puffing up so that its flesh split farther, grease and something that might have been blood spilling from it in fat, poisonous droplets and dripping down its suit, spattering to the floor. Fool saw one of Wambwark's maggots crawl to a drop of Catarinch on the floor, touch the edge of the liquid, and immediately curl itself into a tiny ball, wringing itself around and around until it stopped. A tiny wisp of smoke rose from it as it crumbled apart.

"Lower your voice," said the angel. "You are in no position to demand, demon. Hell has transgressed, and Heaven cannot take this lightly."

"We have not!" shrieked Catarinch. "It is Heaven who has transgressed, breaking the border agreements, making unfounded accusations. Hell demands—" and then it stopped.

For a stretching second, the room was silent and then Catarinch's head slipped strangely, the neck slithering apart along a neat diagonal line, the rotten skull with its red-glow eyes and teeth and foul breath dropping gracelessly away and tumbling to the floor with a wet thud. Its body held its stance for another moment and then, a puppet with its strings cut, collapsed. Blood sprayed from the exposed stump of its neck, thick and fetid, a single long spurt that trickled away to nothing. The foremost angel of the Delegation withdrew its fire, the thin band of silver flame snapping back into its hand, whiplike, leaving snakes of light branded on Fool's vision.

There was a noise from the corridor beyond the room, a rattle and a crash.

"It is decided," said a new voice. The angels on the other side of the table were not speaking, simply standing with their mouths open, their eyes rolled back so that they showed as plain white orbs in those perfect faces, and the voice came from their mouths at once, a single voice from every motionless angelic mouth in the room.

"Hell has sinned," the voice said. "The time of sadness is upon us. The Estedea are awake. We are coming."

Mayall stopped folding the piece of paper. He placed it on the table in front of him and looked up, his face breaking into a wide, toothy smile. He clapped, once, a single sharp note of things beginning, and then rose, stepping off the table. He had formed the paper into the shape of an angel and it stood sentinel in his place looking at Fool, its folded face eerily alive.

Another crash from the corridor. Fool glanced at the door, back at Mayall. "What's happening?" he asked.

"Go and see."

Fool hesitated and Mayall nodded, smiling. Fool went to the door and opened it.

The corridor was empty but all along its length shards of glass lay on the floor, glittering. The pictures of the Estedea were swinging back and forth on their cords, the frames bumping back against the walls and the front of them now empty of glass except for tiny fragments still jammed around the edges of the frames like brilliant, brittle teeth set in old dark gums. Fool stepped into the corridor, hearing the shards crack and snap under his soles. As he neared the first picture, it swung away from the wall and fell back with a loud crack, the picture within the frame now almost entirely filled with the rear of the cowled figure, only slivers of a gray and bucking ocean visible around the edges. A gust of wind, thick with the scent of a cold and salt-heavy sea, blew across his face. The wind came from within the picture itself.

The figure in the picture backed another step toward the frame and then leaned so that its dark-clad head and shoulders came beyond the edge of the picture. Fool stepped away, retreating toward the room as the shape emerged almost horizontally, robes flapping heavily but not falling from the still-hidden head. There was a low tearing sound as the Estedea's wings unfolded, pulling out from its back and stretching into the corridor. They were huge and black, the upper edge of them a thick cable of muscle and bone from which hung rippling sails of feather-covered flesh. They opened fully, scraping the far wall, knocking the pictures that hung there and from which figures were also emerging. With a sharp flap, the first figure lifted out of its picture and tilted upright, its long body slipping out of the frame in a wash of cold, briny air to hover in the corridor and then drop to stand in the space's center.

A figure was emerging from every picture frame and the corridor was filled with dark shapes.

They were huge, tall, and thin, their heads bowed and still brushing the ceiling. The one closest to Fool drew its wings back in, folding them around itself where they merged into the long, hooded habit. It seemed to absorb any light that fell on it, as though shadows had been woven together into cloth and the cloth stitched into the angel's robe. The angel of the Estedea stepped forward, giving space to those that were still arriving behind it, and as it did so it came close to Fool, was standing over him and looking down.

There was nothing in its cowl, only a patch of darkness that was depthless and lost.

Fool stopped walking, knees locking, breath freezing into something hard and frigid. He caught a sense of sadness, of regret from the angel, a sense that grew rapidly until he felt like letting it bury him, letting it crush him down to nothing with its weight, prostrating himself before the angel and begging for an end to the sheer misery he felt. It was like nothing he had ever experienced, this sadness. It was a thing of cold unremitting mass that rolled out from the angel and took everything in its grasp.

The darkness in the cowl roiled, briefly forming empty eye sockets and a mouth of wrinkled lips the color of old sheets that opened in a humorless and flat grin. Fool fell to his knees, letting his chin fall to his chest, holding his hands out to his sides, knowing that the angel was bending in behind him, that its mouth was opening, splitting wider and wider, and he welcomed it, he wanted it, anything to escape this sadness, this feeling that he might explode in shame and regret, might drown in old, trapped miseries. Closer still, and it was ready to feed, to draw everything from him and leave him a husk, and he was ready, he was nothing, he was a speck in the infinite eye of God's saddest angels, and then something grasped his collar and yanked him away.

"Not yet, Thomas," said Mayall, hauling Fool simultaneously back into the room and to his feet. "You may not be one of the saved, may be one of the damned, but you are still our guest of sorts and the Estedea may not have you."

The angel in the corridor straightened, shaking itself slightly, and Fool saw the face in the space beneath the hood fade away to darkness again before the head bowed and the cowl hooded the space completely. It crossed its arms over its front, its hands emerging from the ends of its sleeves momentarily. They were as pale as ivory, almost impossibly long and angular, the skin as smooth as river-washed bone and tight to the skeleton beneath. Its fingers flexed, once, the nails at the tips curved arcs that were even whiter than the hands, and then the sleeves came together and the angel was hidden once again, robes seamless as behind it the others lined up in silent ranks.

"The Estedea," said Mayall from behind Fool, letting go of his collar. "They have been watching and have decided that the time is now. For the first time since the time of the great Fallings, their judgment is that Heaven is at risk. The saddest angels move once more and Heaven will be protected and Heaven will be avenged."

As they watched, the Estedea turned. They didn't appear to walk or fly but spun and then glided along the corridor, moving away from the room. Their robes flapped around them, slow and elegant and heavy, occasionally parting enough to reveal those long, thin hands or feet that were slim and white and clawed and crowned by smaller wings wrapped around their ankles. None spoke, and they made no other noise.

The pictures on the walls were simply framed landscapes now, the Estedea fully emerged, just nondescript images of indefinite places. Several of the flames had fallen from the walls and lay broken on the floor, the glass twinkling like distant stars. From others curls of mist fell, warm air and cold twisting around each other like tongues, and from at least one spills of rain sprayed into the corridor. The air had gone cold, smelled of snow and sea and mountain.

"It begins," said Mayall quietly.

At the far end of the corridor the last of the Estedea filed away, leaving emptiness behind them, and Fool heard the sound of countless wings beating as Heaven and Hell went to war.

PART THREE
WAR

22

They were prisoners.

Fool, Summer, and Gordie had been escorted back to Fool's room after the Estedea left, Mayall at Fool's shoulder and Benjamin behind with the other two. Wambwark was at the rear, flanked by the angels from the Delegation. Mayall did not dance or jig as they walked, and Benjamin's face was a set of stone.

They walked in silence along the corridors of the Anbidstow, their feet crackling the glass that was strewn across the floor, past hundreds of figureless pictures and empty frames. In some, distant seas shifted ceaselessly, and in others fields of corn moved in the wind or snow-storms raged, each one different yet linked by a common thread; in all it was windy, as though the Estedea leaving had dragged the air into chaos, and as they walked the air buffeted out from the pictures and the wind followed them as they went.

When they reached Fool's room he and Gordie and Summer were ushered inside. In his absence two more beds had been added and there was little space to move except carefully along the narrow gaps between bed and desk and wall.

"You will be treated fairly," said Mayall as the door closed, "until we decide what to do with you." He grinned as the door shut, lips splitting back from his teeth in a smile that seemed to take up the whole of the lower half of his face, a flash of the old Mayall, that manic light flaring briefly in his eye, and then the door sealed against the jamb and they were alone. Experimentally, Fool tried to open the door but it was locked, the first time it had been since he arrived.

"This is all wrong," he said when the sound of their captors had faded to nothing.

"That we're prisoners? It's a war and we're part of the enemy," said Gordie. "It makes sense they'd want to know where we are."

"No, not just that, none of it's right. What we saw in the cave wasn't a normal demon, was it? You know these things, Gordie, was it like anything you've heard or read about?"

Gordie thought for a minute. "No," he said eventually. "But if it's not demons, if it's not Hell, what is it?"

"Marianne said something had been found at one of the slaughters in Hell—a pincer? And we found a claw and a scale in the Sleepers' Cave?"

"Yes," said Summer, "but demons have pincers and claws and scales as well."

"But they don't dance, they don't move that way," said Fool and he was thinking as he spoke, his thoughts running faster than his words. He held the feather as he let the ideas stream out of him, tasting them on his tongue, spitting some away and letting others free.

"It's something that moves oddly," he said. "It looks like it's dancing, like lots of pieces working together. They're connected, working with each other as though they're part of one mind. The thing in the Sleepers' Cave, it came apart but never completely, it was linked and worked together. It filled the space with itself."

"You know what it is?" asked Summer.

"I do," said Fool. "I think it's the things that live in the places outside of everywhere. Catarinch told me they're always searching for a way in. What if they've found it? What if they've found a way to tear through at last? What if this isn't Hell or Heaven but the things from outside?"

There was silence in the room for a second, and then Gordie asked, "What are they?"

"I don't know," said Fool.

"More importantly, how do we prove it? How do we stop them?" asked Summer.

"I don't know," said Fool again. How often had he said that? How often had he been asked a question and not known the answer? Too often. In Hell he'd come to expect it, that his world would be hunched with questions that had no answers, that was the point of Hell, after all, but here in Heaven? He'd expected more, had expected things to be smooth with answers.

"FOOL, YOU MOTHERFUCKER, WHAT THE FUCK IS GOING ON?" howled a voice, and at the same time Fool screamed as the skin of his belly tore open. Summer shrieked and leaped back from Fool as he collapsed to the bed, and so violent was Mr. Tap's arrival that his skin was already slick with blood by the time he managed to tear open his jacket and shirt. Gordie made to come to his aid but Fool managed to gesture him back. *They haven't seen this, have they, they've not met Mr. Tap,* he thought abstractly. *Oh my, they're in for a treat.*

Fool dragged himself back along the bed so that he could prop himself against the wall and stare down at his rent stomach. Mr. Tap's face was open there, and the demon was breathing hard. *Panting.* Had the tattoo ever breathed before? Fool didn't think so.

"Fool," it said again, and its voice was barely controlled fury. "What the fuck have you done?"

"I investigated as instructed," said Fool. "But events overtook me." His whole body was twitching now, the pain from Mr. Tap radiating along his limbs. It was as though the demon was poisoning him, its rage sending a sickness into him.

"'Events overtook' you? For shit's sake, Fool, we sent you there to calm Heaven down. You were supposed to solve their little problem so that we could use your success to gain an advantage over them in the trade and border discussions. What fucking use are you if you can't even do that?" Mr. Tap opened its mouth wide, revealing that long, long throat with its lining of teeth, descending an impossible depth, deeper than the thickness of Fool's body, and bit down on the skin below its lip. The tattooed face thrashed, the image blurring as it harried at Fool's flesh, and Fool screamed, screamed as a piece of him tore away and was swallowed.

"Did you like that, you pathetic human scum?" said Mr. Tap. Fool groaned, waving a hand at Summer, who had risen and was moving swiftly toward him. In her hand she held the knife Fool had used to cut his food, although what she expected to do with it he wasn't sure; cut Mr. Tap out of him, maybe. He waved at her, shaking his head. Uncertainly, she sat again. Gordie put his arm around her, holding her. Fool tried to smile at them but the expression felt warped on his face and he suspected it looked like a grimace, let it fall away to nothing.

"ANSWER ME!" said Mr. Tap and tore at another section of Fool's skin, swallowing again, the teeth clicking against each other as the pink scrap disappeared into the gullet.

"No, I didn't," said Fool, and his voice sounded weak, papery.

"Tell me why I shouldn't keep on," said Mr. Tap.

"I did my best," said Fool, and now there was an unpleasant wheedling tone added to his voice, a pitiful begging that he didn't like, "but the angels wouldn't see the dead as murders and then something attacked us and took one of the named angels."

"Something?"

"Heaven thinks it was a demon. They found a tunnel they say leads to Hell. They think you've been attacking them."

"I know!" said Mr. Tap, and it sounded calmer now, more thoughtful. "We've been sent a formal communication pinned to Catarinch's fucking head! A declaration of war! We're at war, Fool, Heaven and Hell joining in the final battle, but we didn't do it and we're not fucking ready."

"No," said Fool and then because he couldn't help himself, "it's not nice, being accused of things you didn't do, is it?"

"Fuck you, Fool," said Mr. Tap. "This is your fault, you little grub, you little shit. If you'd done what we sent you to do we wouldn't be in this position. We haven't attacked Heaven, Fool, but they've attacked us! Dancing things have been seen, Fool, by murders and fires. We have things burning, and have you solved that? No, you useless turd, you haven't, you've solved nothing.

"We have demons missing, Fool, demons and people both."

"Perhaps the Evidence took them," said Fool and then screamed as Mr. Tap tore another part of him loose, chewing it furiously and then swallowing it with a noisy, tearing slurp.

"The next time you speak to me like that I'll chew you apart," said the tattoo. "Understand?"

"Yes."

"Good. We didn't do any of this, Fool. We can only think Heaven has been coordinating the attacks in Hell to force this outcome. Fucking God and his plans, eh?"

"I don't think it's Heaven."

"No?" and now Mr. Tap's voice sounded something other than angry; it sounded eager. *Even you're afraid of Heaven,* thought Fool, *even you don't want this war, because you've no idea if Hell will win or if you'll survive. You want an exit, a way out of this.*

"I think it's the things from places outside."

"The things outside of everywhere? Really, Fool, you believe that those swirling bastards are doing this?"

"Yes. We have some evidence."

"Enough to convince that sanctimonious bastard Mayall? Enough to get them to call off the fucking Estedea?"

Fool thought about the claw and the scale and the dancing and the thing he had chased and said, "No."

"Then I ask again, what fucking use are you? I may as well feed on you and then go and get ready for the war."

"No, wait," said Fool, aching and sick and weary. "I can find proof. Give me some time." He saw Summer, the expression on her face quizzical, Gordie looking horrified, and tried to nod reassuringly at them. *I can,* he thought. *I can, I just need time.*

Time and a fucking break.

"We haven't *got* time, Fool, this is happening now! When their army is ready, they'll descend and we'll be at war." There was a pause and then Mr. Tap continued, its voice calmer.

"Fuck it, you mongrel bastard, you can have until then," said the tattoo, said Fool's flesh, teeth clicking constantly. "But know this: if the war isn't to be averted, then I will take the greatest of pleasure in, just before the first battle, visiting you and speaking the name of every demon I know while tearing you piece from worthless piece and then saying my own name and watching as each piece of you is further split."

"Fine," said Fool and collapsed back on the bed as Mr. Tap's face broke apart and his skin knitted itself back together. Where Mr. Tap had chewed on him his skin healed unevenly, leaving a set of ugly raised scars across his stomach. Fool, exhausted, tried to sit but the muscles of his stomach refused to contract and he flopped back, helpless. Summer and Gordie came to help him and gently lifted him into a sitting position.

"Has that been happening ever since you arrived?" asked Summer.

"Yes. Sort of, it's not normally that bad," replied Fool. Summer took him in her arms and hugged him.

"You poor, poor man," she said. "No one deserves this."

"You don't know that," said Gordie quietly.

"Gordie!" said Summer, her voice shocked against Fool's neck as she held him.

"No, he's right," said Fool. "You don't know. You don't know what I did to be in Hell. Maybe this is just punishment."

"This isn't just," said Summer, pulling back from Fool, a horrified look on her face. "This is . . ." She stopped, unable to find the words to describe it.

"It is what it is," said Fool. "And it's not over yet, I'm afraid."

"No more, please," said Summer, her voice hard. "Please."

"It won't be as bad," said Fool and then held up his arm and rolled back his sleeve. The blood that had soaked the front of his clothes was cold against him, smelled of old metal and earth left, sunless and wet, under abandoned buildings.

"Marianne," he said. "Marianne, can you hear me?"

As he waited for her to reply, Fool looked at the face described by the tattoo. It had become even sharper since he had last looked, more detail added on each viewing, and now it was an accurate representation of how Marianne looked. In the inked image, her mouth was smiling, her brow slightly crinkled as though thinking, her eyes open and inquisitive. Her short hair was swept up, twisting above her head in little curls and tangles, and he wondered how soft it was, whether it smelled like Summer's did, and then the tattoo twitched and he managed to prepare himself before the skin of its mouth split and Marianne said, "Hello, sir."

"Thomas," said Fool without thinking. "Hello, Marianne. How are things?"

"I'm still breathing, I'm still here," she said, and her voice was little more than a whisper. "The Evidence are everywhere. We've been moved out of the offices now, they've taken your room and all the rooms except the mess and some of the toilets. That's where I am now, the mess. Something's happening, sir, something big. I can feel the tension, but it's more than that, I can feel their uncertainty."

Something. The war between Heaven and Hell. Something. "You're right," said Fool, "and it's serious. Marianne, have you still got the picture of me?"

"Yes. Hold on," she said, and then there was a pause. "I've got it and unfolded it."

Fool closed his eyes, seeing again the strange, flattened version of Hell that the picture allowed him to view. Marianne was holding the picture in front of her, and her face was set with lines, worry etching across her forehead and in her eyes. "I'm scared," she said.

"I know," Fool replied, knowing there was nothing he could say that would help. Fear was good, fear was the right thing to feel, Marianne was surrounded by danger and threat and to suggest otherwise would be pointless. "Marianne, can you get outside? I need to speak to the Man again."

"I'll try," she said. There was a longer pause, during which Fool had to open his eyes; the control-less roll of Hell in his paper view was sickening, made his belly flop, nausea inside the still-throbbing pains of Mr. Tap's visit.

"We're here," she said after a few minutes. Fool closed his eyes and saw, once again, the rear walled garden of the Information Office. The gate in the far wall was hanging open now, swinging drunkenly down, held in place only by its bottom hinge. The upper hinge, still attached to a lump of concrete, hung from the upper part of its frame, and he could hear it clanking through his paper ears as it swayed back and forth. The statues that had stood around the garden were now in pieces across its uneven paved floor, and some of the bushes and trees that had sprouted in the gaps between the flags had been uprooted and cast aside, their roots gnarled clumps of frond and earth, drying and crumbling to death.

"What happened?" asked Fool, already thinking he knew the answer.

"The Evidence," said Marianne. "I heard them the night after we were here last. They're out of control, they do anything they like now. Some of the Information Men have vanished, sir. I don't think anyone's safe."

"No," said Fool, thinking about judgment without justice, about Mr. Tap's near-feral children, the bauta, running amok along Hell's streets yet having the veneer of officialdom. *I did this,* he thought. *Even if the war isn't my fault, this is. I created the space into which Mr. Tap and the Evidence fit. I made them.*

"They're taking demons now," said Marianne, and her voice was flat, toneless. "I heard people talk about it. I'm still trying to do my job, but it's almost impossible. All I can do is listen and try to avoid being seen."

"Listening is important, Marianne," said Fool, trying not to let the pain show in his speech. "You're doing well but I'm not sure what you heard is right. I don't think the Evidence are taking demons, I think it's something else. It's why I need to talk to the Man."

"How do I call him?" asked Marianne, Fool's skin splitting and moving to form the words.

"You don't need to," said the Man, and the plants in front of them twisted, the stems and leaves forced into a new shape. It was humanoid again, the large body with its indications of arms and a belly topped by a knot of branch and twig that could easily have been a head, leaves placed for eyes and tangled into rolls to create the lips. *Even now, he's re-creating the body he had,* thought Fool, *fat and gross and imposing.*

"Hello, Fool," said the Man. "What news?

"I hear rumors, Fool, that the angels have led us to war. Is it true? Have I had angels trespassing through me and not noticed? Which ones, I wonder? Those of Gabriel or Malachi, or ones whose provenance is less sure, created for a single terrible purpose?"

"I don't think it was angels," said Fool. "Trespasses have happened in Heaven, too. I think it's something with access to both, setting one against the other. I think it's . . ." He paused, unable to remember if he'd mentioned the things outside of everywhere in his discussions with the Man or if they'd been something he kept back.

"Yes? Tell all, Fool!"

"I know what made the tunnels."

The Man waited a moment before answering, and his tone, when he did, was one of surprise. "How did you know? Have you spies other than me, Fool?" The Man, the plants that formed the Man, rose up, stretching away from the ground and puffing up. Fool heard the snapping of dead stems as he moved, heard Marianne's gasp as the plant figure became larger, looming at them.

"No, I worked it out," Fool said loudly. He remembered a word that Gordie had used once, and added, "I deduced it."

"Did you indeed? Then share your deductions, Fool, share them now," said the Man, sinking back to the earth in a rustle and crackle of relaxing growth.

"It's the things that live in the places outside of everywhere," said Fool. How many times would he need to say it? It didn't matter, he supposed, whether his lies and omissions were discovered now. There was simply the coming war and his attempts to stop it; everything else he'd deal with afterward.

"You mean there are new things in Hell, things for me to know about? Tell me all about them, Fool! Tell me how I can find them, now!"

"No."

"Fool," said the Man, starting to stretch again, voice dangerously low and pleasant, "I insist."

"No. A trade. I'll tell you everything I know after, when I've stopped the war."

"And how do you propose to do that?"

"By proving it to the Bureaucracies of Heaven and Hell. I'll show them, and they'll have to believe me. Especially if you tell them what you know, tell them about the trails through the forests you found and the earth that's been tunneled through and closed up again."

"Reveal myself? Never, Fool, have you gone mad?"

"Help me, and I'll tell you everything. I'll tell you about Heaven and I'll tell you about Mayall and I'll tell you about the Malakim and the tunnels between worlds. I'll give you the feather."

The Man did not reply for a long, long time. The plants dropped in on themselves, and Fool began to think he had left them until they suddenly raised themselves and looked straight at Fool's face on the paper, straight into Fool's eyes.

"I agree. I'll tell them everything, but it will have to be here in Hell. I cannot get to Heaven and they won't believe you if you simply tell them what I've said."

"Where?"

"Assemblies House. Get them to the House, I can come to them there. Bring them all, Fool, and I'll tell them what I know."

"Okay. I'll do what I can."

"Do more, Fool. I hear the Estedea are coming, and they're merciless in their sorrow. If the war starts and they arrive, nothing in Hell is safe, not human or demon or even me. Move fast, Fool. Move fast."

"Yes."

The Man collapsed, the essence of him leaving the plants in front of them and dissipating through the garden and away. "Marianne," said Fool.

"Yes?"

"Stay safe, keep hidden, I'll need your help. I'm coming back, I'll be there as soon as I can. I'll keep you safe, I promise."

"Please," said Marianne and then, consciously or unconsciously echoing the Man, continued, "Move fast."

The link was broken. Fool sighed in relief as the splits along the tattoo's black lines sealed, the now-familiar itch of healing skin scratching at him like a returning friend. He opened his eyes to see Summer and Gordie staring at him, Summer at his arm and Gordie at his face.

"That's how they've made you communicate," Summer said again. "It's awful."

"It's not so bad," Fool said, and knew that Summer knew he was lying even as the untruth escaped his lips.

"How are you going to do it?" asked Gordie. "How are you going to stop the war?"

"I don't know," said Fool and thought, *It's that fucking phrase again.* "I just know I have to try."

And I made a promise. I have a promise to keep.

"We need to look at the tunnel again," said Summer. "Maybe there's something there we missed?"

"I agree," said Gordie. "The tunnel."

"How are we going to get there? We're locked in," said Fool, still bleary with the aftereffects of pain, and at that moment the door shook as something crashed into it and a great howl was raised in the corridor beyond the room.

23

Summer's hand jumped immediately to her thigh, to where her gun would have been strapped if she had still had one, and slapped in frustration at its absence, at the plain expanse of linen. Fool, even as he was rising from the bed, pushing himself through the weariness, saw the gesture and grinned humorlessly; she had always been a natural Information Man.

There was another crash at the door. Gordie rose but the lack of space made movement awkward and he stumbled, falling over the bed in front of him as he tried to push past Summer to get between her and the door. Fool moved slowly, pushing himself along the bed in a half-risen stance, trying to find his balance. Straightening was difficult partly because of the ache in his stomach muscles and the feeling that they had become like wet rope, unable to tauten, but also because his skin felt tight and lacking give. *Fucking Mr. Tap,* he thought, still moving, *my new scars are knotted too tight. I can't stand properly.* Hunched, he found some kind of balance and pushed past Gordie. His gun was on the table and he picked it up as another crash sounded, the door shaking violently in its frame.

"Who's there?" he asked, but the only reply was a roar, low and rumbling. The door jerked, hard, and began to shiver as something or someone pushed against it from the outside. The lock held, but the wood, thick though it was, began to bend in at the top of the door. Something flowed through the gap, two sluggish white streams that seemed to undulate as they crawled across the wood, moving across the inner face of the door until they met and merged. The door bowed in farther and the streams thickened, grew faster. Droplets were falling from them now, things that bounced to the floor and then began to move toward each other.

Maggots.

"Wambwark," said Fool, stunned. After everything that was happening, after the trouble they were in, the silly bastard still harbored this grudge? Blamed Fool for the turn of events?

Yes. The streams were moving swiftly now, the area where they met forming itself into two clasped hands. Bugs fell from the streams, gathering on the ground and massing up, forming the start of legs. From behind him, Fool heard Summer cry out. When he looked around, he saw that a line of bugs was making its way toward Gordie and her, cutting them off from Fool. Summer began to stamp at the line, and the noise of the maggots popping under her feet was terrible, a molasses spray of a noise. Gordie joined in and the air soon stank of the demon's stench, rich and corrupt and sour. Their shadows moved constantly around them like the arachnid dance of some vast insect.

"Wambwark, stop!" shouted Fool, hoping to be heard over the roaring, but the only reply was another crash against the door. The screws of the top hinge popped partially loose of their wooden home, their heads jolting out perhaps half an inch. The door's top section bent farther, more of Wambwark crawling around it, forcing itself in, and there was a sharp crack as the upper panel began to splinter.

"I'm so sick of this," said Fool, more to himself than to anyone else, raising his gun to roughly head height. He pressed it against the door, forcing it into the growing mass of maggots, and then more loudly said, "One last chance, Wambwark. Stop this, please, and piss off."

Another crash, another roar, and the door was bending back on itself with a sound that groaned and cracked in equal measure. Fool could now see Wambwark's head and what passed for its face. It was lower than he expected, presumably because so much of it was already in the room, and its eyes glittered, red and insane.

Behind Fool, Summer shrieked. Without moving, he glanced over his shoulder and saw that she was on the floor with her hands splayed out, the left swarmed by maggots. They moved fast, covering exposed skin in seconds, and she shrieked again, yanking her hand back, shaking it furiously. "It burns," she cried out as the bugs were flung from her. "*They* burn."

Gordie took hold of the collar of Summer's shirt and pulled her back, simultaneously pulling a sheet from the bed and using it to beat away the remaining bugs from her hand. Fool glimpsed her skin, red and blistering, and then his own hand was afire.

The maggots had bulged up around the barrel of his gun, forming a bridge that led them to his fingers. Summer was right, they *burned* as though they were fat with poison. He jerked back, shaking his hand as Summer had done, knocking the little white bastards off. One had started to burrow into the skin of his knuckle, blood welling around it as it surged its way into his flesh. He grabbed it by its wriggling rear end and pulled and it came free in a bubble of bleeding and pain. Fool was horrified to see that the fucking thing had turned pink from feeding on him and he dropped it with a cry, stamping on it and then moving back to avoid any more of the things reaching him.

Wambwark's face, in the gap, split into a wide grin, maggots falling from its lips like fleshy saliva.

Fool stuck the barrel of the gun into the gap and pulled the trigger, and Wambwark's head exploded in a spray of maggots and blood and yellow slime. Instead of falling back, the demon leaped forward and crashed into the door as Fool made a compensatory jump back. His knees caught on the edge of a bed and he fell, only just holding on to his gun. His hand was throbbing, sending waves of a sick, dizzying pain up his arm.

The door buckled, snapping over to reveal Wambwark's top half. Already maggots were flowing up, re-creating its head. Fool pointed his gun in the direction of the demon and fired again, and this time part of the thing's shoulder exploded as the bullet tore through it, maggots spinning away in an arc of yellow streaked dark red with blood.

Wambwark yowled, punched, and kicked at the lower part of the door, shaking it. The lock held, more of the maggots falling into the room as Fool fired a third time, this time aiming as carefully as the situation would allow, placing the shot into the demon's chest. This had more impact, tore a hole through the creature and punched it back. It slammed into the far wall of the corridor and pushed itself off the wall in one clumsy movement, but before it could come back to the door Fool's new bullet had formed and he fired again.

This time, Wambwark was clearly wounded. The bullet opened a path near its shoulder, merging with the hole from the previous bullet so that its chest was mangled. It spun back against the wall and this time did not bounce back but slithered down it, leaving a trail of dark liquid in which maggots wriggled.

The bugs in the room began to surge back toward the door. "Don't let them get back to him!" Fool shouted, struggling upright, but Gordie had already started to hit at them, toppling one of the beds so that he could use its flat edge as a weapon, crushing legions of the things at a time.

In the corridor, Wambwark let loose a long, desperate wail and tried to use the wall to lever itself up to a standing position. It was much smaller now, too much of it separated from its main body, the damage to its chest and shoulder not healing properly.

Fool kicked aside the bugs, treading on them as he did so, and stepped to the broken door. Looking down at the demon as the sound of Gordie's exertions behind him became louder, he said, "You brought this on yourself."

He fired again.

This time, Fool aimed for the head and watched, detached, as it exploded apart again. Maggots moved sluggishly to reform the dome, but as soon as his bullet was there, he fired again, and again, and again.

Eventually Wambwark stopped trying to rise. The demon moved in disjointed arrhythmic surges, its eyes still glittering like spots of angry blood in a face that was damaged and collapsing.

Fool leaned on the bottom half of the door and, with difficulty, put his gun back in its holster. Its barrel was hot, hot enough to be felt through the leather and the material of his pants, but not as hot as his hand had become. He held it up in front of him, watching as the skin bulged, as it swelled. His fingers looked like fat sausages and he could bend them only a little. Veins rose, red and angry, across the back of the hand, the redness extending toward his wrist. Clear, foul-smelling liquid dripped from the hole that Wambwark's maggot had made.

When he turned to Summer, Fool saw that she was in a far worse condition.

Her whole arm had started to swell, had become red, glistening with sweat. Where Fool had been bitten or burrowed into by only one bug, Summer had been punctured by several and her fingers and palm and wrist were slick with blood and the same weeping, clear fluid. She was holding her arm at the elbow and crying, her face crunched into a pained wrinkle, tears dripping down her cheeks and off her chin. As Fool watched, the crawling redness popped the veins up farther and farther along her arm, the swelling and pain traveling back toward her body.

"Help me," said Gordie, crouching behind Summer and propping her up against him. "Bring me the water."

Fool hobbled to the table and picked up the jug of water. He had to pick it up using his wrong hand and he slopped it as he lifted.

"Be careful, we need it to clean her hand," snapped Gordie and then, to Summer, he said, "It'll be okay. We'll make it better."

Don't promise that, thought Fool, *don't ever promise that.* Silently, with waves of sharp pain starting to encircle his wrist and stretch into his forearm, nausea flipping his already abused belly, he carried the water over. Gordie took the jug and Summer stretched her arm, the skin shiny with tension and glowing with the furnace heat of poison. By her elbow the sleeve of her shirt was puffed and taut as the flesh below it swelled.

"It'll be okay," Gordie said again and poured the water over Summer's hand.

She screamed.

Steam and smoke boiled away from her flesh where the water hit it, the vapors roiling up the color of old shrouds. Water splashed off her and spattered to the discolored floor, threaded with strings of blood and yellowing slime. As Gordie poured more water, steam billowed from Summer, filling the room with sour-smelling clouds that hit the walls and condensed into bitter, trickling tears. Summer screamed again, weaker, and then broke into fitful gasps.

When the steam cleared the swelling in Summer's hand had gone down and the red veins had receded, their color burning away to their more usual blue. The holes in her skin still bled, but now it was mostly blood, red and thin and spilling across the floor. She flexed her fingers. The movement forced more blood from her wounds and Gordie poured another splash of water across Summer's damaged hand. This time, no steam rose.

"Your turn," said Gordie to Fool, moving Summer gently aside and leaning her against the bed.

"Use it on her," Fool said. "My hand's not too bad."

"Bullshit," said Gordie. "Your hand's bad. It's poisoned you."

Fool didn't argue. He was growing dizzy and sat on the floor next to Gordie, holding his arm out. Lifting it hurt, as though it had become three, four, *ten* times as heavy. It prickled fiercely and heat radiated from it like a sickness.

"Brace yourself," said Gordie. Fool took a breath, held it, and Gordie poured.

A wave of the purest agony Fool had ever experienced crashed along his arm, blooming in a whitelight roar that he welcomed because even as it smashed through him it *cleansed*, burning away Wambwark's bitterness and poison. Strings of steam, thinner than those that had billowed away from Summer, rose above Fool and hit the ceiling. Water fell to the floor and slithered away through the rough boards, carrying with it the last of Wambwark's bilious seed.

When the pain receded, Fool found that he could move his fingers again. The hole by his knuckle was still bleeding, an open bore into his flesh, but the redness around it was fading now, the color of his hand returning to its more usual tone.

"Thank you," Fool said.

"Pleasure," said Gordie. "I hoped the water would be pure, holy somehow, that it would neutralize the damage."

Fool nodded. For once, the situation had worked in their favor. He wished he could believe it would happen again.

There was a feeble groan from the corridor, breathy and distorted. Fool rose and walked to the shattered door. Wambwark had struggled into a sitting position as more bugs made their way back to it, but it was in poor shape. Its head had reformed lopsided, the temple bulging on one side and collapsed in on the other, and the chest had stitched back together unevenly, so that it was hunched forward and over. Fool, feeling the pull of his own new scar tissue and the effect it had on his posture, thought, *Good. I hope it hurts.* The demon looked up at him and hissed, maggots falling from the mouth that opened in its head, eyes gleaming dully. It reached out a short and deformed arm that wept bugs, and tried to claw at Fool. The attempt was pitiful and its arm fell back after only a few seconds of extension, coming to rest across its thighs. It lost definition for a moment, the bugs wriggling and merging with the legs, and then came together again unevenly. Wambwark hissed at Fool again.

"Don't you know when you're beaten?" said Fool. "Even now, you try to attack. We're stronger than you think, and I'm tired of it. I'm tired of you and Mr. Tap and Rhakshasas and Catarinch and that little shit that looked like a horse challenging me, threatening me. I'm tired of all of you.

"You could have left us the fuck alone. We were never your enemy, not here in Heaven anyway. You're just like all those things in the Houska and the farms and the factories in that other fucking place, so sure you can hurt us and nothing will be done and we won't fight back, and you know what? We aren't in Hell, and you aren't my master, and today I will not fucking stand for it."

Fool drew his gun and fired, a last time, and Wambwark's head broke apart in a wet mess of maggots and slime and something that might have been blood but might equally have been dark brains, and it collapsed back against the wall. This time, it did not reform. The mass of it that remained lost its shape and fell apart, the maggots that had made it crawling away, no longer acting in unison, just a set of aimless bugs trying to escape.

"Thomas Fool," said Benjamin, "in the name of God, what have you done?"

The angel was hovering at the end of the corridor, his shadow stretching out before him like a fat snake. He twitched his wings and moved toward Fool, his feet several inches above the ground. "You killed it," he said.

"Yes," replied Fool, "I did. He would have killed us."

"It was defenseless and you killed it," said Benjamin, and Fool was astonished to hear sorrow in the angel's voice. "You showed it no mercy.

Thomas Fool, that was an awful act, a *sinful* act. But then, what else am I to expect? Perhaps I should remember that you are one of the damned and not one of the saved."

"Sinful?" asked Fool, a worm of anger turning in his stomach. "It's a fucking demon, it's evil and was trying to murder us. You should thank me for killing it."

"No mercy," said Benjamin, now hovering over the dead thing's corpse. "You damn yourself again, Thomas Fool, damned a thousand times over."

"I don't *care*," said Fool, finally losing what little control remained over his temper. "You act so innocent but you and Israfil and all the other angels, you can be violent when you want to be, just like you can avoid even noticing violence when it suits you. Don't call me sinful, you hypocritical bastard, you're just as bad!"

"Thomas Fool, watch your tongue," said the angel.

"You watch yours. Have you considered, Benjamin, that this is all Heaven's fault? You drag me down here and then set me to investigate several murders and then you block me at every step of the way. The kindliest angels take the bodies away before I can give them anything but the most basic examinations. Israfil and you refuse to see anything but what you want to see. Mayall kills the only thing that might have helped me work out what's going on here and everyone smiles and smiles and says, 'Oh look, it's Heaven, isn't it so fucking lovely?'

"But it's not lovely, is it, because people are dying and things are changing and you don't know why or how any more than I do and you've still got the gall to criticize me and call me a sinner? Well, maybe I am, but you angels aren't much better, are you? You were quick enough to kill Catarinch when the situation allowed you to do so but never so quick to give me the time I need to try to sort things out and find a solution to this mess. Heaven's blindness and stubbornness triggered this war, and the war made Wambwark scared and small and powerless and it lashed out the only way it knew, by attacking me because it thought I was the cause of all its problems. Don't lecture me on right and wrong, angel. How many people will die in this war? How many will the Estedea kill? How many angels will be torn to pieces like Israfil, how many little demons scurrying around Hell and hiding from things larger than themselves will be slaughtered without you even noticing?

How many Joyful or Sorrowful will be sacrificed for this war, a war that doesn't need to happen?"

Fool stopped, panting. He couldn't remember ever speaking for so long, saying so much, or ever being so angry, the fury raging in him. Letting it all out, attacking Benjamin, hadn't dissipated his rage at all; if anything, it had made it worse, like stoking a fire. He took a deep breath, letting the anger simmer inside him, letting it coalesce into something hard and sharp, something that overrode his pain and weariness, and then carefully climbed over the broken door into the corridor. His feet squashed more of Wambwark's bugs as he stood.

"Go and tell them, Benjamin. Tell them this is their fault, that their war is based on a lie. Tell them that Heaven is fallible."

"Be silent, monkey!" snapped Benjamin, his skin darkening, the feathers around his groin ruffling, his wings opening, starting to move back along the corridor. "You are sinful, Thomas Fool, and Heaven will judge you for your actions today."

Fool grinned, mirthless, and gestured for Summer and Gordie to follow him. As the angel reached the end of the corridor and went around the corner, Fool called, "All of the dead can be placed at Heaven's feet, all of them. You were so concerned by being perfect that you ignored what was happening under your noses. You judge me because that's still easier than admitting you've made a mistake, isn't it? And you have made a mistake—this wasn't Hell any more than the fires and deaths in Hell were Heaven's doing. This is something else, something from outside, and if you can't see that, won't at least consider it, then fuck you.

"Fuck you, Benjamin. Fuck you, and all of Heaven."

24

"Where are we going?" asked Summer.

"We're going to the tunnel," said Gordie. He sounded a little shocked, and had looked at Fool oddly as he climbed over the broken door and then glanced down the corridor to where Benjamin had gone but had said nothing. *The old thinking is creeping back in,* Fool thought, *the thinking from before he died and came back. He's seeing the risks, seeing the chance of retribution. The tension, it's slinking back in, and we're finding our old behaviors, our old cautions. Heaven is becoming like Hell.*

"I know we're going to the tunnel," said Summer, also climbing over the broken door, "but where are we going *now?*"

She had a point. The three of them had left the room and gone down the corridor, following Benjamin, but the corner led them only to another identical corridor. Branching off from this were more corridors as well as doors to rooms, all locked, and Fool recognized none of them. Or rather, he recognized them all because they were all the same. So they walked, trying to remember the route from the rooms to the meeting rooms, and they made little progress.

They were walking along another of the Anbidstow's corridors. It, like the others they had come down, was lined with framed pictures of landscapes, the images moving and empty of figures. Standing in the corridor and looking into the pictures was like looking through the windows of a building out onto a wild landscape of roiling sea and, two or three feet farther on, verdant forests and past that, through another window, sand-whipped deserts. It was dizzying, and Fool wondered what would happen if they were to climb over one of the frames, if they would clamber into one of the pictures and get lost, be forever trapped in the landscapes of the Estedea. He thought maybe they would. Here and there glass lay across the floor in random scatters; in other places it had been swept into neat piles that glittered ferociously as they went past.

Fool realized he was limping. The new scarring on his stomach refused to give and he was forced to walk, lurching slightly, with his upper body twisted and his gait uneven. Their passage was slow. When Summer tried to help him, he shook her hand off, *proud Fool*, and carried on unaided.

"We're lost," said Summer after they had passed along another corridor. The Anbidstow was silent and, besides themselves and the images behind the frames, nothing moved.

"We are," agreed Gordie.

"We're not," said Fool. "This is Heaven and nothing here is lost, nothing here can be lost, didn't you know? Heaven is the place of things found that were once lost."

"Don't be sarcastic," said Summer.

"I'm not," Fool said. He was being irritable, he understood, but couldn't stop himself. After the adrenaline rush of the conflict with Wambwark and the flowering of his anger at Benjamin, now he was on the downward swing. He hurt, he was confused and worried about Marianne in Hell, had little other than the vaguest notions of how to proceed. He limped along, battered, with Gordie and Summer in tow. This war was with the things from outside of everywhere, he was sure of it and had the evidence of the claw and scale. Marianne had found the pincer in Hell and he was also sure they'd match if he could only bring them together and show them as a set. But what did they prove?

They proved that the same things were attacking Heaven and Hell, that they weren't attacking each other.

And how was he going to get the Bureaucracy of Heaven to go to Hell to hear his evidence? Come to that, how was he going to get Hell's Bureaucracy to listen to the Man tell them about trails and earth churned and tunnels created and filled?

Fool limped. The hole by his knuckle was still bleeding, the flow a mere trickle now but no scab formed over it. Summer, who had been more severely attacked, had wrapped a clean piece of the blanket around her hand before they left the room, but it was soaked through now and drips fell from her, leaving a trail behind them. *At least we can follow it back to where we started,* he thought and was then horrified at himself. *What have I become, that I can even think that? That I can joke about my friend's injuries like that?*

They came to another T-junction, the two arms stretching away in bland uniformity. "Which way?" asked Gordie.

"I don't know," Fool replied. *There. There, it's that fucking phrase again, "I don't know," the measure of my ignorance.*

"We guess?"

Fool thought about Hell, about the Evidence and the making of assumptions, about being set, blind and spinning, into an investigation in Heaven that most of the angels refused to even acknowledge the need for, about Catarinch's head dropping to the floor, about claws slicing through his face, and about being lost, and suddenly he was angry again, livid. "No," he said. "No, no more guessing. I'm tired of guessing, I'm tired of being two steps behind and a step to the side, I'm tired of being treated like I'm a toy to be set rattling and jigging for their amusement, I'm tired of it all. No more guessing. Now I'm going to ask."

"Ask?"

Fool didn't speak. Instead, he took the feather from his pocket and looked at it. Which angel was this from? he wondered. Israfil? Benjamin? Or one of the nameless caretakers? How long had he possessed it now? Three days? Four? It was impossible to remember, time in Heaven seemed as elastic and mutable as melting wax. He simply knew it was his, and he knew what he had been told; angels were creatures of truth and their feathers could not lie. It was time, he thought, for some truth.

"Which way do we go to get out of this building?" he asked aloud, and let the feather fall. It spiraled slowly and calmly to the floor, coming to rest with its spine pointing along the left-hand corridor. He picked it up, holding it out horizontally in front of him, balancing it on his palm, and marveling at its lightness and softness.

"Which way do we go to get out of this building?" he asked again and moved his hand so that the feather fell. Again, it landed pointing left.

"We go left," he said, and started along the corridor. Summer and Gordie followed.

When they emerged from the Anbidstow, they did so into a large court-yard filled with angels.

They were in ranks, hundreds and hundreds of them, maybe thousands, standing motionless as the Estedea moved between them. The saddest angels, taller than their compatriots, were easily visible, dark and thin and silent as they drifted down rows and back along columns, occasionally stopping to carry out some hidden task. Fool and Gordie and Summer stayed behind the half-open door for a few minutes, watching, as more angels flew in, landing and being directed by the Estedea to their places, standing neatly with their wings folded and their heads down, posed like the Estedea themselves.

"What do we do?" asked Summer.

I will not say "I don't know" again, thought Fool. *I will not.* "We walk out like we have every right to be there," he said, "because we do."

"We're escaped prisoners," said Gordie softly, as though to remind Fool of the fact.

"No," he said. "I am Hell's Chief Information Officer and I was invited here to solve a series of crimes, and that is what I'm doing."

"Are you sure that'll work?"

"No," he answered truthfully, "but we don't have much choice, do we?" He stepped fully out into the courtyard, feeling the sun warm his skin almost immediately. He tilted his head back to it, letting it wash across his face and closing his eyes, unable to stop himself. How much longer would he be able to feel this? How much longer until he was back in Hell, where the only sun was a flat disk throwing out grimy light and everything stank? Not long, he thought. Wherever this was taking them, Fool had the sense that they were almost there, that the endgame was looming ever larger and closer.

"We should go," said Summer, stepping alongside Fool, her voice wary.

"Yes," said Fool, opening his eyes. He looked around, saw the fields beyond the far side of the courtyard, and started to walk toward them.

They kept close to the Anbidstow, knowing it wouldn't shield them but hoping to conceal themselves in the shade that gathered at the junction of wall and floor, to become simply part of the background.

Fool knew that all three of them were doing what he thought of as the Houska Walk, that hunched-over gait that said, *Don't see me, don't notice me, I'm small, I'm insignificant, I'm nothing you should even see.* Gordie had his head down, was staring studiously at his feet, and Summer was looking ahead and walking as though she had seen something in the distance that had absorbed all her attention, eyes forward, not glancing at anything but her destination.

The Estedea ignored them. One or two of the angels stared at them curiously but did not break rank, good soldiers that they were. "Why are they letting us go?" asked Gordie quietly without looking up.

"Because they're preparing for war and we aren't important," said Summer, "not in the grand scheme of things." She spoke almost without moving her lips, her voice as quiet as Gordie's, her gaze never wavering.

It made sense, thought Fool, but he didn't think Summer was right. Something about the whole situation had been bothering him, and as he walked he tried to let it play through in his mind, letting the rhythm of his steps give a structure to his thoughts. Why had no one come while Wambwark was attacking them? They had made enough noise, after all, and surely not every angel was being trained and organized by the Estedea? And after, walking through the Anbidstow, why had they seen no one, heard no one? It was as though things were being left to play out without obstruction, and the Estedea's studied ignorance of them seemed a part of this, too. But why?

What had Mayall said? That Fool was a moment of chaos in Heaven's order, something like that? That Mayall wanted the chaos, or liked it, that he was enjoying it? Was this part of that? Was that it? Was Fool being used as part of some bigger game, to see what he would do and to see where it would take things? Neither helped nor hindered but left, to be observed, to see if what he and Summer and Gordie did was fun? Was interesting? Was useful?

Yes.

Yes, it fit. *I'm being used again,* he thought, thinking of Elderflower and the fires that had burned through the Houska and the smoke that had risen and a shadow that suddenly seemed huge and horned. *It's happening again.*

Were the attacks of the things outside being used as an excuse for the war? But if they were, why let Fool carry on? *Because there're other ways to come to victory,* he thought. *If I prove that the things outside are responsible, then the war can be against them, and Heaven and Hell can work together, both trying to infiltrate and manipulate and gain a subtler win.*

So why don't I just stop? Let this play out without our interference? Let them go to war and just stay in our room and be kept prisoners, safe and warm and fed? Surely that's the best thing?

No.

Why?

No, because of justice. Because of truth. Because of the dead.

Because of Marianne.

Yes, because this isn't our business, this is too big for us to face, let the angels and the demons work it out themselves.

No.

Yes.

They had reached the fields, smooth sweeps of crops ahead of them. Now was the time, if ever. Turn back or go on?

Turn or go?

Fool took out the feather again, held it aloft, and said, "Which way?"

He let go. The feather spun as it dropped, twisting on unseen zephyrs, and came to land on the edge of the field. It was pointing out, into Heaven, and Fool didn't care whose truth it was, whether the feather was obeying Mayall's dictates or simply reflecting his own beliefs or being used by some other, greater, power, because it had given him his answer.

They went on.

They skirted the first field, walking up one edge and then following the boundary around, moving down the gap between the hedgerow and the planted crops. Fool asked the feather several more times which direction to head in, and each time they followed its lead, moving deeper and deeper into the farmland. They passed one or two smaller groups of the Joyful, one mass of them standing motionless in the center of the crops and another clustered around a small stone farmhouse. This second set, unlike the first, were spinning and dancing slowly, and Fool wondered if they might eventually stop and become like the first; if they would all, in the end, need the attention of the reaping angels, the ones he had seen cut the Joyful loose from the growths the day before, or the day before that, whenever it had been.

They saw no caretaker angels and nothing moved in the skies above them.

On the far side of the fields, after walking several miles, the land altered. Here, the earth was planted not with crops but with green, short grass and copses of trees in which wooden benches were standing empty. The gap between crop and hedge widened as the crops fell back and the hedge came to an abrupt end in a neat caesura. Ahead of them was a road, a black metal strip leading to a small town.

It wasn't like anything Fool had seen in Heaven before. The buildings were clapboard and old, baked into submission by a sun that suddenly seemed terribly hot. The sidewalks were dusty and what little breeze there was picked up the dust in motes and turned them as though examining them for flaws. Joyful peppered the sidewalk, dressed in old and faded smock shirts and trousers, the women in long dresses. All had their faces raised to the sun and most were tanned a deep brown by its heat, some turning slowly, others still. Wagons were standing motionless in the center of the road or pulled up to the sidewalk in front of the buildings, their canvas rears fluttering slightly in the small breaths of wind. Heavy cords tied the canvases to the wagons' wooden frames, and the canvases themselves were bleached by the sun and looked dry and brittle. The fronts of the wagons had yokes, but there were no creatures of burden attached to any of them.

"Do we go through? Or around?" asked Summer.

"Neither," said Fool, letting the feather drop again and looking at the direction it pointed them to. "We go away."

They walked again, away from the town, and soon the grass had given way, becoming at first scrubland and then shifting into a sandy place of cliffs and rocky earth with little plant growth. The feather led them into an area shadowed by cliffs and huge, tumbled formations of rock and scree before guiding them into a dry gorge that rose in ragged steps to a cliff-top mesa. They reached the top, panting with exertion, and Fool wished they had brought water. His mouth felt hot and cottony, thick with a clinging skin of dust or sand.

From the top of the cliff they were sent down the sloped far side to a dusty, barren landscape of rocks and stunted bushes. At the point where the slope leveled out, a spring bubbled in the center of a small patch of greenness and all three drank deeply. The water tasted clean and fresh and slicked through the coating in Fool's mouth, washing it away with each delightful swallow.

"Were you thinking about water?" asked Summer.

"I was," said Gordie, "when we reached the top of the cliff."

"Me too," said Fool.

"We all thought about it and it was there," said Summer. "Is that what happens here?"

"It might be," said Fool. The sense of their being allowed to move freely, of being observed for what they might achieve, hit him strongly again, and he wondered if Summer was right, if the water had been provided for them because they'd all thought about it at the same time and strongly enough for Heaven to hear. Was it Mayall? The Malakim? Or some other part of Heaven as yet unmet, watching over them and making sure they reached whatever goal had been set for them in vast plans he would never be a party to? He mouthed a silent thanks, unsure whom he was thanking, and they carried on.

The path led through the center of the plain, jagging back and forth, moving around large rocky outcrops and between dust-bowl areas thick with red, rough sand. Creatures moved around them, too small to see, indistinct apart from the skitter of their feet and, once, a hiss that might have been a warning.

"I wonder how far away it is," said Summer, moving back to the center of the path and looking suspiciously at the knotty plants near the path's edge that the hiss had come from.

"We'll see the chapel," said Gordie, "and then we'll know we're close."

"No, things change, don't they? Heaven changes all the time, we can look out of a window one day and see fields, look out the next and see the sea. The tunnel mouth could be anywhere, couldn't it?"

"No," said Fool, emphatic, "Gordie's right. Whatever else has changed, it'll be by the chapel. The tunnel came out there for a reason, because the things from outside wanted the books in the graves. The graveyard's huge, and hundreds of graves have been opened and robbed; whatever happened there has been happening for a long time. The tunnel and the chapel are linked. When we find the tunnel, we'll find it by the chapel. Keep looking for the chapel."

Plants covered in spikes and thorns grew sparsely along the path, and all three sweated as they walked, the sun above them seeming lower and closer and hotter than any other part of Heaven they had visited. It was directly above them, puddling their shadows squat around their feet. There were Joyful here as well, most of them still, some of them sitting down, all with the red dirt smearing their clothes and faces. They appeared unaware of the sun. Farther back from the path Fool saw several Joyful lying down, their bodies partly obscured by mounds of dust and small rocks. *What must they be dreaming of, to create this landscape?* he thought. *What kind of people are these, to love somewhere so rough and harsh?*

If I was dreaming, what landscape would I make? An angelic version of Hell, the place I know best? Or somewhere from a past I don't remember, haven't ever been able to know, some space that meant something to me before I was born into Hell?

The sun blazed, huge and yellow in a sky that shimmered with heat, and they walked and the sweat gathered in their boots and rolled across their foreheads. Fool's clothes had started to smell, the dried blood upon them beginning to flake and crust, and he wished he had taken the chance to rinse them at the spring. He wished they weren't black.

He wished, and knew wishes were the bastard children of hope and that hope was dangerous.

How long they walked, Fool wasn't sure. It felt like it should be nighttime but it was still day and he wondered, *Is that because I'm so tired or is that because the time of day is like the landscape, different in different parts of Heaven? I entered the Sleepers' Cave in daytime and left it in night, but had enough time passed to make it night or was that just Heaven, just the changing of Heaven?* He took his jacket off and draped it over an arm, wanting to drop it by the wayside but not daring to because the next place they came to might be cold, might be one of the seascapes in the Estedea's painting, the air gray and bitter and filled with stinging needles of spray. Besides, it was his, the skin he wore as an Information Man, and he couldn't simply drop it and leave it behind. Even marked in his own blood and the blood of others and the thick, clinging dust, filthy with sweat and dirt, it was his and he would keep it because he had nothing else.

"There," said Gordie and pointed at a distant shape. Fool squinted at it as Summer raised a hand to her eyes to shield them as she stared.

"Yes," she said.

They had found the chapel.

As they approached the chapel, the temperature dropped and the air began to feel heavy with rain. The clouds that gathered above the angels were gradually expanding, their edges slithering out, the mass ballooning across the sky and shading the earth from the sun's gaze. Here and there lightning flashed in the clouds, the sharp white streaks illuminating the grayness around them and sending skittering leaps of shadow across the ground. The wind was picking up, chilling the air and making Fool's clothes flap. He put his jacket back on as a larger spike of lightning, still contained within the cloud, flashed. There was no thunder.

The landscape changed as they came to the chapel. The arid, rock-strewn gulches and cliffs eased, and although the fields that had surrounded the chapel the last time they were there did not reappear, the earth did flatten and smooth. They came to the wall that surrounded the chapel and the graveyard, now made of old stone and tumbled down in places, and walked along it until they could see the tunnel.

There were angels around the opening in the earth, although their number was fewer than in the period after the initial attack and Israfil's taking. They were standing facing the tunnel's mouth in the earth and each had their flame already burning, coils of fire held down and steady, curling around their feet while above them clouds gathered and churned. They ignored Fool and Summer and Gordie as they watched them from beyond the wall, their attention never shifting from the tunnel.

"What do we do?"

"The graveyard first," said Fool. "We didn't get a chance to inspect it properly last time and I want to look around."

"Will they let us?"

"Yes," and he was confident they would because, like the dead Joyful, they weren't supposed to be here, so the angels wouldn't see them. They were invisible unless they made themselves visible by pushing themselves into the foreground, except perhaps to the likes of Mayall.

"Come on."

They clambered over the wall and made their way to the building. Gordie went to go around the far side but Fool pulled him toward the tunnel and its attendant angels.

"No," he said, "this way. This is the direction the things from outside would have come from, and we have to go where they've been."

For all his bluster, Fool was nervous. This wasn't his territory and he understood too little to be anything other than anxious. The sound of his footsteps seemed terribly loud, echoing even over the increasingly powerful gusts of wind, and his breathing roared in and out of him. Surely the angels would hear, would turn to see what was creating this clamor, would see them then and respond? But no; the angels remained transfixed by the tunnel and ignored them as they made their way to the chapel's front.

Its door was open and Fool couldn't help looking into the chapel as they passed it. The inside of the building was plain, with neither decoration nor furniture, and it was filled with books. They were piled in huge towers, taller than he was, carefully lined up so that they balanced perfectly, some of the columns joined at their upper heights by carefully constructed bridges of larger books, overlaid so that the weight of the upper tomes was borne by all those below. The books were worn and, in some cases, damaged, spines etched with lines and cracks, the edges of covers fraying and loose. The effect was to make the space into a strangely worked lattice that appeared both elegant and decaying.

"I think they're waiting to be buried," said Gordie. "Look."

He was pointing at the far end of the chapel, where another series of columns made from books was standing, these shorter and draped with cloth, each cloth stitched with symbols. Fool saw crosses and stars and half circles and other sewn shapes, neat and small and regular in the cloths' weave. By the piled books, on the floor, were scrolls and what looked like pamphlets, their printing cheap and uneven.

Fool backed away from the door. The sight of the books was unnerving, things that had never been alive but that nonetheless now looked dead, collected together, stacked and sculpted and awaiting disposal. Awaiting burial.

"Let's go," he said and carried on along the front of the chapel, glad to turn his back on the dead tomes and walk away. Turning along the chapel's side, they started toward the graveyard.

Even with the light made gray by the clouds and the wind pushing and pulling at the air, Fool could see the signs now that he was looking for them. There were long striations in the earth alongside the base of the walls, as if something had skulked low and dragged itself along the chapel's side. Some of the scores were older, had grass growing in their depths, were overlaid by newer marks in which the only growths were the tiny blue flowers. Indentations around the marks might have been made by clawed or pincered feet.

The chapel was made of rough, dark stone, and when Fool turned his Information Man's eye on it, he saw the marks of the things' passing here, too. Long scratches had been dragged into the stone, hard cara-paces or shells scraping the building as the things went by. The scratches were at all heights, from just above ground level to above Fool's head, too high for him to reach even when stretching. The marks undulated in irregular jags, as though whatever had made them had been moving unevenly, jerking from point to point.

"Summer, stay here and see if there's anything else," said Fool after pointing out the scratches on earth and wall. "See if they left anything physical, like the scale, that we can use. Look properly, Summer; you were an excellent officer and I need you to be one again. Gordie, come with me."

The two men went around to the rear of the building, hurrying now. In pallid daylight, Fool saw that the graveyard was far larger than he had realized. It stretched off into the distance, the rows of stone mark-ers and occasional gnarled, twisting trees eventually blurring together and then down to nothing and merging with the horizon. There were no angels here, and Fool and Gordie were free to walk among the gap-ing, ravaged mouths of the graves and to see the disinterred and dam-aged books without distraction.

The holes were rough and uneven, the earth of the graves ripped apart in the things' desperation to reach the buried tomes. Around the graves' lips were tears in the turf that exposed the rich, dark soil below, and at the bottom of the holes were the fragments of books. Now that he was able to observe without obstruction and to take a little time over the viewing, Fool saw that the books had been buried in large shrouds of the same stitched cloth he had seen in the chapel and that these had been torn open by the grave robbers, the material ripped to strings and peeled back like the skin of one of the bodies on Tidyman's or Hand's tables. The damp earth had stained the material and the paper that remained in the graves, painting everything with a dirty brown luster.

"Be fast," said Fool to Gordie. "See if there's anything that'll help us persuade Heaven or Hell what's happening here. We need to move."

They looked around, spreading out their search and calling to each other as they went, but found nothing. Fool gestured Gordie back to him and they went to the edge of the graveyard, staring out over it and trying to see what they had missed. *There must be something, some-fuckingthing we've not grasped, some other way of reading this place, surely,* thought Fool, feeling the tension knot inside him. They had to be quick, to be quicker than they were; otherwise all this was going to be for nothing and the war would start despite them.

"The books are evidence, aren't they?" said Gordie eventually. His voice was whipped around by the growing wind, and Fool had to concentrate to hear it and to raise his own voice in reply.

"They don't prove anything by themselves," said Fool, snapping, frustrated. "They're just books, buried and dug up. If we show them to Mayall he'll say, 'Yes, we know, the demons that came from the tunnel did that,' and if we show them to Rhakshasas he'll say, 'So fucking what?' We need more than this. We need something solid. We need *something.*"

"Solid? Like what? There's nothing here, not that we have time to find," said Gordie, almost but not quite shouting. "We have the scale, there's the pincer in the office in Hell, the claw, what else can we show them?"

"I don't know," cried Fool. "I don't fucking *know!*"

"How about this?" said Summer, coming around the corner of the chapel and holding something up for them to see.

At first Fool couldn't tell what she was holding. It was swinging in her hand and, by the look on her face, it wasn't pleasant; she was carrying it away from her, and when it swung back in toward her she twisted away from it. What was it? A bag? A dead bird?

No, none of those things, he realized; it was a demon.

It was small and dead. Summer was holding it by its hands and feet so that it was bent double, hanging loose and swaying at the end of her outstretched arm.

"It's a dead demon," said Gordie.

"It's not," said Summer.

"It is," said Fool. "Look at it, Summer. Fuck, if Heaven sees that, it'll confirm every suspicion they've got. 'This is Hell's doing,' they'll say. 'Look, we have a dead demon as proof!'"

"It's *not*," said Summer.

"It is, Summer, it's a demon. A dead demon, not a thing from outside," Fool said, and then carried on, almost to himself, "I was wrong. This was Hell all along." *Little confused Fool, little wrong Fool.*

"Fool, will you look," said Summer loudly and tossed the demon at him. The thing spun in the air, lazy and flailing, and its intestines spilled from it as it spun, fluttering down to the earth below. It hit the ground by Fool's feet and slithered toward him, still spilling itself, and Fool took an involuntary step back. His heels dug into air and he teetered on the edge of a grave before Gordie gripped his arm and pulled him forward, stabilizing him.

"You weren't wrong," said Gordie when he'd let go of Fool's arm and knelt down by the dead demon. He started pushing through the thing's guts, now lying in a pale fan behind it, his fingers turned and teasing at the intestines.

No, not intestines, not guts, something else, something dry and pale, something that rustled and crinkled. Something that fluttered in the wind, rose up off the ground, and danced and dropped and spun.

Paper. The demon was filled with paper.

Fool knelt as well, took hold of the demon, and lifted it. It was light and came up from the ground easily, hanging limp in his hand. As he lifted it, it unfurled and more paper fell from it, spilling into a messy pile at Fool's feet before being picked up by the gusting wind and leaping away from him out of his reach. He took hold of the demon's clawed feet and small, clawed hands and pulled it flat and stretched it in front of him. Flaps of its skin sagged away from it, dangling in a parody of angels' wings, but the thing had no real shape. "What?" Fool asked aloud and then saw, really saw, and dropped the demon with a cry of disgust.

The thing had been hollowed out and its skin used to carry the unearthed books.

The demon had been split up its back, along the line of its spine, and the whole of its chest cavity had been opened up and the contents besides the spine itself removed, the ribs and intestines and heart and lungs all gone, assuming it ever had them. The job had been done inexpertly and the inside of the little thing's skin was still crusted with gobbets of flesh, now dried and dark. Paper had stuck to the blood and lined the thing like clumsy decoration, rustling and crackling as Fool poked at the body with his toe cap, flipping it over and over and feeling a curious mix of disgust and sorrow. Even demons didn't deserve to be treated like this.

Its eyes had fallen in, were still attached to the skin but popped and dry now like old fruit skin left in the sun, and several joints of its spine had been snapped to make it bend back on itself. Fool forced himself to pick it up again, not liking the way its flesh felt in his hands, and folded it up. Its skin had been stretched and torn, the holes placed so that the thing's hands and feet could be used to keep the skin up, turning it into the sides of the makeshift bag. Its head hung down limply, staring back at itself as though shocked by what had been done to it. The back of its head was crushed, and gray brain matter bulged from the wound, dry and old. It stank, the rotten stench of its dead flesh making Fool's eyes water. He put it back onto the ground and wiped his hands on the wet grass.

"I found it behind the wall," said Summer. "They needed something to carry the books in, so they used it as a bag. It's proof, Fool; demons wouldn't do this to other demons."

"No," Fool agreed, because Summer was right; demonkind violence was only ever toward humans, toward the Sorrowful.

Could this be the Evidence, then? Was this what they did? No, they simply vanished things into the shadows and never returned them, and besides, they were in Hell, not Heaven. And what had Mr. Tap said, that demons were vanishing that the Evidence hadn't taken? This was the work not of Hell but of something else, some other terrors attacking Hell, killing its denizens.

This was the things from places outside of everywhere, breaking in.

Yes, *yes,* because that's what this was, it had to be, two sets of attacks carried out at once, the assaults on Hell and the assaults on Heaven, one fueling the other, parallel lines of savagery and violence. This little thing and how many others taken from Hell and used in Heaven, Israfil and the Joyful and the books taken from Heaven and used where? Used how?

It didn't matter. The *where* and the *why* could come later, after he stopped the war, because if the war went ahead, so many would die and both sides would be distracted, weaker, ripe for a head-on assault rather than these sneaky, secretive stabs.

"Gordie, get one of the cloths from a grave," said Fool, "one that's not too badly damaged. Put the demon in it and some of the damaged books. Have you got the scale and the claw?"

"Yes."

"Good. Put them in as well, we'll take it all. We'll show Rhakshasas first, get him to understand. If he listens to us and to the Man, he may help us persuade the rest of the Bureaucracy and might be able to speak to Heaven, to Mayall or whomever it is he needs to speak to. To get them to come together and listen."

"Will that be enough?"

"I don't know," said Fool. "But we have to try. At the very least, we have to try."

"There's something we haven't thought about," said Summer. "How do we get back to Hell?"

"The angels told me that the Flame Garden was the link between all the worlds, but I don't have time to find Heaven's version of it, the Garden of Earth and Air, and I don't know how to get into it. Even if I could find it, I don't know if we can travel those roads only if we have angels or demons with us, so there's only one way to go."

"How?"

"The tunnel. We have to go through the tunnel."

25

They gathered up the evidence, putting the demon in the bag first and then covering it with the ripped remains of the religious texts. Fool knelt and filled his pockets with torn paper for reasons he wasn't completely sure of, and then turned and watched as Gordie took the scale from his pocket, looking at it carefully, lifting it to the sun, and rotating it slowly. Fool watched him, the question unasked, waiting. Gordie's brain was analytical, kept facts in a viselike grip, but sometimes it took him time to make connections.

"There's something," he said after a minute. "I don't know what, but this is strange. It's odd."

"Odd?" *Again, odd.*

"Odd," the man repeated helplessly. "I can't work out why, though."

"Gordie, it's from outside," said Summer. "Of course it's odd."

"Maybe," said Gordie and dropped the scale into the bag and then tied it around the rip so that the contents would stay safe. The bag was large enough to still have long strips of canvas loose after being tied shut, and Gordie used these to fashion a clumsy strap so that he could hang the bag over his shoulder. When Fool tried to take it from him, Gordie simply shook his head and looked at how Fool was standing, still twisted and hunched, pulled around by the badly healed scarring across his belly. Fool didn't have the time to argue, so he simply nodded and turned, heading for the tunnel.

The ground between the chapel and the tunnel's entrance was now thick with blue flowers. It was as though, now that Heaven had allowed itself to see and acknowledge the intrusion, the flowers could bloom fully. Some were as high as Fool's knees and left clinging oily streaks across his lower legs as he pushed through them, and the smell of them was horrible, thick and cloying and sick. He heard Summer choking as they made their way to the tunnel, with its flanks of guardian angels, and when he turned he saw her vomit across the flowers. What emerged from her mouth was little more than a thin gruel of bile and saliva, and he wondered if she and Gordie had eaten at all since their rebirth.

When had he last eaten? He thought of food, of the clean water he had used to wash himself and the way his hair had felt after he had used the soap on it, the way it had squeaked as he ran his fingers through it, and then realized he had stopped walking. Summer and Gordie were looking at him, and it was their turn to have unanswered questions written in their expressions.

"It's nothing," said Fool, thinking, *Is this how it works? You get distracted, fall into a reverie that becomes a daydream that becomes a sleep? Forget? Is this how it is in Heaven, the grandest distraction there is?*

No. No, I have to focus, I have to avoid the distractions. I have a war to stop. He started walking again, one foot in front of the other, aching body finding as comfortable a rhythm as possible, concentrating on the angels ahead of them. None of them turned as they approached and they did not stop Fool as he reached the rear line of them and started to thread his way among them. They glowed, pale and low, in the gathering dark, their feathers ruffled by the wind, their hair blowing across the faces and lifting from their scalps in untidy halos. They were identical, statues carved by the same hand to the same beautiful design, their arms and chests muscled and their bellies taut with strength. They wore nothing and, like Benjamin, their groins were feathered, the overlapping lines of them sweeping down from just below their navels to the tops of their thighs. Their eyes gleamed, violet and bright, but none of them turned their gaze upon the humans in their midst.

Fool made his way among them, careful not to touch any of them as he slipped between them, seeing that Summer and Gordie were taking the same precautions behind him. It took several delicate minutes to get through the ranks, but he eventually found himself at the tunnel's edge; the closest angels were around three feet back from the lip and Fool was able to walk out into the space unchallenged.

"Why aren't they stopping us?" asked Summer, emerging from between two of the angels and joining Fool, Gordie behind her.

"Because we're not supposed to be here, so they don't see us," said Fool. "It's the same as it was with the bodies, with Benjamin and Israfil."

"No," said Benjamin from above them, "in this you are wrong, Thomas Fool. It is not that they do not see you, they do; it is that they were created for a single purpose, to stop anything emerging from this hole, and until you try to do that, you are of no concern to them."

The angel was hanging in the air above the hole, wings flapping slowly to keep him aloft. Against the clouds his body gleamed, his wings perfect arcs, his arms low and folded across his stomach, and his legs apart, the smaller wings at his ankles beating easily. Fool couldn't help but notice that the wings on one leg did not beat in the same rhythm as the other leg; each pair worked independently of the other, correcting the angel's position whenever the wind tried to turn him. Benjamin let himself drop so that, although still over the tunnel's mouth, his head was at Fool's level and said, "Thomas Fool, I have something to say."

Here it is, then, thought Fool. *The end of it. They've watched us long enough, seen what they needed to see, and now Benjamin has been sent to gather us back up, to bring us back into the fold, little lost fools that we are.* His hand dropped to his gun and then, realizing how hopeless it would be, he moved it away again. "Well then," he said, dropping his chin to his chest and sighing, weary, "let's get on with it."

"You are wrong about the angels here, but about the bodies you are correct. About the help that you were given, or rather not given, you are correct. About me, and about Israfil, you are correct. Thomas Fool, I have come to apologize and to offer myself as your servant."

It wasn't what Fool expected nor, judging by the surprised gasps that came from Summer and Gordie, what his companions expected either. Fool raised his head and looked at the angel, still bobbing gently in the air above the tunnel, the expression on his face one of contrite concern, a faint smile playing around his lips.

"I was wrong," said the angel, his voice calm yet clear against the still-rising wind. "We have become complacent, I think. I have become complacent, too confident in myself, and have committed the sins of pride and hubris. I would make amends, Thomas Fool, if you tell me what amends need making."

"I need to stop this war," said Fool. It was getting colder, his breath misting before him as he spoke, "or at least, I need to *try* to stop this war. I need to get to Hell, to speak to Rhakshasas."

"And he will stop it?"

"I don't know. It depends how much they want it—Heaven and Hell, I mean. If the war is part of some bigger plan that we're only small cogs within, then it won't stop no matter what I do, but I have to try. People are already dying, and going to war over a mistake is going to mean more people die."

"They are already dead," said Benjamin, "and those in Hell are sinners. Perhaps they deserve the punishment?"

How could Fool explain? That no one in Hell knew their sin, only that they had sinned somewhen before, and Hell's punishment was the one of injustice in the moment, of not knowing, and that this was fair in the long run because the atonement of sin could take any form? Fool had come to understand it over the past months, since the Fallen, that what made Hell *Hell* was precisely the sense that everyone there was being punished, knew that the punishment was just but felt its injustice because of the blank space in the center of themselves where memories should be. Death in the middle of a war between Heaven and Hell would not be fair, it would be *unjust*. What he said, though, was simply, "I have no choice. It's my job."

"Yes," said Benjamin. "And I will help however I can because I have said I will and because amends must be made. Please, tell me what you want me to do."

"I need to get to Hell," said Fool.

"We cannot go to the Garden," said Benjamin. "The link between the worlds has been, at least in part, closed while the conflict plays out. We can use the tunnel, however, although I don't know where in Hell it comes out. I can take you as far as the border but won't be able to enter Hell with you. Without the protection of the Estedea, I would burn the moment I emerged into its atmosphere."

"That's fine. Thank you," said Fool, and at that moment the clouds above Benjamin started to weep.

It wasn't rain. What dropped from the clouds were fat white flakes that plunged down in great swoops, looping around each other, thicker and thicker and thicker until the air was filled with them. Where they landed on Fool's skin they burned with cold, melting slowly. He held a hand out, marveling as the flakes hit his exposed skin and collapsing, shifting from crystalline white shapes to tiny puddles that trickled away.

"What is it?" asked Summer, her head back and her mouth open. She stuck a tongue out and a flake landed on it, melting to nothing.

"It's water!" she exclaimed. "Water! It's so cold, but it's water."

"It's snow," said Benjamin. "The sky is reflecting the moods around the tunnel. Do you not have snow in Hell?"

"No," said Gordie, head also back. Snow had gathered across his forehead, was crusting his eyebrows and catching in his hair, was decorating him with flickers of whiteness. Fool suspected he looked the same and brushed at the snow that had clung to his jacket. His hand came away streaked with pink as the snow melted and drew the dried blood in his skin back to liquid. He shivered, cold.

"It's beautiful," said Summer and she was right, it was beautiful. "I wish I could draw it."

Gordie reached up and brushed snow from Summer's hair. "You're beautiful," he said, so quietly that Fool thought only he and Summer had heard him. She didn't reply but reached up and took his hand and drew it to her face, kissing his fingertips.

"Thank you," she said.

"We should go," said Benjamin and flew to them, opening his arms. He took Gordie and Summer into his right arm and Fool in his left, shifting a few times to get the weight of them set to his satisfaction.

"Wait," said Fool, looking around. He raised his hands to his ears and reached inside them. His fingertips brushed against what he sought and he pulled out the two pieces of Benjamin's dried spittle carefully. Closing his eyes, he heard that music again, the endless song of songs, the voices and timpani and lute and mandolin and piccolo and everything else as well. Like the snow, it was beautiful, filled the sky inside his head. It was, he suspected, the last time he would hear it.

Finally, Fool opened his eyes. "I'm ready," he said.

Benjamin flapped his wings, once, gently. They lifted from the ground, rose, and then moved out over the hole. Its black maw opened to greet them, and Fool had to swallow a surprisingly large lump of sorrow as he looked around. His last view of Heaven was of a motionless rank of beautiful, somber angels surrounded by falling snow and, behind them, the chapel of all faiths standing alone and mute in the storm light.

They descended.

Fool had expected the flight to be choppy, to feel the movement of Benjamin's wings, but he did not. Although he could hear the wings' beating and feel the slight ripple of air caused by their flapping, Benjamin held them close and they dropped smoothly and easily.

Once they were below the opening of the tunnel with its fringe of exposed roots and dying grass, darkness crept after them. Away from the sky and the whiteness of the snow, the only light came from Benjamin himself and it illuminated only the walls around them, so that it began to feel to Fool as though they were traveling in a bubble of glimmering, pale glow. The tunnel's walls were dark, rough earth that glinted slightly as though it had melted and then solidified into a glaze, and although Fool tried his best to look for them, he saw no sign of the things from outside. Once, he thought he saw the blackness of the wall bulge as they passed, but he couldn't be sure, and soon the place above them was lost to view. The air warmed so that their breath no longer misted in front of them, and the silence that hung about them was thick and furred.

"Won't you get in trouble for helping us?" asked Summer.

"No," Benjamin replied. "Angels who get in trouble Fall, and that's not something I'll do. I'm no rebel or challenger. I have permission to do this."

"From whom?" asked Gordie, echoing the question that had been forming on Fool's tongue.

"Mayall and the Malakim," said Benjamin. The tunnel kinked slightly and they spun as the angel corrected his drop to take them away from the wall. They were so deep now that it was no longer soil they moved through but rock, fissured and cracked and with tiny white roots growing in the cracks.

"They know you're here?"

"Of course. I am a creature of permissions, Miss Summer. I cannot act without instruction. The Malakim told me that, if I felt it necessary, I could help Thomas, and Mayall concurred. I have to join the army when I return, and I shall do so gladly, knowing I have carried out my duty, that I have balanced things as far as I can.

"Now, may I ask you a question?"

"Of course," said Summer. *Miss Summer,* Fool thought and smiled in the darkness. He could no longer see the walls and had the sense that the space around them had opened up and that, at the same time, it had closed in, so that he could reach out and touch its edges if he wanted to.

We're not traveling through earth or rock anymore, he thought. *We're traveling through nothing, through the spaces between the worlds.* He hoped Benjamin's grip was firm.

"Thomas Fool has two names yet you do not, neither you nor Master Gordie. Why is this?"

"It's always been this way," said Summer. "We're given our names when we're fished from Limbo and given our roles. We have no choice."

"I wondered if it was a signifier of a person's importance," said Benjamin. "Given the role Thomas Fool played in the changing of Hell and the importance Mayall and the Malakim clearly place upon him and his skills, that would make sense."

"No," said Fool, emphatically. "I have two names because I have two names, Summer and Gordie have one because they have one. That's just how it is. I'm no more important than anyone else."

"Are you sure?" asked Benjamin, and then, with a dizzying shift in perspective, they were no longer dropping down but were upside down and rising feetfirst. Fool's clothes flapped down, covering his face, and he heard Summer gasp. Gordie grunted and something swung hard into Fool's chest. He slipped, slithering through Benjamin's arm before tightening his grip and feeling the angel do the same. Once he was secure, he reached up and pulled the tail of his jacket away from his face as Gordie reached and took a better hold of the homemade bag, pulling it back across the angel and away from Fool.

Fool looked up at his feet, craning his neck against the newly inverted gravity to see that an opening had appeared below their feet through which he could see the roiling skies of Hell.

Another shift, and they were rising, head up, to the hole.

The skies above them were red, stained by fires he could not see but knew were there, and the clouds that scudded and churned in the sky were black and stained. Already, the smell of Hell was drifting down to them, the thick miasma of fires and mud and unwashed bodies and fear, so rich and dense, so unlike the delicate fragrance of Heaven. Fool breathed it in, remembering, and felt the lump in his throat once more for everything he had been allowed to see and then had taken away, suddenly mourning soap and clean water and air that tasted good and snow.

"We are here," Benjamin said and flapped his wings once, hard, so that they spun loosely about, coming to a new upright just below the opening's edge. "I can go no farther. I am unable to fly past this point, as we would be in Hell and angels cannot fly in the place of no freedoms or joys."

Benjamin allowed himself to drift in close to the wall, now the glazed dirt again, and allowed Fool to use his arm as a step to reach up for the edge of the tunnel. He clambered up, back into Hell, and then turned back to help Summer first and then Gordie, hauling on the man's arms to bring him and the load he carried up safely. Doing so made his belly ache, pulled at the skin, and made him wince. The smell was worse now that he was out of the tunnel, made him gag again, and he wondered how he had ever not noticed it, how they breathed every day. It burned at his throat, making him swallow repeatedly to try to moisten away the pain.

"Thank you," he managed to say to Benjamin. "I'll try to find Israfil, if I can."

"Thank you, but Israfil is gone," said Benjamin, beginning to drop away. "Without her wings, she is as good as dead. Remember, Thomas Fool, in the war that comes all the rules will change and the old accords will be dismantled. I cannot fly in Hell now, no angel can, but the Estedea will be able to when they arrive because in conflict all the old rules are unwritten. Take care, Thomas Fool, Miss Summer, Master Gordie."

"You too," said Fool and watched as Benjamin sank into the tunnel's darkness. His last view of the angel was of his pale face as the shadows swallowed him, his eyes sad and his mouth no longer smiling.

"We're back," said Summer.

"We're back," said Gordie, as though confirming something he could not quite believe.

"Yes," said Fool, turning, wanting to know where in Hell they were, and then Gordie's hand was on his shoulder and was dragging him so that he stumbled, and Gordie hissed, "Get *up*," and they were running and then they were crashing into bushes and Gordie was pushing him to the ground and hissing at him to be *quiet*, be *quiet*, and Fool rolled, found himself peering back through the undergrowth at where the tunnel had emerged and realized that he was in a place of greater horrors than he had imagined possible.

26

Fool found himself lying in a damp patch of foul-smelling dirt surrounded by a clump of thin, straggling bushes. His ribs and shoulder ached from Gordie's grip and subsequent crash to the ground and he could feel fresh earth smeared across his face. Gordie, panting, was by his side. Summer had landed on one of the bushes on the far side of him and was trying to move across so that the branches did not dig into her or scratch her face. Gordie put out a hand to still her.

"Gordie, what—" said Fool, but Gordie interrupted him with a low, wordless hiss and pointed through the bushes back toward the tunnel entrance. Fool, following the line of his finger, squinted through the bushes and across the tunnel and saw what Gordie was gesturing toward.

They had found the missing Joyful.

The tunnel came up from Heaven into what looked like a small clearing hemmed by the bushes that Fool and the others were now hiding in. The plants formed a rough circle around a muddy space perhaps two or three hundred yards across at its widest point, and in the space were thousands of humans. There were more than Fool had ever guessed had been stolen from Heaven, and he wondered just how long the thefts, or kidnappings, or whatever the fuck the crimes were, had been going on for—certainly longer than he'd been in Heaven, far longer. Another lie by omission, another half-truth told to him so that they didn't have to admit any kind of mistake or any kind of imperfection, and damn it all if he had known, he might have approached this differently, might have achieved something more.

Could have done better.

Maybe. He might have been able to put more pressure on the kindliest angels to leave the bodies for longer before removing them so that
he could examine them in more detail, he might have been able to persuade Mayall to let the scribe alone so that he could question it. *So many
mights and maybes,* he thought, *so many times I could have made things
different.*

Thinking about Heaven was a distraction from seeing what was
before him, but eventually he had no choice and he had to study the
scene carefully. The Joyful were naked, staked to poles that filled the
clearing beyond the tunnel's mouth, and most were battered and bloody.
Fool thought some might be dead, their skin marked with traceries of
vein and their legs dark with old, thick blood that had seeped downward to the bottom half of their bodies. Each human's feet had been
lashed to the bottom of the pole with thick cords knotted around their
ankles, the braids digging into the skin and crusted with blood that had
clotted into whorls and pellets, and their arms had been pulled tight
down and around the back of the poles so that their chests were thrust
out and their shoulders strained forward. Most appeared unconscious,
heads hanging loose, hair swinging, but some were awake, heads up,
and as they looked around they were wailing and crying and screaming.

Here and there caretaker angels hung by their wings, pinned to the
stakes with huge rusting nails.

In among the Joyful and the angels were metal braziers, drums with
punctured sides in which low flames guttered, the smoke rising from
them greasy and black. Beside each brazier was a knotted sack that Fool
recognized as being made from the material from the graves by the
chapel. They'd found the remains of the books as well, it seemed.

Fool went to speak again but another hiss and gesture from Gordie
stopped him. He was pointing at the far end of the clearing, where the
creature from the Sleepers' Cave, or one similar to it, was making its
way out of the bushes and was approaching the Joyful. Its movement
was jerky and hard, looked painful in its stretching and twisting but was
still fast, and it covered half the distance between the wall of shrubs and
the tunnel in a few seconds.

It was a different creature than the one from the cave, Fool saw,
smaller and more compact, with fewer of those segments, each joined to

the others with those twisting, writhing strips of blackness that flexed
like fingers with too many knuckles. In Hell's light it was slightly easier
to see the creature than it had been to see the one in the cave, and Fool
could make out more of it. He was struck again, as he looked at it, how
much it seemed as though an entire spiderweb had come alive and was
moving around.

Each individual part was different; most were vaguely humanlike but
tended to hunch over, limbs dragging until it needed to do something
other than move, at which point it would straighten up and assume a
more upright posture. Some of the parts had arms, he saw, others limbs
that flailed or wriggled. He saw a mess of faces, some with no eyes and
some with many, mouths open or closed, teeth large or small. Sometimes, the bands contracted and pulled two of the pieces together where
they knotted into each other, creating a single mass that could break
apart when needed, the two heads and multiple limbs working together.

As Fool watched, a part of the thing detached itself from the central
mass and moved out, dropping low and sniffing the ground. Even on
all fours it was clumsy and uncoordinated, jerking and twitching as it
swept back and forth, searching for something. Searching for them?
Fool suspected so, and held his breath as he waited to see if it would
find their trail.

It came closer, head so low that it pushed furrows through the mud,
curls of dirt peeling away from it as it drove on. Its face, covered in striations and marks, was strangely familiar to Fool, long and square and
topped with opaque black eyes above a pair of wide, pulsating nostrils.
Its mouth was wide and filled with square teeth, drool spilling over lips
that were black and pulled back from the teeth. Why did Fool think he
recognized it? Was it one of the things from outside of everywhere he
had watched in the tunnel between Heaven and Hell, what felt like a
lifetime ago?

It must be.

It came closer, the sound of it harsh, its inhalations ragged. It was
making another noise, under the snapped intakes of breath, a low keening that reminded Fool of a kettle coming to a boil. It pushed through
the soil, closer still, only a line of bushes separating them from it. Gordie took Fool's hand and squeezed and from the corner of his eye Fool

saw that the man's face was ghostly white, his eyes wide. His lips were trembling as though trying to contain the scream that was massing in his mouth, the same scream that was building in Fool's own mouth as he bit back on it and the thing pushed closer.

Its nose was now edging against the far side of the bushes, its eyes looking through the twisted stalks and leaves at Fool, black orbs peering. He tried to shrink back noiselessly, hoping that his black clothes were a camouflage and painfully aware that his face would be cast as a pale circle against the dark behind him, that if the thing looked even slightly to Fool's side it would see Gordie's and Summer's near-white robes and the bag Gordie carried.

Another long sniff.

It blinked, a milky film smearing across the glistening eyeballs, and then pressed itself lower into the earth, pushing against the bushes. Fool wriggled back, looking over the thing's head and shoulders at its back. Its shoulder blades were ridged out, and between them a thick knot of the black connectors pulsed, buried into its flesh. It sniffed again and the cables surged, clenching and unclenching along their length.

Another thrust forward and its head came between the bushes, was inches from Fool's own and he was staring into its eyes. It blinked and more of the film smeared across them, covering the blackness, thick pus squeezing out from the edges of the blink. *It's blind,* he thought, *it stinks,* and hoped that Gordie had seen it as well, would stay as quiet as he could.

The thing's arms came around, questing through the earth by Fool, not hands at the end of the arms but pincers flexing open and closed, the dark earth coating it, and then the connectors contracted, pulling it back, and it jerked its way across the clearing and rejoined the main mass of the thing.

Another piece of the mass came loose, this one larger, a low bulky thing that spread out across the ground like an oil stain, the connectors in its back surging and pulsing as it moved out, its limbs grasping the ground and dragging itself along as though it was climbing a vertical wall rather than scuttling across horizontal earth. Fool tensed, risked reaching down to draw his gun, pushing it ahead of him. The thing was too big to kill with a handgun, but he might be able to delay it long enough for them to run, although where they would go and whether they'd be fast enough, he had no idea. Instead of coming toward them, though, the piece of the thing from outside went to the nearest Joyful and slithered up her back. Its face was wide and dark as it rose above the woman, pulling her head back so that her throat was exposed, and Fool thought it was going to slice her open and drink her blood but it did not.

Its face stretched, mouth opening wide, and it clamped onto the back of her head with an audible crunch. The Joyful opened her eyes and shrieked, blood running down the sides of her face. The thing sucked at the back of her head and the cables emerging from its back pulsed, throbbing as whatever it was taking from her flowed down them and back to the larger mass. Each section within the mass twitched as the pulses reached it, limbs spasming, cables between them twisting over each other and tangling. The woman screamed again, her voice cracking at the top of the scream, her face flushed red underneath the blood, saliva spilling from the corner of her mouth in long, foamy strings.

Eventually, the thing let the woman go and her head fell back to her chest. Her hair was sodden with the thing's spittle and her own blood, dark with them, and she moaned as she swung on the pole, the skin of her tethered legs stretching around the cords, tearing slightly and bleeding. The thing retreated to the mass behind it, moving slower now, replete, and another part took its place as it slithered into the black bulk and the cables swarmed around it and took it from view.

This new part did not approach a Joyful. Instead, it went to the nearest brazier, taking a pile of the torn books from the bag, and dropped them into the flames. Sparks leaped as the flames suckled hungrily and the smoke thickened. Faces appeared in the smoke, emerging from the random chaos only to fall away to nothing again. The faces were open-mouthed, eyes clenched shut, and they screamed silently as they were born and lost again. Were they the owners of the books, he wondered, or were these the faces of the books themselves, howling as they burned?

Its job done, the segment also retreated to the mass, and the thing slithered away, edges swelling and collapsing as it went, until it was gone from sight among the distant bushes.

Fool stood first. Gordie followed, then Summer, and they stepped out of the cover and into the clearing. Fool went to the nearest Joyful, tilted his head back so that he could see the man's face. It was older, the skin a rich brown, the eyes shut but not still, the lids constantly moving as the eyes beneath darted back and forth. Fool stroked the man's face, wanted to say something to soothe him but could think of nothing. What comfort was there, after all? This was Hell.

Fool was turning away from the man when he saw it, a faint glow from just past the plant line. The plants were taller here, over head height, and the glow was coming from within them. He hesitated, torn between carrying on and investigating.

Carry on and stop the war.

Investigate and maybe find the thing that would stop the war, maybe find the piece of evidence that neither Heaven nor Hell could ignore.

Carry on.

Investigate, because that was what he did and it was what he was and the choices he had were limited and small and dictated by the Information Man that he had been and was still becoming and the Commander of the Information Office that he had no desire to be but was anyway. Investigate, because that was, really, all there was.

He started toward the glow, walking quietly, aware that there were probably more of the things from outside all around him. Did they sleep? Or were they always alert, wary of the place they had come to and the dangers it contained? He held his gun loosely and tried to watch all sides at once as he went to the glow, and it took him less than a minute to find out what was causing it.

Israfil.

The angel had been bound much like the Joyful and her compatriot angels, her feet lashed to a fat pole that had been driven into the earth and her arms pulled tight behind her. Her fire was down to almost nothing now, mere flickers of flame like match-head sparks igniting and then flaring out. Her hair had been shorn and lay around her in long hanks that had been trampled into the mud.

When he went behind her, Fool saw that the stake had been jammed against her back between the remains of her wings, the bloodied stumps forced apart by the wood. The wings by her feet had been torn away, the wounds of their removal still bleeding, rubbed continuously raw by the ropes that bound her. The rear of her head was covered with countless tooth marks and splits, some still weeping thick red liquid, others wearing crusts of dried blood. A single large scab hung, half torn away, above Israfil's right eye. Her left was gone, a gored hole in her face where the orb used to be.

At Fool's approach, Israfil lifted her head and looked at him. He could tell that she wasn't able to see properly, kept squinting and opening and closing her remaining eye.

"Israfil," he said, "I'm so sorry."

"Fool?" she asked, and her voice sounded like two ropes dragging together, dry and rasping and torn. "You found me. You're a better monkey than I thought."

"We all are," said Fool. "We'll help you."

Fool went to untie the cords around her ankles, but pulling on them made Israfil cry out. Her flame blossomed for a moment, the fires skimming across her skin in a shallow wave, but then faded back. He pulled again and she cried again, the sound choking away to nothing. Close to, he saw the cords were made of thick vines that had been wrapped around each other and pulled so that they frayed into each other, forming a tangle that was impossible to untie.

"What can we do?" Gordie had come to stand beside him, was staring up at the angel. Even battered and bloody, she was beautiful. Summer reached up and tried to wipe the blood from the angel's face, but she moved her head away, avoiding the touch.

"You'd burn, little girl," she said. "Even like this, my skin is hotter than you can stand. Thomas Fool, the monkey from Hell, are you still here?"

"Of course," he said, stepping into her view. She smiled at him, lips splitting back from teeth that were as white as the snow in Heaven had been. Her tongue traced the line of them, emerging from her mouth, a dark pink worm that slipped delicately out to play along her upper lip, tasting her own blood.

"Little monkey," said Israfil, sounding almost fond of him. "You found me when no one else has managed it. Do something for me?"

"I can't get you free," he said, wanting to hold this beaten thing in his arms but not daring to. "We haven't a blade to cut and the knots are too tight for us to loosen. We could find a rock and try to rub them apart."

"No," she said, "I don't want you to. I'm tired and I hurt and I'm nearly done. My soul will return to God when I die. I have faith in that. No, the thing I want you to do is simple."

"Anything."

"Avenge me. I'm an angel of war, Fool, an angel of fire and sword and vengeance. Be my fire. Be my sword. Be my vengeance."

"Yes," he said simply, and knew that he would be, or would die trying. That she had treated him so badly didn't matter, he would still do it because that was right, that was justice. He would be the vengeance of Heaven for damaging something so perfect, so wonderfully, terribly beautiful. "I give you my word."

"A monkey's word," she said. "I suppose, at this point, it's the best I can get. I'm grateful. It's fair. Go, Fool. I have no advice to give you but to be yourself. You've done better than I ever believed you could, and you're still free, unlike me. Go. Be my revenge."

He didn't answer, instead holding his gun up and pointing it at her, muzzle inches from her forehead. She smiled.

"No," said Summer. "You can't."

"Better this than leaving her to be fed upon any more."

"I don't mean that, I mean you can't because they'll know if you do, the things will know you've been here. They'll know we're trying to stop them. It's too dangerous. Israfil, I'm sorry, truly, but he can't."

"She's right, Fool," said Israfil. "Just go. My soul is free once this body dies, and I've enjoyed my life and will enjoy it more yet. Go."

"We need to go," said Gordie from behind Fool. Fool nodded and backed away. As he lost sight of the angel in the plants, the last thing he saw her do was nod once at him, still smiling, and then her head rested down again and she reminded him of the things that were sometimes strung up in Hell's fields to scare the smaller flying demonkind away from the crops.

Still walking backward, still looking at the angel even though he couldn't see her, Fool led them back to the clearing in silence. Once there, he set off swiftly around its edge, around the massed and waiting Joyful, almost running, body complaining at every step, and he ignored it because that was just pain, just feelings, and he had to drive on through them because this was almost too big to hold now; this was growing and escalating almost out of his grasp. *Keep hold, little reaching Fool,* he thought, and then they came to the first of the paths leading from the clearing. Continuing around, he found two more, each well used, each heading in a different direction.

"Which one?" asked Fool, handing over to Gordie. He had always had a better grasp of Hell's geography than Fool, and he didn't disappoint now.

"This one," said Gordie, picking a path that sloped down from the clearing. "I've got a theory. I may not be right, but I think perhaps I am."

"A theory?"

"A theory. I'm right or I'm wrong, this is as good a one as any at this point."

Fool couldn't argue, didn't have the strength, and they set off. The path was narrow but passable and they moved quickly, Fool leading and Summer at the rear, Gordie in the middle carrying the bag of torn books and the demon and the scale.

"Where are we going?" asked Fool, each word escaping on a pant.

"I think we're heading to water," said Gordie. He sounded, if anything, more tired than Fool did.

"Why water?"

"Because I think we're on one of the islands in the middle of Solomon Water," said Gordie. "I think we're out behind the banks of mist that sit in its middle. I said—didn't I?—that I'd seen them on the map, that'd I'd been hearing rumors for a while about them."

"There are always rumors," said Fool.

"But these were consistent," said Gordie. "They said the same things. Or at least, they were before I . . . you know."

"Before you died," said Summer. "Before you died, Gordie. You have to say it. You have to be clear about your past, about the part you know about, at least. It's the only thing we have that's ours."

"Yes," said Gordie. "Before I died. The map confirmed it, and I think that's where we are."

"Why?"

"I don't know. It's just a feeling."

The bushes at the side of the path were crowding in now, track narrowing, the leaves brushing against them, snagging at Fool's jacket and trousers. He pushed the branches ahead of him aside, stopping them from swinging back until Gordie and Summer were past them, crouching because the ceiling of wet leaves and interlocking branches was lowering, separating them from the sky, and then something at their side groaned.

Gordie stepped in front of Summer, trying to protect her from whatever attack was coming, but she wouldn't let him, pushing him so that they stood alongside each other, waiting.

Nothing happened and then the groan came again, long and loose and hoarse.

"What now," said Summer, her own voice low. Fool went toward the groan, gun held out, motioning behind him at Gordie and Summer to stay still. Another groan and the bushes were thicker yet, straining against him so that he had to use his weight to push through, and then they were apart and he was at the next stop of this mystery, looking at demons bound in boxes.

It was another clearing that opened ahead of Fool to reveal a muddy, shingled shoreline, a long and thin space that stretched out before him, and it was full of crates. They were made of branches lashed together with more of the vines; looking up, Fool saw that the trees that lined the clearing were riddled with the clinging growths. Here and there, vines hung down, their ends showing the signs of rough cutting and slashing.

Each crate contained a demon.

The demons were, if anything, in a worse state than Israfil was, each battered and torn and savaged. The nearest to Fool was a skinless thing from Solomon Water, and its flesh was covered in gashes and what looked like burns, a cluster of weeping holes dotted up high on its back. Its ankles and wrists had been tied together so that it was forced to lie on its front trussed up like a parcel, and in the dim light Fool saw that its claws had been torn away, the tips of its fingers bloody stumps that still dripped. The crate it had been forced into was too small, and the wooden bars, chopped branches, were pressing against it, leaving it no space to shuffle or move. Its breathing was shallow and uneven.

The crate beyond it was larger, the demon it contained a fat globule of muscle and skin covered in eyes that peered at Fool myopically, blinking. Past that were more crates, of different sizes, and all around them, on the ground, were the trimmings of the branches that had been used to make them, leaves and smaller twigs. Here and there, they had been swept into piles, and Fool was reminded of the glass in the corridors of the Anbidstow, patiently awaiting disposal.

"What are they?" said Summer from behind Fool, and he knew she was talking not about the demons, but about the things that had put the demons there.

"They're from outside," he said. "I told you. They're not us and they're not angels and they're not demons. They're . . . other."

"Can we go?" asked Gordie. "I hear something."

So did Fool, the crackle and crack of something approaching. Glancing over, he saw that the bushes and trees at the clearing's upper edge were moving, trembling in a rhythm that wasn't caused by the wind. "Let's go," he said.

"If they're on an island, they must use boats to get into Hell," said Summer. "We need to find them."

"Quickly," said Gordie. Something had started to gather in the shadows of the trees, the darkness moving, coagulating, and pushing forward. Shadows had started out into the clearing, thin tendrils of blackness that writhed across the ground toward the crates. "Quickly, before they see us."

They went as fast as they could to the water's edge and started along it, their feet splashing in the mud and water. Behind them one of the demons screamed, and then another and then another, until it was impossible to make out individual voices in the cacophony, the sound of it rising into the trees, raw and battered and hopeless. As the coast curved around, Fool glanced over his shoulder, running now, and caught a glimpse of the black tendrils slithering over the edge of the crates, forcing their way between the bars, and knew that the things from the places outside had come to feed.

27

They ran, the three of them, keeping the water on their left and the land on their right, moving so that they were abreast and could see each other. Fool was flagging now, various parts of his body going into stitch and cramp, and he stumbled, only just avoiding falling. Summer hooked an arm under his and held him up as they came around a small headland and found, at last, a collection of moored boats.

They were small, little bigger than coracles, each dragged up onto the shingle and into the cover of the trees. Around them, in the mud, were the tracks Fool had started to become familiar with, the footsteps and striations and undulating waves that spoke of the things' presence.

Gordie took one of the boat's keels and began to drag it toward the water, the noise of the hull grating across the pebbles terribly loudly, terribly *noticeably* in the quiet. Fool slumped, sitting at the top of the beach with his back against a tree trunk, gasping, trying not to retch. His skin throbbed and itched where his tattoos split and moved, his belly hurt where the new scars were being pulled, his face ached where the slashes were still healing, his legs hurt from the running, his heart hurt from the fear, and his soul hurt from the pain and misery.

"Where are we going to go?" asked Gordie, getting the boat to the water but not pushing it fully in.

"The Information Office," said Fool, catching his breath, biting down on the pain. "We need to get Marianne and the pincer. Then to Assemblies House to try to get Rhakshasas to listen to us."

"Okay," said Gordie and began to cry. His shoulders began to rack as great sobs were torn from him, moaning low and long, raising his hands to his face and covering eyes that were already leaking tears.

"Gordie," said Summer and went to him, taking him in her arms.

"I'm sorry," he said, "I'm sorry but it's too much, I can't take it. All the pain, the horrors, I'd forgotten. Those poor people, those poor *demons*, all of them used that way, for food. And we were dead and then in Heaven and it was like we had a chance but then we're here again, we're back and I'm scared. All of it, it's so awful."

Awful, thought Fool as Summer stroked Gordie's head, soothing him, *that's not even close. Maybe there aren't even words for what this is, for an angel staked in a field and its fresh pain and horror eaten, for those snatched away from their most joyous places and brought here. Maybe the words will never exist for it.*

"It's okay," said Summer even though it wasn't, it wasn't even close to okay. "You can cope. We can all cope. We've been through worse, we've seen worse. We've *died,* Gordie, died and come back, and we aren't different, we're us, we're the same, they haven't managed to change us. They can't do anything to us that hasn't already been done."

"Can't they?" asked Gordie, and Fool thought of the Joyful, tied to their stakes and being fed upon, and thought that maybe Gordie was right not to be sure.

"No," said Summer firmly. "Now we have to go. We have a war to stop."

"You make it sound so simple," said Gordie, sniffing back snot and tears. "Like we'll stroll in and just say, 'Hey, stop it!,' and they'll agree."

"Maybe they will," said Summer, finally letting go of Gordie and pulling the boat fully into the water. "Maybe they will."

They climbed into the boat. It was cramped, not meant for three, and rode low in the water, but none of them cared or suggested taking two. It was important for them to be together, Fool understood. It was important for them to be with their friends.

There was a set of small oars in the boat's belly, and Gordie took them and started to row, pulling them out into the lake. There was a bank of mist ahead of them, and as they entered it, Fool let his head drop back, let his body relax, and he drifted into something almost like sleep while he put the pieces together.

"The things are other, they're outside," he said aloud, eyes still closed, "and what do they want? They want what Heaven and Hell have. They're always trying to find a way in but they never manage it, and Heaven and Hell get lazy, get complacent, and when the things finally find a way in they don't notice.

"So they're in, but they can't launch an all-out attack straightaway."

"Why?" Summer, always the more direct of the two, closer to the point.

"Maybe they're unsure of what they're facing, maybe they're too weak, maybe they can only get a few things in at a time, so they start somewhere small. Not Heaven, their corruption would be impossible to ignore for too long, so they come and hide in Hell and they start taking demons.

"Does that sound right?

"Yes," he said, answering his own question before Summer or Gordie could, "because this wasn't recently, this was months ago, back when Hell was all chaos and uncertainty, and who's going to notice a few missing demons when everything's changing all the time? They set up on the island because nothing's here and they feed and they get strong and then they're ready for the next stage; they start traveling over the water and lighting fires and carrying out slaughters. The fires aren't about the damage so much as the fear they cause, not in the general populace, because we're frightened most of the time anyway, but in the Bureaucracy, who can't work out what's happening, they're a distraction. At the same time, they have the strength to force their way into Heaven, they tunnel up through the space between the worlds and they follow the same pattern there, starting small, taking the books at first to light the fires, bringing them to corruption, a blasphemy written in flame and paper, and then they take one or two Joyful, and then more and more."

"Why the Joyful?" Gordie this time, the collector of the arcane, Gordie with his brain that could hold so much, taken from so many places.

Fool thought for a minute. "Because they feed off the strongest emotions, and those poor bastards have known perfection, have known exultation and the most perfect joy, and then suddenly they're in a place of such pain and such terror and good fuck how sweet must their fear and disgust and confusion taste, so much stronger than that of the demons in Hell, who are used to this kind of misery. How much stronger it must make them!

"So they get confident, they've done these things and nothing and no one had linked it to them, they take more and more, raid the pool and the beach and finally the caves where they have the greatest chance of all, to take an angel, not just a caretaker but a fucking *angel*, and now it doesn't matter that they've been discovered because they're strong and they're confident. They want the war to go ahead. They leave a dead demon to set Heaven against Hell, and then they sit back and wait.

"They wait for war."

"Because they're the unknown in the fire," said Summer, "the unexpected in the chaos."

"Yes. And in the middle of the war, or maybe at the end, they'll rise up, pour through the gaps and tunnels they've made, flood off the island, and whoever's won, they'll be weak, not able to fight back against a second, surprise war.

"The things outside of everywhere will be *inside*, and they'll have a chance to win, to be in control. No more Heaven, no more Hell, just two vast feeding pens, demons and angels and Joyful and Sorrowful all staked out and being fed upon. And when they're empty, done? Simple: they take more from Limbo, from the oceans of the damned, and from whatever Heaven's equivalent is, and they never stop, just feeding and being inside and being the victors."

Fool stopped. Neither Gordie nor Summer spoke. *Is that how it is, how it's going to be?* he thought.

Yes.

No.

No.

No.

Fool opened his eyes, sat up, struggled to focus, but the last image, of Heaven and Hell being reduced to little more than cattle pens in which nothing moved except the feeders, in which everything was staked and battened upon and lost, lodged in his head, the horror of it unshakable. "Where are we?" he asked.

"Near the shore," said Gordie. "I think we're somewhere on the edge of the farmlands from what I can see. Once we land we should be able to reach the Information Office fairly easily."

"We have to work fast," said Fool. "Things are reaching their climax. If it starts, we may be too late."

"Maybe we should let it," said Summer quietly. "Maybe Benjamin was right. Maybe we should just let them fight it out between them. Heaven might win."

"And it might lose," said Fool. "I'd like to think they'd win but there's no guarantee, especially with the things from outside joining in. We can't risk it. We're the only chance, the only chance to save Heaven and Hell."

"You want to save Hell?" asked Summer.

"Yes," said Fool and was surprised to find he meant it. "It's my job. It's our job. What else is there to do?"

"Do you really think we can?"

"Yes," said Fool, and then his arm screamed at him.

The pain was intense, a sudden white-heat burst from under his sleeve that made his arm clench. Fool started in shock and the movement caused the boat to tilt violently. Water splashed over its side and threatened to swamp it, the tiny craft beginning to wallow. Summer cried out and started to bail with her hands as Gordie pulled the bag up around his shoulders and then joined her, the two of them scooping frantically. Fool curled around himself, arm tucked against his belly as it screamed again, and this time he heard a word in the cry, a single clear utterance in the center of the pain.

He heard his own name.

"Fool," the voice cried again, and this time he recognized it: Marianne. He sat again, the boat rocking, and tried to pull his sleeve back. It had gotten wet and was sticking to his skin, refusing to move, so he tore it along the inner seam, splitting the material apart in a flurry of thread and ripping. He tugged, lengthening the tear, to reveal Marianne's tattoo face.

"Fool," she cried again, "please help. Where are you?"

"Marianne, what's wrong?"

"They're coming," she said, voice still wavering, loud and fearful. "They're here. They're inside!"

"What are?"

"The dancers," she said, "the dancers are here."

"Where's 'here,' Marianne? Where are you?"

"The office," she said and then screamed again.

He closed his eyes. Immediately, his vision was filled with the flat gray view looking out through the picture and his ears were filled with the familiar noise, as though he was hearing everything from a long way back and the space between was filled with wind. Behind the wind he heard a crash, other screams, the sound of windows breaking.

Where was he? The paper him? The sketch? He was tilted, the angle of his vision disconcertingly uneven, and he had to open his eyes briefly to try to adjust. Gordie and Summer were bailing, looking at him. He closed his eyes again, ready for the off-kilter perspective this time, coping with it slightly better.

He was on the floor, he thought, dropped and knocked there in the confusion. He could see what he thought was a chair or table leg, blocking part of his view, and beyond it a door. Was that his office?

No, the door was too large. It was the mess hall, he thought, the main door of the mess hall. It had a makeshift barricade across it, a broom slipped through the two handles to hold them together.

"Can you get out?" he asked Marianne, trying to remember if the mess had windows. "Where are they?"

As if in answer, the doors shook.

"Are you alone? Have you got your weapon?"

The doors shook again, harder.

"Marianne," he snapped, "pay attention. Focus on me. Are you armed?"

"Yes," she finally replied. "It's here." A hand appeared at the top of his view and picked him up, lifting him and turning him so that he could see her. She looked exhausted, her eyes fearful, ever moving, ever watchful. Her other hand, holding her gun, appeared briefly, wiped at her forehead, and then was gone. Everything shook; Marianne, trembling as she held him.

"Put me down, you need both hands free," he said, and she did, placing him higher *On a table? In one of the food alcoves?* and facing the door again.

It shook fiercely and something on the far side of it howled. He remembered; the mess had no windows and only one door. If Marianne was to escape, it had to be past whatever was on the other side of that fragile wooden barrier.

"What's happening?"

"Sir, it's got so much worse," she replied. "The Evidence aren't even hiding that they're taking people now, and Mr. Tap's been gathering demons in the streets. The Evidence have been trying to train the demons to use weapons, but they can't communicate and more often than not they end up fighting the demons they're supposed to be training. Humans have been pulled away from their jobs and—"

The door rattled again, this time hard enough to send the broom handle rattling back several inches.

"Tell me," said Fool. "Quickly, Marianne, it may be important."

"We, the last of the Information Men, were told that we would be heading up troops of humans because we had experience."

"Experience in what?"

"They didn't say. Following orders, or giving orders, I suppose. They told us to stay here until orders arrived."

"How many of you are there?"

"Not many."

"Are you all in the mess?"

"I'm alone. I don't know where the others are." Marianne started to breathe hard, ragged gasping hitching her up and down.

"Calm down," Fool said. "Calm down now, or you'll die. You have a chance, but not if you panic."

The door banged in its frame. The broom splintered but did not break, bending and cracking. Fragments of wood flew from it as the door opened part of the way and then slammed shut again, only to reopen at speed. Marianne's gun appeared in Fool's view, pointing at the door, shaking violently but aiming nonetheless. Her breathing was under control at least.

"We were waiting upstairs when the windows downstairs broke, all at once, and the screaming started," she said, her voice almost conversational, talking to distract herself. "The Evidence were on the ground floor in the offices and I think the attack started there. It sounded like they were being slaughtered, like someone was killing newborns on the floors below. The screams were awful."

Marianne's voice had attained a tone of flat resignation. "And then I heard it, or them, come upstairs and I ran. I used the other staircase but the foyer was full of figures and shapes and screams and I came in here.

"You didn't come," said Marianne. The barrel of her gun steadied, facing the door, which banged again.

"Marianne, be ready," Fool said as the door smashed open again. This time, the broom snapped with a single clean sound and the door flew all the way open. Marianne shouted and Fool opened his eyes without thinking to see the mouth of his tattoo yanking apart and exposing the meat of his arm. Summer, still bailing, cried out as Gordie rowed furiously, trying to get them to the shore now visible over his shoulder. Fool gasped, gripped the arm below the tattoo to try to stifle the pain and throbbing, and closed his eyes again.

Marianne's gun had gone, removed from his sight, and there was an Evidence Man standing in the doorway.

It was crouched low, head swinging, tusks dripping blood and saliva, and its piggy eyes mad with fury. It saw something to Fool's side, presumably Marianne, and *Fuck I need to see I need to see I can't turn I'm paper I need to see* it leaped into the room. Marianne shouted again, furious now, and then there was the sound of a gunshot. A part of the door frame blew apart behind the Evidence Man as it landed several feet inside the room, its face feral and wild.

"Be calm, Marianne!" shouted Fool. "Be calm and aim!"

The Evidence Man crouched as Marianne fired again, the shot tugging at its hair but doing no damage. More screams came from the corridor beyond the door now, and then a new thing filled the doorway.

Marianne screamed, the tattoo shrieking, and fired, the shot going wide as the bauta turned to watch the thing from outside flow in. The front part of it leaped at the bauta, clumsily, springing sideways and slamming into the smaller demon in a flail of limbs, the black tubes connecting it to the central mass throbbing and tangling behind it.

The Evidence Man yowled from under the thing from outside, scrabbling against it. Blood sprayed but the thing carried on attacking, arms slashing mechanically at the Evidence Man, striking it again and again. When it was weak enough, the outside thing turned the bauta over and battened on to the back of its head and started to feed.

The rest of the creature moved into the room behind the front part of it, and for a moment there was an opportunity. "Marianne, *move!*" shouted Fool. "Move now!"

She moved, appearing at the edge of his vision briefly, but it was already too late. The creature darted, each part of the web moving out, stretching, so that the far side of the room was blocked off. Marianne backed away and knocked against whatever it was that Fool's paper self was balanced on. Upended, he fell, spiraling, and the last thing he saw before he opened his eyes as the boat ran aground was the thing from outside leaping to where Marianne had been standing, and the last thing he heard was Marianne scream his name.

The office was in ruins.

They had come to land as Fool had screamed Marianne's name, and then screamed it again, to no avail. His view through the paper Fool *little paper Fool, little helpless Fool* circled down and ended up as one of darkness, the paper having landed facedown against the floor, and when he opened his eyes the darkness came with him and clouded about him, hemming him in. He blinked, trying to flush it away, and managed to focus on the tattoo of Marianne's face.

"Marianne," he said, hoping that she had managed to dodge the thing, had managed to run, but she did not reply. Already, the split skin along the lines of the tattoo was knitting, healing, the itch and burn of it like the scurrying of poisonous ants along his arm.

"Marianne," again, hope as forlorn as torn clouds in his voice. The edges of the tattoo closed together, the final part to seal Marianne's mouth, leaving her looking at him, silent and still. "Marianne?

"Marianne?" and still nothing and the skin was smooth now, the tattoo just a tattoo, and he knew she was gone and Fool threw back his head and howled, howled to try to tear the pain from him, howled to try to spit it out in blood and bile, howled to bring her back, howled to sing her on her way.

Howled because she was gone.

Finally, Fool stopped, his throat raw. Pulling the sleeve of his jacket together over Marianne's face, he said without looking up, "We need the pincer. We can check on her while we get it."

"Fool," said Summer, "I—"

"Don't. She's gone, that's all. This is Hell, this is the way it is, let's go." She did not speak again, and neither did Gordie, as they climbed from the boat and started walking.

Gordie had been right, they had beached somewhere in the hinterland between the farmlands and the Bureaucracy, and it didn't take them long to walk back to the place they had worked and lived in. For Fool, the journey was a fragmented thing, a time of single steps and feeling as though he was looking at everything from behind a thick sheet of glass. *Marianne,* he thought, *I failed you. I said I'd be there and I wasn't, I made a promise and I broke it.* He cried as he walked, letting the tears come, welcoming the bitter sting of them.

The three of them went along quiet streets, streets normally filled with demons or humans, past closed bars and a Seamstress House whose doors were shut and locked. Hell was quiet, eerily so, and even the usual background lament of the factories and the groan of the train wheels against stone was absent.

"Where is everyone?" asked Summer.

"Preparing for war," said Gordie, pointing to a large sign that had been nailed across the front of a brothel. The sign simply read:

Gather

The edge of the sign flapped in the breeze as they drew alongside it, and the noise of it followed them down the street like sardonic applause as they walked away. They passed more of the signs en route, some standing nailed to poles like dead and suffering Joyful, others strung across alleyways or painted across the front of buildings. They were all single-word messages, mostly GATHER but also with several repetitions of PREPARE and once the confusing FIELDS. During the walk, they saw no one and heard nothing, and above them the clouds were still and high.

Finally, they came to the street containing the Information Office and slowed, the understanding unspoken but clear between them that whatever had happened here might still be happening. Fool went first, gun outstretched, still feeling as though this was happening to someone else, that this was someone else's life he had accidentally stumbled into, and knowing it wasn't. This was his and his alone.

The door to the office was intact but the windows were all broken, glass littering the sidewalks, and he could hear no sounds from within. He opened the door slowly, letting it swing back to reveal the foyer beyond, standing away so that nothing could come out at him. *Would I care if it did?* he thought. *Would it matter?*

Yes. Yes, because I failed Marianne but I may still keep my promise to Israfil and I may still protect Hell and Heaven and everything and everyone in them. I may still do some good, even in Hell. Tightening his grip on his gun, he went in.

There was more glass on the floor of the lobby, masses of it sparkling in sharp patterns atop the floorboards. There were bloody footprints in the glass and a handprint on the wall. Blood had trickled from the heel of the handprint in a long, thin string. "Hello?" Fool called. "Is anyone still here?"

There was no response.

"Gordie, go and find the pincer," Fool said. "It's in the evidence room."

"We didn't have an evidence room when I was alive," he said.

"On the first floor. It used to be your room. Be careful and don't take any chances, you aren't armed. If you see anything you can use as a weapon for you or Summer, bring it. Summer, with me."

Fool led Summer through a set of double doors off the foyer as Gordie peeled off to the far staircase in search of the pincer. The corridor beyond the doors led to a second set of doors that Fool pushed open with his foot, peering into the darkened space beyond. Here, the signs of damage were more obvious. Something had scored along both walls, leaving long, torn trails in its wake, and a number of room doors had been broken in or torn from their hinges and pulled out. More blood had sprayed across the floor and ceiling, and a bauta's head gazed at Fool and Summer from the base of the wall. There was no sign of its body and it blinked, once, as they passed. Summer stepped away from it, feet crunching across broken wood, and then they were at the mess.

Summer arrived at the door just before Fool, looking in the room and then turning before Fool could enter, pulling the door closed behind her. It hung awkwardly, the bottom grating against the frame, the top pulled away from the hinge. "Fool, don't. Stay here. Let me go in," she said, her hand gentle on his shoulder.

"Summer," he said, "thank you, but no. I need to go in." She was standing, deliberately blocking his access to the room, and when he moved to go around her, she moved in counterpoint, staying in his way. What had she seen through that open door?

What had she seen?

Fool tried to move forward but again she blocked him, reaching up and taking his face in both of her hands, pulling his attention down to her face. She smiled at him, sadly, and said, "No.

"There's no point, Fool, *Thomas*, let me. You don't need to do this, you already know what you'll find in there. Do you really want to see?"

"Want? No," he said, "of course I don't. But I should, and I will. I owe her that much at least. I wasn't here, I didn't protect her. I need to see, to remember her."

"Not like this."

"Exactly like this," he said and stepped past her. This time, she didn't try to stop him.

The mess floor looked as though it had been washed with blood, a huge puddle of it filling the room and smeared from one wall almost to the other. Most of the tables and chairs that the Information Men had eaten at were stacked against the far wall, except for a single table that now lay on its side in the middle of the blood. *Was that what I was standing on,* he thought, *little perching paper Fool? Was I on that when I watched her die?*

But he hadn't watched her die, had he? And he still had hope, still had that faint glimmer of something almost too weak to be called hope but there nonetheless, that she might somehow have survived. He stepped into the pool of blood, so fresh that it hadn't started to thicken yet, was still thin and slippery, and saw the body of the bauta.

It was lying crumpled against the far wall, back upright and knees drawn up and fallen sideways. Its chest had been torn open to reveal the matter within, the rib ends startlingly white in the redness. Something that might have been its heart had tumbled out and was lying in its lap, and its head had been wrenched sideways and was facing down as though peering at the organ in surprise. One of its tusks was gone, the other slick with blood, and its eyes were open wide. Fool turned away from it, feeling no sympathy. "You died free and moving," he said aloud and then he was looking at Marianne.

She was lying in the far corner of the room, and at first he thought she might simply be unconscious; she didn't seem to have been marked. Her head was lost in the shadows of the room's corner and he walked toward her, saying her name.

"Marianne? Marianne?"

No reply, and then the shadow wasn't shadow, it was a thick pool of blood, staining her short hair and smearing the floor around her. The back of her head was open and pieces of her brain flecked the blood, fragments of bone scattered among them. The thing had fed on her, rough, had bitten through her skull and shredded the skin of her head. Fool crouched by her and reached out, taking one hand, the first and last time he would ever touch her. The skin of her hand was soft, the fingers still flexible. She was still warm.

"I'm sorry," he said, almost whispering. "I'm so sorry."

Summer's hand fell on his shoulder. "Gordie's got the pincer," she said.

"Just give me a minute," he said. He let go of Marianne's hand, closing his eyes. He inhaled through his nose, hoping to catch her scent, but all he smelled was blood and death.

"Fool," said Summer.

"I know," he said. "I know. Let's go, then. Let's go and find Rhakshasas. Let's go and stop this fucking war."

28

They went back through the Information Office and out into Hell's deserted streets. Gordie, as well as finding the pincer, had found a piece of window frame that had broken off during the attack and that was smooth enough to hold at one end. The other was studded with broken glass fragments and would make a good club if they were attacked. Before they left, Summer picked up Marianne's gun and fired it experimentally; as expected, it refused to work. It was Marianne's, would work only for her, and they left it on her body.

Outside, the wind had picked up and paper blew along the streets. A piece caught against Fool's leg and he picked it up. Like the signs, it contained a single word:

Prepare

Fool looked at the paper and wondered, Was this war preordained? Had this paper sat in one of Hell's warehouses for months or years, awaiting the time someone would open the doors and the wind would whip it all away, carry it and the message it contained out to seed?

Summer, seeing Fool look at the paper, said, "It doesn't matter."

"What doesn't?"

"You're wondering if all this is part of a plan, aren't you? Everything, I mean? The things outside, the war, the deaths, whether everything's been planned to happen this way."

"Yes."

"It doesn't matter. You were right, we have to do this, and if we're part of a plan, fine. Plans can change, Fool, or be part of bigger plans. How do you know that your disrupting this plan, if you can, isn't part of an even bigger plan in which the disruption is the right outcome? You can't give up."

Fool considered what Summer had said, thought about it and felt the shape of it, and then felt it *turn* in his mind so that he was looking at it from the other side, from Summer's side, and grinned. At first he tried to keep it to himself but he couldn't, it was too big to contain, and he grinned at Summer as well. Something in his face scared her, because she stepped back, eyes hooding. He tried to turn down the grin but it wouldn't go, crawled across his face like a sickness, aching in his cheeks and rippling around his eyes.

He was the plan within the plan, the joke within the seriousness. He was Thomas Fool, and he would not stop, because he no longer could, even if he'd wanted to.

There were no trains in evidence, so they walked. The Information Office was on the outskirts of the Bureaucracy, somewhere in the blending point between that area and the Houska and the nearest edge of Eve's Harbor, and Assemblies House was perhaps a couple of miles away. They had decided to try to find Rhakshasas there, reasoning that it was likely to be preparing for war with the other Archdeacons rather than at its dwelling in Crow Heights. They covered the distance quickly, without incident, and soon found themselves at the entrance to the Bureaucracy's headquarters in Hell.

For once, the building's main doors were open, and Fool was able to walk in unchallenged, Summer and Gordie behind him. The foyer beyond the doors was a mass of movement, with what looked to be hundreds of small, nameless demons scuttling back and forth clutching pieces of paper and scrolls and ledgers. Fool saw at least one holding a map pinned to a board nearly as big as it was, peering over the top of it as it exited one corridor and made its way to the entrance to another. The war, it seemed, took some serious organization.

"Wait here," said Fool. "Keep small."

He left Gordie and Summer standing as unobtrusively as possible against the wall of the foyer and went to the main desk. Usually there was nothing behind the raised wooden reception, but today there was an officious little demon there, staring down on the scurrying before it and nodding in pleasure. *An administrator,* thought Fool, *a consumer of pointless information, a lover of the process.*

"What?" said the demon as Fool approached. It was wearing a jacket styled for a human shape, torn to accommodate the fins of bone and gristle that emerged from its shoulders. Its face was a mass of ridges and overlapping bony plates that grated together as it spoke, giving its voice an unpleasant strained quality.

"I need to see Rhakshasas."

"Ha! Fuck off!"

"I need to see Rhakshasas," Fool repeated. He reached into his pocket to find his badge of office but it wasn't there; at some point he'd lost it. Suddenly panicking, he reached into his other pocket and, thankfully, found the feather still safe in its depths. He'd forgotten it in the horrors of the last few hours, and touching it calmed him, reassured him.

"I don't give a black enameled shit what you need," said the demon, leaning down so that its face was mere inches from Fool's. "Rhakshasas has better things to do than parlay with little people. Besides, why aren't you at your staging post?"

"Staging post?"

"Why aren't you in the fields?" it shrieked, its voice rising, wobbling, as it found a thing out of place, a thing out of order. "Why aren't you preparing?"

"Preparing?"

"For the war, you muzzlescum? There's a curfew! There are rules! You should be with the others!" Muzzlescum? It wasn't an insult Fool had heard before, and he wondered if the demon had made it up.

"Get me Rhakshasas." Fool was tired of this now, tired of the obstructions, tired of the struggle.

"I'll have you pulled to pieces, you little deserting bastard!" the demon screamed, and the plates on its face were vibrating, it was so angry.

Enough. This had gone on long enough. He straightened as best he could and spoke.

"I am Thomas Fool, Commander of the Information Office of Hell, and I have returned from Heaven. Tell Rhakshasas that I require it meet me in the courtyard in the center of Assemblies House. You can tell Mr. Tap the same thing, and the other Archdeacons, if they're around."

"They're not," said the demon without thinking and then, "Thomas Fool is dead. He killed demons and now he's dead. You aren't him. Fuck off."

Fool removed his gun from its holster and looked at it, studying its long lines and the dark mouth at the center of its barrel. They had picked up an audience, he knew, everything in the foyer staring at them while trying to not look like they were doing so. The movement about them had slowed.

"My name is Thomas Fool," Fool said carefully, "and I am not dead. My gun fires only for me. Would you like me to prove it works?" He turned it toward the demon behind the desk, not pointing it exactly at it but *intimating*, letting it appear a casual gesture full of intent.

"You've picked that up from the street," said the demon.

"Are you sure?" Fool twitched the barrel, was pleased to see the demon flinch, and then he fired. The shot was loud in the walled space, the sound of it echoing back and forth in waves. A piece of ancient plaster-work above the desk exploded into a spray of dust and fragments that rained down on the demon's head. Fool, still casual, brought the gun back around so it was pointing directly at the thing's chest. *Now,* he thought, *let's save its face.*

"I understand you're busy and I don't want to cause you trouble, but Rhakshasas and anything else that's available need to see me. I have news they need."

"Give it to me, I'll pass it on."

"I can't. It's information for Mr. Tap and Rhakshasas and the Arch-deacons only. I mentioned I have returned from Heaven?"

"Yes."

"Then what do you think the information I have may be about?"

The demon paused, and then understanding flared in its eyes and it almost leaped back from the desk, from Fool, as though burned. "The war?"

"I can't say," said Fool, playing hard on its fears, "but I can tell you that what I know may change the events of the next few hours and days

dramatically, and I'll be sure to tell Rhakshasas and the others person-
ally how helpful you're being. Assuming you're going to be helpful, of
course." Another twitch of the barrel, another flinch as it weighed its
options, as it felt the weight of various potentialities settle on its finned
and bony shoulders.

"Rhakshasas?" it asked eventually.

"Rhakshasas. And the others, if possible."

"I'll pass the message on."

"Thank you. And get someone to show us the courtyard, if you please."
Fool put the gun away as the demon held a clawed finger up to a scuttling thing and, with obvious relief, sent Fool away to be someone else's
responsibility.

"Why the courtyard and not one of the offices?"

They were sitting on one of the stone benches on the courtyard,
waiting. They had been there for maybe an hour and they were being
stared at. Three sides of the courtyard were walled by the Assemblies
House's windowed sides, and demon faces appeared at the windows to
peer down at them every few seconds. Fool wasn't sure about the other
floors, but the ground floor was a corridor and the demons that walked
it could stare at them for the length of their journeys. The fourth wall
was blank brick that, if Fool's grasp of Hell's architecture was correct,
was the rear of the garage space in which the transports were kept.

"It's the best place," said Fool to Gordie after a few seconds. He was
leaning forward on the bench, head down, and even to himself, his
voice sounded like an old man's.

"We're a talking point," said Summer, and Fool knew she was watching the demons watching them.

"We've been noticed," he said. "We made an entrance." Marianne
was lying dead in a pool of her own blood, a dead bauta behind her, just
meat abandoned on the floor.

"Why is it the best place?" Gordie again, always searching, always
wanting to know.

"Look around you." Even speaking seemed hard, each word aching
as it emerged.

"It's a courtyard," said Gordie. "Is it safer than a room inside? I don't understand."

"Fool means it's the best place because I'm here," said the Man of Plants and Flowers, his speech an oily rasp of leaves and branches. The overgrown bushes that grew around the courtyard's walls and in ornamental beds that had been made by lifting flags from various points around the courtyard shivered slightly as the Man arrived. Or maybe he'd been here all along and was simply showing himself now; Fool didn't know.

"Hello," said Fool, still not looking up. Just in front of him one of the ornamental beds was filled with oddly colored flowers and they turned toward him; he made them out in the upper edge of his vision but did not look up at them. One of the plants stretched out from the bed and pushed itself between his feet, its single open bud a mass of fleshy petals that tilted back to face him, as though peering at him.

"Fool," said the plant, and the voice from it was high and lisping and strangely feminine, the petals moving to form the words, the leaves below it trembling.

"Yes."

"'Yes'? Is that all? You are returned from Heaven, Fool, you must have so much to tell me."

"No. I've got nothing for you. You keep your end of our agreement and help me persuade Rhakshasas and then I'll tell you."

"You've come so far, haven't you, my little dancing Information Man? Making deals, standing against demons, standing against angels. You worry that you're moving in tracks left by others but you aren't, Fool; you're hacking your own trail through Heaven and Hell now. You're wonderful!"

"Am I? No. Not wonderful. I'm tired, is all. There's no wonder left in me."

"Ah, but you're grieving, aren't you? For the lovely Marianne, left on the floor with her thoughts exposed in the meat of her brain? You should be used to death now, Fool. You've been in the graves of books, Fool, seen so much pain on the island, so why does this one death bother you so much? It can't matter, not in the grander picture, can it?"

"Fuck off," Fool replied.

"For pity's sake, can't you let him be?" asked Summer.

Fool looked up in time to see the Man's bodies twist, his attention shifting to Summer and then Gordie. The plants were still for a long, drawn-out moment and then there was a rustle that Fool could have sworn was surprise spread out along his branches and stems. For the first time, when he spoke, the Man seemed unsure, confused.

"But you're dead," he said. "The two of you, dead. And yet, here you are, alive. How has that occurred, I wonder?"

"You were dead and now you're not," said Fool.

"Touché, Fool, touché. You didn't tell me about them, though. You've been keeping things from me."

"Of course. You taught me well."

"Ha! You're priceless, Fool, *priceless*! You make things so interesting! We'll talk about this in more detail later, I hope. And now, I think we need to prepare. Who's coming to this little friendly meeting?"

"Rhakshasas. I hope."

"No one else?"

"I asked for Rhakshasas and Mr. Tap and the other Archdeacons, but Mr. Tap and the others aren't here, so they tell me. They're out getting ready to fight the war, I suppose."

"Rhakshasas it is, then. It's a start. Well, I'll wait for your sign, Fool. It's up to you now."

A start? Fool was about to ask the Man what he meant when another voice spoke.

"This had better be fucking good, Fool, you little grubbing shit," said Rhakshasas. The demon was emerging from a doorway in the corridor, pushing itself into the courtyard, its intestines wriggling as it came, surging and thinning to allow it access through the gap. The demon was wreathed in a cloud of flies, dark with them, and its face was twisted into an expression that was beyond rage or any other recognizable human emotion. Its eyes glowed a bursting yellow, the color of infection and pus, of bile and vomit. Fool stood.

"Good? No, it's not good, Rhakshasas, but it's important."

"How do you know what's important, little thing? How could you have the first comprehension of what matters to Hell? Or to Heaven, for that matter? How could you know anything?"

"I know that the war you're about to go to is based on a lie. I know Heaven is wrong and that you'll battle each other over a mistake."

This brought Rhakshasas up short, and even in this grandest, foulest demon Fool could see uncertainty take root, blossom. "A lie?"

"A lie, or a mistake, it doesn't matter what you call it. I told Mr. Tap but maybe he's not passed the message on. Heaven thinks you attack it, you think Heaven attacks you, but neither of you is right. You've been manipulated into war, Rhakshasas, you and Heaven both."

Rhakshasas stepped into the courtyard fully, dripping, its flies buzzing, and seated itself on the bench opposite Fool. Even sitting down, its head was level with Fool's. The demon turned its burning eyes to Gordie and Summer and asked, "Who the piss are these two? They're not Hell's, are they?"

"They used to be. I don't know whose they are now."

"Then they do not belong. Remove them, or I will."

"No. They're with me."

"No? Who the fuck do you believe you are, Thomas Fool? You exist because I and the other Archdeacons allow you to, you and every other little piece of human scum in Hell." Rhakshasas's guts began to slither loose from it, heading for Summer, who was closest to it. She stepped back and the guts moved faster and Fool lifted his gun and fired.

He didn't hit Rhakshasas; he hit a point in front of the moving guts so that chips of stone and sparks sprang away from the impact as the bullet ricocheted up and tore through the bushes before burying itself in the wall. Rhakshasas's guts reared back, curled, pulsing tubes of it lifting from the ground like worms.

"You dare?" asked Rhakshasas. "You dare to attack me?"

"No," said Fool, "but I dare to try to save Hell from the mess it's about to find itself in. Listen to me, Rhakshasas, listen. Please."

The demon considered Fool and then said, "Very well. Talk, but talk quickly and be aware that if I am not convinced when you've finished, I will tear you into pieces, you and your friends."

"That's fine," said Fool and started to talk.

He told Rhakshasas everything, everything that he'd seen and heard, everything he'd done, the conclusions he'd reached. Gordie got the pincer and the scooped-out demon and the scale and the claw and the torn books out of the sack and showed them to Rhakshasas, setting them on the ground in front of it. Finally, Fool told Rhakshasas what he thought had happened, about the secret place on the island and the incursions from the island to Hell's mainland, about the thefts of the Joyful for food, about the demons in boxes and what it all meant.

"It's the things from outside of everywhere," he said finally. "It's them, they're doing this."

Rhakshasas didn't move or speak, sitting on the bench, its eyes dimmed to a pale flicker as it thought. Fool, exhausted, sat back as Gordie gathered the things from the ground and placed them back in the crude bag. There was just the Man now, his contribution to the story; then it would be over. Fool nodded at the bushes and then sat back, waiting.

"It's true," said the plants, rising up in front of Rhakshasas. "I never died. I've been here all along. Allow me to be the thing that confirms Fool's story, Rhakshasas. Something has used Hell's empty spaces to plan this attack, and it isn't Heaven. The island exists and the graves Fool saw have all been emptied."

There. It was done. They'd said all they could now, and showed everything they had. Either they'd be believed or they wouldn't, either the war would be averted or it wouldn't.

Either the things from outside would win or they'd be beaten.

As he sat waiting for Rhakshasas to respond, Fool thought about everything. Setting it out for the demon had churned it up in his mind, thrown the pieces into the air, and now they were drifting down, settling into new patterns, and something started to feel wrong, started to nag at him like an aching tooth that needed probing with a tongue to find the gap, find the rottenness. What was it?

It didn't fit.

Fool's head was suddenly filled with questions, all clamoring for his attention at once, yammering and squawking and flapping their panic at him. He groaned and placed his hands to his temples, pressing, trying to reduce the noise in his brain, trying to see it one piece at a time.

If the things were from outside, were so *other*, why did they need the Joyful to feed on?

If they used the boats to come from the island, why the filled-in tunnels in Hell's deserted spots? Why use boats at all if they had tunnels?

"Fool," said Gordie.

"Not now," said Fool, thinking furiously.

"Now," said Gordie insistently, "listen. *Look*. This isn't a pincer."

"What?"

Gordie held it out in front of him. "Pincers are hollow when they're not attached to the living creature, they're made of shell with meat and veins and blood inside them. This is *solid*. It's like a carving of a pincer."

How did the Man know about the graves and the island? How did he know how Marianne's body had been left?

Gordie reached into the bag and took out the scale and began to bend it; it snapped, breaking into two pieces. "I've realized it, the thing that's wrong. This isn't a real scale, like the pincer isn't a real pincer; real scales are flexible," he said urgently.

Orobas. The thing that had pushed itself through the dirt at them on the island, the blind thing, was the demon Orobas. It was an Information Man, one of Fool's troops.

The demons in the crates, they weren't being fed on, they were being *used*.

The Man knew because he'd seen them. Because he'd been there.

"Fool, these are imitations," said Gordie.

"It's you," whispered Fool, turning to look at the Man, the shape of him in the bushes.

"Of course it is," said the Man and tore Rhakshasas in half.

The ground under the demon churned as the plants there burst violently up and plunged into its flesh. Stems grew from Rhakshasas's eyes and mouth and pulled away from each other, splitting its head apart with a wet, sloppy noise. In the now-exposed flesh of the neck, tendrils of vine turned and twisted, slicing through the meat. More, thicker stems pushed out of the demon's belly and cracked its ribs as they forced their way out from between its bones, the pop of them breaking as wet as the sound of its head splitting had been. Fool jumped back as a spray of Rhakshasas's blood arced through the air and only just managed to avoid being caught in it.

Summer screamed and a part of the Man lashed out and wrapped around her neck, choking her to silence. Gordie dropped the two parts of the scale and tried to simultaneously pick up his window frame club and go to Summer, but a thick branch whipped around and caught him across the forehead so hard that it broke, a section of it falling at Fool's feet and Gordie spinning back across the courtyard and slamming into the wall, his club flying into the bushes and lost from view. His head hit the bottom edge of a windowpane and it cracked, the crack starring through the glass as Gordie slid down, unconscious.

Rhakshasas's guts reacted fast, flinging themselves away from the attack and landing on the ground in a greasy slither. They moved rapidly across the courtyard but were not fast enough; as they went over one of the beds, shoots exploded from the earth and tore into them, the tubes punctured and ripped. Brown liquid and semi-digested chunks of something unidentifiable spilled from the intestines as more growths burst through them, lifting them from the ground so that they hung, suspended and oozing, two or three feet above the earth. Rhakshasas's flies abandoned the body, but again the Man was too quick; hundreds of stems and branches rose from the bushes around the courtyard to form a thick, impenetrable ceiling, each lined with buds shaped like mouths that opened and snapped closed rapidly, eating the insects.

Rhakshasas's now-naked body slumped, one part falling from the bench and the other tilting back and flopping loosely. Thick ichor spattered to the ground below, a rainbow pool of red and yellow and green that stank and that almost immediately congealed into a thick scum.

The courtyard was dark, the only light in it that which came in from the windows of Assemblies House, through which demons looked on as they continued to scurry and dart. None reacted to the scene below them, because this was Hell and who was to say what was normal and what was wrong here?

"Now, Fool," said the Man. "Shall we talk?"

29

"It was you," said Fool again, not asking, watching blue flowers sprout in the earth around his feet.

"Oh, Fool, of course it was. I spent my death exploring and I found that I can tunnel, Fool, when left alone I can build the most beautiful tunnels between all the worlds, can go anywhere! I'm not angel or demon, Fool, nor human anymore, and I'm not tethered to any world. I'm strongest in Hell, of course, but I can reach everywhere, Fool, everywhere! So I thought about what I wanted, and what I would have to do to get it, and then I started.

"I lit my fires to cause worry, and I slaughtered to do the same thing, to make the Bureaucracy feel the sting of uncertainty, I took the Joyful from Heaven and I imprisoned them in Hell. I took demons and nameless angels and I unearthed the old books and I burned them. I did it *all*. Everything to this point and beyond, me, just me. I want this war, Fool. I want it to rage and howl and I want the dead to pile up in drifts, and I will make it happen, Information Man. I will make it *explode*.

"But you were always a danger, Fool, always the thing that might right the balances I was trying so hard to upset. You being sent to Heaven was a godsend, if you'll pardon the pun, because it focused angelic eyes on the presence of Hell and made them more prepared to see the blasphemies being committed, but you might also have shown them that it wasn't Hell committing them. You're better than you realize, Fool, more aware than you give yourself credit for, so I kept as good a track of you as I could and then I distracted you by letting you think that the things from outside were breaking through and I set you chasing your tail."

"There are no things from outside?"

"I'm sure there are, Fool. You told me you'd seen them the first time we spoke with you in Heaven, after all, but inside the beautiful kingdom of Heaven or this foul place? No. They remain where they have always been, outside. I just pushed you in the direction of thinking they weren't. You gave me the idea, Fool, gave me the means to so easily fool you, little Fool. A pincer here, a claw there, a scale in a bed. Simple.

"And my demons, those sad things I turned into puppets, they helped, too. I never got their movement right but they gave me ears and eyes and fingers and teeth in Heaven and in Hell, in the places I couldn't reach, and you thought their movement was something wrong, didn't you? And you made up your own stories, gave it details I could never hope for. You've been so *helpful*, Fool!"

Helpful Fool, little helpful betrayed Fool. "And you killed Marianne?"

"I did. I wish I could tell you I felt some sorrow, Fool, but I don't. She was a useful way of keeping you off balance, so I killed her when I knew you were back in Hell. I smelled you through that demon, Fool, and decided to make sure you were distracted. You introduced us, Fool, you let me see her and see how much you liked her, and I used that information at the point where it was most useful, where you presented the most danger, where if you had been thinking clearly you might have still got ahead of me and turned this all around. I always said, Fool. I always said that information gives power, and you've started to learn it, haven't you, in the secrets you kept from me in Heaven, but you aren't a good enough liar. I could always tell there were gaps, tell the untruths. I can always judge where you are on the journey, Fool, better than you can yourself, and I watched as you wandered the trail I'd laid for you and I knew you'd try, you'd try so hard, but that ultimately it would be to no avail.

"It's too late. This day is mine, Fool."

"Why? Why do you want this war?"

"Why?" replied the Man. "Why not? Because I can have it, Fool, just because I can and because I *want*. Because I want to see Heaven and Hell burned to the earth and see the burned earth salted with the bodies of their dead."

"But why?"

"Why anything? You tell me, Fool."

"Because you want to take over." It seemed so obvious now that he said it, the part he'd been right about all along, not about the things from the places outside but the Man all along, a manipulation within the wheels of other manipulations, a third element that he had missed, been tricked into missing.

"Of course I do, and what better way than to have Heaven and Hell war with each other?"

"And you'll step in at the end, when things are at their most awful, and you'll be unstoppable," said Gordie, sitting up. His face was a mask of blood, his forehead torn open by a gash that stretched from temple to temple. A flap of skin hung down and covered one eye, and broken glass glittered in the wound.

"You've trained them well, Fool; they're almost as observant and smart as you are, even the ones that have been dead," said the Man and sent a branch, almost casually, to wrap around Gordie's neck. It tightened and he, like Summer, began to choke, twin sets of breathing on either side of Fool that whistled and caught.

"So, Fool, the question is, what now? The war is almost begun and I am ready to ascend, but what do I do with you?"

"Let me go. Let us go?"

"I think not," said the Man. "You're still dangerous. Until the war is in full spate you might still, by some miracle, stop it. There are Archdeacons other than Rhakshasas who might be persuaded to listen." As he spoke, the Man sent tendrils out from his base and snared the pincer and claw and pieces of scale, dragging them back into the denseness of his growths. The demon and torn books he left.

"And now you don't have those. I feel better this way," he said.

"You can have my feather," said Fool, removing the angel's feather from his pocket and holding it out.

"Fool, if I wanted your feather, I'd have taken it. Besides, I have a whole angel I can take feathers from."

"You tore her wings off," said Fool. "She hasn't any feathers left."

"There are more angels coming, Fool, a whole Heaven's worth of angels, and they all have feathers. It's over. It has been a genuine pleasure, but now I have other things to attend to."

Fool thought, trying to force his brain to speed up, to fucking con-

centrate, but it was so hard, too hard to push through. Nearly everything he'd thought was true was a lie, and again he'd been manipulated
and played, sent like a spinning top into the worlds about him and
snapped back at the twitch of a cord. What did the Man want? Power?
Control? No, not just that, he wanted to be the thing at the tip of the
hierarchy, that everyone and everything else looked up to and relied on.
Everything the Man had ever done or been, Fool saw, had been building
to this point, the point where he could take over.

And he'd helped, keeping Heaven and Hell focused on him as the
Man crawled around in the background, setting things into play that
were now almost beyond stopping.

"We're done now, Fool. This is my time and I intend to savor it," said
the Man. The limbs of plant began to tighten around Gordie's and
Summer's necks, lifting them up onto their toes and then farther so
that they were dangling, suffocating.

In the distance, Fool heard horns, clear and sharp.

The Man relaxed some of his limbs and the ceiling above them fell
away, revealing the sky again. The vine holding Gordie, which had
reached down from the ceiling to grasp him, relaxed but did not let go,
and he slumped back to a seated position by the wall, whooping, his
face blue under its mask of drying blood.

Tiny black spots were swarming across the underside of the clouds,
and Fool at first thought it was flies from Rhakshasas that the Man
had missed, that were making their escape, but then he realized with
a sudden perspective shift that these were far away, high above them.
The Man's parts all twisted to see, eyes that didn't exist turning toward
the sky and watching and mouths made of buds and stems opening
as the black spots grew larger. "It begins," he said, his voice quiet, antici-
patory.

This was Fool's only chance.

The courtyard was large, and although there were plenty of flowers
and bushes for the Man to occupy around the edges and in the spaces
left by the lifted flags, there were still large open areas that he could try
to move through. Fool knelt and swiftly grasped a mass of the ragged
paper from the bag in one hand and the broken part of the branch
used to strike Gordie in the other. Moving swiftly, he wiped the books

into the remains of Rhakshasas, jamming them hard into the exposed innards of the demon, and then slapped them onto the end of the stick, working them around the wood so that the tip was covered in them. Rhakshasas's fluids burned Fool's skin and he wiped them on his jacket and then all he could do was wait, wait and hope.

"What are you doing?" The Man, attention down again, peering at Fool.

"Fuck you," said Fool, *brave Fool, wishing Fool,* and then the books, the holy texts, reacted to Rhakshasas's drying and unclean fluids and burst into flame. The end of the branch caught alight and Fool thrust it at the nearest mass of the Man. He reacted immediately, the branches coiling away, and Fool stepped forward, pressing his advantage, thrusting the flames into the greenery. It caught in a mass of sparks and thick smoke, the burning plants whipping back and forth in an approximation of pain. A vine lashed away from the wall and struck at Fool, who jumped back, stumbling and ducking at the same time, just avoiding being hit. The Man roared, but his attention was now on the fires that had caught within him and he lost his grip on Summer, the wooden noose loosening and letting her tumble out of its grasp.

She fell and Fool managed somehow to hold her in his free arm, backing away, still holding the torch in front of him. Something whipped toward him and he ducked, the movement awkward with an unconscious woman in his arms, waving the burning branch low in a circle around him. There was a path back toward Gordie and the door and he started to move along it, half dragging, half carrying Summer. She moaned dully and spat, the drool thick, landing on his shoulder and rolling slowly down his arm.

"Fool, this is pointless," said the Man. A thick branch speared forward, missing Fool's head only because he saw it coming and dodged at the last second, shoving the torch at it and making it retreat in wisps of smoke and the smell of burning bark.

"Really, Fool? You think I can be killed by fire?"

"No, but I think you can be hurt," said Fool and again jammed the torch into the nearest mass of greenery, occupying one of the missing flagstone beds. The flames snatched at the plants there immediately and they writhed, and they *screamed,* a high-pitched agony that sounded like steam escaping from a narrow spout. The Man threw another spear of wood forward and it slammed into Fool's side, skewering him, and he felt it punch out of his back. He screamed and slammed the torch against the wood, which lashed back out of him in a spray of blood.

Fool dropped to one knee, feeling his foot bang against Gordie behind him, losing his grip on Summer and trying to hold the torch up. She moaned again and rolled onto her knees. A writhing mass of plants came at her side, and Fool leaned over her and thrust the torch at them, singeing the closest few, making them retreat. The move sent a spike of pain through his stomach, less abrupt than the splitting of the tattoos, deeper, a tearing and rolling pain that branched out in waves.

Fool clambered to his feet as another spike burst from the mass, not a javelin of wood thrown, he saw, but a branch forced to grow grotesquely fast, its tip bulging and expanding toward him. He stepped out of its path as another came at him from the side, puncturing his wrist and forcing its way between the bones of his forearm. He gasped and staggered sideways as it yanked itself out. He kept hold of the torch, barely, and swung it, forcing the Man back. He had to move, and move now; the torch was already burning down, the wood little more than a charred remnant.

The Man was all around him now, every part of him moving, approaching, bursting from the beds and surging from the walls. Fool stepped over Gordie, shouting, "Get up!" Gordie grunted and started to rise, and a part of the Man, a curling scythe of greenery, burst out of the bushes. It laced through the air with a noise like tearing silk, heading for Gordie's neck. Fool managed to get the torch in its way and it tangled around the wooden stave, snapping it, the flaming tip falling to the ground and rolling to the gutter, harmlessly, in the center of a stone flag.

Gordie grabbed Summer by the shoulder as Fool drew his gun, although how he'd shoot plants he did not know. They backed toward the door as the Man roared and tried to follow, still burning, the flames catching and leaping from part to part of him. Blue flowers in the nearest bed began to slither over the stone toward them, the flag next to the bed bucking up as their roots swelled, grew, and forced the flowers on. As they came close they rose up and spat, red globules spraying them. Where they hit Fool's exposed skin, the globules burned.

The attack was unnervingly silent, the only noise their own breathing and the rustle of leaf and root and stem as they moved.

Fool stamped on the nearest plant head, the fleshy bulb bursting in a mass of thick red slime under his heel. Stamping caused another wave of pain to ripple across Fool's midriff, the upper edges of it meeting the pain flowing back along his arm, and he grimaced and gritted his teeth. He loosed a single shot into the Man, the noise terribly loud and echoing, and then his back hit something.

Fool thought it was the Man at first, but it gave against him and he realized it was the door back into the corridor. He pushed harder, still moving backward, calling Gordie and Summer. His heel caught against the bottom of the doorway and he fell, crashing across the space and hitting the far wall hard. He dropped his gun, scrabbled for it feeling woozy and sick, as Gordie appeared in the doorway, a patch of dark shadow against the sky beyond. He was still pulling on Summer's shoulder, dragging at her.

Demons, little ones carrying the administration of the war, skittered around Fool and studiously ignored what was happening as he pulled himself around and up, wincing again as the pain in his arms and stomach flared, and then Gordie was in the corridor and Summer was behind him. Plants surged up to the edge of the doorway, tendrils slashing through the air into the corridor, their reach falling short of Gordie and Summer. Another red flower appeared and spat as the Man roared Fool's name, a long and furious echo of sound. Fool fired past Gordie and Summer into the Man, not because it would achieve anything but because he was angry, he was fucking *livid* at the pain and the manipulation and the deaths, and then another of those wooden stems, fat and jagged, burst from the mass in the doorway and punched into Summer's back and tore out between her breasts and pinned her to the far wall of the corridor.

There was a pause that lasted a sliver of a heartbeat and forever and then Gordie shrieked, not just a scream but a scream torn raw and inside out, and grabbed at the part of the Man that had transfixed Summer. He pulled and his hands slipped in her blood and he cried out again and pulled again and this time the Man drew back, roaring again. Fool grabbed at Gordie and yanked him down as the spike burst out of the mass in the courtyard again, missing Gordie by inches and slapping back when it failed to find its target.

Summer collapsed to the floor, her eyes rolling back in her head to white before closing, and a gout of blood sprayed from the ragged tear in her chest. She hit the corridor's tiled floor with a wet thud, and a pool of dark blood immediately began to spread out from her, so much blood, too much. Gordie scrambled over to her as the Man attacked a third time, and this time the spike impaled a little demon that was too inquisitive and that had come too close, lifting it as it slammed through it in a spray of dark gray fluid. The Man roared again and started whipping the spike back and forth, trying to dislodge the demon as Fool pulled Gordie away. Summer's hand came up and held Fool's wrist for a second and then fell away, leaving a last print of her blood on his skin.

"Come on," he gasped. "Come on, Gordie."

"Fool, no, she could be alive!"

"She's dead, Gordie," said Fool, still watching as the blood pool expanded, Summer and Marianne both left lying in puddles of their own wet insides, both invaded by the Man. Both dead. He pulled on Gordie again, hating it, hating to separate them but knowing that the Man wouldn't stop. As if to prove him right, the Man shook the dead demon off and sent another spear toward them. It fell short, the two of them finally out of his range, but stabbed into Summer's neck, jerking her head and snapping her eyes open in a look of startled wakefulness. Instead of withdrawing the spike, the Man curled it around like a hook and began to drag Summer's body back toward the courtyard.

Gordie, seeing her begin to move toward the doorway, howled and tried to go after her but Fool pulled him back again, arm screaming its own lament now, blood dripping from the hole above his wrist. He pulled a last time and the two of them fell back, farther away from the door and the Man, and watched as Summer slipped into the roiling mass of plants. The last they saw of her was her legs and then she was gone.

There was a moment of silence as the few demons in the corridor skittered away and then the Man let his plants fall back, retreating into the soil and leaving torn pieces of Summer scattered in a bloody swathe behind him.

Gordie cried out and tried to scramble toward her again.

"No," Fool said, unable to shout, voice on the crumbling edge of tears, still holding his friend but with no strength. "No, Gordie, it's what he wants, to get us back into his range. Gordie, we have to let her go."

"I can't."

"You can. You have to. We will have revenge for her, but not now. Not here. I have a plan, a thing that might work. We can still stop this. Please, help me."

"How?"

Fool stood. "I need a room with a tube, and I need a canister and paper and thread," he said. "I need to summon the Archdeacons."

Fool staggered along the corridor, opening doors at random, until he found one that contained a desk and a chair and a pneumatic tube in the corner, this one dropping into the floor rather than rising into the ceiling. There was a pile of canisters on the desk and he took one, unscrewing its lid and emptying out the message it contained.

"I need paper," he said. Gordie, who had followed him into the room in a kind of hopeless shuffle, ignored him and sat in the room's chair.

"Gordie, help!" Fool said, insistent. "Mourn her after. We'll mourn her and Marianne together, but now, for fuck's sake, help. I need paper and ink."

Gordie looked at him dully and then got up and began to empty the other canisters, tipping out the messages they contained until he found one that was short, holding it out wordlessly. Fool, meanwhile, was rooting through the desk drawers until he found a bottle of ink. Removing the feather from his pocket, he opened the bottle and dipped the feather's end in the liquid it contained.

Taking the paper from Gordie, Fool scribbled out the message written upon it and then wrote his own message there. His writing was untidy and large, wavering, but he didn't care. As long as it could be read.

Come to the flame garden now

Message complete, he wafted the paper in the air to dry the ink and then rolled it and inserted it back into the canister. He couldn't tighten it because of his arm, so Gordie took it from him and finished sealing it.

"Thank you," said Fool and then knelt in front of Gordie. The man's white shirt was filthy, but some cleaner threads hung from the seam up the side, and he took one of these and pulled on it, dragging loose a long white cotton string. This he wrapped around the canister and tied with a clumsy knot and then carried the canister to the tube. Dropping it in, he said, "This goes to all the Archdeacons. All of them."

The tube sucked the canister away and it was gone.

"Will it work?" asked Gordie and his voice was low and dead.

"Maybe. I hope so."

Fool went back into the corridor, gesturing Gordie to follow him. They went back to the foyer, fighting their way through the thickening flow of administrators and clerks. Walking seemed to be a problem, one foot falling not in front of the other but loosely, to the side, the strength going from his ankles and his knees locking and unlocking in irregular bursts. He leaned against the wall as the horns sounded again, louder this time, loud enough so that the building itself seemed to rattle and shiver. Or was that him? he wondered. Was it him rattling and shivering, his body jittering along the lines of his pain and exhaustion?

They arrived at the foyer and pushed through the throng. The demon behind the desk had gone and had been replaced by a large column of smoke with something solid but unidentifiable at its center, strings of black vapor stretching out from it to point or gesture as other demons approached the desk with questions or requests. Fool paused, catching his breath, buffeted by the passing demons, and then set off again, heading for the doors.

Halfway across the floor, Fool realized that something was happening. The clerks and scribes and archivists, all the little things, had stopped and were craning their heads around, some pressing themselves up against the windows and peering up. The foyer fell silent and Fool heard the horns for a third time. One of the demons whimpered as the outside visible beyond the windows blackened with descending figures. Fool felt dizzy, his arm and stomach burning, the world pitching around him, and as the first of the Estedea landed in Hell's streets he collapsed to the floor and into a blackness as deep as Solomon Water.

———

When he awoke, Fool found himself propped against a wall in one of Assemblies House's smaller offices. Gordie was leaning against the wall opposite, knees drawn up and head down, and all around them were demons, small and large, silent and still. There was little light in the room and the air was thick with dust and sweat and the sour exhalations of the mass of demons.

Distantly, Fool could hear shouting and a terrible flapping sound, and then a heavy crash. The building shook and dust shivered out of old cracks that lined the ceiling.

Fool tried to move and lean away from the wall, but something pushed on him and held him back as a wave of dull, intense pain coiled inside his belly. Looking down, he saw a hand in the center of his chest, long-fingered and demonic, the arm behind it scrawny and ropey with veins and scrappy muscle.

A demon crouched over Fool, holding his injured arm and trying to feed. Fool jerked away. The demon moved without looking around, reaching out and grasping Fool's elbow and not letting go. Its grip was strong, holding Fool's arm in place despite his best efforts to draw it away, and then he thought, *An arm holding my elbow, a hand in my chest, a hand holding my wrist, and another hand there by its face on my skin. It has four arms.*

He shouldn't have been surprised, but he was. He'd spent the past week or so in a place of perfect shapes, and this distortion of the normality he'd become used to was jarring.

You were attacked by a man made of fucking shrubbery, he thought. *Nothing should surprise you anymore!* The demon, finally acknowledging Fool, looked around at him. Its face was smooth, mouthless, had only eyes and two rapidly expanding and contracting slits for nostrils, and it was not feeding on him.

It was inspecting the stitches that now sealed closed the holes in his wrist.

"They fixed you," said Gordie. When Fool looked at his friend, he hadn't moved, had spoken down between his legs so that the sound was muffled and flat. "While you were unconscious. They stitched you and bandaged you. Me too."

As Gordie spoke the demon started to wrap Fool's lower arm in a white bandage, the dressing tight but not uncomfortable, pinning it at the wrist and just below the elbow to keep the material in place. Finished, it nodded at Fool and then moved away. It had feet attached directly to its waist, no legs, and its arms were longer than its torso, so that it knuckled across the floor and into the shadows.

"Where are we? What's happening?" asked Fool.

"Why didn't we ever notice?" asked Gordie, apparently ignoring Fool's question.

"Notice?"

"The *smell*," Gordie replied. "It stinks here."

He was right, it did, not just in the room but in all of Hell, it stank of fear and violence and blood and death and rottenness and vomit and shit, and they didn't notice because it was their air, it was all around them all the time. Fool didn't know what to say to Gordie, so instead he simply moved across the room to sit next to him. Moving ached and lifting his shirt showed him that another bandage had been wrapped around his stomach. A bloom of red, small and delicate, had soaked through the bandage about two inches in from the edge of the midriff and the same distance up from his hip. He twisted, very slowly, and felt something slip in his flesh, two planes moving along each other.

"They said to say it wasn't serious," said Gordie, still not looking up.

"'They'?"

"The demon that helped bandage you. You'll be okay."

"Why did they help me? Gordie, I know you hurt but you need to talk to me."

"We helped," said a new voice, reedy and thin, "because we are scared."

Fool looked around and found that a demon had crouched by his side without him noticing. It was tall, its skin a murky brown, and it was covered in eyes. There were hundreds of them, different sizes, different types, and different colors. Fool saw predators' slit pupils, all-black orbs, almost-human irises, golden eyes that glowed, all of them set into the thing's chest and belly and across its shoulders like a pelt. They blinked in unison, and moved independently, glancing about the room.

"You're scared?" asked Fool.

"Of the war. Of what will happen to us. We're not soldiers, human. We don't want to die." It gestured back behind itself, taking in not just the room but the demons in Assemblies House, the demons outside the House that just wanted to be left alone to scurry and dart and do their jobs and feed on scraps. Fool couldn't help but feel a momentary flash of cruel pleasure. *You're scared,* he thought. *Welcome to our world.*

"But why help me?" He raised his bandaged arm and looked at it again.

"Because we heard you say you could stop it, after the thing killed Rhakshasas and the woman," the demon said. It leaned in close and now all its eyes were staring at Fool, their gaze intense and unflinching. "I'd eat you if I could, little man. I'd suck the memories from your head without thinking about it, but at the moment you're more useful to us alive. You kill my kind and I hate you for it, but now you say you can stop the war and so we have to help you because we don't want to die."

Fool pulled himself to his feet, slowly, using the wall as a support. The demon stood from its crouch, its face keeping level with Fool's own as he rose.

"You will help us?"

"Get out of my way," said Fool. "I'll try to stop the war. Not for you, you fucking freak, but for all the little humans out there that you'd eat in a second and that'll die in this war alongside you if it carries on."

The demon stepped aside and the ones behind it scuffled and crabbed out of the way as well so that a path to the room's door opened up.

"Gordie," said Fool. "Come on."

Fool thought Gordie was going to sit there until he collapsed and fell to dust and blew away, but then he pulled himself up, too. His movements were weary. His head was bandaged and he looked very young and as though he was only partly there, was looking at some other place through lidded and half-closed eyes.

"She's dead," he said, his voice still flat and uninflected.

"Yes," said Fool. What else was there to say? "She and Marianne and all the others because the Man wants to take over Heaven and Hell. We can try to stop him, Gordie."

"Will that bring her back?" Gordie met Fool's gaze for the first time since Fool had come around, and his eyes were red, raw and bloodshot.

"She came back before, you both did," said Fool and hated himself for making the hope grow in Gordie. He watched it blossom in the man's eyes, *little manipulating Fool, making him hope just because you need him,* and he put a hand on his shoulder and said, "We can try."

"What do we do?" asked Gordie. His eagerness was almost pathetic, it was so transparent. *Is this what I've become, or have I always been this way?* wondered Fool. *Is this the real me, revealed layer by layer the longer I survive in Hell?*

There was another crash from somewhere in the building and a long shriek. The demons around Fool cringed and he thought they might have recognized the sound, heard something in it that spoke to them, of demonic pain and suffering and death, and made them see their own approaching ends. He looked down at himself, at the torn and blood-stained clothes and the scars and the dirt and the bandages and the tattoos that even now slipped about his skin like eddying water, and smiled. *They think I'm their only hope and maybe I am. I'm Hell's angel of survival.*

30

The streets were chaos.

Of course, Hell's streets were always chaos, but it was usually a controlled form of disorder, one with hierarchies and rankings and structures, humans below demons below the Evidence below the oldest things. What Fool saw when he looked out the doors of Assemblies House was like nothing he'd seen before.

A train had been overturned in the streets and was burning, flames leaping in its broken windows, filling them. A single Estedea was walking along the side of the train, now its roof, flowing between the fires as Evidence Men attacked it. The angel flicked the little things away, long, white hands appearing from its robes and making tiny gestures that sent out strings of old and dusty fire. The street around the train was littered with dead demons and humans, and the kindliest angels flew among them, fluttering down to stroke the torn and battered bodies. When they touched the flesh of the dead, blue sparks sprang up that they caught and swallowed. Above them all, the atmosphere was black with smoke and flying figures that carved trails through air thick with cries.

The sky was the color of diseased skin.

Gordie and Fool watched as more angels dropped from the sky to form a phalanx beyond the train and demons boiled from one of Hell's alleys to attack them. These weren't just bauta, but a mass of the things that usually walked the Houska or worked the fields or swam in Solomon Water, all of them armed with their own versions of the angels' fires. Fool saw columns of smoke rising from some demons' hands, others holding writhing coils of what looked like living dirt. As the two armies met, the noise in the street rose, a caterwauling blanket of cries and clashes and sizzles and burnings and screams. In among the demons were humans, chained around the necks, held captive in metal collars. The demonkind used the humans as both weapon and distraction; Fool watched as one chained Sorrowful was spun so hard by its demon captor that its feet lifted from the ground and it crashed into an angel. The angel tried to shake off the Sorrowful, but its chain had wrapped around the angel's head, confusing it and pulling it over, and then the demon coiled its weapon of living filth around the angel, and flames and smoke rose from it until its head rolled free and bounced to the street. A burst of light exploded from the angel's sundered neck as its body collapsed and then the Estedea from the train was arrowing through the air and its own cracked and bitter light was reaching out and both human and demon fell to pieces alongside the angel. The Estedea picked up the demon's head and shoulders, the line of severance through the center of its chest still smoking, and fed off the remains. As it did so, the demon's body crumpled as though the Estedea was sucking the very essence from it, finally dropping it when there was nothing left to suck free. A kindly one dropped and swallowed the light from both human and angel; the demon it left alone.

As the battle raged, Fool and Gordie stepped into the street and began to move in the direction of the Flame Garden, hoping that the Archdeacons had obeyed and that he wasn't too late. His battered body wouldn't run no matter how hard he pushed it. He felt as though there were ropes around him, pulling and tautening, dragging against him. He needed to be fast, to be *faster*, but he wasn't, he was slow and clumsy and worried that time was slipping by more and more quickly and that he was late, so very late.

Too late.

An Estedea landed in the street in front of Fool and Gordie, its robes opened into huge wings as it descended and then wrapping back around itself as its feet hit the ground. In the black depths of its cowl a pale face shifted and teeth flashed and eye sockets gleamed and then it was coming at them.

Fool didn't draw his gun. Instead, he stood his ground as it approached and said, "We're not your enemy." In response, the angel opened its arms, the robes pulling back from those impossibly long and bone-white hands, and produced its fire. This wasn't the flame of Benjamin or Israfil but something older and darker, a fire that was made of smoldering dust and old shrouds caught by embers, but it moved quickly, lacing its way through the gap between them and encircling them.

"We're not your enemy," said Fool again as the fire closed in. The urge to pull his gun from its holster was pulsing in him but he fought it, no aggression, no violence, giving the Estedea no excuse. "Look at us. We're no threat. We're human, we're the damned, not demons."

The Estedea tilted its head, its *hood*, and the blackness underneath the cowl looked at him quizzically. The gray fires tightened slightly, ready to snap closed, but didn't touch them. Somewhere behind them there was an explosion, a dull crunch of sound that sent flurries of dust dancing around them on gusts of heat, and then horns sounded again. Over the Estedea's shoulder Fool watched as a squad of demons and chained humans emerged from a side street and ran to the entrance to a farther street, bauta outlying the squad and harrying it along. None of them looked around.

"Please," said Gordie. "Please, listen." The Estedea took another step toward them and Fool could smell it now, could smell old stone and rain and damp earth and ancient paper as it leaned in, peering at them, assessing them.

Judging them.

The string of fire came closer but Fool felt no heat from it even as it touched his skin. He smelled burning hair and then it was gone and the Estedea was stepping away and then something came at the angel from the side and swallowed it.

It happened fast, a creature like a mass of spiders riding a living web rising up in the alleyway between two buildings and surging forward, parts connected by constantly moving cables, and the whole of it fell on the Estedea, and now Fool saw it for what it was—not a thing from outside but demons, demons controlled by the Man like some parasitic host, his branches thrust into their back and sides and making them do his bidding the way his own flesh had once been manipulated by a Falling angel.

How had he not seen? How had he missed it, been so convinced of his own rightness that he hadn't seen the obvious? The thing he had chased across the Sleepers' Cave, the thing that had fed on the Joyful on the island in the middle of Solomon Water, all demons as captive as the humans themselves. *That's why the Man needs the Joyful, as captive food for his captive demons, all of them in boxes until he needs them, and then he takes them out and makes them his puppets.*

The Estedea thrashed against the Man, against the demons controlled by the Man, and its fire curved through the mass that gathered around it, cutting chunks of the demonkind away, but for every piece that fell another took its place, more and more emerging from the alleyway to consume the angel. It shrieked, a sound that was the absence of sound, a silence torn wrong ways out that filled the street like oil and pressed against Fool's ears, making him wince.

The Estedea rose into the air, carrying its attackers with it, and then the weight was too much and it crashed down. This time, as it hit the ground, the mass flowed over the top of the angel, crushing it. It made that heavy not-noise again, its cry rising into the air and expanding into the clouds. There was a sharp tearing sound, and the Estedea's fire, twisting around itself like a dying snake, was tossed from the struggling confusion and flopped into the street. The Man began to drag the angel back toward the alley as it howled, the silence louder than ever, destroying the noise of the war and the fires and the distant rumble of trains, filling Hell with nothing.

"We have to go," Fool said but heard nothing, made no sound. He tried again but again his words were absent. He shook Gordie's shoulder, pointing; the Estedea's cry had summoned help and more of the saddest angels were looping in the sky above them, searching for their fallen companion.

There was a sudden pop, and sound rushed back in, the clamor of Hell shocking after the nothing. "It was Fool!" screeched the Man, still pulling the Estedea back into the darkness of the alleyway, still battering it down. Another piece of its fire was cast aside and then a flapping thing that might have been a wing or might have been a section of its robe was tossed to the street to lie, pulsating weakly.

"It was Fool!" the Man shouted again, and then was gone, taking his prize with him. The Estedea above them began to close in, crackles of dry fire slithering across the ground, searching. One of them hit the now-still wing and immediately they were all crying, their noise a grand muteness that had weight, had mass, weighed down on Fool.

"They'll kill us," Gordie mouthed at him, and Fool simply nodded and they ran and fuck his aching flesh, fuck its infirmity, Fool was running because that was the only hope there was, and if that was his only hope he would damn well keep hold of it.

As they reached the end of the street, the mass of the Estedea arrived and the earth shook with their landing. A tongue of fire curved over their heads as they went around the corner, but it didn't grasp at either of them, instead scoring a line across the front of the building ahead of them and then snapping back to its owner in a flash and a stench of burning brick.

They came around onto a street that was pitted with the remains of old fires, some still smoldering, and that was littered with dead demons and angels. The burned remains of the Sorrowful were piled against the buildings, their flesh split and smoking, blue crackles still slithering across the piles as the vestigial remnants of their souls burned free to rise in the air like fireflies.

A single bauta ran out from a building ahead of them. It saw them running at it and shrieked, wheeling about and loping away, its head down, matted hair dragging across the dirt. As it reached the end of the street a spear of fire appeared from the clouds and impaled it, pinning it to the ground for a second before retreating and leaving the thing for dead.

Another street, another battleground. Here, the angels had come off worse and their dead outnumbered the dead of Hell, although chained remains of Sorrowful were plentiful in the debris. *At least there'll be a lot of space to take new souls out of Limbo,* Fool thought darkly as they went past the mess of bodies and death. *We won't need Delegation discussions about that for a while.*

Another corner, and they were at the top of the Houska now and the war was here, right in front of them.

A second train, this one still upright, had been driven along the Houska's main street, blocking it. From its windows demons were attacking angels as the latter swooped and flew around them. Fool came to a halt and watched as an angel was caught by two demons, dragged in through the train's window, and vanished from view. Fires, angelic and demonic weaponry, and the flames they brought into being crackled across the train's engine compartment, smoke pouring from the vents that lined its sides, and its wheels ground over the dead and dying as it moved slowly forward.

The Man was there, sending his demon slaves to collect the still-living from where they fell, dragging angels and demons back into spaces and buildings, as Evidence Men scurried around the street, slashing with their tusks and claws, gibbering and capering. Mr. Tap walked through their midst, its angular frame and warped face dark, trying to marshal its troops to fight back effectively. An Estedea fell upon it but Mr. Tap grasped it, easily tearing into the angel's wings, shredding them so that it couldn't fly up from the street.

Before the bauta could reach it and finish what Mr. Tap had started, the Man had swallowed the fallen angel and stolen it away.

Fool and Gordie went along the Houska's street, skirting the skirmishes and staying close to the buildings. In some, he saw hiding Sorrowful and demons, for once not attacking or being attacked, simply sharing the space and fearing for their lives.

Behind them the train veered across the street and crashed into one of the Houska's brothels, grinding its way into the building's interior, tearing brickwork loose, sending a cloud of dust and ripping, grinding noises out behind it. A moment later, the building's roof collapsed, burying the front of the train. Angels flocked to its rear, the demons inside it still fighting, the Estedea still hovering above it all, occasionally swooping in to feed on the fallen and the damaged.

"We're losing," said Gordie.

They were. Even now, Mr. Tap had started to retreat, calling the bauta back to its side, the little demons forming a shield around it as it went. The Estedea massed above it, not attacking but not giving ground or air. Mr. Tap found a covered street between two buildings and disappeared into it, and the Estedea followed, and the horns sounded again, loud and triumphant.

"Come on," said Fool.

With the Estedea following Mr. Tap, the battle moved away. Angels still clashed with the demons on the train, but the street itself cleared, leaving more of the dead and air thick with dust and the odor of sizzling flesh. An angel's wing, white and feathered, lay against the wall in front of Fool and Gordie and they had to step over it to carry on. Blood trickled from the ragged stump that had, until recently, connected the wing to the angel's back, and then the Man's roots and stems slithered out from the building behind the wing and tangled around it, tugging it back in through the broken window. Feathers blew away from the wing as it vanished, and Fool remembered what the Man had said, that he'd be able to have all the feathers he wanted, and put his hand in his pocket. His own feather was still there, still safe, and he held it for a brief space, reassured by a cleanness and purity he could feel through his fingertips and palm even though he could not see it.

Another street, this one quiet. They made swift progress, wary, reaching the end without incident.

Another street, more of the dead, mostly Sorrowful here, a great chain of them, their bodies tangled together and blocking the path so that Gordie and Fool had to step into the road to go around them. On the far side of the pile was a Sundô, sitting and weeping. Gordie went to go to it but it looked up and hissed at him, its black face a mask of misery and pity and anger. They went around it and carried on.

The rest of the journey became a thing of pieces and segments and disconnected incidents. A building burning, demons on its roof throwing fire at angels flying around them. An angel crashing to earth in front of Fool and Gordie, its wings glaring arcs of flame. An Evidence Man leaping at them and Fool shooting it. He thought they might have passed along Solomon Water's edge at some point and seen a creature as vast as anything he'd ever seen in Hell churning in the water, watching its sucker-covered tentacles lifting into the air and striking Estedea out of their flights as more angels hauled on ropes of fire to bring the creature up, sickly-smelling steam and smoke rising from the battle in equal measure.

Had he seen a swarm of Sundô carrying body after body aloft? Seen demons using the chained Sorrowful to flail at the flying angels? Heard screams and howls and the Estedea's silences, felt the heat of flames and the ache in his muscles and tears on his cheeks, watched as the Man stalked through the chaos and took what he wanted, stealing the barely living away for his secret purposes? And, forming and reforming in the smoke above them, was that the face of Elderflower, grinning?

Yes, he thought, yes, and the memories were like curses in his mind, writhing and feverish and scorching.

The war ebbed and flowed around them and the dead filled the streets until it was impossible to see them, until it was impossible to take it all in, and they simply ran and they dodged and they hoped.

And Hell burned.

The war hadn't reached the Flame Garden and it was quiet when Fool and Gordie arrived.

They approached along the wide road through the fields, walking in the center so that they were not too close to the Man. *He's everywhere,* thought Fool as they came to the Garden, *all over Hell. How can we hope to beat him?*

Because we have to hope, because if we don't then we may as well die now. Besides, he had the impression that the Man still wasn't as absolute as he made out, that he was still limited, and that his attention was directed elsewhere at the moment. Fool was counting on it.

"You finally came," said a voice from by the edge of the Garden. It was angry, thick, as though the speaker had a mouth of snot and mud. Fool looked around and saw the Archdeacons huddled by the entrance to the Garden. Beyond them, the flames reached up, staining the sky with swirls of soot and heat.

"We were summoned," said a different voice, one that dripped with disgust and fury. "It thinks to summon us using the white thread of command, and then it doesn't turn up to greet us."

"I'm not sure if you've noticed," Fool said, too tired to be polite or deferential, "but the streets aren't exactly safe or quiet at the moment."

"It dares to speak to us like this?" said the second voice, and a demon that appeared to be part pig and part cow emerged from the group, clearly electing itself spokesman. Its eyes blazed red and in its cloven hands it held what looked like a bell that it rang after everything it said, as though to punctuate itself.

"I'm not daring anything," Fool said. "I'm trying to stop what's happening."

"And how would you do that?" *Ding.*

"How will you, hiding by the Garden?" asked Gordie.

"The other little human talks!" *Ding.* "It speaks, little nothing that belongs to neither Heaven nor Hell. Be quiet, little nothing." *Ding.*

"Shut up," said Fool. The demon was startled into silence, its brown eyes flaring wide, its nostrils twitching open. One of the demons behind it, a thing dressed in dirty red and green rags and with long straggly hair covering its entire frame, simian and low, started to come forward, its legs scratching at the ground like a horse given to panic.

"Stay still and shut up if you want to live," said Fool. "You're losing this war, the Estedea are too strong for you. The only chance you've got is to trust me."

"Trust you?" *Ding.*

"Trust me," repeated Fool, "and stop ringing that damned bell. We have to persuade Heaven that the war isn't just."

"And how do we do that, little Information Man, little friend of nothing?" *Ding.*

Fool drew his gun and, before anyone could move, fired at the demon's bell. It disintegrated, the bullet carrying on and punching into the demon's side and shattering its wrist as it passed. The demon grunted and fell awkwardly to a sitting position in the dirt. "I said to stop ringing it," said Fool. "Now, listen to me, and listen carefully.

"All of you, you need to go into the Garden and stay there, but stay where you can be seen from the entrance. Take the injured one and go, now. Stay on the path, stay where I can see you, don't go too deep, and be prepared to fight."

"And if we don't?"

"Then stay here and hide, or go back and die. Kill me if you like, I'm too tired to care. Either you do things my way or I'm done and you can find yourself another Commander of the Information Office, find yourself another fool to toy with. War is here."

Behind them, back toward Hell, light flashed in the sky and a column of smoke was rising up from somewhere in the Houska. The sounds of battle were getting louder and the shapes in the sky were growing larger. Another explosion shook the air, a distant ball of flame and smoke lifting and spreading and then flattening out against the low clouds before rolling away to nothing.

"And you, Fool? What will you do while we follow your instructions?" The demon in red and green, its voice the gruff and deep drone of flies and far-off machinery. It sounded scared, hopeful, desperate.

It almost sounded human.

Fool unbuttoned his shirt and looked at the bandage around his waist. The red bloom had dried to a dark maroon stain and the edges of the dressing had begun to curl over. Dirt had found its way under his clothes and smeared across the white material in black streaks. Fool found the pin holding the bandage together and undid it, unwinding the long strip and folding it carefully over his arm. His belly was a sunrise of bruises and scratches, the newest one the puncture inflicted by the Man, which had scabbed thickly. The lines of tattoos were just visible among the marks and the discolorations, and he poked at them deliberately.

"I," he said quietly, "will be speaking to Mr. Tap."

31

"What the fuck do you want?"

The tattoo Mr. Tap spoke tersely, its tone clipped, the tattoo less expressive than usual, the throat through Fool's guts not opening to its usual depth. "I'm a little busy."

Fool took a deep breath. Here it was. Here he went. "Busy hiding in the middle of your little men?" he said. "Busy running away?"

"What?" Mr. Tap sounded stunned at Fool's reply, the tattooed face of it glaring, the eyes opening wide, and now the throat clicked open, now it was a hole deeper than Fool was thick, now it had teeth.

"I wondered how you were going to win this war if you kept running away? I saw you running. Elderflower saw you," said Fool, invoking the only name he thought might scare Mr. Tap, Elderflower the cleric, Elderflower the unknowable thing. *Further and further in,* he thought. *At least I have the consolation that whatever happens in the war, I'll be dead anyway. Mr. Tap will murder me for this.*

"You little shit, I'll eat you alive," said the tattoo calmly. *Even now, even in the middle of all this, it can't help but react,* thought Fool, and then the face on his stomach grinned, wide, and its mouth opened. Teeth glinted behind the lips, and for the first time, Fool grabbed at his own split and splitting flesh. It felt like him and not like him at the same time, like himself and Mr. Tap overlaid, and it sent a shiver of wrongness up his arm. He placed one hand on the image's lower lip, pushing it out to stop it biting at him, ignoring the bolt of pain the action caused. *Another step,* he thought, *here we go,* and with the other hand he punched at Mr. Tap's eye. The tattoo blinked at him, startled by the blow that Fool felt as another throb of pain.

"I'm tired of being threatened by you," Fool said. "You're a coward."

"I'll eat your fucking *soul*, you little turd," said the tattoo and gnashed at his fingers, trying to snap them away. *If he managed, would the fingers be in my belly or its throat?* wondered Fool. *Where would they go when it swallowed?*

Still holding the mouth apart, he said, "You're not a coward? Prove it."

"What game are you playing, Fool?"

"Do I have your attention, finally?" said Fool. He had it, the demon head of the Evidence, had it angry and concentrating on him, but it wouldn't last. This was his opportunity. "I did my job, Mr. Tap. I went to Heaven and I was an Information Man, a proper one, not like your silly little demons or ghosts or whatever the bauta are. I did my job and now I can make my report.

"I'm at the Flame Garden. If you want to win this war, come here and bring the bauta, bring what's left of the Evidence with you. We can end this war, demon. Surely you want that, or are you so confident that you'll win? Come. After I've told you what I need to, you can eat me if you want." Mr. Tap didn't reply. "We're at the end of things now; surely you want to be here in person?"

The tattoo stopped trying to bite at him and the lines of it sealed in from the edges, itching and burning as they did so. Before the mouth closed, Mr. Tap's voice emerged from it a last time, muffled and dense.

"I'll be there soon, Fool. I'm coming for you."

"You're not the only one," said Fool quietly as the tattoo finished sealing. After the burn of pain had receded, he turned to Gordie and took the remaining pieces of the torn books from his jacket pocket and gave them to him.

"You know what to do?" They had discussed the plan before they arrived at the Garden. It was ill formed and unstable, but it was all they had.

"Yes."

"Wait until you're sure, Gordie. Wait until you're positive."

"I will."

"Summer and Marianne and all the others, this is how we can remember them and honor them properly," said Fool and held his friend's gaze. He took the man's hand on his own and clasped it tightly.

"I'm glad I had the chance to see you each again, you and Summer both."

"I am, too," said Gordie and then broke Fool's gaze and grip and went to just inside the Garden. He sat at the edge of the wall, his back to it, careful to lean away from the flames coming up from the beds below, and then allowed himself to slip sideways, playing dead. The heat must be tremendous, Fool thought, but Gordie didn't move. The Archdeacons, farther along the path and still huddled together in a protective clump, looked on, confused. There was only one more thing to do now.

It was time to call the Man of Plants and Flowers.

Fool walked to the edge of the field that ran close to the edge of the Garden. He removed his gun from its holster and pointed it at the earth, fired so that the shot tore into the soil and through plants. After the echoes of the shot had died away he said, loudly, "I want to make a deal." As an afterthought, he took the feather and brushed it along the tips of the grass, carving a gentle figure eight in front of him.

There was a pause. The air popped with distant explosions and a hazy flash crawled across the sky over Fool and then the grass twisted up into a semblance of a person.

"The feather's touch never gets old, does it?" asked Fool.

"What do you want?" the Man asked. "You burned me in the courtyard, you fight me, you shoot me, Fool, and I am not at all happy with you." Fool stepped back. There were no branches here to force to grow into spears, but he was wary nonetheless; the Man had proved himself capable of attack in unexpected ways.

"I already said; I want a deal," said Fool.

"I have my own feathers," said the Man. "I don't need yours."

Fool, remembering the wing being dragged away, said, "I know. The feather isn't on offer, it's mine. What I'm offering, what I can give you, is the rest of the Archdeacons. I've already gathered them together for you." He stepped farther back, letting the Man see the demons on the path through the Garden in case he had not already noticed them.

The Man paused, and when he spoke again his voice was quieter, friendly. "And you want?"

"I want some peace," Fool said, and it was true, it was so true. "I ache. My body hurts. I'm so tired I can't even see properly or think properly. I give you the Archdeacons, which means I give you Hell. In return you let me go, let me go and be somewhere quiet. I won't bother you and you leave me alone."

The Man paused again, longer this time, the sound of him the rustle of his thinking. Finally, he spoke again, and when he did his voice was even softer. "You're more like me than you thought. You're capable of coldness, Fool, coldness and betrayal."

"You have your war, do what you want but leave me out of it."

The Man thought for a long moment and then said, "Agreed, Fool. It's a fair deal. Keep your feather and find your peace. I'll take the Archdeacons and then I'll take Hell and then Heaven."

"They're in the Garden." It was so tempting to step aside, to let it play out that way, to be left to find some peace. "Come and get them."

"No. Send them out."

"If I send them out, they'll know something's wrong and they'll scatter before you can take them in one go and then you'll have to track them all over Hell. You'll break our deal claiming I've broken my end of it, and I'm too tired and too hurt to play this game again. Come and get them. They're waiting." He stepped aside and gestured at the Archdeacons. "Yours for the taking. Do that, and Hell is without leaders, or at least, without leaders who have any grasp of what's happening. By the time the ancient ones on Crow Heights have organized a replacement set, by the time Elderflower has decided what to do and done it, you'll be in control of enough of Hell to be able to defend yourself."

"Come and get them."

The shape of grass collapsed. All Fool could do now was wait.

Mr. Tap arrived first, traveling in a dusty black transport with holes in its windows and a series of dents up one wing, its paint cracked and the bare metal beneath exposed. Twin columns of bauta followed behind, hundreds of the Evidence Men trying to keep ranks like soldiers but failing, their lines ragged and ever distorting. Some of them were injured, others covered in blood that Fool thought probably wasn't theirs. One of the bauta at the head of the procession carried a damaged angel's wing, small and limp, and waved it like a flag.

Mr. Tap climbed out of the car, its long limbs casting arachnid shadows on the ground, and came to stand in front of Fool.

"Thomas Fool, Commander of the Information Office of Hell," the demon said, and it drawled the words, the warped lips drawing back from its distorted mouth. The tattoo on Fool's belly twitched, and for a moment the voice came from his own body as well as from the thing in front of him, and then the demon waved its hand and the tattoo sealed again. Fool was briefly grateful for the unsundering of his flesh and then Mr. Tap leaned in and whispered, "Should I slaughter you now?"

"No," said Fool, gun still in its holster. "Save your energy."

"For what, Fool? For what?"

"For your real enemy. For the Man of Plants and Flowers. He's behind this, the whole war, not the things from outside. I was wrong."

That brought Mr. Tap up short. It reared back and peered at Fool. "You're lying," it said after blinking several times. "The Man is dead."

"Tell him that," said Fool and pointed behind the bauta.

The Man was coming along the road.

The fields were bursting with plants as the Man forced the bushes and grasses to explode into frenzied life so that he could knot the stems together into vines, could force branches out and keep his horde of puppet demons moving. There was a mass of them jerking along the road, and they were the dancers, their gait uneven, convulsive and leaping as the Man controlled them. *All of them at once,* Fool marveled even as his fear flowered. *All of them, but he's not doing it perfectly. That's why they dance, that's why they're irregular and uneven.* The connecting cables between them, which Fool recognized now as branches, roots, and vines, constantly broke and fell away as new growth shoots snapped out of the fields and attached themselves, pulling the mass on, keeping it moving. It was like watching bitter poetry in motion.

The Man was fast, faster than the bauta had been, and fell upon the rearmost Evidence Men with a noise like a thousand dull knives being drawn.

It was what Fool had hoped and counted on: that the Man was strong when he was at his most diffuse because he could slip around unseen, but that when he was forced to act, when he was forced to concentrate himself, he became a target, could be fought against; that Mr. Tap would respond to Fool's summons because it wanted to win the war and revenge for the slight of Fool's insults, and it would bring its army with it. Fool had brought them together and hoped, and now their natures had taken over, the violence in them having sway over the situation.

They joined battle.

Mr. Tap reacted quickly, darting away and shrieking orders to its troops, trying to get them to organize, but it had little chance of attaining any real control. The bauta, aggressive and feral, responded to the attack as a disorganized pack, and soon the demons controlled by the Man and the Evidence Men were fighting in the dust, scrappy and vicious and filthy.

More of the Man's slaves were coming up the road behind the first mass, more bushes exploding from the dirt of the fields to allow the Man to keep control of them. *He must be using so much energy,* Fool thought as he backed away, stepping onto the path into the Garden. The new captive demons joined the battle as Mr. Tap climbed on top of the vehicle and tried again to make itself heard. It clapped its hands and a spiral of what looked like old fur and hair twisted out from it and lanced rapidly into the melee, snapping taut around one demonic part of the Man's force and severing it from the main body. The slave demon immediately collapsed and Evidence Men fell on it, tearing it to pieces.

Mr. Tap howled, the sound joyous and wild in the hot afternoon, and sent another lash into the struggling crowd. With an audible sizzle, another part of the Man's army fell away and was torn to shreds.

The Man couldn't have stolen that many demons or Hell would have noticed, and some had presumably fallen in the other battles of the war; his plan had to depend on waiting until the two armies were weakened and stepping in then, but Fool had, he hoped—and there was that word again, that fucking word—forced his hand. By making him try to take the Archdeacons and putting him in conflict with the Evidence, the Man was, perhaps for the first time, at risk.

The Man and the Evidence were tearing each other apart.

The bauta had the advantage of speed and ferocity and numbers and a mindless lack of fear, but the Man had *mass*. He could also use the plants on either side of the road as additional weaponry, and Fool saw several of the Evidence Men snared or speared by his forced growths, tangled by them or impaled and pulled into pieces.

The Evidence Men swarmed the mass of captive demons, their tusks piercing and goring, snapping the connecting cable of branch and stem. The disconnected demonkind fell to the roadway and were trampled or set upon by their enemies. Mr. Tap's strings of hair, or fur, or whatever they were, snaked through the battle, snapping and tearing at the Man's troops, lopping off limbs or heads or snipping through the mass and cleaving it into pieces. Sometimes the Man managed to send new growths out from the fields to reconnect the severed section, but for each time he managed it there was a section he failed to reach before Mr. Tap's piglike troops ripped it away and harried it down to nothing. The Man, for his part, set his demons to crowd the smaller things, slashing at them, tearing them, ripping them piece from piece, surrounding groups of them and tightening like some terrible, grand noose, pressing in, leaving the things in its center dead.

Soon, the road was filled with the dead, bauta and captive demons and plants, the sides not exactly equal but neither managing to gain any kind of true advantage over the other. They fought, and they weakened each other amid the stench of spilling blood and baking entrails and sap and shit and hair and fear and rage, and they carried on and on, until what was left were pale shadows of the numbers that had started the battle.

Eventually the two opposing sides had little choice but to draw apart and face each other across the churned bodies of their dead and injured, gathering themselves.

Now.

Fool finally drew his gun. He pointed at one of the demons in the Man's tattered web and fired, shooting the thing in the forehead. The back of its skull exploded and it collapsed in a shower of brain and meat. He fired again and another fell.

"Fool," said the Man from in the field, the shape of him rising up, larger than Fool had ever seen him before. He was still human, or at least, retained a human form, a huge fat man made of greenery sitting in a field overlooking a battle like some malevolent scarecrow. "What are you doing? We had a deal."

"We still have," said Fool. "Come and get the Archdeacons if you want them. I'm waiting. I'm just clearing myself a path out of here. It looks like you'll have to come yourself, though; your demons can't get past the Evidence. Can you do it, do you think?" He fired again and this time a bauta fell, the Evidence Man's face torn away by the bullet.

"Fool," hissed Mr. Tap, turning, and the Man struck.

A mass of wooden stems burst from the center of the Man's bulk and spat across the space between it and Mr. Tap. The longest of them punctured the center of Mr. Tap's back and the rest slapped across its shoulders and wrapped around the demon tightly, creating a shifting carapace of greenery about the demon's chest. The stems stretched between the Man and Mr. Tap and they *pulsed*, bulging and shivering, and then they snapped, the broken ends connected to Mr. Tap contracting, violently slamming into it, tightening and holding on to the demon's back. Mr. Tap let out a strange gasp, elongated and raw, took a single step, and fell from the vehicle to land, hard, on the road with a crack.

Nothing moved and then the mass of the Man's demons collapsed. They fell together, suddenly lifeless. *Being used this way must exhaust them*, thought Fool as he watched the bodies roll apart, remembering the trapped demons in the crates, the Man's supply. They needed to feed, needed the strength the tainted memories of the suffering Joyful gave them to survive, and they had no access to that in the war and it had killed them. *He's taken them too far. It was only being a part of the Man that's kept them alive in the battle, and now he's gone and they've died.*

The Evidence Men, thinking this meant victory, sent up a collective whoop and leaped on the now-lifeless enemy, tearing into the bodies, chewing at them, worrying into bellies and chests with their tusks, gnawing them into bloodied chunks. Fool tried to ignore them, watching for Mr. Tap. He hadn't expected it to be this way, hadn't really known what to expect; he just had a sort of diffuse, helpless hope. His hand tightened on the butt of his gun, fear hot and sour in his mouth. This was it, this was the end, everything turned on what happened now.

Mr. Tap stood up.

The demon rose unsteadily. Its left arm was broken above the elbow, snapped from the landing, and was held awkwardly across its body. It turned, its head rolling, mouth opening and closing, three eyes blinking, body shaking. Fool took another step back into the heat of the Garden and then another, passing the still-recumbent Gordie. "Wait," he hissed. Gordie didn't reply.

Mr. Tap took a step forward, unsteady. It stretched out one leg and then the other, placing each on the ground and bouncing up onto its clawed toes and then down again. It was, thought Fool, like watching a man try on new clothes. In a way, that's exactly what it was.

"Fool," said Mr. Tap, taking another step, steadier now. The mass on its back shifted, tightening, and the next step it took was more confident.

Fool took another step back. "Hello," he said.

"You'll suffer for this," said Mr. Tap. Its voice was hoarse, the teeth in its throat clicking, wriggling, making its neck undulate. "You've been an interesting thing to watch and I might have stuck to the deal if you'd been fair with me, but you've not. You orchestrated this."

"Yes," said Fool. Another step back.

"You've made me inhabit this *thing*," Mr. Tap said, its voice thick with disgust.

"You chose to," said Fool. Another step. "I simply created a situation where you had to, but you always had a choice. You could have walked away. Flowed, grown away. Whatever it is you do."

"This is your doing, Fool."

"Yes. I suppose it is."

"I'll kill the Archdeacons, and then I'll kill you."

"No," said Fool. Mr. Tap took another step forward, steadier again, and then another, faster now.

"No?"

"No. I'm stopping this now."

Another step back.

"It isn't yours to stop, Fool."

"As Hell's Chief Information Officer, as Commander of the Information Office, I'm stopping it. This is over. Go, now, and we might yet still be able to make a deal."

"I think not," said Mr. Tap. "I think not, indeed, Fool. Your time has come."

Mr. Tap started running, ungainly but fast, covering the distance between them alarmingly quickly. Fool managed to snap off a shot, the bullet tearing into Mr. Tap's shoulder and spinning the demon that was now functioning as the Man's vehicle. It dropped to one knee, turning to glare at Fool as he took another step back and then another. Was the Man far enough in yet?

No.

"I'm going to rule Heaven and Hell," said the Man, and his voice sounded less like Mr. Tap now and more like the voice Fool was used to, the voice of the Man of Plants and Flowers. It was hoarse, scratched, and blood spilled from the demon's mouth as it spoke and Fool thought that maybe the Man wasn't using the vocal cords properly, that he was simply forcing the demon's throat to form the words by grinding it together as it forced air through the constricted tube. It was probably painful, and he wondered if the demon could still feel or if the Man had overtaken it completely.

He felt no pity for Mr. Tap.

"You could have had a peaceful life, Fool, but that choice is closed to you now," said the Man and rose. Blood dribbled from the wound in its shoulder and Fool fired again, but this time it was too fast, the Man was too fast, and it dodged away, still scrambling forward.

The Man hit Fool hard, its bony shoulder striking him in the stomach and tearing open the clotted wound in his side; Fool felt it rip, felt the planes of himself tear away from each other as he flailed back and fell. He lost his grip on his gun and it skittered back toward the Archdeacons, who still hadn't moved. *They're bureaucrats,* he thought, almost incoherent. *They've forgotten how to fight because they haven't had to in an age or more. They've not been threatened before, only been the ones doing the threatening.*

Mr. Tap stood over Fool, staring down at him. The Man, tight on its back, had sent more growths burrowing in the demon's flesh, Fool watching as the greenery burrowed under its skin, Mr. Tap's worms crawling along the ridges and furrows, and the wounds dripped an oily blood on the ground around Fool. Under the warped skin of Mr. Tap's face the vines burrowed, fat and hungry, the worms in Mr. Tap's creased face dropping away, knocked loose by the invaders beneath.

"You've lost, Fool," said the Man, using the demon's mouth. "This day is mine, this world is mine, and soon all the other worlds will be mine, too."

"Fuck you," said Gordie behind him and scattered the paper in a fat line across the path.

As Gordie threw himself down, the paper sparked and then burst into flame, the tainted earth of Hell befouling the paper and setting it afire in a violent burst that was almost white. The smoke that rose from the torn books formed into faces and words, twisting and writhing, black and dense, and it screamed and screamed and screamed.

The heat from the burning books was greater even than that of the Garden, Heaven burning in Hell, and it scorched Fool's skin and he tried to crawl away without taking his eyes from Mr. Tap. The demon, standing over Fool, took the force of the blast harder and it shrieked and shielded its eyes from the glare. It turned its back to the flames and hunched itself over, staring at Fool. Flames played across it, gaining little purchase on the thick, solid cage of the Man's flesh, burning out as quickly as they caught.

"This is it? Your plan?" the Man asked. "To trap me here behind a wall of flames? Why, Fool? Even Heaven's flames can't last forever. They'll burn low soon and then I'm free again and we revert to where we were and everything is mine."

Fool crabbed farther back, found his gun, took hold of it, and brought it around. "No," he said, "that was only the first part of the plan. This is the second part."

He fired, the shot tearing into Mr. Tap's knee and spilling the demon and its rider to the ground. It thrashed, trying to stand, but Fool had pulled himself to standing and fired again, this time at its other leg. It took the shot in the thigh and the leg buckled sideways, the bone splintering, the flesh tearing. Mr. Tap screamed in the Man's voice. *It can feel pain. Good.*

"And this," said Fool, gasping and dropping to his knees, "is the third part." He took the feather from his pocket and used it to scratch into the ground a single word written in large and jagged letters:

Mayall

Mr. Tap screamed again. The Man forced the demon to stand despite its broken limbs and it managed to achieve a kind of uneven, ungainly balance. The Man used Mr. Tap's good hand to brace its damaged knee, bent low, and began to hobble away. The fire from the books was still burning, lower now, and Mr. Tap turned toward it, the mass on its back loosening and slithering up to its shoulders. Fool fired again but his shot went wild and cracked into the low wall at the side of the path, sending chips and sparks into the air.

Mr. Tap shuffled on, approaching the wall of fire. It had burned so hot that the ground itself was buckling and bubbling, cracks zigzagging through the stone. The Man stumbled, Mr. Tap's flesh giving up the uneven battle with its injuries, and fell. It rolled and came up, still holding its knee together, blood trickling from between its long fingers. It groaned as it stood. *More pain. Good, good, it hurts good good good.*

Gordie, clothes charred from being close to the burning books, the material smoking, skin and hair scorched, stepped into Mr. Tap's path.

"Move," said Mr. Tap.

Gordie didn't immediately reply, instead tilting his head to one side and studying the rippling mass of the Man that controlled the demon. The skin of Gordie's face was red and blistered, some of the blisters popped and weeping. "You killed Summer," he said eventually.

Mr. Tap lashed out at him but Gordie stepped back and avoided the blow easily. Separated from the main mass of his body, split away from the soil, forced to inhabit a demon's flesh, injured, the Man was slower, easier to dodge.

Weaker.

But still dangerous. The Man risked letting go of Mr. Tap's knee and clapped its hands together, and although what emerged wasn't as strong or even as fast as the weapon the demon had been able to produce in the battle, the line of filthy hair that rose from it and coiled toward Gordie was fast enough to score across his shoulder, tearing through his blackened clothes and into the flesh beneath.

Gordie, blood spraying from his wound, stumbled as Fool fired again, this time more accurately, the shot hitting Mr. Tap in the back. The momentum sent the demon staggering forward and it fell, dropping first to its knees and then over onto its side.

The fires across the path guttered, flared back up, and then guttered again, gaps appearing, greasy black smoke spewing up from the hot stone where the flames had been a moment earlier. Mr. Tap twitched, tried to rise, and then fell back, too damaged to move. The branches and stems around Mr. Tap's upper torso detached themselves from the demon, flopping away from its body in a slithering pile. Mr. Tap twitched violently again, its abandoned body leaking from masses of punctures, its head smacking onto the ground as it fitted, dying.

The Man, exposed and isolated now, hunched himself up onto thin limbs created from twisted vines and tried to scramble away. Gordie, seeing it, threw himself forward as Fool, crying from exertion and pain, clambered up and began to run.

Gordie landed on the Man and then thrashed over, jerking back so hard that he hit and then rose from the ground before pitching back down in a violent spasm. Tendrils of the Man punched into Gordie, clamping on to him, tightening around him as they burrowed under Gordie's skin. Gordie tried to tear the Man's questing fingers away, ripping at his skin and clawing at himself, screaming, his voice cracking and hoarse.

The Man tightened again, pulling himself close to Gordie so that Fool didn't dare risk firing in case he hit his friend. The Man tried to make him stand, but Gordie was still fighting him, and his control was loose. Instead, the Man forced Gordie to his knees but he twitched and leaned back, overbalancing and falling. He twitched again as the Man tried to puppet him up a second time, and then he was forced to his feet and took two wavering steps, outlined against the flames, shambling and burned, before falling, collapsing outstretched.

Fool watched as if in slow motion as Gordie's head plunged into one of the patches of flame that still burned on the path.

His hair caught fire, sizzling and shriveling back even as Fool reached him and pulled him away, beating at the fires that now flowed over his scalp and face like liquid. He was still jerking, the Man trying to make him move, arms ratcheting out, legs wheeling as he tried to find some control, more of the stems and growths punching in through Gordie's chest and neck as the Man sought extra purchase.

Ignoring the Man, Fool tore off his jacket and wrapped it around Gordie's head, suffocating the flames. He could feel the heat through the material, watched as the cuffs charred, beat at the fires as they emerged from the edge of the covering. As he pulled the jacket back strings of Gordie's flesh came with it, long wet strips that smoked and stretched and snapped. Fool gagged at the smell of him, at the roast of his meat, and then Gordie punched him in the stomach.

The Man had achieved enough control to make Gordie lash out and then stand, stiff-limbed, face dripping and raw, eyes molten and bursting. Fool fell to the path with a grunt, then Gordie stepped forward and kicked at Fool. The kick missed, whistling in front of his face, and he raised his gun but couldn't fire at his friend. The Man pulled Gordie's foot up, swayed, and then kicked out again, faster than Fool would have believed possible. The kick took him on the side of his head, clicking his teeth together with a snap, and sent him sprawling, his vision blurring. For a dizzying moment there were two Gordies, each indistinct, each turning and shambling toward the flames, each trying to escape to the outside.

"No," Fool said and stood, staggered after the Man. He hit Gordie in the back and then, before the Man could react, plunged his hands into the tight branches and pulled. Gordie grunted as some of the Man's fingers came away from him with a wet snapping sound. Other pieces snapped and left their tips buried in Gordie's flesh. He smelled of blisters and smoke and meat, and Fool cried out miserably and pulled again.

Gordie sat as more of the Man came loose, spitting blood and bone fragments as he did so. The plants flailed, trying to twist out of Fool's grasp and reattach, but Fool held the mass away, ignoring the pain that the Man's whipping stems caused across his wrists. One more pull and the Man came completely away, more blood spraying out of the holes in Gordie's flesh. He turned his ruined face to Fool, exposed muscles sweating pus, ruined eyes weeping blood and bubbling gel, and mouthed, "Thank you."

Gordie fell, folding over, and did not move again.

Fool turned back and began to walk into the Garden. The Man thrashed in Fool's arms, parts of him whipping at Fool's chest and face. Something slashed across his eyes, and his vision blurred again, his right eye searing in pain. Something else tried to push into his skin but it was weak and he managed to hold it out, far enough away that it couldn't reach him. Something punctured his wrist, finding its way through the bandages and into the edge of the stitched hole beneath, and for a stretching, awful moment the Man was inside him, was nuzzling his way into him, and he had a sudden flash that *yes the Man was his friend and he should walk out, walk to the field* and then Fool yanked him away, wordless, and threw the Man to the ground.

They had reached the point where Fool had written Mayall's name. The Man hit the ground by the words and flipped himself over, strands of him contracting and stretching. He started to scuttle away, slow, small now, just a mass of branches and grass and stems holding the Man at its heart.

Fool saw the feather on the ground and picked it up. He stepped over to the Man, a trail of green slime now oozing behind the mass of plants as it moved, and thrust the feather barb-first into the center of the mass, impaling it.

The Man shrieked, tried to keep moving, dripping more of the liquid that was sap or blood or something between the two from around the feather's white shaft. Fool tried to hold the Man down, keep him still, but even now he refused to stop fighting, was able to pull away, still crawling, parts of him reaching out and dragging himself forward against Fool's efforts, lurching and pulling Fool over, still trying to get back to where the soil could replenish him. The Man shot a single stem back toward Fool, fast, and it punctured him above his collarbone, turned inside him, and then hooked back out in a spray of blood. Fool let go of the Man and tried to reach his gun, but the Man lashed again and sent the weapon spinning away. It came to rest in one of the patches of fire by Gordie. Fool rolled and the Man sent another spike out, this time into Fool's leg.

Fool looked at the Archdeacons, still standing together, and willed them to come and help, because even now the Man was pulling himself on, had removed the barb from Fool and was crawling, crawling, but the Archdeacons ignored his look and remained where they were. Fool groaned, tried to stand and couldn't, leg muscles finally too tired and damaged to function, managed to get to his hands and knees and crawled after the Man and reached him as he was crossing the now-extinguished line of fire.

Fool reached out, taking hold of the feather that was sticking out of the Man's back, his other hand burning against the baking stone ground, and twisted. The Man jolted, tried to pull away, but Fool wouldn't let go. Another barb punched into him and pulled out, then another, weak, only barely breaking his skin. He gripped the feather tighter and said, "No. No," although whether he said it out loud or only in his mind he couldn't tell, and then Mayall was rising out of the fires of the Flame Garden, huge and spinning, wreathed in smoke and grinning.

He landed in front of Fool as the Archdeacons scattered, running from the angel. Mayall ignored them, crouching to look at Fool.

"You came," Fool said, still not letting go of the Man even as he continued scrabbling to escape, trying to drag Fool with him. His voice sounded like it was coming from some great distance, sounded echoing and dry, sounded old and lost.

"You called," replied Mayall, casually knocking away another of the Man's shoots as it quested around his feet. "You have something to tell me?"

"This war is wrong," said Fool. He felt sick, his face burning, his eyes stinging, and his side throbbing, the new hole at the bottom of his neck feeling wet and hot. Grotesque waves of pain were coursing through him, making him dizzy and bilious.

"This war is just," said Mayall.

"No," replied Fool and then vomited, splashing the angel's feet with bile. Speaking was an effort, breathing was an effort, everything was folding in on itself. He pushed on, forcing the words out.

"Hell never attacked Heaven. I thought it was the things outside of everywhere, but it wasn't. It was the Man." He gestured at the still-crawling mass of vegetation. "It's him." He lost his grip on the feather and lowed, desperate, as the Man began to move away from him. A high keening sound rose from the Man, the whistle of air through reeds and grasses.

Mayall smiled at Fool and then stood. "And so we are brought around in our circles," he said, "to the end that is as the beginning was, brought here by a fool."

Mayall walked to the Man and lifted him, gripping him by the feather and by a string of stems that thrashed wildly. "Be still," he said quietly, and there was no humor in him now, only a gentle compassion. Fool watched as he leaned in close to the Man, whispered something to him, and then kissed the top of the mass gently.

The Man sighed and burst into a ball of fatty yellow flame in Mayall's hands. A moment later, there was nothing left of him but ash, white and dry, that fell to the ground along with the unmarked feather. Fool vomited again, the action tearing through him. He could still smell Gordie's burned flesh, felt that he would always smell it, always remember the strings of him peeling away with his jacket, knowing that *always* wasn't going to be long and being grateful for it.

"I thank you, Thomas Fool," Mayall said. "Because you said it, it has become true. It just took someone to see, to be prepared to fight for it. All of Heaven and Hell now knows that this war is not just, and it is over."

Fool tried to nod, tried to be glad but couldn't; his head wouldn't lift up but carried on falling, tilting down so that his chin hit his chest and his forehead struck the wall and the pain rose up through his body, all over him, swallowing his head, and then the blackness was crashing in from his sides and his final thought was *Marianne, Gordie, Summer, I'll be there soon, I'm coming.*

I'm coming.

EPILOGUE

They were in an office in Assemblies House, anonymous and bland.

Fool was sitting naked in a chair facing the new head of the Arch-deacons, his body covered in scratches and stitched wounds and blisters and striations and burns and bruises, bloomed with the colors of healing and pain. He stared at the demon on the other side of the long table and waited. Rhakshasas's place had now been taken by the thing dressed in red and green, who had not introduced itself but whom he'd heard called Quailknife as he was being escorted there. Mayall was sitting at the end of the table, not behind it and pointedly not alongside the demon, but still facing Fool.

"How are you feeling?" asked the angel.

"I hurt. I thought I was dead." *I wanted to be dead, I wanted this to be over.*

"No," said Mayall. "That reward was not granted to you."

Fool waited but no one spoke. He looked down at himself. Under the sullen hues of his injuries, the tattoos burned into him by Rhak-shasas remained but were still now, long lines and patches of blackness that ran through the bruises from his ankles to the edges of his wrists. Marianne's face still looked back at him from his forearm, her expression unreadable.

He was still alive, still hurting, Gordie and Summer and Marianne were still dead, escaped before him. He ached, inside and out.

"Is the Man dead?"

"The Man of Plants and Flowers is no longer your concern, nor a concern for Heaven or Hell."

"That's not answering my question."

"No."

Another pause, another silence. He felt as though he was behind a sheet of glass, just he and his pain, separated, everything muffled and flat. Outside, he could hear the sounds of construction, of the face of Hell being smoothed over so that the evidence of the war, the damage and destruction, was gone. No one had mentioned the conflict so far, and he didn't think they were about to. It was done and gone, and forgotten.

"Why am I here?"

"For judgment," said Quailknife, the first time it had spoken since the three of them had gathered in the room.

"Fine." He didn't care.

"And for reward," said Mayall.

This brought Fool up short, snapped through the muffling silence around his head. He looked at Mayall, in his brown coat and off-color collarless shirt and stained trousers, and said, "Reward?"

"You brought the truth into the light," said Mayall and stood. His feet were beginning to twitch, his fingers beginning to snap. "That deserves reward, does it not?"

The angel did a little shuffle, oblivious of the looks that Quailknife was giving him. He'd start to juggle soon, thought Fool, and then something would get broken.

"Judgment," repeated Quailknife.

"And reward," said Mayall firmly, spinning a full circle, arms swinging, legs kicking high. One of the angel's feet caught the edge of the table and it bounced up, but before it could crash down Mayall caught it and began to tilt it this way and that, letting it fall from one hand to the other.

He's juggling a table, thought Fool and couldn't help but smile. Mayall, seeing the smile, said, "That's the ticket! Life's always nicer when we smile, don't you think?"

"I don't know." *That phrase again. Fuck it.*

"Oh, trust me, Thomas Fool, it is. Take it from me, I know. Now, your reward. What would you like?"

Fool remained silent. What could he ask for? His friends to be returned? To be allowed to die? To be Elevated, to become one of the Joyful?

Mayall let the table fall back and skipped to Fool, crouching in front of him so that their faces were level. The angel's breath smelled of mint and something else, something sweet and old. As he crouched he calmed, the manic light in his eyes fading, and he became serious again. "Would you like to know what you did, perhaps?"

"What I did?" *In the war? In Heaven, or in Hell?*

"What you did before, the things you did to bring you here," said Mayall, cupping his hands around Fool's face and making them into a tunnel, pushing his own face into the other side of it so that the whole world was Mayall, the whole world was Mayall's calm, deep eyes.

"I can tell you," said Mayall quietly. "It might help you make sense of your time here. It might help you understand why this punishment, if you understood the kind of monster you were."

Quailknife spluttered, somewhere outside the tunnel. "No," it said, "that is not to be offered."

"Nonetheless," said Mayall, still quiet, still Fool's whole world, still the kindest eyes peering at him from across the gulf of that short space, "it is available if it is wanted."

"No," from Quailknife again.

"It is not for discussion," said Mayall and finally broke the tunnel, let the rest of the world back in. "Well, Fool, what do you think?"

Fool looked down at himself again, at his battered body, and thought. To know what he had done, to know if he had been a monster, to know what kind of monster? Would that help? He looked at Marianne's tattooed face, at her eyes and her smile, at the lines on his stomach that were still almost Mr. Tap if he looked at them right, and raised his head to look at Mayall.

"Thank you, but no," he said. "Whoever that person was, it's not who I am now."

"A wise choice," said Mayall. "So, then, what will it be?"

"Can I have my skin back?"

Mayall grinned, mouth open and teeth huge, eyes gleaming. He flicked his head, sent a string of hair back from his forehead, and said, "Of course."

The angel leaned forward and pinched the skin of Fool's ankle, trapping one of the tattoo lines between his thumb and forefinger.

"Not this one," said Fool suddenly, placing his hand over Marianne's face. "Leave her. I can't lose her again."

"Of course," said Mayall again and *pulled*. The tattoo unspooled from Fool's skin in a long string, its end still pinched between Mayall's fingers, slithering away from him and spilling on the floor around his feet. It took perhaps three seconds, the lines emerging from his skin painlessly, the only sensation a flowing warmth as though someone was rubbing a gentle, moist tongue over him.

And then it was done.

Fool lifted his hand, finding Marianne's face still looking at him. He smiled at her. Mayall gathered the lines of tattoos into a bundle and thrust them into his pocket.

"I'll have fun with them later," he said, grinning broadly.

"And now," said Quailknife, "judgment. You brought things into Hell that had no existence, things that should not be." For a moment, Fool couldn't work out what the demon meant, and then realized: Summer and Gordie.

"True," he said.

"You shot more than one of Hell's Evidence Men, you brought Rhakshasas to his death, you lied in your reports."

"All true," said Fool, still looking at Marianne, still looking at what might have been.

"You have colluded with angels," said Quailknife, "and this may be the worst sin of all."

"This is Hell, he is supposed to sin," said Mayall.

"You killed Wambwark with no mercy," said Quailknife.

"Is there mercy in Hell?" asked Mayall.

"Angel, you are not helping," snapped Quailknife. "Your function here is complete, you have no further part to play."

"Be careful, little demon," said Mayall.

"I'd listen, he kills demons," said Fool helpfully.

"We are embargoed from killing you," said Quailknife, looking at Mayall, hatred in its eyes. "So Elderflower has decreed that your punishment is this: You will remain here in Hell, Thomas Fool, and continue as head of the Information Office, but nothing will talk to you and no one will count you as friend. You will do your job in Hell's silences. That is Hell's judgment. The mark of Hell is on you, now and forever."

The Archdeacon rose and, in silence, went out. On the table in front of where it had been sitting was a new uniform, folded neatly, and on top of this was his gun. He picked it up, feeling its weight, looking at its burned and scorched barrel. Would it still fire? He turned it and pointed it at the wall, but Mayall stepped in his way.

"No," the angel said. "There's time for that. No more for now. There has been enough shooting." He nodded at Fool and then turned to go, wings already unfurling.

A moment later, the room was empty and quiet. Fool was alone, would live in a silence born not of peace but of war, was an outcast thing.

He was Thomas Fool, Commander of the Information Office of Hell, and knew what he had become.

Pariah.

ACKNOWLEDGMENTS

No book is ever written without help, and the following all deserve a touch of the hat brim and a nod, and probably medals for putting up with me:

Mum and Dad, for everything.

Rebecca and Adam, for the same everything as Mum and Dad.

Rob Bloom at Doubleday and Michael Rowley at Del Rey, for still taking a chance and for all the excellent editorial suggestions.

John Berlyne at the Zeno Agency, for still having faith and being a great agent.

Steve Marsh, for the friendship and the support and the music.

Andrew Worgan, for the friendship and support and the nights before the hangovers.

The owners of Duo Café in Sedbergh, where most of this book was written, deserve a particular mention for serving excellent coffee and never apparently minding my sitting in the corner, muttering to myself, groaning, and then typing in frenzied bursts.

During the writing of this book, two of my heroes died: Rik Mayall and Robin Williams. Both were huge influences on me as I grew up, and without them I'd see the world and relate to the things around me very differently. Although I never met either of them, their losses made me feel the lurch of unstable ground beneath my feet, and I miss both of them still. Whatever you've gone on to, gentlemen, travel safe.

ABOUT THE AUTHOR

Simon Kurt Unsworth was born in Manchester and lives in a farm-house in Cumbria, in the United Kingdom. He is the author of *The Devil's Detective* and many short stories, including the collections *Lost Places*, *Quiet Houses*, and *Strange Gateways*.